ROBIN HOOD
DEMON'S BANE
MARK OF THE BLACK ARROW

COMING SOON FROM
DEBBIE VIGUIÉ AND JAMES R. TUCK

Robin Hood: The Two Torcs (August 2016)
Robin Hood: Sovereign's War (August 2017)

ROBIN HOOD
DEMON'S BANE

MARK OF THE BLACK ARROW

DEBBIE VIGUIÉ ✦ JAMES R. TUCK

TITAN BOOKS

ROBIN HOOD: DEMON'S BANE

MARK OF THE BLACK ARROW

Print edition ISBN: 9781783294367
E-book edition ISBN: 9781783294374

Published by Titan Books
A division of Titan Publishing Group Ltd
144 Southwark Street, London SE1 0UP

First edition: August 2015
2 4 6 8 10 9 7 5 3 1

This is a work of fiction. Names, places and incidents are either products of the author's imagination or used fictitiously. Any resemblance to actual persons, living or dead (except for satirical purposes), is entirely coincidental.

A CIP catalogue record for this title is available from the British Library.

Printed and bound in the United States

Did you enjoy this book? We love to hear from our readers.
Please email us at readerfeedback@titanemail.com or write to us at
Reader Feedback at the above address.

To receive advance information, news, competitions, and exclusive
offers online, please sign up for the Titan newsletter on our website:
www.titanbooks.com

To my husband, Scott, who will always be my hero.
–DV

To the Missus who is always on target.
–JRT

THE SCENT OF
SMOKE AND DUST

PROLOGUE

Screams. The howls of dogs lusting after blood and the shouts of men wanting the same. Her own ragged breathing. All these sounds drowned out the whispers of the forest as Finna ran as fast as she could.

"Don't let her make it into the forest," the master of hounds shouted. "The witch knows it well!"

Aye, she knew it well. There were creatures in Sherwood that would help her, shield her. The old magic wasn't gone from the world, just retreated and hidden from all except those who could wield it.

She was only a stone's throw from Sherwood's borders. A few long strides to freedom. She should have been able to hear the spirits calling to her, but there was too much noise. The baying of the hounds, the tattoo of booted feet, the huff of men's breath, the rushing-rapid *shoosh* of her own blood racing through her veins. Fear pounded through her, and she wondered if the fey had abandoned her to this fate.

It couldn't end this way.

Her work wasn't finished.

The children were special. She had been sent to train and educate them, prepare them for their destiny. The fate of all rested upon it, and she'd had so little time with them.

One of the dogs, faster than the rest, snapped at her ankles. She should have poisoned the monster when she had the chance. Pain seared from her heel to the top of her spine as the creature bit down on her leg, sending her crashing to the ground. Rocks and twigs scratched her face. Dirt filled her eyes and mouth and she couldn't scream as it choked her.

She kicked and clawed, trying to get away, but the beast had her in its grip, tearing at her limb, ripping into it. Her chin bounced off the ground, teeth cracking together as it shook her back and forth in its massive jaws. A gobbet of her own meat tore free in a gush of hot pain and the beast backed off a step. She could hear it choking down her flesh as though she were some animal it had brought to ground.

The monster was going to eat her alive.

Her hands closed around a dead branch and she lashed out, swinging it backward at the animal. It caught the stick in its jaws and jerked it from her grip, tearing her palms. She pushed up off the ground with bloody hands, then twisted her head, blinking rapidly to clear her eyes of the dirt and tears. She saw the monster clearly, jaws stained red, some of her skin stuck between two of its fangs, and eyes that glowed with an unholy light.

"Demon!" she spat.

Its mouth opened wider, jaws cracking apart, as though it were laughing at her.

Her mind raced. She knew no spell that would cast it hence. That it walked the earth at all was a sign.

The time of the prophecy had come.

She had failed to ready the child.

The master of hounds arrived, holding the rest of the brutes jerking and heaving at the end of a fistful of chains, a long bullwhip trailing from his other hand. Men followed him, and they circled around her. They were no better than the dumb animals that snapped at one another. They looked down at her, mouths open to reveal jagged teeth, eyes heavy-lidded in their sockets. The master handed off the pack to one of his followers and jerked his head. It took both the man's hands to control the pack. They flailed at the end of their leashes as he dragged them away.

The master of hounds stepped toward her.

"Get her up."

They pulled her to her feet and her stomach tried to crawl up her throat. Her left leg hung, swaying beneath her on stretched tethers of gristle, bitten almost completely off. Screams of anguish ripped out of her, something she could no more stop than the beating of her heart.

"She cannot walk," one of the men grunted.

"Then let the witch fly," the master sneered. "Fly, witch! Or do you need a little motivation?"

He flicked the whip against her back. It cut through her thin dress, and parted flesh from bone just as easily. She screamed again as she fell. Desperately she pulled at her center, trying to stave off the panic that threatened to obliterate her sanity, trying to find the magic inside her through the throbbing pain and the howling fear. The earth was beneath her hands, but she couldn't feel it—not its energy, not the life it gave. All she could feel was death closing its dark hand around her while the men laughed and the air stank of her own spilled blood.

"Enough!"

It was a new voice, one laced with authority, and with something else.

"The lord wants her alive."

She looked up and saw an older man, a soldier by his dress. The others parted before him, out of fear more than respect. She struggled to a sitting position as he approached.

"The witch cannot walk," the master of the dogs said.

"Then you shall carry her," the newcomer replied, "and next time you'll know better than to let your filthy beasts feed on human flesh." With that, the soldier turned to go.

The master of hounds stared at his broad back. The murder-eyed creature that had taken her down stood with its chest out, a rumble grinding from inside it. Its master looked down, then back at the soldier. His hand twitched, fingers twisting into a sign. The beast lowered itself, coiling to strike.

"Watch out!" she cried.

The monster leaped, and the soldier turned in mid-stride, hand pulling a sword from its scabbard. With one quick motion he plunged his blade into the beast's chest. It fell with an inhuman scream. Black blood poured from its wound and began to smoke and sizzle along the length of steel.

"What in the name of God?" The soldier turned, eyes gone dark with anger.

"This witch has summoned forth all manner of evil," the master cried.

"The beast was his!" she protested. The master backhanded her across the face. Four of her teeth tumbled out of her mouth as she rocked back. They rolled across the dirt like wet dice in a game of chance.

"Shut up, lying filth!"

The master grabbed her hair and raised his hand to strike her again.

"Stop," the soldier commanded, but the master struck her in the temple with a thick calloused hand. White sparks flew across the back of her eyelids. She braced for another blow, praying to Hecate that it would send her on into darkness, away from the pain.

The blow never came.

A gurgling noise and a jerk of the hand that held her made her crack a swelling eyelid. The master of hounds still held her, but his face was splayed open in shock as he looked down nearly a foot of steel that had burst through his chest.

The steel slid backwards, rolling blood down the man's leather jerkin. The body dropped to its knees, slumped forward, and fell next to her. Blood from the gushing chest wound sprayed across her.

The soldier bent down until he looked her in the face. He had a scar over his left eye that was familiar to her. She had seen it once in a vision.

"I will take you back to my lord, but I will not raise a hand to protect you against him."

She spit blood on the ground.

"Blessed are you, man of the sword, for it will be your honor and duty to protect he who will one day protect all. The darkness is coming. You have seen it with your own eyes, and you cannot deny that proof."

"I have seen enough darkness to last a hundred lifetimes," he told her grimly.

She wanted to tell him that what he had seen was nothing, in comparison, to what was coming. Yet the pain proved too much for her, and she collapsed in his arms.

Finna woke screaming. Her injured leg was on fire with pain. It convulsed, and a half-dozen rats that had been feeding on it scattered—but they did not go far.

She shivered as she reached down to touch her wound. The leg was swollen, feverish. Someone had wrapped it in a filthy rag that had bonded with her blood, crusting to the wound like a scab. A leather thong cut into her flesh below her knee, cutting off the flow of blood—it was probably the only reason she was even alive. Weak from blood loss, she could feel that a poison had already started to taint what life she had left. Even if the lord decided not to burn her as a witch, she was still as good as dead.

She cast around in the darkness of her cell, looking for anything she might use to defend herself, if only against the rodents whose eyes glistened at her in the darkness. She would rather die by her own hand than allow them to eat her alive. She found nothing save the moldy straw beneath her, and the damp stone beneath that.

Footsteps sounded in the gloom. A wizened man bearing keys arrived in the company of a large man whose head nearly scraped the low ceiling. The old one opened her cell. The large one stepped in and effortlessly picked her up, slinging her over his shoulder. He knocked her head against the ceiling in the process. She struggled to hold onto consciousness even as she was bounced around like a child's doll. Hanging upside down, her head swam as she banged against his body with each step. She retched over and over, but her stomach was empty and nothing came out.

Outside the light blinded her. The giant put her down, her back to a blackened iron pole that had been driven into the ground and surrounded by piled, pitch-soaked wood.

They were going to burn her.

"No, please!" she choked out even as she was lashed to the pole.

"You are a witch, and you will burn for it," the old man informed her in a calm voice, as though he were discussing nothing more than the weather.

Around them were gathered people from all stations in life, come to witness the execution. She glanced around frantically, looking for a friendly face, but found none.

"You know me!" she cried.

"We know you as a witch."

It was no use.

Once she had been sentenced to burning, none would dare speak in her defense unless they desired to share the same fate. Lord Longstride was there, his face hard. Beside him stood his oldest son, Robert, all of four years of age and yet already a miniature copy of his father. On the lord's other side stood his wife, the lady Glynna. Their infant son was not with them, though, and Finna looked frantically for the boy.

She finally spied the child in the arms of one of the servant boys, the one they called Little John—though at nine he was already almost the size of a man full grown. The baby's mother had refused to touch the child since the hour of his birth. A darkness had seized her mind at that moment, and she had sworn that it was a fey changeling and not her own child.

On the night of his birth, she had taken a pillow and tried to smother the child. He had been saved by his father, who had entered just in time. Nothing he could say or do would convince his lady wife to suckle the child.

He had searched for a wet nurse, and Finna had seen her chance. Though childless, she had mixed a potion that allowed her to take the child to her own breast and give him sustenance. His father had placed the boy wholly in her care, and while their mother was not well, the older boy had been her responsibility, too.

These last four months she had done what she could to relate the knowledge of the old ways to both children, telling tales and stirring within them the inborn knowledge of the magic that once held the Isle of the Mighty safe and secure against the forces of darkness. She had tried to be careful, but she had not been careful enough.

Someone must have overheard.

Someone who hated her.

Finna's eyes drifted back to the children's mother, and a sickness grew deep inside. A fiendish light danced in the Lady Longstride's eyes, as though she was beholding something for which she had fervently wished.

The old man who had spoken her fate struck flint to iron, throwing sparks onto the head of a fuel-soaked torch. The tiny fires caught in the fabric, jumping to flame almost immediately. The cruel man picked it up and moved toward her.

"Listen to me, my lord," she called to the boys' father. "There is a great evil coming to this land. Only a Longstride can defeat it. The signs are all coming true. It will happen in your lifetime—sooner than you think."

"Is that true, Father?" the oldest boy asked.

Lord Longstride frowned as he put his hand on the boy's head. "Don't believe anything a witch tells you, Rob."

"You must protect your sons," she begged. "Teach them both the old ways, and the ways of Christ."

Lady Glynna leaned into her husband, whispering.

Finna strained to hear. A small incantation in her mind sharpened her ears

"We should throw the changeling onto the fire with her," the lady said, her face twisting viciously.

"No! Don't listen to her!" Finna shouted.

"The creature sucked at the witch's teat," the lady continued. "Who knows what evil she has imparted to it?"

"Woman," the lord hissed, "I will not hear another word from you against my son." He spat on the ground. "Let's be done with this filthy business." He gave a short nod to the old man who tossed the torch onto the pitch-soaked wood.

Within moments the pyre was lit and flames were engulfing Finna's feet. The baby started to scream and it cut through the pain already climbing up her, breaking her heart. Her skin began blistering, pain eating its way up her legs and leaving nothing below them. Oily smoke from her own blackening flesh made her eyes stream tears. It all began to swamp her mind, stealing her from herself, and she held onto one thing.

Regret.

Finna regretted so many things: not having children of her own, failing in her mission to prepare the Longstride children.

Most of all she regretted not taking that Longstride bitch with her to the grave.

CHAPTER ONE

The sun did not reach the ground. It tried, pounding away at the top of the green canopy, beating against interlocked boughs of ash, oak, and birch.

The majestic forest kings held the rays at bay, allowing only the softest, verdant light to spill into the heart of the lonely wood, turning it into a permanent emerald twilight. Here and there a giant had fallen, crashing through his brothers' embrace and leaving a gap. These small pockets bloomed and blossomed, filling with flowers and grass not found beneath the trees.

Few ever saw the beauty. Sherwood was vast and it kept its secrets well. Travelers avoided traveling its length or breadth. Indeed, they tried to skirt the mighty forest altogether. If they could not avoid it they stuck to one of the known roads, many of which were roads in name only, and actually little more than deer paths that men and horses had sought to widen. The forest constantly sought to reclaim them.

Robin crouched in the underbrush at the edge of a hidden meadow. He waited, weight over the balls of his feet, rendered invisible by stillness so complete that he barely breathed, and by the hooded hunting jerkin he wore, its thin deerskin dyed a green to match his surroundings.

Eyes narrowed, he stared across the clearing where a sleek-sided doe grazed the low-growing sweetgrass, mouth moving rhythmically as she ate. Two spotted fawns frolicked around her, leaping and nudging each other in a game of keep away. They flashed around, white tails flicking, tiny hooves digging the soft earth. Their mother ignored them, head down, enjoying the clover in her mouth.

They didn't know he was there. If they had, they would have fled, abandoning the sweet food for safety in the wood.

His hand tightened on the bow, fingers whispering softly against the leather-wrapped yew. He could almost hear the wood whispering to him, reassuring him that its aim would be true.

He could make the shot. He could take one of them. Rise, draw, pull, and release in one smooth, fluid movement. He could pin an arrow through the doe's chest, stopping her heart in an instant. She would drop to her knees and then slowly fall to her side, dead before she even felt the pain. Yet leaving the fawns to die without their mother's protection and guidance would make the meat, however needed it might be, taste of guilt and shame.

No. The family for whom he hunted was not that hungry.

Not yet.

He stayed there in the itchy undergrowth, thighs burning from crouching, and he waited.

The mother led her fawns into the meadow. There was no hesitation in her step, no pause to even look for danger. She ate in total security, oblivious to the world around her and her children.

So she wasn't alone.

His eyes scanned the forest behind the doe, trying to pierce the gloom just beyond the tree line. There, deep in a pocket of near dark, he saw a flicker—the tiniest movement of something.

He focused, teeth gritting, pouring his will into the dark.

Come out. Show yourself.

The doe raised her head.

The fawns continued to play.

I know you're there.

The doe stepped back to the edge of the clearing.

Something massive moved in the dark.

The fawns stopped, dead still.

The largest stag he'd ever seen stepped into sight. It towered over the doe, a massive rack of antlers spreading from its skull in a crown of bone, a fortress of spikes and tines. Thick fur lay in a mantle across shoulders and a back wide enough to carry the entire world. Its bones were carved timber. It was majestic, magnificent, and primordial, the avatar of every stag that ever existed.

The Lord of the Forest.

Awe fell on Robin, like thunder across the sea.

He couldn't take a creature such as this.

The mean spot of his humanity rose up, filling his chest with the very desire his awe denied, and splitting him like lightning. The urge to destroy such beauty, to conquer such strength, raged through him and he wrestled, wrestled *hard* within himself to contain it.

His fingers touched the notch of an arrow in his quiver.

The stag stepped forward, lowered its mighty head, and began to eat, trusting the doe, its mate, to watch for danger.

This was the moment.

His fingers closed on the notch and stayed, gripping tight, as he fought inside himself. His father's voice sounded in his mind.

Kill for food, never for the pleasure of the kill itself. That is a road that leads to Hell.

He pushed away not the message, but the messenger.

Centering himself with the thought of the families who could eat through a winter with this one act, he laid the arrow across the bow.

Rise.

Breathe in.

Hold.

Draw.

And...

"Robin!"

A voice split the silence, an axe through a piece of dry firewood. The stag jolted at the sound. Almost too fast for his eye to follow, the mighty beast swept its antlers around, driving the fawns and their mother into the trees. With a snort of contempt, the Lord of the Forest disappeared like quicksilver.

Robin released the tension on the bow, and exhaled.

Another day, fine fellow.

Quivering the arrow, he turned and began making his way through the trees to find the person who had spoiled his shot.

I can't see anything in this blasted place. Will Scarlet sat straighter on his horse, stretching to peer further into the gloom that bordered Merchant's Road. The horse ignored his movements, standing between shallow ruts of dirt packed hard by countless rolling wheels, and cropping a mouthful of grass.

Will shifted his gaze from side to side, picking out shapes in the darkness. Dappled light fell around him, following the curving line of road where the tree canopy had been thinned.

"Damnation, Robin, you know you're supposed to be back by now." His voice was low as he grumbled. The horse's ears twitched, but it didn't look up from its mouthful.

Will brought his hands back to his mouth, drawing in air to bellow once again.

"I think we've had about enough of that."

Will jerked in his saddle, slender hand snatching at the handle of his rapier. Seeing who had spoken, he relaxed his grip.

Robin stood at the edge of the road, bow in hand.

"Where did you come from?"

A smile pulled Robin's face. He slung the bow across his back.

"Perhaps I've been here all along."

"Sneaky bastard." Will shifted in his saddle. "One day you'll show me how you move so quietly."

Robin pointed at Will's embroidered boots made of suede calfskin, dyed a rich vermillion to match his surname.

"You can't be stealthy in boots as loud as those."

"So it's a choice? Either style or stealth?"

"Not in your case."

Will sniffed. "I'd choose style over stealth every day."

"Perhaps one day you'll choose substance over style."

Will rolled his eyes. "I am a *paragon* of substance."

"Perhaps," Robin replied, sounding doubtful. "Your style is substantial, though, I'll grant you that."

"I've seen you dressed well," Will replied. "Even then, you're so quiet it's spooky."

"Ah, cousin, maybe I'm half-ghost." Robin's smile grew wider. "Don't you think Sherwood is haunted?"

"Haunted by you? Almost certainly."

"Not by me." Robin waved his hands. "But the spirits of the wood are benign." A serious note crept into his voice. "Mostly."

"Tell that to Cousin Requard," Will snorted. "He claims to have been held captive by them one night, and hasn't been the same since."

"Ha! Requard was held captive by too much mead from the monastery, and a briar patch he fell into while trying to catch a glimpse of the Latimer twins at their nightly bath in the river. He wasn't even in Sherwood proper." Robin moved closer until he stood next to the horse. "Now, why have you come out here calling my name as if it's your own?"

"I was sent to fetch you—by Uncle Philemon."

"Fetch me?" Robin's face darkened. "Fetch *you*," he spat, and he turned to leave, lifting the hood over his head.

"But the feast is tonight," Will protested. "We have to attend. By order of the king."

"Fetch him, too," Robin said, but his voice softened slightly. "I have no use for feasts when there are families who starve."

Will sighed. "What starving families? The Lionheart is a good king. Everyone eats."

"Some eat better than others."

Will shrugged. "Such is life."

"Fetch *that*," Robin said firmly. "I'll make a difference."

"You *do* make a difference. We all know you hunt for the poor. It's why you're allowed to hunt in Sherwood at all. Well, that and your father's fervent support of King Richard."

"Fetch my father most of all." Robin's mouth twisted into a scowl.

Will held his tongue. His Uncle Philemon was a hard man—he had to be when responsible for so many, and he tasked his sons accordingly, yoking them with the expectation that they would become copies of him. With Robert, the oldest, it had been no difficulty—the boy took after him in so many ways. With Robin, however, it was different, their relationship full of enmity. Will had been party to many of their fights, and saw that his uncle knew no other way.

He and his youngest son were much alike.

Time for a new tactic, he decided.

"Don't eat the king's food then," he said. "Hell, steal your portion and give it to your poor families, but before you refuse to attend, bear in mind that *she* will be there."

Robin fell silent.

"She'll be wearing a fine dress," Will taunted, "and she'll be available to dance. If you aren't there, then who knows with whom she might partner. Maybe I'll ask her to spin around with me—" He shrugged. "—If Locksley doesn't get there first."

A low, animal sound came from beneath Robin's hood. Will looked closely. Robin's face had flushed red, jaw bulging as his teeth clamped together. He looked like a madman.

The horse balked, loosed a shrill whinny, and amble-stepped away. Will put a hand up, pulling the reins with the other. His voice dropped, switching to a melodious, soothing tone he used for dealing with injured animals.

"Ease yourself, cousin," he said. "I jest too much. You know she has no interest in him."

Locksley's great-great-grandfather and Robin's had been brothers—twins, actually. Their father had wanted to leave them each with an inheritance. In return for his service to the crown, the elder Locksley had been allowed to split his land in two, giving the first portion to his elder son and the second to the younger, along with the new title of Lord of Longstride.

While the arrangement had suited the brothers, their descendants on both sides had chafed at the division. To this day Locksley longed to have the land reunited, under his control. The same was true of Longstride. The hatred and rivalry between the two families only increased with each generation.

On more than one occasion Locksley had suggested that Sherwood should be put to the torch, its majesty and mystery destroyed for the sake of more land to be plowed, more land to be coveted. Robin took this particularly to heart.

He stared now, eyes narrow and black in their sockets. Will watched his cousin warily, feeling an itch to grab for the handle of his sword. It dug into the back of his neck, worming its way toward his spine. Teeth clenched, he ignored it. To listen would end badly.

Then something appeared in Robin's eyes, flickering behind tightly-slitted lids. His head dropped. He drew a deep breath and held it as a tremor rolled through his wiry frame, chasing along the lean muscles of his arms and shoulders. It passed, shivering out of his fingertips. He released the breath and looked up.

His eyes were clear, face nearly back to its normal dark coloring.

"It's true," he said. "You do jest too much, cousin."

Will's body unclenched in a rush that made his head spin for a moment. He smiled and cocked an eyebrow.

"One day it'll be the death of me," he admitted.

"Probably," Robin agreed. "But not today."

"Good." Will leaned forward, separating them from that conversation. "Now about this feast—your father was insistent, and I promised I'd bring you."

"Well, if it means preserving the good word of Will Scarlet, then I guess I must." Robin reached his hand up. Will grasped it, pulling to help his cousin swing up behind him.

Instead Robin leaned back, yanking the slim man from the saddle. As Will tumbled to the road, Robin smacked his hand flat on the horse's rump. It reared and jolted forward, racing away and disappearing around a bend of the road.

Will leapt to his feet, frantically beating dirt from his linen trousers and suede boots as he listened to the diminishing sound of the beast's hooves.

"What the hell did you do that for?" he demanded.

Robin chuckled. "If I must go, then I will walk, and get there in my own good time. Since you came to fetch me, you can keep me company."

"But these boots aren't made for hiking," Will protested. "They come from the Iberians!"

Robin slung his arm over Will's shoulders. "The Iberians make fine boots, cousin. I think you shall survive. A little fresh air and exercise won't hurt you." With that, he began walking.

Will scowled as he followed.

"If my boots are ruined, I will hurt *you*."

Robin's laugh echoed through the forest.

CHAPTER TWO

Much, the miller's son, shifted the pole across his shoulders, easing the sore crease of flesh forming under its weight. The basket on each end swung with the motion, roughly scraping along the outsides of his legs. He had calluses the size of his palm on each calf—rough patches of skin with no hair.

One foot in front of the other.

Step by step he walked the Merchant's Road, carrying loads of fruit for the family larder, a fair trade for two sacks of ground wheat. The fruit was lighter than the wheat, but still heavy enough to turn each step into hard work. Work he was used to, but work still.

His mind conjured thoughts of what his mother would make from what he carried home. Damson jelly, perhaps a quince pie. She would *definitely* make blackcurrant jam, since his father liked that. His eyes slid over to the basket on his left, looking at the mound of dark berries.

Hopefully his father would distill some sweet currant brandy. *That would be heavenly.*

There was a short, stout door of thick wooden planks that stood in the back of the mill. Never had Much been allowed inside his father's den. The old man—far *too* old to have a son as young as Much—would often go inside and shut the door tight. What lay beyond was for his father and his father only.

He'd asked his mum about it.

"Men need a place to go and be themselves, to shed the skin that being social makes them wear," she replied. "You'll see. One day you'll have your own place."

Even at that wee age, he'd already understood.

Then last season, when his father had taken him aside, and led him to the door, Much's stomach felt trembly-tingly, like it did when he had to climb to the top of the mill wheel and unclog the waterspout. The pipe that fed river water to the top of the mill started in a wide scoop that narrowed quickly, forcing the water to rush, squeezing it faster and faster until it had the force to drive the wheel forward. That turned the mighty gears which spun the grinding wheel, the gigantic round stone from a quarry in the north.

Sometimes the scoop would catch something coming down the river and suck it in, blocking the flow of water. Much would have to climb then, pulling himself up hand over hand by the spokes until he reached the top. He'd cling there while he wrestled out whatever debris clogged the pipe. Pull too fast and the river would jet out of the pipe, driving into him like a hammer on a nail. If he slipped, if his balance wavered for even a second, then the mill would toss him to his doom far below.

It made him feel as if he'd been slit across the belly and a hand inserted that juggled his innards, clumsy and without care.

Standing in the cool air at the front of the door gave him the same feeling.

His father grunted. "You're tall enough to have to stoop, so you're tall enough to enter." With a calloused hand, he pushed the door open, ducked, and then squeezed his large frame inside, shoulders scraping either side of the door as he hunched over and passed through.

Much followed.

The cubby was small. Simple. Built in the style of a monk's cell, it contained a high window covered in thin oilskin that turned the late-day sun into a warm, sallow glow. There were two chairs—one a worn wooden frame covered with a deer hide older than Much himself, its hair polished away by use save for a handsbreath that fringed it. The other was newer, the wood freshly chopped into shape and the deer hide still furred and stiff. They stood on each side of a small clay firepot which offered more than enough heat for the small space.

A ledge circled the room, its narrow space crowded with objects. There were stones polished by the river, a small bird skull, boxes and bins of various sizes, and a series of wooden carvings—people so intricately cut free from the wood that Much could read their expressions.

His father lifted a small box from the ledge. It was made from a dark wood Much had never seen before, such a rich brown that it looked almost black. It wasn't until his father passed it through the light that Much saw the carvings that wrapped the sides. Some serpentine creature with scales smaller than a river trout wove in and out of itself. It reminded Much of the ancient knotwork on the door of the monastery, carved by the Celts from long ago. His father grasped a second box. This one was larger, but plain and made of dried maple, just like the boxes his mother used to store things in the larder. His father sat in the old chair, putting the plain box between his feet. His ample body completely covered the hide's bare skin.

He pointed at the other chair and nodded.

Much sat. The chair creaked, green wood rubbing where it had been lashed together. He didn't squirm, even though he was uncomfortable, the chair under him as stiff as he felt. The sensation of being atop the wheel ran through him again, like he was on the verge of something new.

Reaching inside his tunic, Much's father drew out a small bronze container with holes in its lid. Lifting the lid he revealed a coal from the hearth fire, still glowing dully orange. Balancing the box on his knee, he reached into a pocket in the deer hide and produced a long wooden pipe. He opened the intricate box and a dark aroma of spice and something heady filled the small space. Without speaking he pulled out a pinch of tobacco, dark and shredded, then used both hands to pack the bowl of the pipe, tamping down and adding more until he was satisfied.

Much just watched.

Lifting the small bronze box his father tipped it forward, catching the coal between lip and lid before it could spill out onto his lap. He blew on it and the coal burned bright, heating to a near yellow before cooling back into sunset orange. Touching it to the tobacco he had so carefully arranged, he brought the pipe stem to his mouth, inhaled three sharp times, and blew smoke on a long exhale. Satisfied, he flipped the coal box up and shut it with a snap.

He smoked for a long moment, eyes half-lidded as he stared at Much.

"You're a good son."

His voice was a shock. Much didn't know what to say.

So he said nothing.

His father leaned forward and opened the plain box. Inside sat a corked jug. A long dead spider had built a web from the box's corners to the neck of the jug, its work covered in a fur of dust. The jug had been there for a good while.

Pulling it out, his father wiped the spider web away. He shook the jug, causing a liquid to slosh, before pulling the cork and lifting it to his nose. Much could smell it from where he sat—a sweet smell so pungent that it cut over the tobacco. The two things combined, mingling and complementing each other until his head swam just a bit. His father lifted the jug to his lips, took a long pull, and swallowed.

Then he held the jug out to Much.

The question of what it was, what elixir he was being given, sat heavy on his tongue. But he didn't ask—he just took the gift he was given.

It was heavier than it looked, made from a thick pottery like chipped stone. The smell was stronger up close, clawing into his breath and threatening to take it. His father looked at him, but didn't say anything.

Much lifted the jug and took a long drink.

The liquid burned sweetly across his entire mouth and made all the air in his lungs go shimmery. He coughed, barking into his sleeve. The room turned wavy and indistinct as his eyes teared up.

Still his father said nothing, letting him work through it.

Much breathed deep, clearing his throat.

"First one takes you by surprise," his father said finally. "Try another, but sip it."

Much tentatively brought the bottle back to his lips. The burn had passed and his mouth still tasted sweet and felt strange. He took a smaller drink this time, prepared for the same burn, only to find his tongue numb. This time he tasted the currant, fermented into a pungent sweetness.

It was *delicious*.

He raised the bottle a third time.

His father chuckled, a sound foreign to Much's ears, and reached out before he could drink.

"We still have work to do, son."

Dutifully, Much handed it over.

His father took a long drink, swallowed, and sighed as he corked it. He held up the jug and gave Much the same look he had when he told him to be careful around the big grinding stone.

"Only when I give it to you," he said.

Much nodded, his head full of the camaraderie of father and son, and his mouth filled with the hot-sweet taste of currant brandy.

Much smiled at the memory and kept walking, peering at the ground.

One foot in front of the other.

"What do we have here?"

The deep voice jerked him out of his thoughts. His head shot up.

Three men-at-arms were blocking the road. They were large, all cut from the same block of wood. Matching mail shirts, dull and storm-cloud gray in the shaded light of the road, contrasted sharply with sapphire blue tabards that showed double rampant lions embroidered in white thread.

The crest of Locksley.

Two of the men leaned on wicked halberds, long oak shafts propped against their shoulders to support their bulk. The third guard, with a thumb-sized birthmark over his left eye that stained the skin a darker red as if he'd been burnt, carried his weapon menacingly in two hands as he stepped forward.

Much stopped walking. He didn't like the gleam along the sharpened edge of the spear's blade, or the matching gleam in the man's beady, dark eyes. His whole body tensed as the armed man stopped in front of him.

"What are you doing, boy?"

"Returning home."

"Where is that?"

"The mill on Trent."

Please just let me pass.

The marked guard's face split wide. "You're the miller's son!" The gleam in the man's eyes grew sharper as he leaned in. "The dullard."

Much looked down again, and his ears began to burn. He knew they were blazing red. People had many words for him.

Dullard.

Simpleton.

Idiot.

Midge.

They would say these things, even in his presence. He never responded, never spoke back, which only added to the reputation. Being quiet planted the idea, staying quiet allowed it to bloom and take root.

The armed man stuck the end of his halberd into the dirt at his feet.

"You must be slow-witted to travel Locksley's road without paying the toll."

Much kept his head down. "This is the king's road," he said. "Open for all."

"Thieves and bandits hide in these woods. Locksley provides us to the people for protection. Thus it is Locksley's road, and a toll is levied."

There were no thieves or bandits in Sherwood—everyone knew it to be true. Ghosts and ghouls and spooks, but no thieves, not for many, many years. Not since the old stories of the Hood, but Much didn't say this. His mind desperately reached about, looking for something, *anything*, that would extract him from the situation.

"I have no coin."

Locksley's man laughed, head back, teeth out to the open air.

"I can see that!" His fingers plucked at Much's tunic, sewn by his mum from sackcloth. It was durable and, at a mill, plentiful. With the butt of his weapon the guard bumped the basket on Much's left side. "But you do have a bundle of sweets."

The other two guards moved toward them, standing to either side of him and closing Much in a circle of menace. Anger sparked. He didn't want to give up any of the fruit. He'd already made plans for it.

And yet...

"How much will the toll be?" he asked.

"Let's see." The guard shoved his hand into the basket, pawing at the fruit and nearly knocking the pole from Much's shoulders. He looked at the guard to his left, the one with a patchy beard being used to cover jowls and a double chin. "You like damsons, dontcha Bartleby?"

Bartleby grunted. "They's me favorites."

"And Quentin—" he looked at the guard on Much's left, the one with a drunkard's swollen nose "—just *has* to like quince."

Quentin smiled. "I like it just fine."

The guard straightened, pulling a handful of small dark berries from the basket. Leaning back, he dropped them into his mouth. It was a sloppy move and most of them spilled off his chin and down his chest to lie in the dirt of the road.

"And me, I love a ripe currant!" He laughed, and the sound of it pounded nails into Much's head. "Leave the entire thing and we'll let you pass."

Much stood straighter, the heavy baskets driving the stout pole deep into the muscles of his shoulders.

Three men.

Three *armed* men.

A basket of fruit.

Slowly Much lowered the baskets to the ground, turning his shoulders to unhook the pole from the rope slings. The guards moved in.

The bushels of wheat his father and mother had ground to flour and carefully bagged.

The miles between the mill and the Donal farm.

The taste of blackcurrant brandy.

Much swung the pole with all his strength before he realized what was happening. It clanged across the top of the birthmarked guard's helmet, bouncing off the curved steel. The impact vibrated the pole, jarring Much all the way to his teeth.

The guard didn't fall down.

As one, the three men turned toward him.

The guard's face was purple behind a deep scowl, birthmark glaring out over his eye like a hot coal. Lifting his halberd in a smooth motion he struck Much in the side of the head with the flat of the wide blade.

Much's head spiked with pain, and black washed across his vision as if someone had thrown ink into his eyes. The metal blade drove him to the ground, hard steel as unforgiving as a hammer to a nail. He lay there, unable to hear, unable to see, held in place by the weighty throb of his rattled brain inside his skull. He blinked and blinked, trying to clear his vision. Slowly the black faded to red, and the world began to come back.

The three guards loomed over him.

The marked guard had pulled off his helmet, sweat-damp hair in a mess. He had one hand pressed against his ear, and his face was still purple.

"Why did you go and do that, you imbecile?"

Much dug his hands in the dirt and pushed, trying to scramble away.

"Pin him down!"

Both of the other guards stepped forward, driving down the butts of their halberds. Bartleby of the patchy beard punched him in the shoulder. The big guard leaned into it, pressing the circle of hardwood into Much's joint, making pain blossom from his elbow, across his chest, and up into his neck. Quentin's halberd end drove into Much's thigh, twisting the muscle before slipping off and pinning his trousers to the ground.

He lay there, unable to move or crawl away.

The marked guard stepped over him.

"You shouldn't have done that, boy," he said. "Now you *really* have to pay the price." He raised the halberd shaft over his head, then drove it down with all his strength.

The butt of the weapon smashed into Much's stomach in an explosion of pain. The air was yanked viciously from his lungs, making them feel as if they'd been turned inside out and pulled from his throat. He folded into himself, muscles jerking him into a knot around his injured midriff, pulling him free from the shafts that pinned him. All he could do was suck air, trying to force oxygen back into his lungs through a throat that had closed like a fist.

From the corner of a watery eye he saw the marked guard raise his halberd again.

Much closed his eyes, and waited.

CHAPTER THREE

"Come, sit child, here beside me."

Lenore put her sling and stone in the pocket of her tunic and moved to her father's side. He was leaning back against the side of their house, legs stretched out. She hopped up and scooted back on the worn log that acted as a bench. Her father smelled of sweat and dirt, the product of work on Longstride land. He bit into an apple, taking a big chunk between his teeth before handing it to her. She took a bite herself, much smaller than his. Her mouth puckered at the sourness.

"I have a bit of time before going back to work. Would you like a story?"

She sat up straighter. "Yes, Da." She took another bite. "Please, one of the Hood."

"How about the time the Hood saved the monastery from a band of sea wolves?"

Her eyes widened. "He left the forest?"

Her father chuckled. "Yes. He did it, but rarely."

Her brow furrowed in thought. "He saved the monastery? This was recent?"

"No, child, this was long, long ago. The monastery was little more than a burned-out hill fort that some industrious monks were living in. This is when the light of Christ was new here. A time when the Northmen would raid the shores in their dragon-headed ships and come a-viking ashore, killing everyone they met and taking anything of value." He shook his head. "Are you going to take all my time with questions, or would you like to hear the story?"

Her face grew solemn. "One more question, Da."

"Come out with it."

"Does he use magic to win this time?"

"No, dear, he uses strength, and cunning."

Her face fell.

Her father winked. "And maybe just a *little* magic."

A tiny glimmer of candlelight spilling through a cracked shutter was the only thing that marked the small chapel from the deep gloom of the woods around it. It crouched in the green shroud of Sherwood as if playing a hiding game. Midday, and yet this deep in Sherwood it was near dark, everything shadowed by the boughs of the trees above.

It lent the very air a sense of otherworldliness, as if the forest had always existed and always would, locked outside of time itself. The footpath to the small circular building had become overgrown to the point that any visitor had to pay close attention to his step, or be tripped by root or bramble.

The low light gleamed off the lithe man's clothing, picking out the brighter threads of his tunic, trousers, and cloak. In the forest he felt connected to the world of the ancient Celt, the epitome of every bard that ever strode beneath the boughs of holy trees and crossed the mythical ground. Here it was still Avalon, still the Isle of the Mighty, a giant sacred grove that once housed the druids and the bards of old.

It made him tingle down to his bones.

His hand moved to his shoulder, to the ancient yew harp that rode there, strapped securely in place. The instrument faced out in its harness, laying in the curve of his chest and arm, ready always to play, able to be protected by him while also letting the harp absorb the world around him, adding to her magic. Slender fingers brushed the strings, calloused tips raising humming notes from the gold, the silver, and the brass. It wasn't a song, just a snatch of sound, a tiny run of notes that spilled out of the instrument that he'd been handed down. The sound danced in the space around him.

The harp itself hailed back to the time of the druid, long before Christ came to England. A bard of his line had carved it from a yew tree born in this very forest. Now it was his to carry, his to use in the tradition of all who came before.

Storyteller.

Minstrel.

History keeper.

Lawgiver.

Myth spinner.

Bard.

There were other storytellers who roamed the land, but none of them had his connection to the ancients, none of them could wield the magic of song as he could. It weighed heavily on him sometimes that, unless he sired children or took an apprentice, when he was gone it would all be lost.

His mind began weaving a song as he walked closer to the chapel. As he stepped on the tiny flatstone threshold, the door opened. The man who stood there was short, thick, and covered in the brown wool of a monk's robe—he looked like a tree shorn of limb and left to only trunk.

A smile cracked the monk's round face. "My dear friend," he said, motioning the bard inside.

Stepping through the door frame, Alan-a-Dale turned to see the monk lean outside and look left, then right before coming back in, shutting the plank door, and throwing a thick iron bolt to lock them in. He turned and opened his arms.

"It's so very good to see you," he said as Alan grasped his forearms in a brotherly greeting. "I trust you did not encounter any of the fey folk on your way here?"

Alan wasn't certain if the monk was in earnest or jesting. Sherwood Forest was rumored to be home to fey: goblins, ghosts, and other such creatures in which some believed strongly, while others scoffed.

Well, scoffed at the fey at any rate.

He had yet to meet a person who didn't think the forest was haunted, even if they didn't believe in faeries.

"None chose to make themselves known to me on this day," he said, choosing his words carefully. "I should have been glad of the company, though. It was a long walk to find you."

The monk returned the grip and pulled, drawing the bard into an embrace of friendship too long apart, clapping him soundly on the shoulders to make sure he was hale and hearty. Alan returned the gesture in like fashion, finding the friar as solid as ever and even more stout than the last time they had met.

"I would not have asked if it were not necessary, my friend," Friar Tuck said, releasing his hold and moving apart. "Of that you can be sure."

"Is there a need to be so secretive?"

"There is a need to be cautious."

Alan raised his eyebrows. "Trouble at the monastery?"

The priest waved his hands. "No, brother, nothing of the sort."

"Is it the new bishop?" Alan pressed. "Has he done something?"

Friar Tuck moved over to one of the rough plank pews that lined the small chapel, motioning for Alan to join him. As they both sat, the priest removed a wineskin from a sack on the bench and passed it over. Alan took a long pull, thirsty from his hike through Sherwood. Inside the skin was a rich mead that coated his tongue with the taste of honey and clover.

Then Tuck began pulling other things from the sack. A loaf of hard, brown bread, a waxy chunk of cheese, and small cooked sausages pinched together in a chain of short links. Alan's mouth began to water as he realized how hungry he had become. A knife appeared in the priest's hands and he began talking as he prepared the food.

"It's not that Bishop Montoya has proven himself untrustworthy," he said. "It's that he is too new to know."

"You monks and your secrets," Alan replied. "You are like ravens, gathering around a corpse and driving off the magpies. You're all blackbirds, but not all equals." He took some bread, sausage, and cheese from the priest, pressing them together in slender fingers.

"That's a colorful way of putting it," Friar Tuck smirked. "Yet I would expect no less from a bard."

"You know I speak the truth."

"You tell stories."

"As do you, my friend," Alan countered. "Does that make them any less the truth?"

Friar Tuck nodded his assent. "The fact stands that bishops come and go, but we monks remain. If things need be guarded, then they need be kept secret."

Alan took a mouthful of food. The bread was a day old and the cheese sharp as a knife, but the sausage was freshly made. The spices of it struck tiny fires of flavor across his mouth. He smiled. His long-time friend knew his palate, after many long meals shared in close companionship. He chased the fire away with another drink from the wineskin and tilted his head toward the door of the chapel.

"I've never seen a prayer house with a bolt on the door."

"Again, some things require the utmost secrecy."

The bard leaned in. "This thing I carry—is it that important?"

"If it is real, then yes, it is." The priest's eyes glittered in the candlelight.

Alan nodded and took the last bite of his food. Wiping his hands he reached to the small pouch on the back of his belt, hidden under his cloak. With one hand he deftly untied the knot that kept it closed, then fished out an object wrapped in waxed leather. He drew it out and handed it over.

"Take it then," he said, "and I hope it is all you want it to be."

Friar Tuck accepted the package, staring at the twine-wrapped leather. After a long moment, he tucked it inside the sleeve of his robe, making it disappear. When he looked up again, there was concern in his expression.

"Did you have any trouble along the way?" he asked. "Were there any inquiries as to what you carried?"

"No, your brother monks in Glendalough apparently kept the secret of it, as well." With that, Tuck relaxed a bit.

"Thank you once again, Alan."

The bard leaned back, stretching his long body into a line of sinewy muscle.

"It was quite the favor, traveling to the Emerald Isle and back to here. I am a bard, not a hewer of wood nor a fetcher of water."

The monk chuckled. "Only you could have made the trip without suspicion."

"A king's messenger could have done it."

"True enough," Tuck said. "But I didn't have one of those lying around."

"Well, someone did," Alan said. "I met one in a tiny village inn, eight nights ago."

Tuck sat up straight. "A messenger from King Richard?"

Alan nodded. "He didn't identify himself as such, but I saw the king's seal on a parchment he kept tucked in his tunic."

"Did you get him to reveal his business?"

"No, he wasn't enough of a drunkard for that. Very wary, he was."

Friar Tuck considered this silently for a long moment. Finally, he waved it away.

"I'll speak with Cardinal Francis about it after the feast," he said. "He sends his gratitude for your effort on the part of the church."

"I didn't mind so much," Alan admitted. "The brothers in Ireland brew a nice dark beer, and they have some lovely manuscripts they allowed me to memorize."

"If only they could cook worth a piss."

Alan sniffed. "I had some delightful meals on my trip."

It was true. Anywhere Alan stopped the families would gather, bringing the finest food and drink they had to offer in exchange for the news of the land, as well as the chance to hear him sing the ancient songs of heroes and gods—to awaken the ancient Celtic blood that flowed through their veins and remind them of the glory they once had, the magic that still resided deep in their bones and nestled in their hearts. Old men would smile, remembering the tales of glory, and children would sit at his feet, rapt with the visions his lyrics sparked in their young minds. Every stop became a feast, a holiday, a celebration of the fact that he had come to their village or town.

"Everyone brings their best for a bard." Friar Tuck swept his hand toward the leftovers of the food he'd brought.

"Truly the best meals are flavored by the company in which they are shared."

"And did you share some lovely company on your travels?" The friar avoided looking him in the eye, and his voice was quiet.

Alan waved it away. "You know as well as I do that the life of a bard is like the life of the monk, in that respect."

"It doesn't have to be, my friend. You've taken no oath." Friar Tuck began gathering up the remains of their food.

"It is still the way of it… my friend," Alan said softly.

"You will need to father a child one day, to carry on after you."

"Times are different. It's hard to find a woman of character willing to raise a child by herself, or nearly so for seven years, only to lose him to his training and wandering the earth with his father. Even then, the last two bards I knew of who managed to find such women could only father daughters." Alan shook his head. "I'm not inclined."

Silence filled the space between them as the moments spun themselves out. Finally Friar Tuck stood.

"There is a feast tonight," he said, "called by the king himself."

"So I have been told, and I am to sing. It was my given reason for traveling back so directly." Alan rose. "Do we know the purpose of it?"

"I've asked the cardinal, but he's keeping the knowledge to himself."

"That must infuriate your Bishop Montoya."

Friar Tuck chuckled. "To no end," he agreed. "Secrets kept drive him mad."

"Then you must have become his favorite, given how forthcoming you are with your clandestine meetings in the dark of Sherwood."

"You know me." Sarcasm dripped from the monk's voice. "I am a people-pleaser and an arse-kisser by nature."

Alan snorted. "Truly they are your most endearing traits, along with your famed temperance."

Friar Tuck chuckled as he leaned over the candle. "You know me well, my friend."

He blew out the flame, leaving them both in the dark.

The blow never came.

Instead a dull *thunk* and an animal howl split the air above him. Much looked up just in time for something to drip on his face in fat gobbets of wet.

His nose filled with the tang of iron.

The marked soldier spun away, screaming and batting at a feathered shaft that now pinned his hand to the wood of the halberd. Much reached up to his face, touching the moisture there. His fingers came away red.

The other two guards jerked around, Bartleby with his spear up and at the ready, Quentin nearly dropping his weapon as his fingers went lax like the jaw that hung down in shock.

Much looked where they did. Two figures moved down the road toward them, one a slender whip of a man, the other rangy and lean, built of sinew and bone, all shoulders and arm. Both men were darkly cast, but the taller one—the one in the green hunting hood—was the one that drew his eyes. He carried a stout bow with another wicked arrow already notched.

Recognition sparked in Much's mind.

Robin Longstride and Will Scarlet.

He scrambled back as the marked guard's halberd clattered to the road, the arrow shaft having snapped from the weight of it and pulled through his palm. The man dropped to his knees, moaning in pain and cradling his injured, bleeding hand.

"Move back!" the hooded archer barked, swinging the arrow point from one guard to the other.

Will Scarlet ambled onto the scene, hand casually draped on his rapier hilt. He waved languorously toward the three men-at-arms.

"I'd do what he says, fellows. He's strung tighter than that bow he holds."

Quentin immediately began moving, stumbling toward the side of the road, putting as much distance between himself and the other guards as he could. Much stood up and took a single step back. Before he could take another, Bartleby reached out, snagging his tunic with a meaty hand. The spear in his other hand swung down, the sharp edge hovering by Much's face.

"Walk away, little Longstride," he said, panic clear in his voice. "This be no concern of yours."

Robin stepped forward, bow still drawn. His jaw bulged as he spoke through clenched teeth.

"Let. Him. Go." It came out almost like a growl.

"He won't tell you again," Will Scarlet said. "I know him, and you've soured his mood." He held up his hand, fingers loosely pointing at Bartleby. "No doubt you made your move with haste, but our good fellow Much here is a poor shield for someone of your... girth. The good Lord Longstride is a fairly decent shot."

The spear in front of Much's face wavered as the guard tried to figure out how to extricate himself from the situation. Taking the opportunity, Much grabbed the haft and shoved back with all of his considerable strength. Bartleby jerked, his halberd torn from his grip. Much spun, almost toppling over from the pulling weight of the wide-bladed spear, but he kept his feet and swung the blade up to point it back in Bartleby's face.

Will Scarlet cocked an eyebrow and smirked under his thin mustache.

"And now you've been bested by the least of us."

The guard raised his hands into the air.

Robin stepped forward to stand beside Much and released the tension on his string. With one deft move, he un-notched the arrow, dropped it back in the quiver, and slung the bow around his shoulders. His hand fell on Much's shoulder.

"Are you unharmed?" He didn't call him boy, or lad, or son. He spoke to Much as he would another man, simple and direct. Much nodded, throat too tight to speak.

"May I?" Robin reached toward the halberd.

Much gulped, then nodded and handed over the weapon.

Robin twirled the spear in his hands, fingers running along the hardwood haft to a wicked hook that curled up from a band of steel a hand span beneath the wide metal blade. Much watched him, mind working hard.

Why would there be a hook...? And then it dawned on him. The hook stopped the spear when it had been driven *through* the body of an enemy.

He fought to hide the shudder that swept through him.

Will stepped close to Robin, his brow furrowed. "What are you going to do with them now, Robin?"

Robin continued his examination of the weapon as Much glanced around. The marked guard knelt on the road, still cradling his hand. He'd wrapped it in the tabard he wore. The blood stained the blue to almost black, but glared out bright pink where it wicked into the white thread of the Locksley crest embroidered there.

Quentin stood ten paces away on the side of the road, arms still in the air, watching Robin with his jaw hung open. One of the baskets of fruit Much had carried lay on its side, apples and root vegetables spilling onto the road.

He'd have to pick those up.

"What *are* you going to do?" Bartleby demanded. He shifted from one foot to the next. His chainmail whispered against itself like conspiring snakes. "Locksley will be none too happy with any o' this."

"Do you know how I feel about your Lord Locksley?" Robin still gazed at the weapon as he asked the question.

"Everyone does," Bartleby said. "I've heard him rant oft enough to know it be a mutual thing."

"Then you will understand the compliment when I tell you this…" Robin spun the halberd in his hands, the blade whistling in an arc. "He does buy the finest of weapons."

The hardwood shaft blurred through the air, swung at the end of long arms and powered by archer's shoulders, faster than Much could see. It *kerranged* off Bartleby's helmet. The guard's eyes glazed over, then closed as he tipped forward and crashed facedown into the dirt.

Casually, Robin swung the halberd around, pointing the blade at Quentin.

"You." His voice was a dangerous growl. "Run away."

Quentin bolted.

Much chuckled as the guard ran, arms and legs flying every which way like the limbs of a disjointed chicken. He didn't look back or side to side, just ran pell-mell down the road until he disappeared around a curve.

Will Scarlet sniffed. "You could've had the decency to remind him that Locksley's land is that way." A slim finger pointed in the opposite direction.

Robin shrugged. "I'd wager he's done working for Arse-ley."

Will waved toward the guards on the ground. "What do you want to do with these two?"

Robin looked over. "Leave them to themselves." He nudged Bartleby with his toe. "This one will live, although his head will ring for a few days." He lifted his chin in the direction of the marked guard. "And he won't bleed out, I used a birding arrow without a broadhead, so before long he'll stop being sorry, and make his way back to Locksley for care."

"He'll hate you for the scar he'll have."

"Let him hate, that's his price for being an arsehole to our friend here." His hand clapped Much on the shoulder again.

Friend?

Robin's hand didn't move.

Friend.

Robin held out the halberd. "Would you like to keep it?" he asked. "You bested the original owner, so it's yours by right."

Much reached for it, then saw the hook on the haft and stopped himself. Pulling his hands back, he shook his head.

"I... I don't need it."

Robin nodded then looked back at the spear. "It is a fine weapon."

"Isn't it too big to fit your bow?" Will asked.

Robin's eyes lit up. "Now *that* would be an invention! A bow that could shoot halberds."

"We are at peace, cousin. Why on earth would we ever need something so terrible?"

The humor and delight fell from Robin's face.

"Things can change in the blink of an eye and the terrible becomes simple necessity. I've had dreams of late..." Robin drifted off without finishing his sentence.

"Dour talk on such a fine day." Will shook his head, blinked, and then threw out his best rapscallion grin. "We have a feast to attend, and you have just guaranteed us an exciting evening when Locksley learns of this."

Robin stared for a moment, then slowly smiled.

"You know, I am suddenly looking forward to the festivities."

Much looked from one man to the other. They might well be a bit mad, but he was glad to be in their company.

Quentin didn't get paid nearly enough to deal with the likes of Longstride's youngest son. Wet-nursed by a witch! The boy had been strange his whole life, known as a black-haired firebrand, prone to violence when provoked. And a lord's son at that.

You couldn't win up against something like that. It was why he ran. It wasn't cowardice, it was good sense. He wasn't about to come under a curse, just because Locksley wanted to collect more taxes.

None of that money went in Quentin's purse.

None that Locksley knew about anyway.

He stopped running when his lungs burned and the muscles in his legs twitched and jerked. He wasn't far enough away for peace of mind, though, so he kept looking behind him, sure that he would turn and see an arrow coming his way.

He left the road and cut across a field, so scattered he couldn't even think where he was and whose field he was in. The sun had sunk behind the trees, the gloom of twilight falling fast. He looked around to get his bearings. The field was full of dead wheat, the shafts of grass hollow and yellow and brittle. No green or color of flower broke the expanse. Then he saw a pillar of stone in the center of the field. It jutted from the ground, leaning slightly to the east.

Dread crept up his legs and settled in his bowels. He knew that stone. It was ancient, placed there long ago by some race of man long gone from England. Maybe the Celts, maybe the Picts, maybe the Fey. Legend had it that Morgana of the Fey, born with the curse of witch blood in her veins, had trapped the mighty Merlin beneath that very rock.

Nevertheless, he'd played around it as a child, he and his friends. It was a game to creep to the stone and touch it, then run like the devil was on your heels. Their parents had chided them, warning them that it was evil, forbidding the game.

They hadn't listened, continuing to play, growing bolder and bolder until one of the older boys took a dare to spend the night beside the stone.

He was never seen again.

Bastion. Bastion had been his name.

People said he'd run off, left to make his way in the world, to escape the hard life of a field hand.

The children never played by the witch stone again.

Quentin heard a step behind him and turned with a shout.

There was nothing. He turned back around and nearly jumped out of his skin. An old man stood in his way. His skin was gray like the stone and so wrinkled it was hard to make out any of his features. Something gleamed in the folds where his eyes should be, but Quentin had never seen eyes like those of this man. He stared at Quentin, looking deep into his meat, deeper into his bone. The old man's mouth opened impossibly large, as if his jaw dropped down forever and left just a gaping black hole in its place. He closed it rapidly, smacking his lips together.

Quentin shuddered and took a step back.

"What the hell are you doing, old timer?"

"Master is coming," the old man said.

"Who is your master?" Quentin asked, praying that the answer wasn't Longstride.

"Master over all this earth. Nearly here."

"You're crazy, old man," Quentin said, backing up further as the hair on the back of his neck lifted. Something deep in his gut told him it would be safer to deal with Longstride than with the ancient creature before him.

Off in the distance he heard a baying, as of hounds.

"Herald his arrival," the old man cackled, lifting hands that were gnarled, gray, and tipped with razorlike claws where fingernails ought to be.

"What does your master want?" Quentin continued to back away, terrified to turn.

"The red."

The old man's face contorted even further and his body jerked as though something were trying to crawl out of it. Black gore seeped from the creature's eyes and mouth, trailing through the folds of flesh, staining tracks along the wrinkled ridges. Quentin turned and ran back in the direction he'd come, back to young Longstride. He had to go back, throw himself on the ground and beg for mercy.

A roar shook the air behind him. He was jerked up off his feet and thrown through the air. He landed hard, bones breaking down the left side of his body from shoulder to ankle in a firestorm of agony. Pushing with his right leg he tried to move, to push through the pain, to keep going. He wheezed once into lungs lacerated by broken ribs, and blood spilled out of his mouth.

Above him, something monstrous and dark appeared against the twilight sky. Then all he could see in his own fading vision were eyes that glowed red.

"And when he comes, we feast," a booming voice said. The creature fell upon him, ripping at his chest with jagged teeth. It stunk of rotting meat as it gnawed into his breastbone, and, with his dying breath, Quentin cursed Locksley and Longstride both.

CHAPTER FOUR

"Milady, you aren't dressed!"

Marian looked up from her cup of tea, her left hand pulling the hem of her dressing gown down over her legs as she dropped from the window ledge. It hung from her, loose and light down to her feet, like wearing air.

"I still have time, ma'am," she said.

The housemarm swept into the room, frizzy head shaking on the end of a long thin neck like a child's bobble.

"This will not do, child. It simply will not do." She whisked over to the wardrobe and swung it open. "Guests will arrive very soon and you are the hostess. You must not be caught unawares."

"I am not unaware, good ma'am. Calm yourself. Chastity will—"

"And where *is* that wayward child? She should have you sorted already." The housemarm continued riffling through dresses, *harrumphing* loudly through her nose.

Marian held her hands up. "If you'd stop and let me—"

"This is last year's Christ Mass gown, but with some accessories it will do." The housemarm turned, arms full of gown, the silk and lace of it spilling over and trailing the floor. She draped the gown across the bed and turned to reach for Marian. "Now let's get you undressed, child."

Marian put her hands up, fighting to keep them from becoming fists. She could feel the skin on the back of her neck heat up, turning red from neckline to cheekbones, anger coloring her skin.

She hated it when people didn't listen to her.

"I am *not* your child."

The woman stopped short, sweeping immediately into a bow.

"Milady, I meant no disrespect."

"And yet you gave it."

"You must get dressed," she pleaded.

"And you *still* give it."

"Milady, the feast…"

Marian put up a finger. "Do *not* 'milady' me again."

The woman's mouth opened to speak, stopped, then shut. They stood eye to eye, neither of them blinking.

Time ticked away.

The housemarm's mouth opened again.

The door to the room crashed open as a stack of luxurious fabric came stumbling through on two legs.

"Oi! Some help here, princess," a muffled voice called from behind the fabric.

Marian turned away from her staring, moving toward the door, when the housemarm pushed past her. The older woman reached the stumbling fabric and grabbed an armful of it, hauling it into her grip to reveal a mountain of curly hair atop a pleasantly round face that broke into a smile.

"Sara!" the newcomer said cheerfully. "Glad you could come. We could use your wiry arms and extra hands."

"How *dare* you speak to the Lady Marian in such a manner?" the housemarm's mouth barely moved as she hissed. "I should have you lashed."

Chastity's face crashed like thunder across the hills.

"How dare you talk to *me* like that?" She pushed past with the shove of a rounded hip. "And good luck with having me lashed." She paused with a sly look. "I just might enjoy it." She dumped the dress onto the bed, winking at Marian where the older woman couldn't see.

The housemarm strode over, determined to regain some semblance of control, and began carefully laying the fabric she held across the end of the bed frame. Marian didn't recognize what it could be—to her it was just mounds of cloth. Sara straightened, and peered with accusation at Chastity.

"Why isn't she ready yet?" she demanded, sweeping her hand toward Marian.

Chastity locked eyes with her. She turned her head slowly, pointedly looking down at the mountain of fabric that lay on the bed, then turned her eyes back up to stare holes in the older woman's face.

"Could be that the dress just arrived," she replied. "Could be that she didn't need to be ready yet. Could be I was off in the stables having a go with one of the groomers."

"You are a disrespectful, low-born..."

Red crept from Chastity's jaw up to under her eyes and her mouth made a hard line. "Careful with the next word you say. I've a feeling it just may be insulting."

"That is *enough*." Marian stepped up. Both servants turned toward her, Sara's face twisted as if it had been boiled, Chastity's glowing with a smirk.

Marian pointed at the door. "I am sure that on such a festive day your services are needed elsewhere. Chastity will see to it that I am properly attired, and positioned at the ballroom entrance before the first guest arrives."

The housemarm stood stiffly, and didn't bow. "Yes. Milady." Turning on her heel, she marched out of the room.

Chastity waved her fingers toward the door. "Yes, *milady*," she sang, voice laden with mockery.

"Don't smirk," Marian said. "It's unbecoming."

"Only for a lady," Chastity replied. "For us low-born, *disrespectful* types it's quite the fashion."

Marian smiled in spite of herself. Chastity could always be

counted upon to lighten the mood, and Marian's had been much in need of lightening lately. For the past fortnight she'd been troubled by dark dreams that caused her to waken, startled, in the dead of night. Once up, she found it impossible to return to slumber. Exhausted much of the time, she felt like a ghost, haunting the castle, roaming the halls when all others were fast asleep.

It had been liberating in its own way, though. The silence found in the deep pockets of night allowed her time to think, and to explore the place where she lived. The castle was built long ago by a sect of masons who constructed a myriad of cubbyholes and pass-throughs that were not revealed on their plans. In recent days she'd discovered two new hidden passageways on the lowest level. They'd been built by her ancestors long ago, one tucked into a wall beside the kitchen, part of it following the back wall of the larder. The stilted smell of vegetation filled its still air.

Another could be reached from inside the privy, of all places, behind her own bedchamber. That one led to a steep, twisting incline that led down to the unused and musty dungeon located deep in the bowels of the building. From the looks of both, she was the only one to have disturbed the dust on their floors for quite some time.

Chastity shook out the skirts of the dress, interrupting Marian's thoughts. The piles of cloth began taking shape.

"Still no whispers about the meaning of tonight's festivities?" Marian asked.

"None." Chastity shoved her arms down the bodice of the dress and wadded the skirts until they bunched against her chest. "Drop your kit and hit the floor, princess."

Shrugging out of the shoulders of her dressing gown, she let the thin fabric fall, catching it at her waist. She glanced at the door, making sure it was closed, though it wasn't her nudity she felt she needed to hide.

"She's gone, princess."

"She might return."

"After that tongue lashing?" Chastity shook her head, tight ringlets of hair shimmering. "She'll find something better to do with her time."

Nevertheless, Marian glanced again at the door. Chastity placed a hand on her arm. It was warm against the skin.

"Do you want me to throw the bolt?"

Lips pressed tight, Marian shook her head.

"No, let's just get this done."

The nightgown dropped as she released it, falling into a pool at her feet. The sunlight from the window washed across her legs, leaving tiny black shadows under the edges of the raised scar tissue that lashed across otherwise perfectly formed limbs.

Chastity shook the dress into which she had shoved her arms, the skirts whispering against her skin. Marian knelt as she was supposed to and the room went away in a muffle of fabric that dropped over her head. Panic fleeted behind her now-blind eyes, a tiny rabbit of emotion nearly too fast to feel. The fabric tightened around her as Chastity wrestled to get the dress over her head.

The girl said something Marian couldn't understand through the swaddle of cloth that persisted in hooding her.

"What?" She yelled to be heard.

"—*tand fup*!"

Marian stood, twisting as she did to push through the folds. Light flooded in as the fabric parted and the dress slipped down her body.

Chastity stood close to her.

Very close.

The act of slipping on the dress left Marian pressed against her friend, the shorter woman's breath warm on her collarbone, her hands lightly on Marian's hips. Marian became completely aware of how… busty her friend was compared to her own lean frame and modest bosom.

The servant girl continued to pull and tug the dress into place, entirely unfazed by the intimacy. Chastity had been helping her dress for years. Together they'd walked the road from girl to woman.

"Have you asked the king directly?"

"What?" Marian said.

Chastity stepped back, studying her from top to bottom.

"Have you gone to the king and said to him, 'Oi! Why all the madness of a feast? What are you on about?'"

Marian smiled. "His Majesty wouldn't let even *me* talk to him like that."

The girl laughed. "Probably not."

Marian stood still as Chastity continued to work on the dress, pulling here and tugging there. It was almost soothing.

"Well, I guess we'll find out soon enough."

It was strange, though—the king, her uncle, usually kept her in his confidence. Not all sovercigns treated their relations in such a way, particularly female relations. She'd heard the king's cousin Henry kept all of his siblings and children at a distance, for fear that they would one day topple him from his throne. He married off all his sisters and daughters save his youngest, whom he sent to a remote school in the crags of the north. There was rumor that he'd had his older brother poisoned as a teen. Of course other rumors said the brother had plotted to have his throat slit, and that Henry had simply struck first.

Even the king's own brother, her Uncle John, lived far away in Ireland and was never mentioned by Richard. He'd been sent away by her grandfather because of some scandal, but Richard had not brought him back. The allure of power seemed to make sovereignty an uncertain thing, causing even good kings to act strangely toward their kin.

Yet she and Richard had shared a close bond ever since she was a child. Whenever her parents left their villa and took her to the castle, he always found time to spend with her, sometimes even making visiting dignitaries wait as he played hide and seek with her in one of his many gardens. Her father always said his brother loved her like the child he never had.

Their bond had strengthened when he'd taken her in after the fire that destroyed her life. His was the first face she saw after awakening from her injuries. He'd raised her as his own. Grief, his over the loss of a brother and sister by law, and hers over the loss of her parents, tied them together.

Once she was well enough, he finished her education, including the skills of horsemanship and swordplay her father had insisted she learn. He'd also taught her the intrigues of the court, including her in matters of the highest importance. Never had he kept anything from her. Not alliances, not military actions, not the quelling of unrest, and not the dispensation of boons. This time, however, whatever his purpose might be, it seemed as if the king kept counsel only with himself.

Chastity stepped back, moving from in front of the mirror that stood beside the wardrobe.

"What do you think, princess?"

Marian saw herself, a slender stick of a girl in a mound of mossy green fabric that seemed twice as wide as she could stretch out her arms. Scallops of cloth layered the dress in a scaled formation from the ground to her waist. A jewel, polished and sparkling, nestled on the edge of each upturned, petal-like section of cloth. They looked like limp dragon scales. This pattern continued up her waist and ribcage, ending at the edge of a laced bodice that drove her small breasts upward to sit just below her shoulders.

The sun coming through the window fell on her in a light haze, catching in each jewel and shining through them as if they were liquid drops of fire. The green fabric threw off the light, glowing but cut through with a pattern of shadow under each scallop. Dark and light caused her skin to glow like ivory and where the bodice straightened her posture and lifted her breasts she suddenly had the form of a queen, with her hair a mess from pulling the dress on perhaps a somewhat wanton queen, but one with power and agency to use it.

Her eyes widened.

"This dress is utterly... *ridiculous*."

"Ridiculously amazing!" Chastity chimed with glee.

Marian smiled in spite of herself.

True to her word, Marian was dressed and downstairs before the guests began to enter. The housemarm stood by the doors to the great hall as Marian descended the staircase, walking carefully, placing each foot deliberately on the step below her since she could not see them beneath the skirt. The woman's mouth pulled into a hard line as she bowed her head and walked stiffly away.

Marian felt the pang of distance between them. Sara meant no harm, she simply didn't take Marian as more than a girl, even though she was indeed old enough to marry and run a house herself.

Something that's not going to happen anytime soon. She wrinkled her nose at the thought. Her station as the king's niece and ward meant that her suitors chased not her, but proximity to the throne.

It made her tired.

Was it too much to ask for the old story to come true? Too much to want love, instead of security? Too much to ask for what her parents had possessed before...

No, it isn't, she thought fiercely, and she was stubborn enough to believe it. Besides, she was more than content to assist in the affairs of the court. Her work with and for the king gave her a satisfaction she would be loathe to let go.

The right man would never ask me to.

With that she swept into position, her skirts flaring around her as they were meant to. The gown hung heavily from her frame, but she had seen with her own eyes how beautifully it complemented her skin. Chastity had chosen well again. Once in place in the foyer, she gave the doormen a sharp nod to open the castle doors.

Outside stood a press of people—noble born, landowners, and craftsmen all heeding the call of King Richard. Shuffling into a line they moved toward her, the first stop of hospitality.

Plastering a smile on her face, she began. As the nobles arrived, each one announced by the herald, she read the opinions in their eyes and their polite murmurs.

Child.

Girl.

Breasts.

Illegitimate.

Looks of lust, looks of dismissal, looks of jealousy, and occasionally looks of genuine admiration. She kept her eyes and ears open, seeking information that could be of use to her uncle. It was amazing what some would say when the person who was listening was *just* a woman. Richard had recognized the advantage long ago. It was part of the reason he always held her in his confidence.

Always… until today.

The initial rush of guests became a blur of touchings, kisses into the air, and fluttering fans.

"How are you this evening?"

"Lovely to see you."

"Thank you for joining us."

"No, I do not know when he will arrive."

"Thank you, my servant chose it for me."

On and on and on. Just as she thought it would be forever, the line ended. There would be a short respite before the herald spoke again, and another guest would stride through to be greeted.

Her brow furrowed as she looked for a particular face.

Chastity appeared at her side.

"Who is it you keep hoping to see?" the girl asked.

"What makes you think I'm hoping to see someone?" Marian countered.

"The excitement on your face every time the herald begins to announce a new arrival, followed by the look of disappointment when another person walks past."

Marian shook her head. Chastity was forever paying attention to the smallest details, yet she was right. There was one face Marian was hoping to see among the arrivals. He'd been in her thoughts increasingly of late, although she hadn't shared that with Chastity.

Then she thought of King Richard.

It seemed as if there were a lot of secrets being kept.

A circle of torches guttered in the night, pushing back the dark and flinging ruddy highlights up the edges of the standing stone. The dead wheat grass had been trampled flat inside the circle. The gray man knelt before two men, his wrinkled head bowed low.

"I serve," he said.

"You have done well," the taller of the two replied. Torchlight glittered on the edges of his armor and painted his hair red. "One more task, and you may find your burrow again."

"Anything to bring master."

"Bring to me an oblation tied to this land, a thread of the fabric."

The gray man tilted his head as if in thought, face turned toward the night sky. After a long moment he nodded and stood, then walked out of the circle of light and into the surrounding darkness.

"So you are that thing's master?"

The armored man turned. "No, princeling, it serves the same master as I."

The shorter man sniffed. "So it is your equal."

"It is a principality. It is tied to this land."

"That's not a denial."

The tall man turned. His eyes reflected the torchlight as small infernos in pools of basalt. "Watch your tongue, or I shall show it to you."

The smaller man stepped back, raising his hands. "Mere curiosity. Nothing more, Sheriff." He sniffed again. "I like this place better than the hovel I was in. It smells better."

When the tall man did not speak he fell silent and waited, listening to the crackle and hiss of the guttering torches.

CHAPTER FIVE

"Your outfit is ridiculous."

Will looked down at his finest clothes, worn for the occasion. The shirt and leggings had been dip-dyed a rich black that patterned from midnight to blue-black in a subtle motif that tricked the eye in the warm yellow of the lanterns lining the walkway. The same tallowed light turned his shagreen vest, dyed a bright cardinal red, into a color more akin to virgin's blood. His Iberian boots had been replaced by low, slouchy, short-heeled shoes from France.

He felt that he looked just enough the villain to turn a head or two this evening. Satisfied, he looked Robin over, head to toe.

"What you should hope," he commented wryly, "is that I can distract the people from *your* clothing."

"What's wrong with my clothing?" Robin had removed his hunting hood and replaced it with a plain leather jerkin, put over the same tunic and trousers he'd been wearing when Will found him.

"Well, it's... nothing." Will shook his head hopelessly. "Nothing at all." They fell into silence as they drew closer to the castle gates.

It was uncommon for the king to call for a feast, and this one was made all the more remarkable by the secrecy that surrounded it. It had come out of the blue, unattached to any holiday or major event. Rumors claimed the king would make some form of announcement, but no hint had been given as to what.

Even as a young boy Will had been fascinated by the intrigues of life at court—who was coming and going, petitions for the king's wisdom and his resources, boons granted and judgments delivered. Being from a noble family, he could hover around the throne room and the meeting halls and listen to the conversations with little fear of being rousted.

As a young man, he'd begun plying the standing of his family—including Robin's father—to insert himself into the machinations of sovereignty. He recognized that he possessed no power, but he did hold a certain reputation, everyone knowing him and most of them liking him.

It was one of many ways in which he and Robin were so different that sometimes he wondered if they were related at all. Perhaps Robin really was a foundling, some strange fey child taken in and cared for by his uncle. Will's mother had once told him that Robin's mother believed him a changeling.

That would explain so much.

He watched the groups of nobles making their way into the castle.

"Look," he said, as he pointed ahead of them. A pair of elegant, fair-haired people were about to cross the threshold with two elegant, fair-haired girls in tow. "It's your family, minus your brother. We should catch up so we can arrive together."

"Hurry on if you want," Robin said. "I will arrive when I choose."

"Don't be surly."

"I'll be better with ale."

"You're not going to save the ale for the poor?" Will winked. "There are thirsty families out there."

"Smartarse."

* * *

Soon the doorway loomed in front of them, stones cut by the masons and stacked to form a double arch. Robin's eyes traveled up the polished rock and hand-tooled mortar until they landed on the one odd stone in the group. High in the right archway hung a rough-hewn block, chiseled into the shape needed to fit the gap it filled. It was the keystone. The master mason himself, generations back, had carved and placed that stone. It alone held the pressure from all the other stones, locking them into their arch, holding them to the task of forming the doorway.

One stone, different from the rest, the only thing maintaining the integrity of the castle gates. If someone were to remove it, the entire front facade would weaken and crumble from its own weight. He picked out the chiseled initials of the master mason, located just below the carved all-seeing eye of God. He had no idea who that long-forgotten man had been, but was fascinated by the idea that he had designed such a work with but a single weak spot.

"Robin, beware." Will touched his arm.

Five men approached from inside—four guardsmen and a stoutly built noble with dark hair and hawk eyes blazing beneath pulled brows. The noble wore a double rampant lion on his tunic, the two raging beasts glaring white against the sapphire-blue cloth. The man's dark face looked as if it had been pushed into a furnace. Rage twisted his features, and his teeth shone wetly behind snarled lips.

Locksley.

Robin's shoulders tensed at the threat that stalked toward him, his body growing tight with adrenaline. Unconsciously his hands reached for a bow and quiver that were not there.

"It is the king's feast," Will whispered harshly. "This is just posturing—no one would do violence here."

Nevertheless, Robin reached to the skinning knife hidden behind his belt. The leaf-shaped blade was only two fingers long, but sharper than a razor.

"I'm not betting our lives on Locksley's manners," he muttered.

"Don't break the law."

"And if he does?"

"Then at least don't break the law *first*." With that, Will stepped in front of him, both hands up, palms out.

"Locksley! Imagine running into you here, at the castle, for the king's feast, where all men are brothers and no man seeks to commit violence upon another."

Locksley's chest bumped against Will's hands.

"Out of my way, Scarlet," he growled. "I have business with that craven scoundrel."

Will dug in his feet, pushing back.

"Let's let cooler heads prevail," he said.

"You attacked my men," Locksley said over Will's shoulder.

"They attacked a boy," Robin responded.

"One of them has disappeared, and another will never hold a sword again."

"Yet he will live, and that's more than might have been said for the boy had I not arrived when I did."

Again Locksley pushed against Will's hands. "You may run through the woods like a wildling, but you will not get away with assaulting my men. You will be taught your lesson."

Robin watched Locksley's men as they began working their way to the left and the right, circling him. With only the skinning knife to defend himself, he'd have to kill at least one of them. The thought sat in his mind, squatting and strange, pushing up against the back side of his brain.

I'll need to take a man's life.

He had been taught that life was sacred, even the lives of simpletons who were stupid enough to swear allegiance to a man such as Locksley. Yet he would not submit himself to them, and so blood would be shed.

A crowd gathered, people drawn by the voices raised just outside the castle gate. It wouldn't take long for the commotion to draw the attention of the guards or, worse, his father.

This needs to end.

"If you have such a grievance against me, perhaps we should

speak with King Richard," Robin said, taking a deep breath. "I'm sure that when he hears that your men have been levying a tax on *his* road, in *your* name, that he will be most interested."

He studied Locksley's face, looking for the moment when the other man would choose just how far he was going to push things. He kept his hand on the skinning blade, muscles tensed and ready. Whatever happened next, it was Locksley's choice. Robin's conscience would be clear.

A sudden footstep sounded behind him, strong and filled with confidence. He knew it so well he did not need to turn.

"My brother is in need of being taught many lessons," the newcomer said. "He is stubborn. I have tried for many years to soften his hard head, and have learned the futility of my efforts. What I do not need to be taught, however, is the value of loyalty—to my blood and to my king. Speak your grievances to me, or stand aside."

Locksley paled. There wasn't a man alive who had the will to challenge Robert Longstride, favorite agent of the king and deadliest sword in the land.

"Little brother, do you have anything to add?" Robert asked.

"Only this," Robin said, fixing his eyes on Locksley. "From this day forth, the Millers are under my protection. *Any* harm occurs to them and *you* will answer for it tenfold."

Locksley turned red. He was angry and embarrassed, but he wasn't stupid. He turned and, without another word or a backward glance, he strode into the castle. His men scurried behind him.

"Why did you say that?" Will asked.

"Because Locksley is a fool, and a proud one," Robin said. "He cannot touch me, but I can see him harming the boy or his family in some sort of childish retaliation."

At that moment Robert stepped up. A giant of a man, he stood nearly half a foot taller than his younger brother, and there was no one in the land with a more regal bearing—save King Richard himself. Like the rest of their family, save Robin, Robert was fair-haired.

"I thought your threat was a nice touch," he said, his voice jovial as he put a hand on Robin's shoulder.

"I'm surprised Father hasn't already informed the king of Locksley's activities," Robin said. "If he had, perhaps the boy wouldn't have needed saving."

"Nor you tonight, eh?" Robert added with a grin.

Robin sighed, but said nothing. He exchanged a glance with Will. At least his cousin understood—Robin hadn't been the one in need of saving. He didn't have to guess what his father would believe, though. He felt his spirits darken.

"Come now, it's time to join the others," Robert turned toward the gate.

"I am no longer in the mood," Robin said.

Robert looked from him to Will, who shrugged. Robert sighed deeply then turned and walked away.

Will leaned toward Robin. "Come now, be grateful, cousin. At least you didn't have to kill anyone." He put his hand on Robin's arm. "Can you imagine what the splatter of blood would do to my wonderful clothes?" He smiled, attempting to liven things.

Robin did not even try to conjure a smile.

"I don't know," he said. "I think it would have added a nice roguish touch. The ladies would likely have found you twice as fascinating."

"Well, tonight, there's only one lady I'm thinking about, and not for my own sake. I refuse to leave this castle until I have seen you dance with the Lady Marian."

"Then for your sake," Robin replied, "I hope she says yes. Otherwise you will have to spend the rest of your miserable life in this godforsaken place."

A hand touched her elbow. Marian turned to find Chastity beside her.

"What was that commotion?" she asked.

"I don't know, but I will find out for you." The girl's eyebrow twitched up at the thought of gathering information. "For now, though, it's time."

"Already?"

"The king was clear that the feast would commence at the beginning of the third watch," Chastity replied. "That time is now."

"Very well. Help me with this dress."

Chastity moved behind her, gathering the skirt into a bustle that drew the hem from the floor so that Marian would be able to walk. As she waited, however, she watched the castle doors.

Through the entrance strode Robin Longstride.

Her heart caught in her chest.

He was like a storm off the ocean, dark and full of violent potential. Fire flashed in his eyes. She was drawn to the play of muscle in his forearms as his hands clenched and unclenched. Something had happened to anger him and she could tell that he was controlling himself, but just barely.

His eyes met hers, and he stopped.

They stared. Unblinking. Unmoving.

Then he took a deep breath. He held it, chest swollen, keeping the precious air caged inside for a long moment. Her own breathing locked, waiting for his. Her heart beat, hollow and rattling inside her like dice in a cup.

With a parting of lips, he let his breath free.

She let hers go, as well. Then, unsure, she gave a smile so barely there it might be mistaken for a trick of the light.

Robin touched his fingers to his brow in salute to her.

"Oi, princess. There you go." Chastity gave a push against her now fastened bustle, forcing her to break eye contact. It was just as well. At that moment Will Scarlet—small, dark, *charming* Will Scarlet—hurried to Robin's side.

Shaking herself, she walked to the center of the room. Robin and Will moved to the side, and, even though he spoke to his cousin, his eyes were still on her.

It bothered her not at all.

Projecting assurance and confidence, she raised her arms

and clapped her hands three times above her head. The room snapped to silence, all eyes turned to her.

"My lords and ladies, gentle folk one and all," she said, her voice loud, firm, and crisp, "it is time for the king's feast to begin."

A cheer went up, hale and hearty and many-voiced. She turned and moved toward the doors of the main hall as they swung open.

The moment all were seated, servants entered from the left, where the kitchen was located. They carried platters laden with all manner of roasted meats, placing them on the tables. Fresh fruit, a particular delicacy, was present in abundance.

Will watched as Robin reached for a leg attached to a roast pheasant, ripped it off with a twist, and pulled it onto his platter.

His father frowned from his place down the table.

"Wait until the entire feast has been served," he said sternly. "It is the proper way." His mother gave him a dark look, her mouth turned down in the way it always did when he drew her attention.

Without listening, Robin continued to pull food onto his platter. Down the line of the table others, inspired by his brazenness, also began reaching in, plucking delicacies and putting them on platters of their own. By the time the cup bearers arrived with wine and mead, everyone had begun to eat. For the occasion the king had provided only the best, right down to drink. As people ate, they began to talk.

"Do you know what country this is from?"

"Why are we here?"

"I'll try that, I've never even seen it before."

"When will the king arrive?"

"I'll start with mead and end with wine."

"Is there trouble in the land?"

"Perhaps he has found a wife to replace the queen, God rest her soul."

Will became less concerned with the reason for the feast as he heartily enjoyed all that was set before him. After several minutes—and several cups of light, dry wine from Germania—Alan-a-Dale rose from his seat next to Friar Tuck and the band of his brother monks who were responsible for providing both the ale and the mead to the feast.

He didn't say anything, simply walked languorously to the center of the room. A hush fell, every eye turning his way. His checkered cloak hung off one shoulder, meticulously pinned in the old Celtic way with folds and creases that made the pattern seem to swirl and shimmer as he moved. It hypnotized, charming the eye and capturing the mind.

Will suffered a momentary pang of jealousy at the bard's audacious style.

Looking into the middle distance, eyes unfocused, Alan-a-Dale reached up and began unbuckling the harp that rode in its case on his left shoulder. He undid the last tiny silver buckle, and the crowd gasped as the ancient harp rolled down his chest, tumbling toward the floor.

He caught it at the last moment and gave a deep bow, coupled with a small chuckle. The warm sound broke the tension and the gathered audience followed it with laughter of their own.

The minstrel let them have their mirth. As Will laughed with his family, even Robin was smiling. Will studied how the bard played the crowd, taking notes in his head for anything he might use to garner attention and curry favor. As much as he strove to insert himself into court, he hated arse-kissers and refused to be one, instead relying on the art of genuine charm.

If Will were an artist, then Alan-a-Dale was a master.

Laughter continued to roll and pulse in the room, slowly dying down until the bard reached up and strummed slender fingers across metallic strings.

"I recently found myself in Ireland," he announced, "and here is a song of the Emerald Isle."

With that he was off, entertaining them all with songs and news of the north. Will had never met the man's match when it came to singing or spinning a good yarn. Around the room the women—including Robin's sisters Rebecca and Ruth—gazed at the singer in adoration. Will chuckled softly to himself. His young cousins were growing up fast, faster than he imagined their parents wanted to admit.

Change comes whether you seek it or not.

CHAPTER SIX

Movement drew their attention. Into the torchlit circle came the gray man. He dragged a burlap sack behind him. One side of his face hung, the wrinkled skin flayed open along his cheek. The thin skin swung from his jaw, brushing against his chest with each shuffling step. The meat that lay underneath was the same pallid gray as the rest of him. In the flickering light it shimmered and moved, covered with crawling maggots.

The gray man stopped three paces away. He lifted the sack, grabbed the end of it, and turned it upside down. One sharp shake and something fell out, landing at their feet with a thump and clank.

Both men looked down. There lay a creature the size of a child, bound in shackles. Its skin was smooth and blemish free except where the iron manacles clamped cruelly against its wrists. There the skin blistered and smoked, thin curls wisping up with each brush against the metal. Its face was fine-boned and smooth, its nose a button between plump lips and liquid eyes four times the size they should have been. Silky hair of the palest sapphire parted around a pair of feral, pointed ears. The eyes flashed with hatred and the plump lips were pulled wide to show rows of needle-thin teeth locked into a grimace.

The smaller man crouched, staring at the creature. "What is that thing?"

"One of the trow," the tall man answered.

The smaller man reached out his finger to touch the creature. He barely pulled it back in time as the trow lunged, teeth snapping where the finger had been.

"Vicious little shite."

"The iron causes it pain."

The smaller man stood. "That why you had me bring this?" His hand disappeared under his cloak, coming out with a long, slender dagger. The metal was a dull gray that nearly disappeared in the dim light. The blade was wafer thin, both edges ground to razor sharpness. The taller man's voice came out dry and sardonic. "I chose you for your ability to quickly grasp a situation."

"But *I* summoned *you*."

The tall man's thin lips twitched in what could be mistaken for a smile.

Drawing their attention, the gray man knelt beside the struggling creature.

"Good enough?"

The tall man nodded. "Near perfect." He passed his hand over the gray man's head and his voice took on a cadence of power. "You may return to your barrow, return to your hole, return to the loam that covers you, return to the effluvium and decay. Lie in wait until root becomes branch and branch becomes root and the worm that dieth not walks free among the tombstones."

The gray man raised his wide, shovel-like hands to his face, covering it completely. He spoke three words in a language that had not been uttered by humans since the Tower of Babel. His hands lifted to the sky and his face turned with them. He stood in supplication for a long moment and everything paused—both men, the creature in its bonds, even the torches ceased their sputtering and burned with steady, still flame.

Finally, the gray man dropped his hands and turned away, shuffling off into the dark without a glance back.

The creature on the ground began to howl, a long, plaintive drawl of noise full of sorrow and threaded through with fear.

The tall man kicked it lightly with a booted foot.

"Stop that."

The creature's mouth shut, cutting off the noise.

"What is your name?"

"So you can use it in your working?" The creature's voice was smooth and melodious, the sound of rain on a leafy bough, of a sparrow's flight. "Not in this world or the next."

The tall man chuckled. "I don't need your name to do what I plan to do." He turned to the smaller man, who still held the iron blade. "Gut him."

"What?"

"You heard me. Stick that knife in his gullet and split him open."

The smaller man held out the knife.

The tall man shook his head. "It is to be by your hand, princeling."

The smaller man looked at the creature on the ground, then at the knife in his hand, then back.

"This is necessary?"

The tall man said nothing.

The smaller man knelt beside the creature, who watched him with impossible eyes. He took a deep breath and put his hand on the creature's chest.

"Wait!" the creature cried. "You don't have to do this. Not this. I can give you what you seek without it."

"You don't know what we seek."

"Two men in a dead field by the witch stone, consorting with a principality… I'd wager that you want power."

The tall man touched the creature's shoulder and spoke. "What power can you give us? You are our captive."

"I am the land here. Me and mine are the guardians. I can give you the strength of the earth, if you take off these blasted chains."

"You would give us your dominion, in return for your life?"

"Dominion's no good if I'm not alive to exercise it."

"Stay true to your nature," the tall man said. "You were asked a question, speak the truth."

"I would trade my power for my life."

The tall man nodded. "The gray man chose well." He lifted his hand and nodded. "Do it."

"Wait, *no*…"

Leaning his weight on the arm that held the creature flat to the ground, the smaller man pushed the blade into its stomach. The knife slid in with a hiss, and he pushed it around the bottom of the creature's stomach, twisting his wrist to keep it moving until it had carved a great furrow from the creature's ribcage on one side, down and around the stomach, and back up again to slide out when it struck the creature's breastbone.

A thin liquid the color of peat moss spilled and gushed from the wound. It smelled musty like swamp water as it washed up the man's arm, soaking his tunic sleeve.

The creature screamed into the night like an animal.

The tall man stepped on the creature's throat, choking off the cries. "Pull it open. Quickly, before the power is gone," he said.

The smaller man lay down the knife. The creature writhed weakly, held by the hand on its chest and the boot on its throat. Each twist of its body made the cut gape and pull. The small man reached with two fingers and gingerly grasped the edge of the flap he'd carved across the creature's midsection. He pulled and it lifted a few inches before it caught on something inside. His fingers curled around the skin and he yanked, pulling it free with a tearing sound.

Inside the body lay organs in strange shapes and configurations. They were not like any animal or human he had seen. There was a coil of something that looked very like a long worm the thickness of his wrist. Above that lay a mass the shape of two fists twined together. Nestled inside a ribcage made of thin, curving bones that wove together in a mesh, lay what he presumed to be the creature's heart, still beating. It looked like the nest of a seabird, a mottled clump of wet weed and broken sticks. He reached for it instinctively.

"No, you fool!" the tall man hissed. "Take the viscera. Hurry, before the life fades."

The prince dug his hands into the coil. It was hard, like boiled leather, and slippery. Fingers clamped around it, he pulled it from the cavity with a sucking sound, one end still trailing back into the twitching body.

"Drape it around your neck."

He did as instructed. The thing lay heavy across the back of his neck, cool where it touched his skin. The tall man held out his hands, fingers twisting into forms that looked to require more than three joints.

"We stand in the blood of this land and lean into the embrace of its flesh," the tall man intoned. "We sain ourselves to this place by this sacrifice and stake our claim to it."

Something changed in the air. The warm trickle of magic crackled along the prince's skin. It raised the hairs on the back of his neck and he found himself erect and throbbing in a push-pull of pain and pleasure. His eyes rolled back in his head as the tall man continued to speak.

"...bend to our will, bow to our desires, we invade thee. We penetrate thy defenses and lay this land bare to us. We cannot be denied. There is no protection against us, no binding of our power, no sanctuary to this land. We are free to work our will and to seek our destiny.

"We declare it in the name of the Three Below, in accordance with the prophecy told and untold, as we speak it to power we will it to become. This sacrifice, this moment, these words, this ritual."

He clapped his hands and lightning from the clear night sky struck the witch stone. The smaller man jumped. The air in the circle swirled, superheated by the blast. The stone glowed, red hot, and the dead wheat grass sparked to fire, tiny flames licking their way across the circle. The prince felt it, felt the tightness break. Since setting foot on this shore he had been bound, his magic shuttered within him.

Now he understood that the land itself had been protected from him, and from the Sheriff. With the sacrifice of the creature, that protection had been broken.

Their plan could now begin.

The Sheriff lowered his hands, face stark in the light of the glowing witch stone.

"So it is spoken, so mote it be."

CHAPTER SEVEN

After several songs, Friar Tuck rose to his feet and walked toward Marian. He leaned a little to the left and walked with the gait of someone determined not to stagger under the load of the enormous amount of ale they had consumed.

He leaned down, moving his mouth by her ear. His warm, moist breath smelled like unbaked bread dough, confirming her assessment.

"Milady, I would like to say something to the people," he said, his voice low. "As hostess, do you mind?"

She nodded her assent and held her breath for a moment, wondering what his announcement was going to be.

While the bard still sang, the monk stalked to the center of the room, big feet slapping hard on the marbled floor. He stood, swaying to the rhythm of the song. Droopy eyelids closed and his mouth turned up in a smile of pure joy. People began watching him, nudging their tablemates and pointing. The priest seemed not to care, lost to the melody of the harp and the bard's voice. His hands rose, hanging limply at the wrist as he waved them in time with the music, shoulders bouncing in a rhythm that didn't quite match.

Paying him no heed, the bard drove on, pushing his voice and his fingers to make the music a rolling thing. His face glowed, his mouth lively and laughing through the song, fingers a blur on the harp strings. Friar Tuck rolled and swayed, bending at the waist and turning at the knee as his hands and arms swirled along with the tune, possessed by the music to move in ways seemingly too fluid for his girth.

The people around the tables were all caught up, the music driving and driving and driving, pulling listeners to the edge of their seats. Everyone leaned together and held their breath, the feast forgotten, the world outside forgotten. Everything that had been, was, and would be swirled into that very moment.

The song ended with a crash of notes and the two men standing close enough to touch. For a long moment no one moved.

Or breathed.

Friar Tuck opened his eyes, his smile growing larger as he found his dear friend standing beside him, harp still vibrating from the last note struck.

"Thank you," he said. His voice was a whisper, but the silence in the room let everyone hear it.

Alan-a-Dale nodded, just once. Slowly he turned, his gaze sweeping the crowd. As his eyes fell on the gathered people, it released them from the hold that gripped them, breaking the spell of the moment. One by one they sat back and breathed again, smiling and still feeling the ebb of rapture in their hearts.

His eye fell to her last, and Marian felt that break.

"That is the power of a true bard," she said, commending the singer.

People raised their glasses, and murmurs of "hear hear!" and "amen!" rang out. Alan waved them away and stepped back to his place at the table.

Friar Tuck shook his head.

"I had something to say, but it seems almost silly now. That was a moment given by the Most High, and I am humbled to quietude by being a part of it."

"Not that humble!" someone cried. Laughter broke among the people and Friar Tuck bowed his head at the jest, taking the jab with grace.

"No, I suppose not," he said. "Well, no more proclamations until the king arrives." He clapped his hands together, the noise like a crack of thunder so loud it made Marian jump in her seat. "However, let us have some dancing!"

All around, people came to their feet and moved to a cleared space of floor. The monks stood. From under their robes and under the table several of them pulled out instruments. Quickly they gathered behind Alan-a-Dale, and the sound of music filled the hall.

Friar Tuck walked over to Marian.

"You, too, my dear," he said firmly. "You should dance while you're young."

She looked at him and smiled, emboldened by his display.

"I'll do that very thing." She rose to her feet and moved to join the others. As she did so, however, she considered the night thus far. Clearly the king planned on keeping everyone in the dark for as long as possible. To what end, she couldn't fathom.

The dancers assembled in two circles, the women on the inside and the men on the outside. She saw Lord Locksley break free from the line, heading toward her with determination.

Her stomach tightened and underneath her gown her skin turned damp and hot. There was nothing wrong with Locksley, save the fact that he was old enough to be her father. Since he was a widower of several years, it wasn't improper for him to approach her for a dance. Yet every time they spoke, she knew that he was far more interested in her lineage than in her self and it left her cold.

A sudden, quick movement out of the corner of her eye made her turn, only to find Robin standing close enough to touch. A smile danced on his lips and his hand extended toward her.

"May I?"

"You may indeed."

The moment their hands touched, her skin calmed and she felt grounded, connected to the earth. Robin paraded her to the formation of dancers. As they passed Locksley she could feel the other man's jealousy.

Robin chuckled softly. "Och, he looks a mite displeased."

"Does he?" She feigned ignorance.

They stepped into position, his arm going around her waist. He stepped close, pulling her tighter than was courtly. Dark eyes flashed down at her.

"I seem to be unable to see him any longer."

"Do you have something in your eye, Robin of Longstride?"

"Only everything, Maid Marian of Lionheart."

The music began and they were off, laughing and spinning, weaving among other couples like frantic planets wheeling across the cosmos. The band of monks, led by the bard, played a jaunty tune that drove them to high-step and pinwheel at the change of a note. Robin moved with the assurance of a practiced dancer, leading with strength. He pulled her through the steps without being rough, allowing her to move in time with him. Her body seemed to fall away from her, becoming weightless and fluid.

She couldn't remember the last time she'd had quite so much fun dancing.

As soon as the song ended another began, the notes of the first flowing into a wistful, slower melody. People scrambled, changing partners, but Robin pinned her with his eyes and didn't let go.

Ready to go again? he asked with a small smirk and a cocked eyebrow.

She replied by smiling silently.

Yes.

They danced again, and she kept dancing with him song after song after song. Flushed and dizzy and tingling with a kind of joy she had never known, she laughed the entire time, until she could no longer catch a breath.

"Enough. Enough!" she said.

Robin swung her into a dip, holding her body close to his, supported only by the strength of his arms. He smiled and the world slipped away.

"I accept your surrender."

"Not a surrender," she protested, "merely a regrouping."

He lifted her to her feet and gave a slight bow. "Till we meet again on the field of battle."

She curtsied. "'Twas a lovely war."

The doors to the great hall swung open with a crash against the walls. Everyone turned as one. Conversations died. The music stopped.

King Richard the Lionheart strode into the room.

He did not turn aside or pause. Walking with purpose, shoulders set, crowned head held high, he wore the sort of look he might in battle—a hardened gleam in his eye and sharpness to his jaw that his oiled beard could not hide. He was the Warrior King, the Unblemished Blade, the Lion of England. The gathered dancers parted before him as he walked to the raised area at the back of the hall, set for the king's table.

It wasn't until he passed that Marian noticed the cardinal walking several paces behind her uncle, his shoulders stooped, his head bowed. It seemed to her as if he walked like a man who had lost something dear.

Richard climbed to the stage. Honey-brown eyes swept the crowd until they found her. He gave her a strange little smile. She returned it through her confusion. Turning away, he raised his arm, even though he already had everyone's rapt attention.

"I have one announcement," he said. His voice boomed across the now silent hall. Everyone held his or her breath again, as they waited to find out the true reason they had been summoned that night.

"There is danger in the Holy Land," the king continued. "The Holy See is calling for men to free the precious city of Jerusalem from a darkness that threatens to overtake it." His hand dropped. "I will heed his call. Within the fortnight I set sail east. Tonight I call upon every lord and free man to join me in this Holy Crusade for the sanctity of our very faith."

The crowd remained silent, stunned now. Marian looked around, noting the surprise on all the different faces. No one moved. No one spoke.

Slowly Robin's father climbed to his feet and raised his cup.

"Let me be the first to pledge a hundred men, all the resources of Longstride Manor, and my own sword, your Majesty."

Across the room Robert Longstride leaped upon the bench he shared with his friends. "I go with my father! Two Longstride swords for the king!"

Richard smiled. "Thank you, old friend."

Robin stepped forward. "But the both of you can't go…"

"Don't prattle." Lord Longstride cut him off with a sharp gesture and a glare. "Sit down. Now."

Robin's eyes, so full of merriment moments before, turned dark again with anger. Without another word he turned and strode out of the hall. As he did so, Marian's heart skipped a beat. To leave an official announcement by the king, without Richard's permission, was unthinkable. She glanced quickly at her uncle, hoping that he wouldn't mete out a swift and terrible punishment.

To her surprise, Richard didn't seem the least fazed by the insult. Instead he continued scanning the faces of all the others present. One by one, several other lords stood and pledged their services to his Crusade. Within moments half the room was promised to board the boats and cross the ocean.

Locksley climbed to his feet, making a show as if the effort cost him dearly.

"Sire, this is madness," he said, his voice strained. "You must turn from this path."

"I will not." Richard's face hardened.

"But what occurs half a world away is not the concern of Englishmen," Locksley pressed. Murmurs of assent rose around the room. None loud, nor clear, but a buzz of agreement.

"Do you think evil stops unchecked?" Richard replied. "Do you believe that once the sacred relics of our faith have been despoiled, ransacked, and blasphemed, that the infidels will be sated?" His voice was a rumble of thunder now. "No! They will continue to spread, destroying any holy place they can find. Evil knows no bounds, lest righteous men find a way to constrain it."

Locksley shook his head. "I will not pledge my support to this."

"You spineless cur, your father would have!" Lord Longstride shouted. He leaped forward, clearing the table before him in a spatter of plates and food, lunging at Locksley. Suddenly the two men were locked with each other and rolling on the ground. The room filled with the *chang* of dress armor on the marble tile, and the dull, meaty thuds of fists. Marian watched Robert striding across the room to his father's aid, and breathed a prayer of thanks that Robin had left.

"Enough!" the king roared.

The two men froze.

Richard lifted his gaze, dismissing the two combatants as if they were irrelevant, daring either of them to continue fighting as he spoke.

"We set sail at dawn in ten days' time. All who support their king should present themselves at the ships." His eyes swept the room. "The rest of you remain safe in your beds as we fight in the name of the Lord Jesu."

Stepping off the stage he swept alone through the room, fierce and majestic. His boots clapped on the floor and his silken capelet snapped in the air behind him. Silence accompanied his departure.

The moment he disappeared from sight, however, the room exploded in conversation. Some murmured in small groups, others argued loudly. Looking around, Marian saw dismay on many faces. It echoed what she felt in her heart.

Why hadn't he told her?

Who would be in charge with the king gone?

Why was he abandoning his people?

Why was he abandoning *her*? None of it made any sense.

Chastity bumped her with a hip and leaned close. "You need to do something to check this mood before it spoils, princess," she whispered urgently. "This could go ugly too quickly."

Marian nodded to her friend. She forced herself to smile, and walked slowly to the stage that had just been abandoned. She was the king's representative in his absence. It was her responsibility.

"My lords and ladies," she said, loudly enough to be heard over the din. "Thank you all for being here tonight. Please, eat and drink your fill." The hubbub died down, and she motioned toward Alan. "Bard, more music. Please."

Alan-a-Dale nodded, lifted his ancient harp, and began playing a jaunty tune that did nothing to elevate her spirits or alleviate the pain she felt, but seemed to soothe the crowd, breaking apart the seething confusion. The implications of Richard's announcement began to swirl in her mind. This would affect everyone in the kingdom. Noble to peasant. Families would be separated, the harvest would be a daunting task, and a portion of the men who could be called to defend the land would be away. England would be vulnerable.

Weakness drew jackals and wolves.

She breathed a prayer.

Stepping from the stage, she walked among the guests, listening to snatches of conversation here and there. The voices strained with concern, but anger seemed to have fled everyone in the room.

Except one.

Friar Tuck had moved to a corner, a goblet in each fist. He glared daggers at the cardinal, who was engaged in conversation and seemed oblivious to the friar's fury.

The cardinal... the king had met with him right before the feast. She thought back to his posture as he trailed in behind her uncle.

He knew all along what the king had planned.

She walked to the cardinal's side and caught his eye. He turned from those with whom he was talking and led her a few steps away. She bowed her head.

"I am sorry, Your Grace, for disturbing your conversation. It's just that..."

He waved a gentle hand toward her, wiping away her apology. "I've asked the king not to go, to just send men in his stead, but he refuses." He sighed and she watched the motion as it shook the parchment skin on his cheeks and throat. "He is a brave one. A fierce warrior. I shall pray every day for his safe return."

The man's words made sense, but his eyes were veiled.

He's keeping something to himself.

She had long ago learned that it was impossible to get a holy man to talk when he chose not to, so she didn't bother asking him to explain. No, she was going to have to speak with the king.

Marian took her leave, and slipped from the hall, walking briskly. Cutting around corners and turning down halls with which she was intimately familiar, she managed to avoid anyone but servants. Within a quarter turn of the glass she reached her uncle's suite. A burly guard, his armor polished but dented from combat, stood at attention by the door.

"Is the king in his chambers?" she asked.

"No, milady." The man dropped his eyes to the ground.

"Then where is he? It is imperative that I speak with him immediately."

"I am sorry, but that is not possible. He is taking in some night air, and has closed himself to visitors."

So he was in the garden courtyard.

She stepped forward. "That does not include me."

The guard lifted his hand, palm out but careful not to actually touch her.

"He made himself clear, milady. *All* visitors."

She stared at him for a long moment, then turned and walked away.

CHAPTER EIGHT

The door slammed open, crashing against the wall. A vase on a table shuddered, rocked, and fell to the floor. Robin expected it to shatter, but it was made of sterner stuff than he realized. Only the rim chipped, catapulting a tiny sliver—a needle of ceramic—that spun away and disappeared into the shadows at the edge of the room.

Turn the vase toward the wall, and no one would know the difference.

Until his father kicked the spinning urn from his path. It skittered across the floor and exploded into shards against the stone wall.

"What were you *thinking*?" His father, Lord of Longstride Manor, vassal to the king, bellowed at him with a face gone purple. Robin felt the kick and rise of his own anger, the beast that slept in his belly, and struggled to keep his voice even. He hated fighting this way, no matter how often they did it.

Inside, however, he prepared to do battle.

"I'm not the one who vowed to strip this family of our resources, and run off across the ocean."

"I'm doing nothing of the sort," Longstride replied. "I'm following the edict of the king."

"Without a thought to your wife and children."

His father jerked back as if he'd been slapped. His teeth ground together, chewing his words.

"How *dare* you?"

Robin pushed out of the chair. "What do you expect Mother to do? Have you thought of how your leaving will affect Becca and Ruth?"

"Your mother is a strong woman, and will manage until I return." Longstride waved a hand toward the door as he spoke.

Robin's voice dropped. "What if you *don't* return?"

His father stopped, his body motionless, his hand in mid-air. His arms fell to his side, and he seemed to deflate.

"God will protect me." He didn't look at his son as he spoke.

"God protects us all," Robin replied, "and yet we all still die."

His father shook his head, wheat-colored hair shifting side to side as if it were blown in the wind.

"Don't speak ill of God's mission."

"I'm not... but you shouldn't go." He wanted to add *and nor should Robert*, but he bit it off. His brother was old enough to stay or go at his own will.

Longstride's eyes, blue and cold as the depth of winter, narrowed. New strength seemed to bolster him as he peered at his son.

"I know what your true concern is," he said.

"Your safety and the wellbeing of this family."

The laugh barked out.

"You do not want to shoulder your own responsibility. You never have. Now you will be without a choice."

"And what responsibility is that, Father? To learn by your side, under your hand, how to one day become the Lord of Longstride? That is something you have taught Robert, but the manor only needs one lord and that was always going to be him. Or was my duty to care for my mother while Robert devoted himself to you? You know she has no love for me. She devotes herself to the others, but not to me, and Becca and Ruth look to me for nothing—neither guidance or protection—as they prepare to someday be ladies of other manors than this."

His father took a deep shuddering breath. "You must act as lord in my absence, even though you are ill-suited to it. There is one thing, however, that you and you alone can do for this family."

"And what is that?" Robin asked.

"You must protect our lands and our title, and the best way you can do that is to woo the Lady Marian."

Robin stared at his father in shock, but couldn't think of a thing to say in response.

"Mark my words," Longstride added, "the man who wins her to wife places his family half a step from the throne. And since King Richard has refused to make a match on her behalf—"

"He has?" Robin interrupted. "Others have tried?"

"Don't be a fool, boy. Of course they have. She's of age. Every lord has tried to persuade the king to wed her to himself or one of his sons. Given the king's stance on the subject, there are only two possible outcomes. Either he intends to keep her a spinster so that no child of hers could ever pose a challenge to the throne, which I know better than, or, worse, he intends to let her choose her own suitor, foolhardy as that is."

"You said every lord had made an offer. Does that mean—?"

"I suggested Robert as a match, naturally. After she gave her dance to you, though, I'm beginning to wonder if I should have put you up instead."

"I'm not livestock to be bartered," Robin said.

"You are, and so is she. If you don't see that, then you're even more of a fool than I take you for." Longstride paused, then continued. "Son, you have an opportunity here to do something for all of us. Locksley is remaining behind. He has made no secret of his interest in her, and he will take every advantage to press his suit. With the king gone, you must not let him turn her head."

The very thought made Robin sick with anger.

"So, be a good lad and get the girl to pledge herself to you, if you can. Prove your loyalty to the family."

The anger beast kicked again.

"I *love* this family."

"Then I am simply giving you a chance to prove it. Grow up and do your duty. *That's* how you show love for your family."

The beast climbed. So his father viewed both him and Marian as no better than farm animals to be sold and bred. Robin clamped his jaw shut to hold the anger in. If he spoke—even one word—the beast would roar out and he would lose himself to rage.

His father felt no such need to bite his tongue.

"I'm sure it's too much to ask, though," Longstride said. "After all, you have *never* lived up to your responsibility. Always playing childish games, and never being a proper son like Robert."

Without thinking Robin began moving, crossing the floor. He shouldered past his father and strode to the door, pausing only to snatch his bow and quiver from their pegs.

His father's voice chased him into the night.

"You will have to stop playing in the woods, and become a man!"

Marian's heart was in her throat. Carefully, she placed her tiny oil lamp on the ledge beside the door, its flame barely strong enough to light her way. The passageway behind her was pitch black, but Chastity was the only other member of the castle who knew this secret tunnel.

She hoped—*prayed*—that Richard would not be angry at her. Yet she had to have answers. The need for them burned in her chest like coal in a furnace.

She opened the door that was hidden behind a hedge of thorny roses, and stepped into the fragrant night air. Moving to the path and looking around, she saw Richard on a raised bench that overlooked a bed of night-blooming buds. Quietly, she walked toward him.

As if sensing her presence, Richard looked up swiftly from the blooms. He stared at her for a long moment, not blinking. She stopped walking, and stood in the moonlight until he waved her forward.

"What is it, child?" he asked, as she came to stand next to him.

"I'm not a child." She said it firmly, but winced inwardly. She didn't mean to start off on the wrong foot.

"No," he said quietly. "I suppose you're not. Time has a strange way of catching up to us when we least expect it. Not that long ago you were a little girl dancing on my brother's feet. Now you're a woman grown, and I am quite sure you didn't tread on young Longstride's boots even once. Quite a feat, since I hear you gave him every dance, much to the dismay of your other suitors."

Heat came to her cheeks and she struggled to keep her composure. They could discuss Robin at a different time. Later, when urgent matters didn't press so hard.

"You should have told me your plans," she said, keeping her voice steady. "I would have kept your secret."

He sighed. "I know you would have, but I had reason to keep close counsel until the very last moment." He paused. "Even from you," he added.

"I don't think you should go," she said. "Send the men, but you are too valuable to risk losing in such a venture."

He looked straight at her, fallen hair casting a shadow over his eyes.

"My dearest niece, this cause is too valuable for me *not* to go."

She took a deep breath, fully aware that her next words would brush against blasphemy, even though she did not mean them as such.

"The pope does not go into the fray himself," she said. "Surely he cannot expect a king to do so."

Richard reached out and took her hand. "He is fighting very hard, just not in the way you are thinking."

"What do you mean?"

He sighed, and it was almost as if she was watching him age before her eyes, his shoulders stooping under some invisible burden.

"We do not struggle merely against flesh and blood."

She blinked. She had heard such words before. One of the monks had spoken them, years earlier, in her childhood, or perhaps it had even been the cardinal. The man who had said them had been quoting from the Bible, and had talked about the spiritual battle that raged around them all—spirits and angels and demons and principalities all clashing and striking and clanging, invisible to the eye. She remembered it vividly, because of how deeply it had frightened her. She had barely slept for a fortnight, convinced that she saw shadows moving around her room, images teasing her and flickers of motion caught out of the corners of her eyes.

She'd been young, and she'd just lost her parents to the fire.

The king continued. "Sometimes there is more to a situation than there appears. Evil lives in this world, and every day it walks the earth, growing stronger. We have an opportunity—" he shook his head, dismissing his choice of words "—a *duty*, to vanquish it now before it consumes everything. If we don't, the world will be covered in darkness, and there will be nowhere anyone can run to be safe."

A chill danced up her spine. "You're talking about more than the infidels."

"Every war is waged on three battlefields. On the earth itself, in the human heart, and in the realm of the spirits. Every so often those three battlefields merge into one."

"I don't understand."

His eyes turned sad. "And I'm very glad you don't. I pray that you never do, because if that day comes, then I will have failed to protect you and England from this great curse."

"If the threat is that great, shouldn't you remain here to protect the kingdom?"

"The kingdom was here before me and will remain after me." He shook his head. "I've chosen another to stand in my stead."

"Another?" she said, her eyes widening. "Who?"

"John is coming to care for the land and watch the throne."

"John?" she said.

"My younger brother. Your uncle. Lord of Ireland."

"Oh." The word went dry in her throat.

Her Uncle John. She had met him only once, on a visit to Ireland when she was a wee child. Her memory of him was hazy and distorted by the passage of time.

"He has been gone so long."

Richard shifted on the bench beside her. "So long that it's difficult to recall why our father sent him to Ireland in the first place. He's not the true king there, just a vassal of England living in a small holding owned by the crown."

"You are the crown."

He tilted his head in assent. "Owned by me then." Richard grew quiet. She let him fade into memories for a long moment as she studied his face in profile. His hair swirled, unruly around his head, giving him the maned look of the lion after which he was named. Finally he shuddered, and blew out a long breath, releasing his thoughts into the world.

He didn't look at her when he spoke.

"Our father was a hard man. I didn't even allow John to come when your father died. I sent word by messenger after he and your mother had been interred. All because of a dead man's insistence."

She didn't know how to respond. Richard never mentioned his father, her grandfather, taken before her birth by a winter pox that had scoured the land.

"It is a good choice." Richard nodded, as if agreeing with himself. "My cousin Henry has long envied the throne, and I would not give him the opportunity to make mischief."

"There are only two choices?"

"I'd thought, briefly, to leave England in your care."

The words hit her chest, echoing as they struck. Before she could speak, however, he continued.

"But you're young," he said. "Too young to be burdened prematurely by such responsibility."

"I would do my best," she said.

"I know." His hand was warm on hers. "But John is my decision. I expect you to help him where you can."

She nodded. "Of course."

"And, if the worst should happen overseas, well, then England will have had some time to adjust to its new king, and he to her."

Marian felt a lump in her throat. "Nothing will happen to you," she whispered. It was more of a prayer. He smiled at her, but she could see sorrow in his eyes, and it gave her a moment of panic. It was one thing for her to fear for his safety. It was chilling to know that he, too, was fearful that he might never return.

He cleared his throat and turned back toward the night blooms. "You should be in bed."

She had been dismissed. She curtsied and turned to go, wishing they'd had nothing more serious to discuss than how many times she had danced with Robin of Longstride.

She stepped from the porch as he leapt off, landing on flexed legs, letting his knees absorb the impact. He turned, drawing short as he caught sight of her.

"Mother," he said.

She looked down on him. He nearly melded with the darkness, blending like a night creature. He was so alien, so foreign. So unlike her other children. Unlike her husband. Unlike her. The spoiled fruit of her womb.

Her curse.

"Mother," he said again, his voice turning stern. "I know you heard the fight. Say what you have to say."

"Feel free to go with your father on the journey."

Robin's face twisted. "He has made it clear that I am to stay."

The thought of him doing so soured her stomach. Working the land, he would be around under foot, a constant reminder, without the light of Philemon or Robert to distract her from his presence. "I do not need you here. You love him, so go with him. Fling yourself between your father and the swords of the enemy."

"You would like that, wouldn't you? To send me off to be killed on a foreign land."

She remained silent.

"I will remain here and I will do my duty to this household, but never fear, I will stay out of your sight." He turned and strode away.

She watched him go until he disappeared into the night, then went inside, making her way to the bedroom she shared with her husband.

He stood in their room, pulling off his tunic.

She stopped at the doorway and watched him. The soft linen shirt slid up his torso and over his head before being dropped to the floor. Philemon Longstride had thickened over the years, padded from a life as a commander of men rather than a worker beside them and cushioned with age, but he still had definition to his body that pleased her. Muscles still flexed and played beneath his skin and his head was still full of thick hair, even if some of it had turned silver here and there.

He was leaving her soon. She did not want it, but understood he was doing what he thought was right. It wasn't the first time he had chased after his king and left her alone. She would miss him.

His hands moved to his belt, unbuckling it.

Desire rose inside her. Tonight she would make sure he would miss her.

Her hand touched the doorjamb, brushing the ancient symbols of protection she had painted there in pigment cut with her own menstrual blood. It was old superstition, woman's magic passed from mother to daughter. Not the right-hand path of the hedgewitches and the herbalists, but the left-hand path of darkness. It was something she had done after the birth of Robin, a ward against allowing him entrance to this room, and he never had crossed the threshold. Her husband had no use for witchery, but tolerated it for her.

He did not understand its origin.

Energy crackled under her fingers, running up her arm and into her chest. It made her head swim like too much wine. Her mouth tasted of clover.

That was new.

She stared at the symbols in wonder until her husband's voice called her to bed.

CHAPTER NINE

Friar Tuck woke feeling sticky and damp against the thin pad of his bedroll. His skull buzzed like a beehive, proof that he definitely had taken too much to drink the night before. That in itself was no mean feat. Noblemen, warriors, peasants, bishops... he had yet to meet the man who could drink as much as he, and still remain standing.

Not that he imbibed often, but when the opportunity presented he gave himself to it body and soul. There was no harm in it... well, what was the point in going to confession if you never had anything to confess?

He had missed morning prayers, and, when he presented himself to the cardinal, the man looked him over with a roll of his eyes.

"Are you aware that gluttony is a sin?" the cardinal asked.

"No greater than lying," Friar Tuck replied. "You told me you had no idea what the king's announcement would be."

There were few above his station to whom he would ever speak that way, but Tuck had known Francis since his assignment to the monastery as a child. The man had been a mentor and a guide in the path to becoming a man of faith. More than that, the friar considered him a friend.

"It was an omission of necessity, I'm afraid." The cardinal's sigh had an edge of frustration. "The king wished it kept absolutely quiet until last night. We... *he* needed to see everyone's reactions upon hearing the news."

Tuck wondered at that. The king answered to no one except the pope, so fear of disapproval couldn't have been what concerned him. The nobles had no choice but to follow his lead in this, as in all things. So, why would he need to see their reaction?

"What was he looking for?" Tuck asked. The cardinal eyed him for a long minute before answering.

"Treachery," he said, dropping his voice. "Or signs thereof. A few of his loyal knights and servants were spread throughout the hall, observing the reactions of those who were present."

Tuck gave this a moment to sink in.

"Did they find anything suspicious?"

"Not that I'm aware of," the cardinal said.

The king's announcement weighed heavily on Tuck's mind, which was part of the reason he'd overindulged. The journey would be filled with danger, the destination even more so. He was a man who enjoyed comfort, such as it was, but here was a way to serve the church in a manner he would never before have conceived. An idea had taken hold of him, and would not let go.

"I wish to go on Crusade with the king and his men," the friar said. "To attend to their spiritual needs, and help with the battle that awaits them." There, he had said it. The words shimmered in the air between them.

When first he had been pressed into the service of the Lord as a child, he'd prayed almost ceaselessly that God would not send him to the corners of the earth, ministering to the heathens, but would allow him to stay in England and tend those who were already among the Lord's flock.

How the years could change a person.

As God was his witness there had been a restlessness growing in him for several years. It came with a conviction that he wasn't doing as much as he could for the Lord or His people. He woke in the middle of sleep, at least once a fortnight, covered in sweat and shouting part of the Lord's Prayer—usually the section about deliverance from evil.

Suddenly things seemed so clear.

The Lord had work for him. In the Holy Land.

"I cannot allow it," the cardinal said firmly. "I need you."

Tuck blinked in surprise. "There are enough here in the monastery to care for God's people."

"And they are fine men. I would trust many of them with my very life." Francis peered at him intently. "You I would trust with my very soul."

"I'm flattered, " Tuck replied genuinely, "but what does that mean?"

"I want you close at hand. I believe God will reveal a way for you to be of use."

"But the Crusade—"

The cardinal cut him off with a hand. "Is nothing with which to concern yourself."

Friar Tuck rolled the words around in his head, wishing now that he'd shown some restraint the night before. It was hard to think and he felt ashamed at having to work so hard at concepts.

"Am I to infer that you perceive the greatest danger not to be in the Holy Land, but here on our own soil?"

"That is precisely what you are to infer," Francis said.

"I still do not understand."

"You know I am a believer in signs, portents, and prophecies." Tuck nodded. The cardinal looked around suddenly, as though concerned that someone might be listening. Tuck did as well, but they appeared to be alone in the chapel.

The cardinal rose and gestured for him to follow. The two walked together down one of the corridors of the monastery. They took a left down an intersecting hallway where the walls were much narrower. Then they reached a section of the wall that appeared to be completely ordinary, and stopped.

Tuck knew what was about to occur.

The cardinal removed a torch from its wall sconce and lifted it high until the light shone on a tiny indentation in the stone, a spot worn smooth by the pressure of countless thumbs over the years. It was such a small spot that only one who knew it was there would see it. The cardinal glanced around hastily before jamming with his thumb and shoving. A narrow section of the wall about four feet tall swung away into darkness. They stooped to enter.

Friar Tuck's chest tightened and his breath grew short. The narrowness of the passage unnerved him, as if it got narrower and narrower with each step, pressing in on him.

Yea, I say unto thee, 'tis easier for a camel to crawl through the eye of the needle than it is for a rich man's soul to enter the gate of Heaven.

Once inside, they pushed the door shut behind them. The torch flickered in a darkness that was otherwise absolute. They proceeded for several feet and the whole time he struggled to stay hunched far enough to not bump his head on the low ceiling, even as he winced at the feeling of squeezing through the passage, the rough stone catching at his robes as though trying to stop him from continuing forward.

They came to a flight of stairs which they had to descend while bent over nearly double. It was slow, painful work and Tuck had never been sure if it was a necessity of the architecture, or a deterrent to keep out all but the most persistent.

When he actually had to traverse the passage he contemplated that it could simply have been the sadism of the masons who built the monastery.

At last they reached the bottom and were able to stand straight. Tuck began to breathe a little easier. They passed through what looked like an old storage room, long since forgotten. At the back of it the cardinal pressed his thumb to another wall and another door opened, large enough for them to walk through quite easily.

Again they closed it behind them. The cardinal set the torch in a sconce and Tuck looked around the room. Even though he had been here but yesterday, it never ceased to fill him with awe. All manner of objects were present, some of them ancient beyond reasoning. His eyes tracked over the shelves, picking out those that had fascinated him since his indoctrination into the inner circle of the Protectorate.

A cup, plain pottery with a worn seal of the House of Arimathea stamped on its side, used at the Last Supper. Not the Sangreal—no, not the Holy Grail—but a cup from which the Christ and his disciples, the first church fathers, had drunk.

A small tin whistle that had belonged to St. Brigid.

A basket with a swaddle of crumbling cloth that wrapped what were supposed to be the shards of mighty Excalibur.

The axe used to take the head of the apostle Paul, its bronze edge still stained with saint's blood.

An arrow removed from St. Sebastian, also stained to the fletching.

The shelves were littered with mundane objects as well. The shoe of St. Simeon, and the diary of St. Boedwyn. His eyes simply passed over them. As had always been the case, the relics that drew him were deadly in their own right. From the first moment he'd been entrusted with the knowledge of the chamber's existence, he'd been fascinated by weapons and objects of war, stained by the spilt blood of the holy. That something meant to kill could be a vessel of God's power and might—it pulled at a place, a small hollow, nestled deep behind his heart.

On a table sat the book the bard had carried from Ireland.

The cardinal turned to look at him, his face awash with moving shadows. He reached out to a low shelf and removed a book bound in black. He held it up.

"Do you know what this is?"

Tuck didn't have to look closely. The binding gave it away.

"The Black Book of Carmarthen," he said quietly. Written in Welsh, the tome contained centuries' worth of poetry and writings both secular and divine, with quite a bit of early history thrown in, as well—particularly when it came to Arthur and the wizard who had always attended him.

"There are more than sonnets recorded in these pages," Francis said. "The book contains prophecies of a time when the king will be absent, and the land has been rendered barren."

Tuck nodded, listening intently.

"I have studied the prophecies, here and elsewhere," Francis said. "Many come from saints, some were made by the druids, and some even by the lost race who first occupied these lands. All point to the same event."

"And that is?" Tuck asked, fear gnawing at the edges of his mind.

"That an age of darkness shall fall upon England, and if nothing is done to counter it, that darkness will soon take the rest of the world. Evil will walk free on the earth, roaming where it wills and killing whomever it wishes."

"How do you know that the prophesied time is upon us?"

"There have been many signs, omens," he replied, "but the final piece of the puzzle fell into place last night. Yes, I knew the king was planning for England to join the Crusade. Until last night, though, I had no idea that he was planning on leading the army himself. He told me shortly before we joined the feast." He looked down, his eyes hidden. "I did my best, argued until I couldn't speak anymore, but I could not dissuade him. The prophecies all indicate that the time of darkness will take root on the day the king sets sail, abandoning his people to their fate."

"But the king leaves in but a matter of days."

"Yes, which gives us scarce time to prepare."

"What is it you want me to do?"

"Pray that I'm wrong, and watch for me. Be my eyes and ears wherever you go. Finally, I need you to protect these relics," he said, gesturing around them. "None of them can fall into the hands of the enemy. The king may be going off to war in the Holy Land, but the real battle will take place here."

"Do the prophecies tell us how to oppose this evil?"

"No, not as such. There are hints, but I've yet to uncover their meaning. There is one thing all of the prophecies speak of, however. A man who will rise and accept the mantle of leadership, to fight a war while the infirm can only watch. But for him Sovereignty itself may be overturned."

"Who is he?"

"If only it were that easy." The cardinal shook his head. "All I've been able to glean about this man is that he will be of Sherwood."

Friar Tuck blinked. "He'll be a ghost then. That's all that lives in the forest."

"I understand no more than you, but I have faith that in time the truth will be revealed to us. Until then, can I count on you to help me?"

"Absolutely," Tuck answered.

He awakened in the grave he'd been buried in for centuries, trapped there by the damned wizard. The creature thrashed, straining at his bonds inside the iron box that encased him. He opened his mouth to hiss and howl in alternating patterns. Black fur flared out, a sign of rage. He howled again, and heard his sister-mate answer.

He redoubled his efforts, wicked claws clacking against the metal as he sought to wiggle his jaws free from the iron band that kept his mouth clamped shut. He had been sleeping long, too long, but at last had heard his master's call, and knew it was time to walk the earth at his side. Together they would rain down destruction and feast on the flesh of the living.

With a terrible screaming sound the metal band around his jaw gave way. Above the prison he could smell dirt. So many smells, so many sins. He thrashed harder, gaining strength as he took in the aromas of human desperation and depravity. Greed, hunger, lust all fed him until he was strong enough to claw his way through the box, then upward through the dirt to finally emerge in the pale moonlight, a monstrous black shadow.

Nearby the ground heaved and a moment later his sister-mate raised her head to the moon and let out a howl. With a final thrusting of her body she was free of her grave, as well. Together they wove in and out of tombstones as they made their way east. They had been called, and it was time to go to work.

The first thing they had to do was find the prince.

CHAPTER TEN

He sat with his back against one of the hawthorns, the ground dry beneath him. It was a tall one, reaching to its height to try and wrest some sunlight from the oaks above. He nibbled absently on one of the small red pommes, not noticing its dull sweetness.

He'd spent the night in the forest, a place that normally calmed the anger he kept inside himself, an anger that was his oldest companion, but his mind had been in too much turmoil for sleep. Instead he had wandered the glens and ridges of the mighty forest and listened as the spirits of the wood danced around him.

Some of the noises in the night were surely animals, nocturnal and on the prowl, but some were unnatural. Voices that sang snatches of melodies and the patter of feet that were not normal creatures. He spent hours chasing them into the depth of Sherwood, but always they stayed out of his sight and just beyond his reach. Finally exhausted, he declared the game over and sat at the foot of the hawthorn.

His body rested, but not his mind. That ran along, faster than even the feet of the fey.

He thought about his father, a man who on many occasions had proven himself more loyal to the king than to his family. Not a full two harvests would pass before he was off with Richard settling some dispute between lords, or riding the land to survey the borders. Lately he'd taken Robert with him. He was never gone long enough to force Robin into the role of housemaster, but he'd also never gone overseas.

Robin did his part on the land—at least the part he was allowed to do—but it seemed as if neither of his parents wanted him around for very long. His father always preferred the elder son, the two of them so much alike it was almost eerie. His mother had never been anything more than distant toward him and, at times, looked at him with an animosity that chilled him to the bone. She spent all of her time doting on the girls or ignoring everything in favor of her own private studies.

Now he would be trapped working the farm under her watchful eye.

Jesu, take me now.

The brush rustled to his left. It was a huge bramble, a thick tangle of thin vines with knuckle-length barbed thorns. In the dim light of dawn filtering through the forest he could only see a wall of darkness.

The bramble shook violently.

His hand closed on his bow, lifting it to his lap while he pulled free an arrow.

A sound rose up, rolling from the bramble. It was like the tearing of cloth in his ears. Loud chuffs of air bellowed toward him, then the vines split asunder, curling in on themselves and sending broken thorns flying through the air.

Out stepped the Lord of the Forest.

The majestic beast walked from the thorny knot with its head held high, the massive rack of antlers spreading like the branches of an oak. Its chest heaved under a thick pelt of fur. It stepped forward, moving until it was only a few paces away. Black eyes the size of Robin's fists stared at him, through him, as the ancient stag turned and presented its shoulder and flank to him. Instantly his eyes picked out the spot half a handbreadth behind the front shoulder. The spot where the ribs opened wider than anywhere else as they pressed against the shoulder joint. The spot that led directly to the heart.

The death spot.

He could do it. He could draw and place his arrow feather deep into that chest. He could put the broadhead into the muscle of that mighty, beating heart and still it forever.

He could take this creature down.

The Forest Lord turned its head to look over its shoulder. Robin stared into that eye, the eye of a creature who may very well have walked this forest from the time of creation, a creature who had lived through all the changes wrought by the years and had been unaffected by any of them. This king of wood and glen was the protector of Sherwood and as long as he lived he would keep this sacred land whole.

The knowledge seeped into him, and suddenly the world seemed right. His father could leave, his brother could follow, his mother could hate him and somehow, as long as this stag walked this wood, then all would be well.

"Thank you," he said, as he came to his feet.

The stag watched him.

He felt its ancient eyes on him the entire way as he walked home to begin his duty.

As morning dawned and pale sunlight kissed the water, Marian stood looking around at the encampment by the sea. The days had flown by, consumed by preparations. Prince John had made landfall and would be meeting them there, at the ships that would carry King Richard and many of his noblemen away to war.

Tents flying colorful coats-of-arms stretched as far as the eye could see. Some of the men had arrived days before and waited, ready to accompany their sovereign on his great journey. The flag with the Longstride coat-of-arms flapped atop a pole. The sight of it caused a lump to form in her throat.

Will Robin be going?

After his display at the feast, she knew he wouldn't want to, but Robin had always been unpredictable. He'd had time to think about this and discuss it with his father. He might have changed his mind, or been given no choice.

She couldn't help but worry that, with so many of their finest warriors leaving, England would be vulnerable to attack. The peace with France was uneasy at best, often preserved by virtue of Richard's strength and the waters that separated the two countries. They wouldn't hesitate to attack if they felt England had become weak. So she said a prayer that the French king had pledged troops to the Holy Crusade, as well, and in such numbers that an attacking force would be impossible to muster.

Noise made her turn, a crunching of boot against graveled rock. King Richard walked up the hill to stand beside her. He took a deep breath of morning air and swung his hand out toward the tents, the ships, and the men bustling with weapons and supplies.

"Magnificent, isn't it?" His voice boomed out in the morning chill.

She smiled at his uplifting spirit. "I cannot deny that."

"I've given the order to break camp," he told her. "We'll be sailing soon."

"But Prince John has not arrived at camp," she protested.

"He has. He came in the night."

Like a thief.

She shook her head to clear away the thought.

Less than an hour later the sun hung a short distance above the horizon, sending a blinding glare off the water. The ships were loaded with supplies and men, the last of them leading blindfolded horses up gangplanks. The war beasts, bred to obey their riders in the chaos of battle, still shivered and whinnied as they swayed up the long, bending boards that took them onto the ships. The salt in their noses unsettled them, and one went off the edge between the ship and dock. It screamed like a woman, floundering blindly in the water.

Two men dove in, managed to secure ropes around the beast, and had it hauled on board. Its flailing hooves struck one of the men and he was dragged onto the ship, unconscious and bleeding.

Blood stained the hull in a wide streak of crimson.

Marian shivered and turned away. Then she stopped abruptly, her eyes going wide.

A man stood there, too close and looking down at her with dark eyes. His arms hung long by his sides and he slouched inside his cloak. The royal crest of England blazed out from a patch that covered his left breast.

"Prince John." Her hand fluttered to her chest. "I didn't see you there."

His lips pulled up in what she thought was meant to be a smile. However, it didn't reach his eyes or move any other part of his face—not his narrow chin or the fleshy pockets at the top of his cheeks.

"Perhaps I came from the shadows, niece," he said. His voice had a slippery quality, slick-sided and like an oily echo of her uncle's. It soothed her and pulled at her.

"I heard you came from Ireland," she replied.

He chuckled, dry and raspy. "They are one and the same, in truth."

"I always found the Emerald Isle to be entirely enchanting." She tried to make her voice sound light, breezy.

"It is a magical place." His eyes shifted and he looked over her shoulder. She turned, following his gaze to the wide bloodstain on the side of Richard's ship. He hummed. "I wonder, is that a sign of how the trip may go?"

She took a step back. "How... what... how could you say something like that?"

Prince John chuckled. "I merely meant that my brother will shed much blood in his Crusade against the forces of evil." Pudgy fingers touched his forehead as he dipped his head toward her in a half-bow. "Some ancient practices actually use blood sacrifice to seal the fate of a voyage, beseeching the gods to shine on them with favor."

"Richard the Lionheart is a Christian king."

"So he is," Prince John murmured, turning from her and walking away.

She watched him cross the dock, moving toward a man who stood looking down at the people gathered to see off their king. His back to her, she couldn't see the man's face. Black armor that gleamed dully in the sunlight wrapped him from heel to throat. She'd never seen armor like it, interlocking plates that fit so close they looked like the carapace of an insect.

One with a stinger... and venom.

The man's hand was bare, and so pale it looked dipped in milk. It rested on a great bastard sword that jutted off a narrow hip, the sheathed blade sweeping out behind him. A shock of white-blond hair hung down his back in a thick braid, glaring out in stark contrast to the ebony armor.

He turned as Prince John drew near him. His face was clean-shaven, the skin smooth over sharply angled cheekbones and jawline, just as ghostly white as his hand, contrasting harshly with a wide furred collar that circled his throat. A straight and patrician nose jutted over a mouth framed with thin, villainous lips.

John spoke to him. She strained her ears to hear what was being said, but the wind off the ocean blew from behind, carrying any sound away from her. After a few sentences the man's eyes flicked up to look at her.

It took everything she possessed not to turn away. Instead, she stood resolute as they walked toward her.

She jumped as a hand came down on her shoulder.

King Richard stood next to her. He pulled her into a hug, his arms tight around her. She had a brief flash about proper etiquette, the decorum of how royalty should behave in public, but the thought was dashed in the warmth of her uncle's embrace.

He'll be gone so soon.

She gave herself over to the moment, embracing him in return, clinging to his strength with all of hers. Finally the king loosened his hold and stepped back. His eyes shimmered in the sunlight.

"Ah, Marian," he said, smiling. "I will miss you. Take care while I am away."

"I will miss you, too, more than you could possibly know." Her voice choked.

His thumb swept the tears from her eyes. "Enough of that—it is unbecoming for a king to weep before his people." Richard cleared his throat and looked at the gathered crowd that waited for him to board.

"It's time."

She nodded, even though her heart had turned to lead.

"Brother, send me in your place," Prince John said from behind her. "England cannot afford to lose you."

"Would that I could," Richard said with a smile. "Alas, the task that God has set before me is mine alone. I need you here, John, protecting England, keeping her safe for me."

"I am but your humble servant in this charge," John said with a bow. He straightened, holding his hand toward the man in the black armor. "I have the finest adviser. Please allow me to introduce the Sheriff of Nottingham."

The Sheriff gave a small nod.

"He will help... *quell* any unrest that stems from your leave-taking."

Richard looked at the man for a long moment, his face a blank.

"Marian knows how I run my court. She will guide you," he said, gesturing to her. "There should be no need of any quelling."

John turned and looked at her. She shivered. His eyes were empty, cold, like a snake's.

"She has grown," he said. "It seems she has become a woman in my absence."

"I do not remember what kind of man you were, or know what kind you have become," she said, subtly putting him on notice that she knew something was different about him. By the narrowing of his eyes, she knew that he had taken her meaning.

At least we understand each other.

She jerked as she felt something like a cold hand brush the back of her neck. Reflexively she turned her head to see who it was, but there was no one behind her.

"Marian?" Richard asked.

"Nothing, sire," she said quickly, to hide her own uneasiness. "It was a chill."

"You should be careful, my dear," John said. "We wouldn't want you to become sick."

"I can assure you that I am in the best of health, and in no danger of suffering such a fate," she smiled, even while she imagined slapping him across the face.

"It's reassuring to hear that," he said.

Yet someone was watching her, she could feel it like an oppressive weight. She glanced around. The Sheriff met her eyes and smiled slowly in a way that made the knot in her stomach twist, and she realized she had begun to sweat. What *was* this man that he had the power to make her feel that way?

"Are you sure you're alright, niece?"

She could hear John speaking, but it was as if he was far away. She felt dizzy, lightheaded, and wished with all her heart that she *was* someplace else in that moment. She took a step back, and then another, struggling to get enough air. She couldn't breathe, and her knees didn't want to continue to support her.

I'm going to faint, she realized.

Then, suddenly, a steadying hand gripped her elbow, holding her up. Everything seemed to snap back into place. She gulped air as fast as she could as she looked up. Robin stared at her, brows knitted together in concern. He had a hand under her elbow and gripped her arm tight enough to keep her on her feet.

"Are you alright?" he echoed.

She nodded as she looked around and realized that she had walked farther away from King Richard than she had thought.

Her head began to clear and she glanced around hurriedly, but didn't see the man with the black armor.

"Yes, thank you. I—I don't know what happened," she said.

"I thought you were going to fall," he said, slowly removing his hand from her arm.

"Thank you for your timely intervention," she said. Her head was clear again and her stomach no longer rebelled. She had no idea what had happened, but was grateful Robin had stepped in when he had.

"I'm surprised to see you here," she added. "Are you joining the crusaders?" The thought of Robin stepping aboard that boat, marching past that streak of blood-soaked wood, made her stomach feel hot and oily again.

Please, no.

He shook his head, dark hair falling over his eyes.

"I came with my father, in the hopes of talking him *out* of going. I failed in that. He's too damn proud, and stubborn."

"Traits you inherited." Her hand fell on his arm. "You do know that, don't you?"

"So he tells me. Often." His hand covered hers. "I just can't shake the feeling that there is some dark hand at work in all of this."

Marian almost told him that she felt the same way, but realized she should be more circumspect. At least for the moment.

"So then you are staying?"

"Someone has to watch Longstride manor, and keep the wolves at bay," Robin said, nodding.

"Those sound more like your father's words than yours."

"My mother's actually." He laughed without humor. "She just happens to think I'm not the watcher she needs."

He looked so wistful it hurt her heart. The enmity between Lady Longstride and her youngest son became obvious within a few moments of watching them together. She knew the ache of missing her own mother, and she couldn't imagine how it would feel if her mother were still alive, but shunned her. It would destroy her.

Her hand moved toward him before she thought, touching his chest.

"You'll prove her wrong."

His dark eyes turned toward her, and he smiled a crooked little smile full of longstanding sorrow. "Not to her, I won't."

They looked at each other for a long moment.

A commotion on the dock broke the stare. As much as she would have liked to stay with him, she had duties to be performed.

"I should return to the king," she said, glancing over at Richard and John.

Robin tilted his head and stepped back. "I won't keep you." Marian gave him a smile before hurrying to Richard's side. Just as she reached him, alongside his ship, he began to speak.

"I appreciate your concern, brother, but there's no need for that," he said firmly. "I will return home soon enough to resume my rightful duties."

John turned away, walking over to the Sheriff, who was back watching the crowd. He spoke to the taller man, and their backs were turned to Marian and Richard.

"What was he suggesting?" she inquired.

Richard turned to look at her. "He voiced concern for the danger of my mission, and whether it might be prudent to give him the kingship now, so that I could focus entirely on matters in the Holy Land."

"But *you* are the rightful king of England," Marian said, outraged at the very thought. "He has no claim."

Her uncle chuckled. "Calm yourself, my dear. I'm certain it was one of his advisers who pushed him to ask. I take no offense, nor should you. For the good of England I am leaving, and for the good of England I will return." He leaned down, dropping his voice. "I am leaving behind the *Kestrel*. It is my fastest ship. I have ordered it to be maintained and ready for service at a moment's notice during my absence."

"For what purpose?"

"If England needs me, if *you* need me, then you send a messenger to Donthos at the dock. He will maintain the *Kestrel* and put your man in that ship with a crew that can be trusted. They will have the charts and maps needed to find me.

"If the need is true, then I will return aboard it immediately," he continued. "You must only use it in the direst of circumstance, but use it if you must. You are the only one to whom I am giving this information."

Realization bloomed in her heart. She was his watchman on the wall then. If John harmed England in any way, her uncle expected her to call him back. With that thought, another seemed inescapable.

Why does he doubt his own brother, his very choice?

Yet she had no time to ask. Already he was preparing to depart. So she pushed it from her mind, determined that she would be true to his request. It was the most trust anyone had ever shown her, and the weight of it was tremendous.

"Thank you," she said, her voice almost a whisper.

"Be strong and of good faith." He kissed her forehead. "I will return." At that, he turned and strode up the gangplank. The crowd cheered at the sight of him. At the top he turned, unsheathed his sword, and lifted it high.

"For the glory of Christ the Lord and the safety of England!"

The crowd exploded with a roar. Richard sheathed his sword, nodded once, then turned and disappeared.

Marian hugged herself. She vowed that she would watch the prince carefully in the days to come.

CHAPTER ELEVEN

Adaryn knelt in her garden, clucking over some of the herbs she'd planted in the spring. Most were doing nicely, but her sage had been much slower to grow than the rest. She puzzled over it. It got the same water and sunshine as the others, and she spoke the same incantations over it at night. The plant should be flourishing. She needed it as a potent ingredient in several of the poultices and potions she created. It had healing properties and was good for all manner of ailments. Burning it could also cleanse a place and ward off evil spirits.

She touched one of the tiny leaves and it crumbled like ash. The spot where it had been attached to the stem was black and oozed some sort of liquid. She'd never seen the like. She dug deeper in the earth, and, when she pulled out the roots, a stench of death and decay came out of the earth with them. It was so strong that her midday meal leapt to the back of her throat.

She looked into the hole left by the plant and saw more of the black ooze. Moving over a few inches she inspected a rosemary plant that was growing well. She carefully dug in the ground, exposing its roots. There was no stench and no black ooze, even though the two plants were close together.

Something was wrong.

The sound of horse's hooves came from the narrow path out front and she rose, wondering who had come to call. There weren't many who knew Adaryn, or where she lived, and that was how she liked it.

She moved around her small house and watched the path that led here. A rider came into view, a woman of fair hair and complexion riding a stallion that matched her. Both had a regal bearing, chests thrust high and necks straight as they came at a good clip. It took only a moment for them to draw close enough that she could recognize the rider.

Lady Longstride.

Adaryn frowned. She had not expected a visit at this time of year. The lady pulled her horse up and Adaryn reached out to hold the reins while the woman dismounted. She then led the horse to a patch of grass a short distance away and tied his reins to a stake driven into the ground for just such purpose.

She turned back. "What can I help you with today, milady? Are you looking to have another child?"

"No, I have my hands quite full enough with the ones I already have. Besides, my husband is away fighting in Richard's Crusade."

Adaryn blinked. News could be slow to reach her, but even she had heard about the Crusade.

"Then what may I do for you?"

"I have no sage. My crop failed this year and I need to dry some before winter comes."

"Milady could have sent her servant to ask for it," Adaryn observed.

"I would never trust a servant with an errand as important as mine," the woman said haughtily.

Yet she had sent her servant, Lila, on numerous occasions. Adaryn suspected that the lady had come with another purpose as well.

"Did all your plantings fail?" she asked.

"No, just the sage. It rotted in the ground. None of it could be salvaged."

Adaryn frowned. To have the same plant be destroyed in two completely different locations smacked of something unnatural. Could there be magic at work? If so, why the sage? There were many herbs that could be used for healing, some far more valuable.

"Why have you squished your face up in such an unattractive way?" Lady Longstride asked.

Adaryn smiled outwardly. Lady Longstride wasn't a nice woman, despite what others might think. She was, though, an excellent client, and one well worth humoring.

"I was just concerned because I, too, have a lack of sage at the moment. I will, however, procure some for you, and deliver it within the fortnight." She would approach some of the others who grew such herbs. It would also give her a chance to see if others were experiencing similar difficulties.

"Do not come to my home," Lady Longstride said firmly. "I will send Lila for it."

"Is there anything else with which I can help, milady?"

"Yes," the noblewoman said. "I need you to teach me another spell."

Adaryn had suspected as much. "What is it you wish to accomplish?"

"I want to increase the strength of the wards for a room."

"To keep out one person, or to keep out all?"

"To keep out all, this time. All but myself, of course, and it must be subtle, so that a person simply doesn't want to enter."

"Of course," Adaryn responded. "Why don't you come inside while I prepare a few things for you." As she turned to lead the way inside her home she wondered exactly what it was that the Lady Longstride wished to hide from the world.

They were a few steps from her front door when the horse screamed. Both women spun to look.

There, not ten feet away was a gray wolf twice the size of any Adaryn had ever seen, its yellow eyes fixed, its mouth dripping blood and foam as it circled the horse. The animal reared, trying to pull itself free from the stake to which its reins were tied. The predator lunged at it, jaws clacking together.

Adaryn ran to the woodpile and pulled her axe out of a stump. She ran toward the two animals that were now struggling together. Just as she reached them the horse kicked the wolf in the chest, sending it flying backward. Adaryn swung the axe at the beast's belly. The metal head barely scraped the creature's skin beneath its fur, but it landed on the ground and its belly burst open, spilling steaming hot intestines onto the ground.

Adaryn bit back a cry of shock.

The wolf thrashed on its back, rolling in its own offal. The ropes of innards crawled with squiggling white shapes, maggots that had been devouring the creature from the inside. She put a hand over her nose and mouth, dropped the axe and turned toward the Lady Longstride. Fear prickled at her scalp as she struggled to appear calm.

Lady Longstride's eyes were wide, watching the wolf twitch, its body slowing into death as its strength spilled into the dirt.

"Wolves don't come near people unless they're starving," she said, "or they have the sickness."

"From the looks of this one, he definitely had some sort of sickness," Adaryn said, though she was pretty certain it hadn't been the kind that the lady was referencing. In truth, it had been dead before it staggered out of the forest.

"How should we proceed?"

Prince John looked startled where he sat. "You ask me?"

Thin lips twitched. "Of course. You are the king now."

"*Acting* king." John immediately regretted the thought, feeling as if he'd been led into it. He was still a prince.

The Sheriff stood by the window of John's chambers with his back to the room. He stood in the thinnest beam of sunlight there was, a wafer of illumination that rendered him pure black, like living basalt except for that streak of widow white hair.

"Yes, *acting* king," the armored man agreed. "A toothless position."

"I'm still king," John replied irritably.

"In name only."

"Names have power, *Nottingham*."

The Sheriff's eyes locked with his. John hadn't seen him turn.

"Names do have power, little prince. They belong to powerful things and... entities." The Sheriff broke his gaze, walking around the room. Slender, pale fingers darted here and there, touching only the things John had brought with him.

A small jewelry box that had belonged to his mother.

A knife he'd had since childhood, given to him by his father.

A bronze cast of a bird skull, the first kill he'd made as a child.

A candelabra stolen from a chapel in Ireland.

A jar containing the finger bones of the thief he'd hired to steal the candelabra.

The Sheriff stopped and turned.

"Kingship is a tricky thing," he said abstractly. "It is not held lightly, just because you possess a throne. This damned isle is a maze of relics and traditions and rituals."

"Richard may die in the Crusade," John offered.

"That may not change anything. You are not a direct heir."

"I could make a claim."

"I have no use in waiting for the whims of human agencies." The Sheriff's face twisted, his mouth and eyes feral as he spoke. Prince John flinched, and hated himself for doing so.

"Then what do you suggest? Regicide?"

"Feh! You royals breed like rats—you would never find all the hidden bastards and illegitimate bitches sired by your kin. No, if we are to proceed, we must find a way to secure *you* as the lawful king."

Prince John leaned forward in his chair. "If not the knife's edge, then how do we clear my path?"

"There is a way."

"Do tell."

"In the heart of Sherwood there is a relic, a symbol of England's Sovereignty, that can bestow upon whomever wears it the kingship of the land."

"I have never heard of such a thing," John said.

"You wouldn't have," the Sheriff replied. "It's old. Older than your lineage, older than your people being on this island, but powerful."

"Then we shall have it."

"How cavalier you are," the Sheriff said, his voice dripping venom. "Possessing the object will be no easy thing."

"And why is that?"

"To begin with, I may not step foot in the cursed forest. It is protected. And even if I could, the way to find this object is steeped in ancient knowledge as recorded in another sacred relic, a grimoire of light. Indeed, the book contains much more, and in the wrong hands it might be used to reveal and destroy creatures of magic."

John blinked. "Such an object would be dangerous... to some." A wry smile played across his features. "I'm surprised you haven't been clever enough to secure it already," he said, with a hint of scorn.

The Sheriff didn't reply. He drew his sword in a long, fluid motion, the blade edge chiming along the sheath's metal throat. The sound sent shivers up John's spine, and then his heart froze in his chest.

The man in black lifted the weapon so that it hung, poised between them. One step closer and it would be near enough to take John's head. The prince's mind scrambled desperately for the words that would halt the Sheriff in place, or cast him to another room, but it was like drowning in the center of the ocean. Frantic and desperate, knowing how to swim and still completely powerless.

The Sheriff stepped forward, drawing back the sword.

John shrunk, trying to crawl into himself.

The blade swiped out.

John fell to the floor.

The sword cut through the tapestry hanging behind the chair in which he'd sat. It was ancient, woven by nuns to depict the Virgin and the Child. It crumpled to the floor, leaving bare wall in its place. The Sheriff sheathed his sword. Wisps of smoke hung in the air.

"Clever has nothing to do with it," he said. "I don't know where it is. It may be in the hands of a practitioner, perhaps even tucked away in some trunk of heirlooms in a peasant's hut. Most likely that damned monastery has it secured somewhere." The Sheriff looked down at John, cowering on the floor. "Get up. You are still the one, little prince. I will not harm you." He looked around. "However, you will redecorate this castle. I cannot think clearly with all of these… decorations to distract me."

John pulled himself back up into the chair. "I'll order it done."

The Sheriff nodded sharply. "And we need to find that book."

"Should I round up the people and demand that it be produced, under pain of death?"

"If it is hidden under protection, and you tip our hand, then you only assure that the book will be burned. They would sooner destroy it than allow it to fall into the wrong hands."

"Why haven't the protectors burned the book before? It seems only logical."

The Sheriff shook his head. "The need for it outweighs their concern. Until the relic is claimed, then the book must remain the guide to it. Without a direct threat to the relic it would simply reappear elsewhere, somewhere out of their control. There is always a grimoire and a relic of Sovereignty. It has been so since Creation."

"And you believe it can be found?"

"I am here for a reason."

"Then a simple seeking spell…"

The Sheriff cut him off with a glare. "You don't think I've tried such a spell? You are a fool. The power that created the relic has rendered such things utterly useless," he spat angrily.

John pushed back into the chair, his body tightly wound, waiting for the Sheriff to lash out again at any second. His mind raced for a solution, something to appease the man in the black armor.

"I have an army," he offered. "Well, part of an army."

"You cannot lay siege to your own country. Not without arousing suspicions."

John smiled. "Then we need a pretense."

The Sheriff nodded.

"I have just the thing for it then."

"It won't work, Lord Longstride."

Robin rammed his chest against the plow, pushing with his legs, shoving with his arms. An ache had settled deep into the base of his spine and fire lit the backs of his thighs. Still the plow's tip bounced off the hard-packed dirt, driving the handles down to club across the bruise his shoulders had become.

He stumbled back with a curse, sweat dripping off his brow.

The ox harnessed to the plow passed gas, its dun colored tail flicking back toward him. The man standing at the fence chuckled.

"See, even the beast knows you're doing it wrong."

Robin looked up. The sun cut behind the man, casting a long shadow for an average-sized person. A stray beam caught the edge of fine steel mail that slipped from under his tunic sleeve as he chewed a piece of grass and watched with a milky eye.

Robin threw his hand at the plow and the unfurrowed field.

"This land hates me."

The man shook his head. "I think it is the opposite, Lord Longstride." A small blue wildflower he'd tucked into the band of his wheat straw hat bobbed in disapproval.

"Don't call me that," Robin spat. "I'm not my father."

"No, you're not," the man agreed. "Your father wouldn't be trying to plow."

"It has to be done, and we are short-handed." Robin braced himself to start again.

The man clucked his tongue, reaching over to push him away. Robin jerked back, hands clenched and up. The man looked down at the fists then back up to his eyes. His voice came, soft but firm.

"Calm yourself," he said. "I'm just going to show how to do this easy, instead of hard, Lord... Robin."

Anger poured from Robin's body like water, spilling out onto the hard soil and soaking away. He stepped back and held his hands up.

"I'm sorry, Old Soldier," he responded. "I'm not a farmer."

"No, you're not," Old Soldier chuckled. "Neither was I when I came to your father's service, so mayhap we can make you a suitable stand-in." The elder man stepped between the plow's handles. "Now watch."

He bent his knees, hooked his elbows under the handles, then stood, lifting the back of the tool off the ground. One hand, a sandwich of rough calluses on the palm and slick scar on the back, held the single rein that ran to the ox's bridle. He gave a loud whistle and jerked his hand. The leather rein cracked the air above the beast's back. The ox lowed and began to move.

The tip of the plow sank into the dirt, splitting it and driving soil up into rounded mounds along a handspan-wide trough. After a few steps Old Soldier dropped his arms and used his hands to guide the plow and keep the furrow straight. He smiled at Robin.

"Let the beast do the work," he said. "You're here to keep order, is all."

Robin watched as the truth of the advice rang in his ears.

He would have rather been with the king, heading now for the Holy Land, but he had been chosen, singled out for a particular mission. He had boarded a ship, true, and many had seen him do it. Only one had seen him shimmy down the far side of the ship and into the water, to make his way back to land.

Dark forces were gathering. The night before departing, King Richard had summoned him to his private chamber and told him the truth of what they were facing in Jerusalem. It had made him all the more eager to go, to fight, and all the more bitter that he needed to remain behind.

Then the king had told him why.

There was darkness gathering in Jerusalem, yes, but there was darkness gathering at home. With so many gone to fight, the king needed to know that some would stay behind to guard the kingdom. He was to be part watchdog and part spy.

The prince sat on the throne. He was an unknown quantity, and the king didn't know how much he could trust him.

"Trust no one," King Richard had told him. *"No one except the Lady Marian."* He could never bring himself to involve her in this, though. She was barely more than a child, and a woman, as well, which meant she possessed limited influence, despite her many abilities.

He was on the path through Sherwood. He had never liked the mighty forest, finding the darkness within it to be unsettling. It seemed to go on forever, and once inside it was easy to become turned around, lost forever. Some said it was the work of creatures that dwelt there. He'd never believed in such things, but given what the king had told him, he might do well to start.

CHAPTER TWELVE

Sweat trickled under his clothes, sticking fabric to skin. The cape and cassock hung heavily across his shoulders, draping on the rounded planes of his body. He moved his arms, watching the square beam of sunlight play over the purple cloth. When he passed it through the light it glistened and gleamed, as if each thread had been hammered from a precious metal.

The color—the brilliant, verdant purple—came from Phoenicia, harvested from small snails whose only purpose was to provide the chemical compound to create the Tyrian hue. Dozens, if not hundreds, had been slaughtered when he ordered his attire, dissected for the glands that held the precious dye.

The thought of all those tiny sacrifices, just so his robe of office could be the correct color, thrilled him somewhere deep inside.

He held a crozier, and, when he passed it through the river of light, motes of dust swirled and eddied. The sun, coming through the sole window in the antechamber, glimmered dully along the surface of the golden staff, rimming along the curl of precious metal at the head. There in the light, it looked like a rod of molten sunshine, the power of the universe formed to his shepherdic symbol of office and rank.

Called to a private audience with Prince John... no... called to a private discussion with the king.

Bishop Montoya ran his fingertips down the thirty-three buttons of his cassock, one for every year Christ had walked the earth. They were made from ivory that came from a trader who had confessed to some heinous sins. He'd been forgiven, but at a price.

Noise made him step quickly from the sunbeam, stand straight, and drop his errant hand.

The doors to the throne room opened wide, swinging apart as the back of a man jostled through. His bandy arms wrapped around several rolls of embroidered fabric. Montoya couldn't see the subject of the tapestries, lost in patches of colored thread, a riot of bean stitching, bird nesting, and buckram.

"Uhf! Where are we taking these again?" The servant was tall, hunched over the bundles.

"Around back to the burn," a voice replied from inside the room. A second man appeared, and Montoya watched the two of them shuffle under their load, moving across the foyer.

"The king will see you now."

At the sound of the voice, the bishop turned. A young servant stood there, looking at him expectantly with wide eyes and high cheekbones. Montoya's hands ran down the front of his cassock, smoothing the material. He stepped sharply toward the boy and followed him into the throne room. His footsteps echoed across the marble flagstone floor and rolled up the carved block walls.

The throne room was nearly bare.

Along the walls, long tubes of rolled fabric lay on the floor, like the ones carried out by the men who had left before he'd entered. He knew immediately what they were. Behind the throne, four servants struggled to pull down the last remaining tapestry. Fixed high above and behind the seat of power, it clung stubbornly to the wall, set there by ancient iron spikes driven deep in the granite and cemented in by mortar. It was massive, stretching two men tall and near forty feet across, and depicted a scene from John's Revelation.

Thousands upon tens of thousands of threads wove together to depict Christ seated on the throne of Heaven as the Judge of all men. The entire tapestry was symbolic. The Savior, anglicized for the region, held a scale in one hand, a sword in the other, and the Book of Life across his knees. At his feet knelt the lamb and the lion, both of them with peaceful expressions on their faces. To the right of Him stood men and angels, hands raised in supplication. On the left side were men and angels bent in agony, surrounded by flames.

Bishop Montoya did not know how to feel as he continued to walk toward the throne, where waited the king-in-standing. This was a religious tapestry, depicting the Christ Himself in Glory, and Montoya's office demanded that he be outraged at its removal.

Yet the tapestry was ancient. Thick threads of embroidery hung loosely along its edges and one area, low by the lion, was worn and threadbare. It long ago had lost its luster, age and time leeching the pigments out until the entire cloth looked tarnished to his eyes.

It was shabby.

It was a disgrace.

And it had intimidated him the last time he'd been in its presence. When he'd first arrived, King Richard had summoned him to a meeting.

It had not gone well.

The king had been warm at the beginning of the audience, smiling and speaking broadly of the good work of the brothers in Christ at the monastery. His mood had turned, however, as Bishop Montoya shared his observances that the monks were undisciplined. He'd confessed that the monastery was near shameful in its shabbiness, the monks too concerned with the poor and needful of the village to maintain a proper place of worship.

"*God is great and greatly to be praised*," he'd said, and He deserved a worthy house. For that matter the bishop himself, as Christ's ambassador in the land, should not be assigned to a hovel, with the barest of creature comforts, a near-blind old maid as a house servant, and a hump-backed gardener.

Pursuing his ideas for rectifying the situation, Montoya had broached the concept of indulgences and tithe. To his utter surprise, the king had ended the audience by standing and leaving the room without another word.

He remembered it well, and it still stung.

Now he arrived at the foot of the dais, following the lead of his escort and stopping at the first step of four that led up to the great throne of England. Prince John stood beside the throne, watching the laborers struggle with the mighty tapestry, his face pulled into hard planes. Montoya couldn't help but compare the man before him to the former occupant of the throne.

Prince John and King Richard had little in common. He could see the family resemblance—the same broad forehead, the same lowered brow, the same jutting chin, all signs of shared blood. On the Lionheart those features, combined with a broad frame and a mass of tawny curls, had lent him the leonine look that became his namesake.

On John those same features gave his eyes a hooded, secretive look, and the jutting chin lent a feral cast to his jawline. His frame was far leaner than Richard's, coiled under a rich brocade tunic and packed with violent potential. He was his brother's shadow.

A dark reflection.

"Cut the mangy thing down if you have to," Prince John ordered. His voice didn't boom across the room like Richard's, but it carried, slithering toward the ear sure and steady. It was the voice of someone used to being obeyed.

One of the servants reached down and pulled a small knife from his boot, the kind used to cut an apple for eating. He handed it up to the man perched high on the unsteady ladder. Taking it from his fellow worker, that man laid the knife's edge against the tapestry and began to saw back and forth with it. Ancient threads parted with small puffs of dust, and the tapestry jerked downward in tiny increments, pulled by its own cumbersome weight.

Prince John nodded sharply to himself, spun on his heel, and dropped into the seat of the wide throne. He leaned back against the arms and propped his knee up.

"What the hell can I do for you?" he demanded in a surly tone.

Montoya bristled. "You called me for an audience."

Prince John's head lolled on its neck, turning to the servant who'd escorted Montoya.

"Who is this?" he demanded. Before the servant could speak, however, Montoya inched forward, his toes touching the front edge of the first step.

"Bishop Donel Montoya, Christ's ambassador to the Isle of England, appointed by the Holy See." He tilted his head just slightly. "At your service."

Prince John regarded him for a long moment, dark eyes taking in every inch of finery wrapped around the bishop. He grunted, then spoke.

"Nice stick."

Bishop Montoya stroked the crozier with his fingertips.

"I am surprised you don't have one, Your Highness."

"I have no lambs that are gone astray."

"But you do have subjects to rule."

"They wouldn't respond to the crook."

"They recognize the rod," Montoya persisted. "A ruler should have a scepter."

Prince John didn't reply, but studied him, most likely trying to determine if he was being mocked.

"And where would I find a suitable scepter?" he said at last.

"Surely Your Highness could have one made by the finest goldsmith in the land."

At that moment the servants succeeded in cutting free one corner of the tapestry. It slid down the wall, fabric hissing against stone like a trapped snake, and then it *tharumped* hollowly on the floor. The servants began moving to the next corner, ready to cut it free as well.

Prince John didn't react, just continued to stare at the bishop. Montoya's eyes remained locked on him.

"Where would I get enough gold to create a scepter fit for me to wield?" Prince John asked.

Eagerness to please the royalty rode Montoya hard, and he said the words before thinking.

"The church will provide." As soon as the words had left his mouth, he wished desperately that he could recall them, but it was too late.

An eyebrow arched.

"The church has gold?"

In for a pinch, in for a pound, the bishop decided, his heart pounding now. "We have some… items in storage that can be procured. We will… *I* will gladly contribute them so my king can be properly attired." He smiled. "As God would want."

Prince John leaned forward, feral mouth stretched to show teeth.

"Then I will accept your *tithe* to me." The words struck like a cobra. Suddenly Montoya felt as if he were falling backward— as if a rug had been pulled from under his feet.

"I… I…" he stammered, but words would not come.

Prince John shifted his body, leaning back again.

"And since the church is so amicable toward helping the throne, there is something I need you to find for me." He fell silent, watching the clergyman intently.

After a long moment, Montoya broke the silence.

"What is it you are seeking?" he asked.

"A book," Prince John replied. "Ancient in origin. Pagan."

"Why would you look to *me* for such a thing?"

"I have reason to believe that at least one of your monks might know where it is."

"Such a thing should have been sent to Rome," the bishop said, stopping himself before he mentioned the secret archives held by the Church at the Holy See.

"Let us hope it has not been," John said. "It is an artifact of this land, and therefore it belongs here. In fact, it should be turned over to the throne. Immediately."

"Yes, of course," he said. Montoya felt himself nodding before he realized he was going to agree. "If you will give me the particulars, I will search for it, and bring it to you as soon as it can be found."

"Excellent," the prince said, a smile twisting his features. "Approach the throne and I will... *impress* upon you the sign of what I seek."

"You've been awfully quiet since the king left," Chastity remarked, breaking the stillness of the room. Marian glanced up from the beautifully illuminated manuscript she'd been perusing, but not truly reading.

"He has scarce gone, but I feel his absence already," Marian admitted.

"I have been wondering if it's that which weighs on your mind, or thoughts of a certain handsome noble, instead."

"I'm sure I don't know who you're talking about," Marian said.

"You know *exactly* who I am talking about," the girl replied. "The one you made such a lovely sight dancing with."

"Oh," Marian waved her hand, feigning surprise. "Robin."

Chastity rolled her eyes.

"You might be able to fool everyone else in this castle, but not me," she said, leaning closer. "I see right through you. You fancy him—I know you do—and any fool could see that he fancies you."

Marian felt her cheeks grow warm.

"Do you think when the king returns he'll ask for your hand?"

"Chastity, I'd thank you to employ your matchmaking skills on someone else," Marian said, returning her attention to the book.

"I grow weary of matching stable boys to servant girls. I desire a challenge."

"Well, then look to finding yourself a husband, and not one for me."

Chastity grimaced. "I have yet to spend more than five minutes talking with a man that doesn't bore me."

Marian could sympathize. Not all men were Robin.

"What have you been reading?" Chastity said, seeming eager now to change the subject, once it was focused on her.

"The cardinal was good enough to loan me a manuscript detailing the life of Saint George," Marian said. "I've been most curious about him since his last feast day, and have found myself more and more drawn to his story."

Chastity squinted, as if trying to think. "He's one of them that refused to renounce his faith, and wouldn't make a sacrifice to the pagan gods, wasn't he?"

"Yes, he's also renowned for slaying a dragon, and saving a lady in the process."

"We could use more of his type around here, especially lately, now that all the good ones have gone off to war." She paused, and then added slyly, "Well, most of them that is."

Marian knew what she meant, but she couldn't help but recall what the king had told her. She pointed to a picture of Saint George.

"Some battles are waged closer to home, and we might have need of men such as this," she said.

"We will if that sorry excuse for a French king isn't doing his duty, to the same extent as our own Lionheart," Chastity responded. "We'd be in a fine mess then."

"Don't let it burden you, Chastity," Marian said. "I worry enough about that for the both of us."

Suddenly there was a shout from another room. Both Marian and Chastity leapt to their feet.

"That sounds like it was coming from the main hall," Chastity guessed. "Best stay here, princess. I'll discover the source." Before Marian could respond two guards entered the room. Their uniforms were covered in dust and rolled up at the sleeves. Dirty leather gloves covered their hands.

"What is happening?" Marian asked, though she didn't recognize either man.

Neither of them looked at her, much less answered. With matching strides they moved toward a large tapestry that hung on her wall, depicting the crucifixion. Each seized a corner of it, and then tore it from the wall with a mighty yank.

"Stop!" Marian screamed, striding forward quickly as they dropped the tapestry and turned to lay hands on another one. The taller of the two looked at her, and she froze in her tracks. His eyes shone, glassy and lifeless. A sick feeling settled in the pit of her stomach. She felt rooted to the spot, as though she couldn't move while pinned by his gaze.

Without pause the shorter of the two tore down the next tapestry.

"I commanded you to *stop*," she thundered, raising her voice, the spell broken as she pushed forward and snatched the cloth from the man's hands. "What are you doing?"

"Following orders," the tall man replied flatly.

"You will address milady properly, and heed her command." Chastity grabbed the arm of the tall guard as he reached for a new tapestry.

"Orders of the king," the shorter one said, as if it explained everything. Chastity looked at Marian with wide, startled eyes.

"Watch them," Marian hissed. "I will go to my uncle, and put an end to this insanity." With that, she passed through the main hall and was sickened to see that everywhere the tapestries had been ripped from the walls and lay in piles on the floor. A pair of servants was busy rolling them up. She quickened her step, and a minute later she saw the new bishop exiting King Richard's study.

He scurried on his way without acknowledging her presence, which surprised her and further served to stoke her ire. She marched into the study and found the prince there. She had to fight down her instinctive sense of outrage at seeing him sitting at the king's table. He looked up from a piece of parchment, which he then dropped onto the desk, folding his arms over it as she approached. Whatever it was, he didn't want her to see it.

"Child," he said, greeting her with a thin smile. "What can I do for you?"

"You can stop the guards from tearing the tapestries from the walls," she said, barely managing to control her temper. He blinked at her, and for a moment she thought he might deny having given the order. Then he leaned forward across the desk.

"I'm sorry, I can't do that," he said smoothly. "You see, the tapestries, they are… outdated. I'll be replacing them soon with some new ones." He spoke to her as if she were a simpleton.

"What gives you the right?" she demanded.

"Why, my brother, of course," the prince replied. "You remember, he left me in charge, and gave me the authority to do whatever was necessary. I'm afraid this is necessary."

"Those tapestries have been there for generations," she persisted. "The king would not wish them removed."

"Well, my dear brother isn't here to protect them," John said, and every pretense of cordiality disappeared from his voice. "Or you, for that matter," he added. "I'd hold my tongue if I were you, niece, lest something happen to it."

She blinked in surprise as she realized he had just threatened her, and without subtlety, at that. He stood up abruptly and leaned forward, his eyes jittering as if he were mad.

"I'm your sovereign now, and, if you forget that, I won't hesitate to remind you in the most direct way possible."

Marian took an involuntary step backward, frightened by the look in his eyes. She had questioned Richard's choice in appointing his brother. Now she wondered if the land wouldn't have been better served by Henry, scoundrel and schemer that he was, than by this man who stood before her.

She desperately wanted to tell John that there was something wrong with him. She also wanted to examine the document that was now lying exposed on the desk. Instead she forced herself to take a step forward and, though it galled her, she dropped her head as though expressing subservience.

"I'm sorry," she said through clenched teeth.

"That's better," John answered. "You'll find that if you keep that attitude, things will be infinitely more pleasant for you."

"I understand," she said.

Reading upside down was something her mother had taught her from a young age, explaining that a lady often had need of more information than the men in her life were willing to give. Unfortunately the language on the parchment was unknown to her, but there were a couple of symbols there, and she hastily committed them to memory.

The effort caused pain to twinge in her skull.

The sigils looked foreign, a language she knew not. She would ask Cardinal Francis about them. Hopefully he would know their meaning. He was a learned man, and had studied many things.

"Good," John said coldly. "Now get out, and don't interrupt me again."

Though she seethed inside, Marian managed to hold her tongue as she turned and departed. The king should know of what John was doing with the tapestries. It was an outrage, yet she hesitated. Was it enough to cause Richard to forsake his holy quest and return home? No, she decided. She needed more information and the cardinal was just the man to help her with that.

She didn't have time to send for him and request an audience. Neither did she want those in the castle who might report back to John knowing her purpose. She cast one more thought at going to tell Chastity what she was doing. After all, her friend would worry when she didn't come back.

Two more servants wearing leather gloves and carrying wide-bladed utility knives made her decision for her.

It could not wait.

CHAPTER THIRTEEN

Adaryn was determined to find some sage for Lady Longstride and answers for herself as she set out to visit a potion maker with whom she occasionally had dealings. The older man had been a friend of her father's, and she'd known him since childhood.

She rarely left her home, and when she did it was usually to barter for something she or a client needed. Barnabas, on the other hand, was a downright hermit, never leaving his hovel for anything or anyone.

When she arrived at his home, after several hours on the road, she was shocked to find that almost everything in it had been stripped bare, and that a cart out front was laden with trunks and sacks. The old man was huddled over another trunk out back, packing things away in it.

"Barnabas?"

He jumped and turned with a cry, then pressed a hand over his heart.

"Oh, it's you," he said, before turning back to what he was doing. "Thank goodness," he muttered.

"Barnabas, what are you up to?

"I'm leaving," the man said, standing up again. His eyes twitched nervously.

"Leaving? You've lived your whole life right here, haven't moved more than a hundred feet. Where are you going to?"

"I was thinking I'd head to France."

It seemed so preposterous she almost started to laugh. The cart out front was no laughing matter, though. Three months earlier, when she'd last seen him, he'd owned no such conveyance.

"But why?"

He leaned in. "Look, there is something happening. I've felt it, and others have felt it, too. Don't tell me you haven't."

She licked her lips. "Maybe I have, and maybe I haven't."

"Whatever is coming, I don't want to stick around and see it. If you're smart, you won't either."

She glanced at his garden. He had spent so many years cultivating it, and now he was just going to abandon it.

"How is your sage growing?" she asked.

"Sage?" he replied. "Sage is the least of my worries. Although it's all rotted, as yours surely is. No one's been able to grow sage in months."

"What does it mean?"

"It means that there's an evil poisoning the earth, destroying anything that can possibly stand up to it."

She took a deep breath. He'd always been prone to exaggeration and a pessimist on top of it all. Still, his words twisted in her mind like something alive.

"If what you say is true, there would be other signs."

"Are you blind, woman? The signs are all around. Blackbirds litter the fields and blot out the grass. Worms crawl across dry dirt. Half the cows in the land are dry." His eyes twitched even more rapidly. "Owls have been flying out of the forest and circling people's houses for weeks. They've been flying both night and day. Death is coming, and not just for a few people. It's coming for everyone. There's scarce a house in all the region that hasn't been visited."

"And how would you know that? You never leave your home."

"I have friends, friends all over, and they tell me," he said, "and now I'm telling you. Leave while you can, before the owls hoot outside *your* door."

"If an owl comes to me, I'll not take it as a portent of death. I'll take it as a visit from *cailleach-oidhche*...or a sign that the mice are growing too plentiful," she said scornfully.

"You mock me, Adaryn, but mark my words. You'll come to a bad end if you stay."

She sighed, not sure what to think.

"Do you have any dried sage I can buy?"

He barked, a short, hard laugh. "Not a stick. Anyone with any sense is using all they've got left over to make wards, cleanse houses, preparing for the worst."

"Do you know if Alderman has any?"

He shook his head. "He left the region more than a fortnight ago. Picked his garden dry before he left, but I can tell you no sage was growing there, either."

She blinked in shock, stunned to hear that the old wizard had left, and without stopping in to say a word to her. They had shared a few summer weeks as a young couple not old enough to know a thing about the world and still enjoyed company occasionally. Something was wrong indeed.

"Best tend to your own house and not worry about others'," Barnabas said, not unkindly. He put a hand on her shoulder. "Take care of yourself, child, for your father's sake. I'd not like to see you joining him in the grave anytime soon."

"Be careful around those French," she said back. "They're an unfriendly lot."

He nodded and then turned away, but not before she saw tears in his eyes. Shaken to her core, she began the long journey home.

It was quiet.

The silence had snuck in, creeping along the walls and windows like a shadow. All of a sudden he realized that the only thing he could hear was the sound of his own breathing. The in and out of air through his lungs rasped along his eardrums, startling him.

The door was shut now, but all afternoon he'd been accompanied by the hustle and the bustle of men and women following his orders, their noise bleeding through the stout wood. Now even those were gone.

He decided to stand, to fling open the portal and find someone, *anyone*, who might be outside.

"She will have to be handled."

The voice came from nowhere, freezing him in place. Eyes jerking to and fro, he searched the room. From the black of a shadow beside a cabinet stepped the Sheriff.

The shadow was not big enough to hide a man.

The armored man stood, pale hands clasped before him. His skin and hair almost glowed against the gloom around him. The wide fur collar outlined his angular face, giving it a cruel, aristocratic air.

John put his feet on the floor, sitting up in his chair.

"I've handled her just fine."

"No, you shut her up."

"That's not handled enough for you? What would you like me to do, cut her tongue out?"

The Sheriff raised an eyebrow. "You have no sophistication, always reaching for the quickest way."

"If that little girl is going to be a problem," John said, "I would rather just be done with her."

"That *little girl* has lived in this castle nearly her entire life, while you have been here for mere days. If you harm her, it will not go unmarked, and there will be repercussions. This island has its protectors." Pale fingers stroked the collar, running through the long fur flecked with tiny sparks of blue. "Our first asset will be knowledge. Find out everything you can about her."

"She's my niece."

The Sheriff's eyes blazed. "I did not ask for what you already know. Find out the things you *don't* know."

"To what purpose?"

"There is something about her that smells strange to me."

Prince John furrowed his brow, and then nodded. "I'll call for records, and question the staff." He returned his attention to the table in front of him. His hands shuffled parchments, moving them into a pile.

Without warning, the Sheriff was there beside him. John didn't jump, but inside his skin he twitched.

"What is this?" The Sheriff's finger pinned a parchment to the table top. The tone of his voice drew the prince short. His mouth moved, but he had no words, unsure of how to respond.

"Did you have these out when your niece was here?" the Sheriff pressed. The words were a hiss, a slip of steel on sheath. "Out in the open, where she could read them? What sort of fool are you?"

"She couldn't read them!" Prince John protested. The Sheriff removed his finger and John fumbled the pages more, trying to shove them together, to make them smaller. The parchment fought him, sheets sticking to each other and crumpling, or slipping and flying from his hands. "None of them have been translated. Some are a struggle even for my mind."

"Leave them be!" the Sheriff roared. John froze, hands in mid-clutch. In a flash of dull sheen off ebon armor the Sheriff snatched one of the loose pages. He stared at it, eyes darting. As the seconds ticked by his face darkened, taking on the color of aged bone instead of corpse white. His lip curled, revealing teeth gone sharp. His eyes rolled black, flicking up to pin John in his seat.

"This is a binding."

Prince John gulped, the noise loud in his ears, sounding like a bucket dropped in an empty well. His mind scrambled.

"I thought it might be needed, with the culmination of our plans."

"This puny enchantment would accomplish nothing. It wouldn't even cause a blink."

"It's Enochian."

"And?"

"I thought..."

"You thought consorting with the enemy might save your arse." The Sheriff leaned down, bringing his face close to John's. "The only thing you can do, little prince, is remain loyal to me. We are bound together, and *that* is the only binding that should concern you. Break faith in our arrangement at any time, and there will be nowhere in this world you can hide that I will not find you."

"How dare you?" John responded. "You need me." Hatred flashed through his chest at the weak mewl his voice had become.

"I need you to provide information about young Marian." The Sheriff straightened. "Everything depends upon you doing as you are told. Obedience brings reward. Anything short of that..." The Sheriff shrugged, leaving the threat unspoken, and all the worse for it.

"We want the same thing," John insisted. "I swear it on my soul."

"You did that back in Ireland."

The prince fell silent, desperate to change the subject. "What are we going to do about the girl?"

The Sheriff said nothing, simply touched his fingers to the fur collar around his neck and blew air from his lips. The push of his breath made the long, black hair wave and trill. Two eyes opened between his long, pale fingers, glowing yellow and feral. The collar shifted, unwinding itself from the Sheriff's throat.

As John watched with eyes grown wide, legs with claw-tipped paws broke free from the dark shape and pulled it up to stand, where it shook and stretched, expanding with each movement until an animal that may have been a cat, may have been a dog, and may have been something else altogether, crouched on the Sheriff's shoulder. The Sheriff turned his face toward it and it lowered a triangular head.

"Find and watch her," the Sheriff murmured. The animal peered at him, comprehension clear in its eyes. It batted his face with a paw, and leapt into the shadow from which its master had stepped.

The Sheriff waved his hand in a motion that John recognized. It had been diagrammed in an ancient Egyptian text for which he'd traded two pounds of gold and two pounds of black goat flesh. His eyes burned as he followed the twisting fingers, and began to water uncontrollably.

When his vision cleared, he could hear the servants shuffling past outside the door.

And he was alone in the room.

The stone was cool under its feet, much cooler than its home. It slinked down the hallway, moving through the ever-present shadow at the base of the wall. Windows were high. The light only dipped so low.

Fat ankles passed by. They puffed out of leather shoes too small for the feet and became stout calves that rose up into a skirt. Tempted it was to swipe out, to let out the tang of the blood trapped in those swollen joints.

It kept moving. It would obey.

The girl. The one that smelled of innocence and lean flesh. The one with narrow ankles. Her it would find.

It stayed near the inside wall, where her smell soaked into the stone. She crackled in its nose.

It moved faster.

"Your Highness." The boy bowed so deeply she feared his hair would brush through the dirty hay. He straightened, looking at her feet instead of her eyes. "How may I serve you today?"

Marian glanced around the stable. She loved riding, and came here often to try different horses, depending on her mood. Today people moved with purpose from one end to the other. It was noisy in the long barn. Of course, there was always a sound of horses, and of people talking and laughing.

This was different.

The clamor inside the stable had a brittle edge to it. Head cocked to the side, she tried to figure out what was unusual. Looking down the line of stalls, she noted that about half were occupied, each with a horse hanging its head over the gate. Ears flat, the majestic beasts nickered and neighed at each other. Hooves clopped and bodies bashed against the walls as stable hands moved from one to the other with sugar cubes and apples, using them to try to calm the beasts.

Her nose filled with a harsh, bitter smell of fire and dust. Glancing up she found traces of smoke curling along the thatch roof.

"Highness?" the boy said again.

"I'm sorry." She smiled down at him. "I need a horse."

The stable boy looked around, eyes wide.

"Um…"

"Do not worry," she said. "I can see that things are not normal here today."

"It is an odd one, Highness," he agreed.

"Then let us follow the simple course," she suggested. "Go to Merryweather's stall and bridle her, but don't bother with a saddle. I'll take her from there in a few moments."

He nodded, touching two fingers to his forehead in salute, and moved off to do as she bid.

Moving over to the tack room, she entered and locked the door. Briskly she moved to the locker where her riding gear was stored, including a small stack of clothing. Opening the wooden door she was greeted by a waft of cedar and horse sweat. She needed to wash her kit, but it would have to wait.

Glancing back at the door to make sure she'd bolted it, she shimmied out of her castle gown, letting the simple cotton shift fall to the ground. Kicking off her sandals as she unfastened her undergarment, she found herself unencumbered. The air in the tack room was warm, but she still felt a chill. She shook it off, telling herself that it was just in her mind, an aftereffect of being naked.

She looked again, and found the door still bolted.

Pulling a linen shirt off the top of the stack of clothes, she jerked it over her body. It lay close to her skin, soft from dozens of washing, and hung to mid-thigh. Snatching up her trousers, she slipped them over her legs, the wool stiff from her last ride and scratchy across the slick scars that criss-crossed her shins, calves, and thighs. She tucked in the shirt and buckled her belt. Next came the leather jerkin that supported her spine during a ride, and covered her breasts for modesty's sake, holding them steady for comfort. Finally she slipped her feet into matching well-worn boots that made her ready to ride.

Dirt did not hold the girl scent like the stone. And the hated sun hung overhead. It darted around the open door, so fast it was a blur as it streaked under the tapestry being carried by the solid men who smelled like dust and sour milk. Their smell helped it separate the girl from the dirt until it found her trail.

She crossed the courtyard. It circled, keeping low around the flowers and bushes as it chased the smell left behind.

Exiting the tack room, she lost no time and went straight to Merryweather's stall at the end of the stable. Inside she found the small chestnut mare with a leather bridle in place and the stable boy holding the reins.

On sight of her, the horse pushed forward, nuzzling her face along Marian's shoulder and neck. She smiled and stroked the sleek muscles along the creature's withers. Merryweather was firm and solid, full of power despite her smaller stature. Marian loved her, always stopping at the stall to give the gentle creature a treat of carrot or apple, choosing her most of the times she rode.

"You are sure no saddle for you today?" the boy asked.

She shook her head. "Not for my girl. We ride better without a barrier."

"Then she is ready for you, Highness." The stable boy bowed his head again.

She reached out and touched him on the shoulder. He wasn't much younger than her, perhaps five years separating them. She was tall for a girl, and he hadn't reached that bone-stretching growth spurt boys seem to get, so he was shorter than her by more than two handspans. It made him look younger than he was. That and his wide brown eyes.

"What is your name?"

"Murther, ma'am."

"Good name. It's distinctive."

He blushed. "Thank you, Highness."

"Murther, I need something more from you today."

"If I am able, I will."

"I would not ask you to lie, but if you are not asked directly, I would prefer you to not speak of me here today. No mention of it as gossip or news."

Murther passed his fingers over his lips, indicating that they were sealed.

The warm smell of rat urine filled its nose. A rat had crossed this space moments before it arrived. The scent made it waver, tempting it to track and kill and eat. Instead it coiled its body tighter, drawing deeper into the shadow, and flicked its eyes up to watch.

The horse lived here.

The girl had taken the horse.

The girl would return here.

It would wait.

Marian and Merryweather broke free of the forest's shadow on a ridge above the Church Road. The sun washed over her, bathing the world in bright yellow and warming her immediately.

Underneath her legs, the horse shook and snorted, also feeling the effect of the high summer sun.

Marian had taken her up the narrow trail through the wood, trying to get ahead of the bishop. Looking down the long slope of the ridge she saw a carriage pull from the forest into the same sunlight she enjoyed. The driver wore the brown robe of a monk, and the team of horses trailed purple streamers from their harnesses.

Leaning over Merryweather's withers, she clucked her tongue and tapped her heels into the horse's flanks. Merryweather took her lead and began to trot down the other side of the ridge, heading across the open pass toward the monastery that stood solid and wide, surrounded by sunlit fields of monks working their crops.

By the time she reached the gate of the monastery's corral, she needed a long drink of water. Merryweather agreed, walking straight up to the trough and dropping her muzzle into it. Marian tossed her leg over the horse's neck and slid down her side. She considered scooping some of the water for herself, but decided against it.

A monk jogged along the track she'd just ridden, one hand holding up his long monk's habit. He stumbled to a stop beside her, dropping forward to put his hands on his knees as he gulped air in great draughts. She looked down on the top of his head. His tonsure had plastered thickly to the shaved portion, held down by sweat and turned ruddy brown instead of what she believed would be a bright ginger when dry.

"Are you alright, Father?" she asked.

He nodded, sweat flinging off his scalp. He took a deep breath and straightened, blowing it out before looking at her. His eyes rolled from her face down to her ankles, and then jerked violently away.

"What brings you here this day, milady?" he asked.

"I need to see the cardinal."

"Ummmmm…" The monk scratched his neck where the robe

had rubbed a thin red crease. He paused as if to gather words, but only repeated the humming sound from his chest.

Anger flared inside her. "What is the trouble?" she demanded. "Is the cardinal here?"

"Yes, milady," the man responded. "He is."

"Then take me to him."

Still the monk hesitated, glancing at her, then the ground, then back at her before motioning for her to follow him. He led her in through a door to a small room. It contained a bench, and not another stick of furniture. A single window, covered in oilskin, let in the sunlight.

"Stay here please," he said. "I will return with the cardinal."

Before she could agree, he darted out the door, shutting it firmly behind him.

CHAPTER FOURTEEN

The room was narrow, but Marian found the bench uncomfortable, and so she paced back and forth, leaving tracks in the dirt floor. As each moment passed anxiety gnawed at her stomach. She stopped moving, and jumbled thoughts rattled through her head

Will I be turned away like a fool?

Dismissed as a child?

Ignored as a woman?

Just as she began to pace again, the door opened. The cardinal stepped inside, his face creased with worry. To her surprise, Friar Tuck squeezed in behind him.

She knelt and crossed herself.

"Enough of that, child," the cardinal said. She rose and he indicated the bench. Dutifully she sat on the end of the hard seat, giving him plenty of room to sit beside her.

"Your Eminence, I apologize for coming unannounced," she said, "and demanding this audience."

"I can only assume that it is urgent," he replied.

"It is."

"Then it is good that I am here."

"I was afraid the father I spoke with wasn't going to allow me to see you."

The cardinal chuckled. "Well, you did cause a bit of a stir. The good brothers here are unused to seeing a woman wearing such attire."

Marian looked down and blushed. Her clothes covered her, but they also clung to her like a second skin. Good for riding, yet inappropriate for a monastery. Before she could speak to apologize, the cardinal seemed to read her mind, and held up his hand.

"All is well," he assured her. "Tell me, to what do I owe this visit, milady?"

She glanced at Friar Tuck. The cardinal followed her gaze, then looked back at her.

"Do not concern yourself," he said. "The good friar has my full trust. You should regard him as you do myself." Looking back at Tuck, he added, "Plus he makes an excellent doorstop, should anyone feel the need to join us."

Friar Tuck rolled his eyes, but he did it with a small smile. Moving to the closed door, he leaned heavily against it.

Marian nodded slowly, then cleared her throat.

"Your Eminence, Prince John has ordered that all of the religious tapestries at the castle be torn down," she said, the words tumbling out. "When I confronted him about it, he... well, he threatened me."

Friar Tuck crossed himself. The cardinal's mouth formed a hard line.

"There's more," she said.

"There always is," the cardinal responded.

"When I entered the king's study, I found the prince reading a parchment. He tried to hide it from me, but I did get a glimpse of it. It was written in a language unknown to me, but I managed to memorize a few symbols that appeared on the page."

"Could you describe them?" the cardinal asked.

"It would be easier to draw them." Kneeling beside the bench, Marian began to draw the first symbol in the dirt. With each drag of her finger, it felt as if a band tightened around her skull, cinching with each stroke. She had nearly finished the symbol when the cardinal reached out and seized her hand hard enough to grind her knuckles together.

Startled, she let out a little cry and glanced up at him.

"I'm not finished," she said.

"Were you about to draw a line through the middle of it?" he asked.

"Yes, that would complete the symbol."

He pulled her back up onto the bench, kicking the symbol clear in the dirt. "Then thank Christ that I stopped you. That symbol is unholy. It is used by those who practice black magic."

A chill raced up her spine. "Does such magic truly exist?" She had heard of such things, but had never seen evidence of them with her own eyes.

The cardinal nodded solemnly.

"And you are certain that this symbol relates to it?"

"Yes." He stroked his chin, silent for a long moment. "Can you describe the other symbols? Drawing them is too much risk."

She did her best, and the cardinal's jaw tightened with each word. So did the pressure in her head.

Finally her memory was exhausted, and the pressure softened.

"What are they used for?" she asked.

"They are symbols used to conjure and control," he replied. "Most often the object of their use is some sort of dark entity, something monstrous. Some such creatures have been known to poison the very earth beneath their feet."

"Surely the prince would not call upon such a thing," she exclaimed. She didn't like or trust her uncle, but what the cardinal suggested was incomprehensible.

"I would be certain of nothing at this moment," the cardinal said, "except that danger has come upon us all, and there are very few who remain to stand and fight." He shared a significant look with Friar Tuck. "I must think and pray and plan."

"There is still one thing you don't know," Marian said.

"Tell me, child."

"The king has left his fastest ship at my disposal, to summon him home in the event of an emergency."

The cardinal frowned, saying nothing.

Tuck pushed off the door. "He is still at sea, traveling in heavily-laden vessels," the friar offered. "He could be caught by a lighter ship."

The cardinal shook his head. "We don't have anything that we can show him as proof, other than a few missing tapestries. I warned him of the dangers of leaving the land unprotected, that a darkness approached, but he chose to go anyway. I'm afraid we'll need much more damning evidence than we have of John's wickedness."

Marian knew he was right, even if she wasn't happy about it. Richard had placed John in control, and she knew him well enough to trust that the decision had not been made lightly. They needed proof that evil was taking root in the heart of the kingdom. She only prayed that they found it before it was too late.

Friar Tuck looked at her thoughtfully. "When the time does come, choose carefully the messenger you send. This might be the one chance we have to undo our fate."

The cardinal nodded. "Wise advice."

The words of both men weighed heavily on Marian. "What are you not telling me?" she asked. "Do not dare to hold back. King Richard kept me privy to his court and I have proven myself capable. Grant me the same respect you would any man."

"It is not a lack of respect, Marian, but a fear for your safety."

The cardinal sighed and fell silent, studying her.

Finally he answered.

"There are prophecies that tell of a time of darkness, when evil will be unleashed upon England," he said. "This malicious force, if left unchecked, will spread across the land, and then the world. The prophetess, Bernadette of Avignon, had a vision regarding it. She said in her writings, 'The lion of the north will range from his home and the jackals of the devil will be free to ravage at their leisure until nothing is left of the land or the people.' She continued in more detail, but you can see what she meant."

"You believe this is that time?" she asked.

"Prophecy is tricky," he said. "But yes, all the signs and portents lead me to believe it is true."

Marian's mouth turned down.

"What is wrong?" he asked.

"I mean no disrespect, Your Eminence—you are far more learned than I—but I have studied the scripture and the writings of the church fathers, including the Revelation of St. John, and even St. Irenaeus."

Friar Tuck started, his wide shoulders jerking. "You've read Irenaeus?"

Her mouth pursed and her eyes narrowed. "Yes I have, and I understood it, as well."

The monk raised his large hands. "I meant it not like that. I thought the only copy of his writings was held here."

"The king had one in his private library, purchased from a convent somewhere in the land of Gaul." A thought pinged through her mind. *If John seeks to harm those, I shall…*

No appropriate punishment occurred to her.

The cardinal raised his hand, gaining their attention once more. "There are words written by mystics of the church that very few have read. Their prophecies are considered controversial, sometimes even heresy. The Holy See keeps them only for their own records. I have spent my life chasing these—I am fascinated and I do not pretend otherwise. It is frowned upon by my brethren, and yet I still search." He put his hand on her arm lightly. "I have lived three times and ten your lifetime. I have read prophecy from saints and heretics, madmen and scholars, pagan and Christian alike. I have found threads that weave a disturbing tapestry, and I think we are on the cusp of a massive attempt by the dark to overtake the light."

She stood. "Then we must not waste another minute. We must find proof of what we suspect and quickly, for all our sakes."

* * *

Glynna Longstride stood in her kitchen alone. The girls were at the market with some of the servants and the men who were left were all out in the field. She could finally fulfill a goal she had long pursued in secret. Her trip to Adaryn had given her the final piece of the puzzle she needed.

She had sought out Adaryn when trying to get pregnant for the first time. It had been Lila's suggestion, though she knew not how Lila was connected to the hedgewitch. Adaryn had given her some herbs to put in her wine and her husband's on the next full moon. Nine months later Robert had been born, a male child and a blessing. Years later she had used herb potions to conceive both Rebecca and Ruth.

Robin had been a surprise, the only child conceived without use of any potions. It was a difficult pregnancy, far more painful than any of the other three. When he was born she had seen light pouring out of his eyes and mouth, and it had terrified her. If not for the intervention of her husband she would have killed the creature then and there.

After that she had carved the symbols into her bedchamber door and mixed the paint to be smeared into the wood, preventing the boy from crossing the threshold. When it worked she went back to Adaryn, seeking to learn more of the woman's magic, to add to the cache her own mother had left within her.

Adaryn had been clear that she did not take students.

Glynna had been so furious she'd almost outed the woman as a witch, the way she had done with the whore who had been wet nurse to Robin as a babe. Fortunately she had thought the better of it. Adaryn had her uses, after all.

Then her mother died, having survived her father by several years, and Glynna discovered her grimoire. Buried in a trunk, it was hidden inside an old woolen cloak that was musty and molded. She did not know if her mother had ever used it, or if it was an antique passed down through the family. Glynna, though, had studied it thoroughly. Much of it was written in other languages, but there was enough that she could read and comprehend to prove to her that what she held was a true relic, a thing of power.

With her husband absent Glynna was able to do something she had long wanted to do. She had come straight home and carved the new symbols into the doorposts. She had mixed herbs in a bowl and sliced deep into the hollow below her wrist, bleeding into the mixture, using it to paint the doorposts on top and both sides. As she did so she was reminded of the Bible story of the Israelites getting ready to leave Egypt, and painting their door frames with lamb's blood to keep out the Angel of Death. She wondered if her blood would only work on humans, or if it would even stop St. Azrael should he come to call. It was a comforting thought as she watched the red blood soak into the faded wood until it couldn't be seen.

When that was done she walked inside and closed the door behind her. An excitement burned in her belly, not unlike the one she felt from time to time when her husband would take her in some room of the house other than their bedchambers. The risk of being caught always made the excitement exquisite. She quivered all over now, in the same type of anticipation.

She stripped naked and allowed herself a moment to revel in how freeing it was to be skyclad, even inside. She had cleared the top of a large, low table and knelt before it. Slowly, reverently, she began to place objects on top of it. Two candles flanked each end. In the center she put a bowl, the same one in which she'd mixed her blood with the herbs. Beside it she placed the dagger with which she'd opened her own vein. It was still stained with her blood, and just looking at it caused a surge of dark joy.

On the other side of the bowl she placed a small, carved figure that she had also found in her mother's things. It was black as the night and had a twisted face that both attracted and repelled her. She found herself staring at it sometimes for hours at a time, and it was as though her mind went elsewhere when she did.

Next to the dagger she placed the sacred book with the spells she had been learning. Turning the hidebound cover, she opened the book and fingered through the parchment pages. Her fingertips tingled as they slid over the symbols and words. She left it open to an incantation that had long fascinated her—the shape of the words, the ink with which they were writ. It sank into the fiber of the paper, bonding with it. It was a reddish brown on the cream-colored parchment, and her eyes found the combination of the two pleasing.

Now she had a proper altar, one that was just for her. Now she could finally attempt some of the things of which she had only been able to dream.

The spell was simple, the words written to spell out the sounds. They were not English, not even similar. She had recited the syllables over and over in her mind, the noises of them rubbing along the inside of her soul.

She began rolling through the summoning without thinking about it, her lips moving just enough to mouth the words. As the spell rolled off her lips she peered at the carved figure and for a moment she swore that she could feel the lightest of touches, like hands caressing her naked body. She closed her eyes and let the feeling wash over her, the touch increasingly more intimate, like some dark entity wanting to take her and make her its own.

Let me in.

She felt herself spreading in welcome as she threw her head back.

"Yes," she whispered.

And with that, she was gone over the edge.

Adaryn arrived home just before sunset. As she stood for a moment, staring back toward Barnabas' home, she fought back her own tears.

A sudden hoot from above her head caused her to jump. She looked upward. A large owl was perched on her roof, staring down at her with cold eyes. A shiver danced down her spine and she hurried into the house.

* * *

When Marian returned, it was with a renewed determination to watch her uncle like a hawk. She was convinced that he was up to something more than just destroying the tapestries. Without proof, though, Cardinal Francis was right—there was no use sending a messenger to Richard.

Murther was waiting when she pulled the horse to a stop outside the stable.

"Did you have a nice ride, Highness?" He held the mare's head while Marian dismounted.

"Yes, thank you."

She followed him inside the stable and watched as he opened Merryweather's stall. Something dark flashed at the edge of her vision, causing her to take a hasty step backward. When she took a closer look, however, there was nothing there. She scanned the stable, but caught no other glimpse of it. Black on black, it had seemed.

Just a shadow, she thought, though she felt a shudder. Dismissing it, she hurried out of the stable without bothering to change back to her gown, her thoughts turning to Chastity and what might have happened in her absence.

She slipped into the castle through a side entrance used by the butcher and headed straight to her chamber, hoping the girl would be waiting for her there. When she walked in, however, she discovered Chastity on hands and knees, shoving something beneath Marian's bed. A distinct scent of smoke filled the room.

"What are you doing?" she asked.

Chastity jumped and gave out a yelp. She twisted, her face pale except for a bruise that spread on her left cheekbone under her eye. She stayed on her knees, and her hand fluttered over her generous chest.

"By the saints, you scared me," she said, struggling to regain her breath, but Marian scarcely heard her as she stepped quickly closer, standing over the girl, her eyes flashing with anger.

"Chastity, what has happened?" Her voice sounded harsh even to her own ears. "Who *dared* to strike you?"

"A knave of a guard did this." Chastity winced and touched her cheek. "I gave better than I got, though."

"Why did he lay hands on you?" Fury burned in her chest. She shook free of it for a moment. "Wait, are you injured? Do you need assistance?"

"Other than this love tap, I'm fine. Him, on the other hand..." Chastity shrugged.

"Tell me everything."

Chastity took a moment, and Marian could see that she was struggling to maintain her composure. Finally she took a deep breath, and spoke.

"All the tapestries from the castle." She stood. "He was burning them... in a pit behind the castle proper."

"No." Marian reeled at the thought. "Surely not."

"By my virtue, it's true," Chastity declared vehemently. "I tried to stop him, and he struck me to the ground. When he turned his back I crowned him with a stone." She sniffed. "Some men just can't deal with a strong woman."

"Did you kill him?"

"No, but he'll wish I had. His skull was already goose-egged by the time he started to get up," Chastity said. "I managed to save three tapestries. They're a bit singed at the edges, but they're intact. One of them is the suffering of Samson. The others were lost."

Marian gasped, for the story of Samson was her favorite. Many an afternoon Chastity had found her staring at that tableau when she was supposed to be elsewhere. The tragedy of the man spoke to her—given all the strength of God, felled to his knees, and finding redemption in the loss of his own life. There was honor, hard-won and learned too late. She often contemplated why such a masculine story would resonate so surely inside her.

Marian strode forward and embraced her friend.

"Thank you."

"Och, princess, lay off." Chastity wiped a tear from her swollen eye, and winced with the pain.

"It's been a long day of turmoil," Marian said, breaking the embrace. "Dark things are afoot, and the only comfort is knowing that you saved something precious to me."

"I don't know which other two I saved, but they're under your bed. You can inspect them later."

"Hopefully we will restore them to their rightful places soon." She lowered her voice. "We must find proof of John's villainy, before I can send word to the king."

"How?" Chastity asked.

"We will have to be watchful, and pray that he makes a mistake. It might take a while so we must be careful, or I fear burned tapestries and bruised cheeks will be the least of our worries."

CHAPTER FIFTEEN

The day after a feast, Will usually felt the worse for wear.

Sir Ferguson had thrown a grand fete for those who had chosen to remain behind when the king set sail. Ferguson with the large house. Ferguson with the winery. Ferguson, who had three lovely daughters of willing demeanor.

Yet the morning found Will dead sober, and it was an unwelcome state of affairs. He was at his wittiest when the mead flowed, which might explain why he had failed to charm any of the ladies the night before.

The truth was, Will had not felt much like celebrating. Not without Robin at his side.

The absence of King Richard and the men he took with him upset the status quo. The effects of it rippled through the town as people were forced to do things for which they had never planned—as in the case of Robin and Longstride Manor. It was bad. Bad for everyone, but especially for Will, who had grown accustomed to life the way it was.

He was in a sour mood as he neared the castle. He had no wish to see Prince John, but he did have need of collecting one of his father's horses—one that had been left behind on the night of the king's announcement.

He was still a good five minutes away when he observed

smoke smudging the sky. Something burned, and for a moment he wondered if it might be the castle itself. He touched his heels to his horse's flanks and the animal sprang forward.

The fast stride ate up the ground quickly and just a few minutes later he dismounted inside the courtyard, where the air was nearly gray. A man, stooped and shaky, stood up from a bench and came forward to take the reins of his steed.

"I've come to collect my father's horse," Will said as he dismounted. "The dappled gray—she bears our brand."

The man nodded. "I know the one. I will prepare her."

"What is on fire?" Will gestured, indicating the hazy air.

The man dropped his eyes to the ground, muttered something unintelligible, and moved off with Will's horse in tow.

Will entered the castle, seeking someone who would be able to explain to him the cause of the fire. He passed through empty corridors, moving in the direction of the great hall. Bare stone hemmed him in. Large squares of the wall were discolored, lighter, and after a moment he realized that the light areas had once held tapestries and wall hangings, things that King Richard had collected and loved.

They were all gone, leaving the surfaces cold and stark. Walking past the staircase that swept from the upper level, he found a person moving quickly into the hall ahead. He recognized the lean figure and dark hair.

"Lady Marian," he called, quickening his pace.

She hitched her step and turned, watching as he drew near.

He swept the hat from his head and bowed low.

"Why are you here?" she asked.

He straightened, startled by her brusqueness. "I'm retrieving one of my father's horses."

"Inside the castle proper?"

"Of course not. A man is fetching her from the stables."

"Good day then, Will Scarlet." She lifted her skirts from the floor and began to turn away.

"Wait," he said. "Please."

"Yes?"

"Why does the castle smell of burnt hair? And where are all the decorations?"

"Prince John burned them." Her voice was flat.

"What?" The answer startled him.

Behind her the doors to the great hall stood open. He looked past her into the room, and saw that, where there should be the grandest and oldest of tapestries, there stood nothing but blank walls.

"Why?" he said.

"You would have to ask my uncle," Marian said, "but I suggest that you don't. Just collect your horse, and leave."

Forgetting decorum he stepped close enough that he could lower his voice to a whisper.

"What is at work here?"

Marian looked away. "God only knows."

"I am serious. This is an ill portent."

Anger flashed across Marian's face. "Watch your tongue, and how you use it."

He stepped back. "My apologies. I did not mean to offend."

"I've known you my whole life," she snapped back. "You never say anything without intention."

"Truly, I misspoke."

He felt her gaze, looking through him as much as at him. Judgment fell on him as she weighed out every interaction they had ever had since being wee children. He knew her well enough to maintain silence and let her follow her own mind.

"Forgiven," she said, her voice softer. "You still should go."

"Milady, bear with me just a bit longer."

She paused, then nodded.

"What does the prince intend by his actions?"

She looked him straight in the eye. "I am not in the prince's confidence."

"Who is?"

She looked at him.

Without speaking, she had just said quite a lot.

"I will ferret out the truth of this," he said.

"If you do, then find me."

He nodded and stepped away, letting her continue down the hall. She didn't look back. Will moved to the doors of the great hall and stood between them, looking at the empty room now completely dominated by the mighty throne of England. After many minutes, a herald appeared, clearly startled to find Will standing there.

"My lord." The man skittered up to him. "No one warned me of your coming."

"I wish to speak with the prince," Will answered, leaving the statement to hang there. The man blinked at him, eyelids fluttering like butterfly wings.

"Why?" he squeaked, then caught himself. "I mean, why... don't you wait here for a moment, while I see if my master is taking visitors?"

Will nodded, turned, and walked into the hall to wait. There he studied his surroundings. The walls with their light patches bothered him. Something was desperately wrong here. Even Marian's manner gave him pause. He knew her, not closely, but for a long time. She was the embodiment of kindness and consideration, even though a fire burned in her belly. That made her perfect for Robin, and he wished they could see that.

Long minutes passed before the herald returned.

"The prince will see you," he said, far more poised this time. "Please follow me."

Moments later, the man stopped on the threshold of the king's study. Will forced a smile across his face and relaxed his posture so that he would appear as cavalier as his reputation would make him out to be.

"William of the House Scarlet," the herald announced. Will entered the king's study, a place he'd never been before. It was much more cluttered than he would have guessed. Shelves were crowded with objects and items, and it held a personal air. It was a room that had been lived in.

Prince John sat behind the king's desk, the only true dark spot in the room. Will studied him closely. The prince lifted his face with an air of insolence that immediately grated across his nerves. The man's mouth curled at the corners above the weakness of his chin. When seen from afar, the day the king had set sail, the prince seemed like most royalty, handsome enough to woo the people. Up close he was a weak imitation of Richard, but passable enough.

Will forced himself to smile even more broadly, trying to compensate with pleasantness for the extreme unpleasantness he felt.

The herald scurried from the room.

"Your reputation precedes you." The prince swept black eyes up and down Will's lanky frame.

"As does yours, Majesty." Will dropped into a sweeping bow, hat in hand.

"Majesty is a word saved for the king," John corrected. "Highness is the correct address for a prince."

"I only say what I see before me, and surely I behold a king." The flattery slipped easily off his tongue from years of practice.

John smiled faintly. "What is it you want from me, William of the House Scarlet?"

"Nothing more than to pledge my loyalty to you and your court," he replied. "I gave you a few days to settle in and take care of pressing matters of state before presenting myself to you."

"Very thoughtful of you." The prince laced his fingers together. "Perhaps you were just waiting to see which direction the wind might blow."

Will shook his head. "Not at all. If you know my reputation, then you know I am a most courteous courtier."

"I understand you have a great deal of influence with the young ladies... and some of the young men."

Will shrugged. "There is a small degree of favor that others harbor toward me." It was an understatement. Will knew he held a great deal of sway over many in the court. His manner and his dress gave him a certain charisma to which others responded favorably. Clearly the prince was already aware of this.

John looked at him with new interest.

"I could use you, I think, as a sort of aide and counselor," the prince said. "It is always convenient to have in pocket someone who has the hospitality of the people."

"Indeed, the king cannot hear every conversation that takes place in his court," Will smirked. "But with the proper people in place, he can surely know what is said."

"So we understand the place you will occupy in *my* court?" John asked.

"I believe so, Your Majesty."

"Then go, and gather ye rosebuds while ye may, Scarlet."

Will bowed again, straightened, and replaced his hat upon his head.

Just before he left the room, he turned.

"Well done in your decision to redecorate. Things were getting rather… stale around here. The air is already clearer without all of those dusty cloths hanging everywhere."

Prince John tilted his head in acknowledgment, then held up a hand.

Will stepped back into the room. "Is there anything I can do for you, my liege?"

The prince smiled. "I am so very glad you asked."

IN THE SHADOW
OF THE GALLOWS

CHAPTER SIXTEEN

King Richard's spy had discovered far more than he had expected. He was back on real English soil after having been in Scotland for a fortnight. There he'd found evidence that the king's cousin, Henry, was indeed preparing to move against the crown.

Nearly a month had passed since the king's departure, and the man chafed at the delay. He tried to school himself in patience. Soon he'd send a report, but there was more information he needed to collect first—this regarding Prince John's activities.

He called for a horse.

The green forest beckoned.

Leaf-laden arms waved Robin closer. The wind through the upper branches and the fragrance of loam enticed him. The shadows beneath the oak and the hawthorn and the ash called to him.

Sherwood ringed the easternmost edge of Longstride land, great and mighty hardwoods only ten long strides from the back door where he stood.

So close.

The sun was in its downward arc, slinking toward the massive, sprawling treetops, hanging perfectly above the yard between house and wilderness, painting the grass boundary betwixt them a fervent, buttery green. The green of summer. The green of planting.

His back twisted at the thought, the sensation running through him like a bowstring with a mis-notched arrow.

So many damned fields.

He looked at the forest and resented the flat expanses that had been cleared long before he was born, by forebears whose only use for the mighty Sherwood had been as a source of lumber and firewood. He had toiled endlessly, yet it seemed as if he had just begun the task of furrowing and planting, and he hated the sun on his neck and the stink of the ox and the ankle-twisting softness of plowed earth.

He remembered the coolness of midday beneath the trees, how it kissed the sweat of exertion off his brow as he rested wherever he stopped. Whether on the ridge or in the hollow, he would find some peaceful place to lean and close his eyes and simply become a part of the forest itself.

He closed his eyes now, sorting through a thousand memories.

Behind him, from the front of the manor, came the dull, distant sound of a door opening and closing.

"Robin!" The sound echoed through the halls, pulsating around corners to lick up to the boots on his feet like a stray cat. He turned and faced the inside of the room. Moving his eyes away from the forest made his chest feel tight. Leaning on the doorjamb of the pantry, he waited for whoever was calling his name. He'd done enough walking today, over turned dirt and exposed rocks.

Let this person come to him.

He realized that he didn't have a weapon, not even the tiny skinning knife. In the field, everything had been shed in the heat and the sun. Yet he was almost too tired to care. His back hurt.

On the shelf to his left, a half pace away, he saw the handle of a thick knife sticking out between two jars of preserves. It would be dull, the edge round and the point blunt—a chopping knife, heavy of spine and handle. But it would be sturdy.

He could reach it if needed.

Robin stood straighter as he waited, keen ears picking up footsteps. A shadow, driven forward by the window light from the end of the hall, loomed outside the doorway. He wanted suddenly to reach over and pick up the knife, to have it in his hand as the footsteps drew nearer.

But he didn't. Instead he took a deep breath and shook out his hands.

The dark shape looked misshapen, as if some fey creature had crossed the threshold and stalked its way toward him, lurching and bobbing through his childhood home.

"There you are!"

Will Scarlet stepped into the door frame. Tension left Robin's shoulders, running down his back and falling away.

"Indeed, here I am," he replied. "Where *else* would I be?"

"Where is everyone?"

"Depends on who you are asking about."

Will looked around. "You're the only one I found here. Where's Aunt Glynna and the girls?"

"At the market."

Will's brow creased. "Why didn't they send a servant?"

"The house servants are helping with the planting."

"Why would you have…?"

"Damnation, Will!" Robin lashed out. "If you're going to call into question every decision I have made, then get the hell out of my house!"

Will raised his hands and pivoted on his heels, sliding away from his friend's fury.

"Easy, easy," he said. "There was no judgment—just confusion on my part."

Robin stared at his fingers. Slowly he turned his back, facing out the door toward the darkening forest outside.

After a long moment he said, "I'm sorry."

Will didn't speak, just let Robin get to the end of it.

"It's been… hard trying to take my father's place here."

"Don't get angry when I ask this," Will responded, "but why are you trying?"

Robin didn't turn, just kept looking at the woods. "There are people who live on this land. They need someone to run it, to lead. My father left us all in a hard way."

"He's trying to do God's work."

"I don't care. That doesn't change things here."

Will crossed himself. Robin hadn't blasphemed, but just to be sure.

"Still, why try to be him? I can assure you, that will never happen."

Robin's head dropped. "He thought the same thing."

Will moved forward. His hand went out to touch Robin's shoulder and stopped an inch short. It hovered in the air, wavering for long moments before he finally let it come to rest. His hand felt hard-packed muscle under the grimy muslin shirt. When Robin didn't jerk away, he spoke quietly.

"Your father's greatest flaw is that he's never understood you—never realized that you are your own man."

Robin turned at that.

"That's what Old Soldier tells me."

"He's much older than me, and certainly not as pretty," Will said, allowing a hint of a smile, "but I'd listen to him nonetheless."

Robin smiled back. "That's good counsel. If I don't start doing just that, he may decide to kick my arse across the fields."

"He *is* a tough old knot." Will leaned close, conspiratorially. "Working with him, have you yet seen him without his mail?"

"He wears that shirt even in the heat of the day."

Will shook his head. "Must be miserable."

"He never shows it."

Robin moved from the door, glancing back over his shoulder at the woods, now just shadows and shapes even though the twilight of the evening was still several turns of the hourglass away. He moved into the pantry, going to a dark cubby.

"You're one to talk," he said, "with your many layers of velveteen and leather."

Will sniffed. "At least I am wise enough to not work a field."

Robin tensed.

Will immediately regretted the words, but didn't take them back.

Robin reached deep in the cubby, drawing out a wide jar with a narrow spout. Red wax dribbled off the cork, sealing the contents inside. He held it up, and Will nodded.

Robin twisted the cork, wax crumbling to the floor.

"Old Soldier chooses to be here, and does so freely. He seems to like this life, dirt and sweat and hot sun and all." He shrugged and took a swig of his father's secret whiskey. "It's lost on me." He handed the jar over.

Will held the jar low to his chest. It was warm from Robin's hand. The vapors rising from the uncorked container took his breath away. Uncle Philemon had a taste for strong spirits, and this one smelled as if it would strip the lining off his gullet. Closing his eyes, he took a swig. His throat seized like a fist and he coughed harshly, keeping the alcohol down, but just barely.

His fist thumped his chest, trying to clear the fireball inside it so he could draw in air.

"Whooo, that's brutal."

Robin shrugged and took another sip. "There was another jar."

"What happened to it?"

"It helps me sleep, after day upon day of monotony." Robin looked away. "And my back hurts enough to keep sleep away without it."

Will nodded. Many deep winter nights, when travel was impossible and he had to remain at home, away from the court intrigue he loved so much, he turned to the bottle to help him fall into the arms of slumber.

Robin took a deep breath, eyes wide and staring away in the

distance. They snapped to focus as he turned toward Will.

"So, tell me why you have come, cousin."

"The new king summons you to his audience."

"He's not the king." The words were out in an instant. "And since when do you do the bidding of the throne?"

"There is something strange going on at the castle," Will said.

"I see," Robin replied. "And you think you are going to untangle whatever the mystery may be?" He didn't wait for a response. "You should leave that nest of snakes alone, before you get bitten."

Will's eyes narrowed. "You know who would say that?"

"Who?"

"Your father."

Robin thought about it for a long moment. "You're right," he replied. "So tell me, what is happening at Lionheart Castle that has you so concerned?"

"Not just I, but Marian as well."

Robin straightened.

That got his interest.

"Let's find a seat, and then tell me all about it."

Smoke still hung on the air, seeping from the charred remains of dozens of ancient tapestries. One lone servant leaned on a wooden pole, its end blackened from stirring the thick folds of cloth so the flames could reach every inch.

The fire had burned and then smoldered for days. Soot smudged his face and arms, making him disturbingly anonymous in the gloom. He looked up and watched her cross the flagstone path leading to the groundskeeper's lodge, his eyes too white in a face smeared nearly featureless.

Her hand moved in a ward to detach his stare. The servant blinked twice, big owl movements of his lids, before he turned and his gaze fell back to the smoldering coals of burnt cloth.

Blessed be, dark Hecate.

Her steps carried her up the steep slope to the long, low, thatch-roof building. The path was treacherous and the flagstones slick to hamper any intruder coming toward the mighty rear wall. As she drew near, she raised the shawl over her silver-threaded hair. The charms tied into it tinkled against one another.

As she stepped onto the threshold, the heavy plank door swung in, dim lamplight spilling onto her. Inside she could see the shapes of people, all in shadow forms and silhouettes.

Something in the back of her mind, some instinct, some niggling little hindbrain memory, cried out for her to run, to turn and flee as fast as she could. It only lasted a moment before being smothered by curiosity, the wonderment that caused her to chase the unknown, the mysterious, to delve into the very secrets of the universe. The thing inside that drove her to be in this place at this time.

Like the feral cat that was her familiar, she was a creature who could not deny her nature. Curiosity called, and she came.

The castle guards did not know where she lived, in the narrow hollow in the narrow house on the far edge of Sherwood, and yet one had arrived on her doorstep two days earlier. A young man, not tall but well-built, one who practiced his drills far more than required. Earnestness shone from his face. He knew her name and gave her the simple instructions.

Message delivered, he simply turned and left.

Now her foot stepped over the threshold and she moved into the gloom of the long building. Inside she found a plank floor, its surface scratched deep. In her mind's eye she could picture the heavy iron tools being dragged across the floor after a hard day of use. These tools hung on the walls, lining the entire left side of the building. Wicked spades with wide blades both sharpened and dulled by the rocky soil around the castle hung side by side with axes and hatchets, their robust heads oiled and filed, and wicked-toothed saws whose cutting edges brought to her mind the mouths of ravening animals.

Lamplight traced along cutting surfaces and keen, spiky points.

The room was full of people. The floor was occupied by a few chairs and benches, all of them empty, for everyone stood. At the far end, the wall held a fireplace that watched her with a dead sooty eye.

This was a plain, utilitarian structure, designed entirely to keep tools locked away and allow a groundskeeper and his charges to rest at the end of a long day, or to shelter them from the elements. As she walked further into the room her eye picked up details here and there—an empty wooden cask turned into a table, its surface holding a pair of carved bones used for gambling. Pegs held oiled cloth raincloaks and heavier winter garments made of wool, their dirty blue color a signal to anyone that their wearers were in charge of the upkeep of the castle grounds. Around the fireplace squatted pots and pans, blackened from time in the flames.

Something in the firebox made her look twice. A nest of many tendrils lay there, stark against the soot and the ash. Bending close, she could see what it was.

A tangle of perhaps a dozen short, knotted ropes.

Prayer ropes.

The groundskeepers would be simple citizens, villagers who worked for the crown in a servitude capacity. They would have been raised in the shadow of the monastery, under the hand of a Christian king. They would be devout, working hard for lord and liege. They would carry these ropes from the moment they woke until they lay down again at night, using them to count out the prayers they spoke at each break of the day.

They would *never* desecrate something they used every day in the name of Richard and his God. The blasphemy struck her like a blow to the face. She did not ascribe to the Christ of the monks, but she was not opposed. Her belief was "do as you will, if it harm none." Belief in Christ did nothing to conflict with that.

Pulling her gaze away from the scorched prayer ropes, she stepped to the wall, put her back to the stone, and watched the occupants of the room with a narrow eye. They were all watching her as well. Most of them stood apart from one another, solitary. A few of them clumped together in twos and threes, whispering with mouth to ear.

Two of them she recognized. A man stood near the center of the room, possessed of bladed shoulders and an enviable height. His face was almost handsome from a certain angle and in a certain light. His hands were overknuckled and crossed his chest to press like knobby, pale spiders against his shoulders. A simple monk's robe of undyed wool suckered to his spare frame, outlining every nook and cranny of him. His eyes glittered with a feverish intensity as he stared at her.

Though they had never met, she knew him by description and by reputation. The Mad Monk. Disgraced and excommunicated for dabbling in the dark arts, he lived in the crags of the northland, above Hadrian's Wall, among the Picts and the fey and the Bean Sidhe. Legend was that he'd attempted to pull an archangel from the heavens and make it a house servant. According to many, he had never stopped trying to pull down his Seraph through incantations and self-mutilation.

She looked away before his eyes could lock with hers, certain she didn't want to gaze upon a soul that dark.

Against the opposite wall leaned a woman, broad of shoulder and thick of wrist like a man, but her features were smooth as unchurned milk, her skin twice as creamy. Knots of hair fell around her shoulders like a cape, brushing past dimpled elbows. Blue fain tattoos swirled on her left cheek, chasing one another in spindly patterns running from her temple to under the corner of her deep-set eye.

Pushing off the timbers with her shoulders—a move that thrust out her bosom to distracting effect—the woman began walking toward her, swiveling hips like a dowsing crystal. She was like some form of feline creature.

Stalking a mouse.

Every eye touched them as the woman stepped close.

"Adaryn."

Her voice was fluid, almost slippery as it wove around the syllables of her name.

Adaryn forced her eyes to stay on the woman's face, avoiding the appearance of what she felt in her knees.

"Agrona."

"Have you finally left your jugs and herbs and smelly roots, and joined the true face of power?"

"I still follow the Path."

Agrona's eyes narrowed. "You always did kiss arse to father."

Adaryn didn't speak. Her sister was right. She clung to their father's way of magic, through communion with nature and harmony with all of creation. He had been her shelter from their mother, a malevolent whirlwind of cruelty who sought power by communing with the dead. Agrona had worshiped at Mum's feet. After the woman died Agrona kept her bones in a box that formed her personal altar.

Her sister lived as a necromancer, while she had chosen to become a hedgewitch.

"If not to change your ways," Agrona said, "then why are you here?"

"I was summoned by a castle guard, just like you."

Agrona's laugh was a vicious knife, stabbing shallow and quick. "Oh, dear sister, no servant called me."

"Then why…?"

"Mother sent me."

CHAPTER SEVENTEEN

The men stood around the throne room in groups of three and five, trying to talk over one another, jockeying for position, establishing dominance in their small circles of nobility. He moved among them, a hawk among hens, stepping into each group long enough to make his presence known, to mark himself as the strongest personality in the room, and then on to the next.

Sometimes the move was simple—step up, and the men parted to make space, smiles latched onto their faces. These groups were the people he'd counted as allies for years, nobles who sided with him when decisions were required.

Bootlickers.

Other groups had a very different reaction to him. They would stiffen as he approached, tensing hands on their belts, always near the dagger or dirk that had become fashionable among the landed gentry. He was the only one who still wore a longsword strapped to his hip. These groups would still part for him, and allow him to stand in their midst as he parlayed and positioned himself. These were Longstride allies left leaderless by a fool's insistence on sailing with the king.

He wasn't an unbeliever. To the contrary, his religion was devout and strictly disciplined, but God was in England. If He chose to allow barbarians and infidels to overrun the Jews, then so be it.

Old Man Minter nodded to him, one eye closed in a permanent squint by an old knick with a dagger caught in a border skirmish long ago.

"Locksley."

The men around him grunted unenthusiastic greetings. He remained silent for a long moment. When he did speak he leaned in, tilted his head, and kept his voice low, sounding conspiratorial.

"Gentlemen," he said. "Good day to you."

Feet shuffled. Eyes flickered to Minter.

So he's the one to bring to heel, in Longstride's absence.

Locksley said nothing more, watching the older lord. His years had barely stooped him, just the slightest curve of shoulder. He remembered a younger version of Minter, a rawboned rogue in his father's hunting parties. He'd known the man near his whole life and he knew to wait, let his patience be Minter's downfall.

Minter rubbed his upper lip with a blunt finger.

"'Tis certainly no feast we've been called to this time," he said, and the group murmured their agreement, the babble of noise rolling around the circle. "Any idea what the proxy wants with us?"

One by one the faces turned toward him. He waited until they all watched him before casually lifting a shoulder and gesturing lazily with his left hand.

"He is the new king, even temporarily," Locksley responded. "This is where he establishes how things will run under his hand."

"I, for one, am not interested in being summoned like a dog," Lord Staunton said.

"None of us are," Minter affirmed.

"He needs to be told," a man to Minter's right said, a thin voice coming from a thin neck. "He needs to understand that our support is necessary, if he is to rule."

The murmurs grew louder, more animated. Other men began to move closer, wedging into the group. Men he had in his pocket.

Excellent.

He responded to Minter's right-hand man, but lifted his voice for the entire group to hear.

"We enforce the throne's decrees, and yet you worry that this king remains unaware of it," he said. "Of the fact that we are free men and landowners, who supply the resources he needs through our own nobility."

The nods and murmurs were vigorous.

He smiled. "Then we shall remind him."

One of his men struck up a cheer, and the others grabbed onto it like a lifeline. Minter held fast to the end, but even he joined in, and with that they were his.

Will fell over his own arms as he leaned forward. Brow furrowed, he tried to make his tongue work properly. "You thee, wha's happeninanin is strange."

Robin sighed. His lower back ached; despite his youth and despite the loosening effect of the drink, it still throbbed a little. He leaned forward in his chair and lifted the jar, draining the last dregs. The movement made his head feel as if he were underwater, reality dragging just slightly with the smallest movements.

"You can obserf... ob... look for yourselb when you come wilth me." Will's words stumbled into each other, sticky in his mouth.

"I'm not going," Robin said stubbornly. Will stared at him with wide eyes and a slight shake of his head that wouldn't stop.

"You *muth*."

"No."

"Buth..."

"Tell Prince John what you want," Robin said. "Or not. I'm staying here."

"Do you not take this seriouth... seri-ah..."

"It has nothing to do with me or this land." He shrugged, and rose to his feet. Standing made the room tilt, but not much. Will pushed himself out of the chair with a lurch. He stopped himself, hands out in the air as if it were a wall to brace on. Nevertheless, he swayed precariously.

Robin grabbed his cousin's arm. "You will be able to ride?"

Will looked at him with a smirk on his face. "I'll be fine." He took a step that made him arc lazily in a quarter-circle. "Walk wif me to the thables."

Robin laughed, and it felt good to do so after the days he'd had since his father and brother left.

"I am pleased to see you all here."

The voice came from everywhere. It wasn't raised, nor shouted, yet every person paid attention. Sounding as if the speaker stood by her side, it brought Adaryn a chill so strong her skin puckered beneath her clothes.

Her sister shivered and stepped back. Both of them—indeed, everyone in the room—glanced around to locate the source of the words.

The shadows at the far end of the hut deepened, coalescing and taking on the texture of sackcloth. They moved from sooty gray to rich midnight. In the center of the veil something pale moved forward, swimming through darkness like a serpent through stormy seas. The shape clarified as it drew near, closer to the lamp's light. A man's face, pale and angular, topped with a shock of white hair that hung straight to the waist. Then two shapes to the side, long fingered hands held in intricate knots of knuckles. He stepped from the pool of darkness, boot heels sounding for the first time as they struck the plank floor, and the knuckle knots relaxed, falling free into simple, normal looking hands.

The darkness behind him broke, tumbling away. As the shadows snapped back to normal, something swept through the room, not a breeze or a whisper, but just a brief brush of *something* that touched them all.

The reaction followed it in a wave. Most of the practitioners in the room shuddered, a few growled like animals, two convulsed. Her sister gasped as if she were with a lover, and the Mad Monk wept, lifting ball-and-joint hands in the air.

Adaryn swayed on her feet, legs gone to water beneath her.

The man at the end of the room walked toward them with an easy gait. He was clad in light-drinking armor. It didn't reflect highlights or make a sound as he walked, save for the *clomp* of boot on wood. The only color that relieved the sheer black lay over his chest and at the pommel tip of the bastard sword on his hip. It was almost a pentagram, the symbol of harmony among the five elements of the universe, yet inverted—its point hanging down over the place where his heart would lie.

Ancient symbols squiggled on the edges of it and whorls cut into it, the whole creating a sigil of terrible meaning. She didn't know it, but recognized it as part of an ancient path of workings that her father had sternly warned her away from. From a distance the symbol had looked to be painted in bright, harsh red but as he drew closer she could see it was actually carved into the armor and the color of it pulsed from within like a slow, ponderous heartbeat.

Midway across the room a dark shape detached itself from the man's shoulders, falling to the floor with feline grace and landing on four paws. The creature looked up, glinting eyes red in the lamplight. Lupine face on feline predator curves, its pitch-black fur stuck out in bristles and juts over a body big enough to be a threat even to a large man. Adaryn did not recognize it. It hissed at them then ran straight for the wall, where crescent claws dug in as it climbed in a streak of ebony and disappeared into the rafters of the thatched hut.

She followed it with her eyes, but lost it in the shadows. The thought of that thing over her head, that it could drop at any moment… another shiver chased her body, and her hand moved instinctively into the protective ward.

The man stopped, glittering eyes turned toward her.

Her sister took a broad step away from her.

"What have we here?" the armored man said.

She wanted to shrink, to pull herself inside her shawl, to climb into the fetish bag around her neck and huddle beside the river stone, badger teeth, herbs, and bird-bone powder that was housed inside.

"I'm Adaryn of Moonmist Hollow."

Suddenly he was there in front of her, so close the air felt tight, as if a blanket had been thrown over her head. Sweat beaded her throat and chest, and her lungs closed like fists. He loomed over her and all she could see by craning her neck was the cleft chin and the thin villainous lips… and the pearl white teeth that smiled down at her.

"I did not ask *who* we have here, little bird." The teeth clicked together, biting off the ends of the words like tails on puppies. "I ask *what* we have here."

Her mouth, her dumb mouth, moved but made no sound.

"To illustrate—" He leaned back, allowing these words to go to the room "—I am the Sheriff of this land. I am the arm of the law and the law is given by the word of Prince John, holder of throne and crown. I am the one who called you forth. You have come by mine own will, whether you admit it or not." He glanced at Agrona. Then his face swooped back down near Adaryn's, mouth so close it could brush her lips in a lover's kiss.

"But *you* I did not call." Air pulled sharply into the blade of his nose, the inhale brushing air across her cheek. "You don't smell like the power I seek." He sniffed again. "You were not summoned."

That's not true, she thought frantically. *The castle guard…* Her mind had become a babbling brook, a hundred thoughts tumbling over one another in an avalanche of confusion.

"*Answer the question!*" He screamed pain into her ear. "*What are you?*"

"I am a witch!" she cried. "A medicine woman and a midwife."

He turned away from her and began to walk around the room. "You are a medicine woman. Yet I am not sick." His hand flicked out, brushing through the dirty red hair of a man wearing a plaid kilt, wrapped in bandages from head to toe, all skin covered save his eyes and mouth. His eyelids looked as if they had stacks of ash on them, the skin dead and white and flaky, tumbling onto his lashes each time he blinked. His mouth lay wide across his teeth.

When you have no lips you're always smiling, she thought involuntarily. The Sheriff slid his arm over bandaged shoulders, ignoring the exposure to leprosy. The man looked up at him with moonish eyes that spun in deep sockets.

"I am much more needful of a plague-bringer like this one," the Sheriff said. Then he pushed the leper away, leaving his arm outstretched. It swung the room until it pointed at the Mad Monk. The tarnished priest flung himself at the Sheriff's feet, knees banging into the floor, robe catching and pulling on splinters. The graying wool blossomed dark as blood from torn and punctured skin seeped into the coarse fibers. His fingers danced along his open jaw and his eyes rolled back in ecstasy while pouring tears down hollow cheeks.

The Mad Monk began speaking, low and jumbled, in a language she didn't recognize. The Sheriff reached down with a pale finger and lifted the monk's chin up, closing off the sounds of the tongues. Then his eyes cut to her again.

"I am born of time and judgment, come forth to walk this land and fulfill my purpose here. I have no need of a midwife." He looked down. "This one has carved himself into a perfect Enochian vessel. *That* I can use."

Turning away from the monk, he took Agrona by the hair, fist gnarled in the tresses rooted at the back of her neck. He yanked, drawing her to her toes. Her eyes fluttered, her chest heaving as it blushed red across her cleavage.

"I have need of the dead and those who intercourse with them. Your sister is valuable to me. A necromancer I can use." He turned his face toward Agrona, eyes still on her. His mouth parted and a tongue, long and wide and split down the middle, licked across the throbbing artery in her throat. Her sister swooned, leaning against the armored chest of the Sheriff. "A hedgewitch I cannot."

He let go. Agrona stumbled across the short distance and fell against her. She grabbed her sister, keeping her from falling to the floor.

"I did not summon you. I had you *fetched*, for there is one role you can fulfill for me." The Sheriff snapped his fingers with the sound of old bones breaking. Instantly Adaryn gasped in pain as blood began pouring from her eyes. Her hands clutched like iron bands as the voice filled her ears.

"I do need a sacrifice."

The sound of the doors caused all heads to turn so fast it looked as if invisible assassins had snuck behind each man and snapped their necks.

Prince John strode in, flanked by guards holding crossbows ratcheted and locked, all of them step-marching through the middle of the room as if they were on parade. The *bang* of boot heel on the parquet floor sounded like a regiment, instead of the proxy king's personal security detail. The nobles parted and Locksley made certain he moved with Minter and his men, to ensure that he retained his hold on them.

The prince wore the crown on his brow, a simple circle of gold adorned with rushing lions. It had been gifted by the cardinal to Richard the Lionheart when he first took the throne. It sat wobbly on Prince John's skull, like a hat too big, and he held it in place as he stepped awkwardly up the stairs to the throne itself. There he turned, and sat. The guards fanned out to each side of the throne, like gull wings.

In his hand he held a heavy scepter made of gold. Prince John smiled with one side of his mouth.

"Come closer, gentlemen," he said. "We have much to discuss."

Before they could look to him or, God forbid, look to Minter, Locksley strode toward the throne. Behind him he could hear the others fall into line. Stopping sharply, he inclined his head in a short bow, more an acknowledgment of the position than of actual subservience.

"Milord, we are here…"

"Stop."

Locksley froze.

"Milord is not proper," Prince John continued. "Refer to me as 'Your Majesty,' or 'Your Highness.' 'Liege' is acceptable, but only barely."

Locksley straightened. This was the acting king, with all the power of the throne behind him, backed by armed guards, but the tone of the man caused him to bristle. He swallowed and started again.

"Your Majesty… we are eager to learn why you have called us from our lands and asked us to meet with you." He looked around. "We assumed there would be refreshments, perhaps a hospitality meal as befits a conference between a king and his nobility."

"Ah." Prince John raised a finger into the air. "There is your mistake. Your presumption, although I do not blame you for it. My brother ruled with a far too generous hand."

A murmur rose around the room, swelling up behind Locksley and pushing at his back. He lifted his hand, and they fell silent.

"It sounds as if you desire to change the relationship established by King Richard," he said.

"I do not care what my brother did on this throne."

Locksley felt the pressure of the men behind him. He needed to say something, but to ask what Prince John planned to do would smack of weakness.

The prince did not make him ask. Shifting on the throne, twisting to the side as if the seat was too hard for comfort, John leaned forward, pointing with the scepter.

"All of you will deliver to the crown one half of your harvest and one third of your retinue, in return for my service as your king. You will acquiesce to the search of your property by crown-appointed tax collectors, so your taxes may be assessed. This will apply to the people living under your purview, as well. What is theirs belongs to you, after all."

Silence fell on the room like a crushing hand.

The men exploded with anger.

"What is the *meaning* of this?" Minter leapt forward, his fist shaking in front of his squinted eye. He shoved past Locksley, shouldering him two steps to the side, mouth locked in a snarl. "We'll not stand for this outrage, you, you… *substitute*."

Shouts of "pretender" and "usurper" rang through the chamber, clanging off the bare stone walls. Fists were raised, some even holding the ceremonial daggers snatched from belts. Locksley watched the other nobles leaping as if their feet were afire. He did not move away from them, but neither did he join in their fervor.

On the throne, Prince John smiled.

He raised a limp hand, flicking the first two fingers toward Minter. In a blur the guard to the left of the throne raised his crossbow and fired. All noise cut short as the thick bolt slammed into Minter's chest, just under his throat, with the sound of a fist smashing a hollow drum.

Everyone froze.

All but Minter, who flipped backward as if struck by a giant, feet flying from under him with the impact. First his curved shoulders slammed against the floor, followed by the dull, melon THUNK *thunk* of his skull bouncing once, then twice. Heartblood splashed up in an arc that mimicked his trajectory, splattering across Locksley's jaw, cheek, and temple.

Minter bled out on the floor, the pool widening around him, a deep claret on the tile.

Lord Staunton leaped forward with a roar. "You have no right!"

A different guard stepped forward, unsheathed his sword, and ran Staunton through in one fluid motion. He resheathed his weapon and stepped back to his place before the lord's body even hit the floor.

The message was clear.

Prince John sat back on the throne.

"You were saying?"

Locksley stepped over Staunton's falling body and spoke without wiping the blood from his face.

"I will command the tax collectors for you… My Liege."

CHAPTER EIGHTEEN

Marian was furious. The king had instructed John to trust her, to rely on her knowledge of the realm and how it was run. It *burned* to be dismissed.

The prince was dining with the nobles, and she needed to find out what was occurring. She'd tasked Chastity with learning what she could, but a growing fearfulness in Marian urged her to have a care for the girl's safety. If John was willing to threaten Marian, in no uncertain terms, then he would not hesitate to kill a serving girl. Especially one who was her friend.

No, she had to find others who were loyal to King Richard, and would be willing to spy for her. To that end she made her way to the kitchens in search of the steward who attended to the prince's needs. When she got there, she was surprised to discover that there was no great flurry of activity, as there should have been in the case of a royal meal.

Indeed, the kitchen was almost empty.

She moved through the large square room, passing tables stacked with pots and pans. A round woman, near the shape of an apple on two sticks, scurried over, wiping red hands on an apron. Jansa was her name, Marian recalled, and she performed a rusty curtsey.

"Milady."

"Please summon the person who schedules the kitchen staff."

"You'd be looking at her."

"You've moved up, Jansa," Marian said. "I'm impressed."

"Beg pardon, milady, I didn't think you'd remember me," the woman said with a smile.

"You fed me sweets the first time I was thrown from a horse, back when I was a child," Marian said with a grin. "How could I ever forget?"

"I thought that arm would never heal," the woman answered warmly. "Praise God it did." She stood quiet after speaking, looking at Marian with her head cocked just slightly to the left.

"Why is there no activity?" Marian asked. "The prince is meeting with the lords of the kingdom."

"I'd thought to be providing refreshment, at the very least," Jansa shrugged. "Perhaps a full meal, but the steward said no, the king was not providing for his guests that way."

"*Acting* king," Marian reminded her gently. "He only rules until the Lionheart returns."

"May it be soon, and God grant him victory over all his enemies." The woman crossed herself, fingers moving quicker than conscious thought.

Marian nodded. "Yes, we should all pray for that."

"What can I help you with today, milady?" Jansa said. "I don't think you've come around looking for sweets. You haven't done that since you were a little girl."

"I'm looking for the steward."

"I'm not sure where he is at the moment, but he'll be back here in an hour to take some food and drink to the king... the prince." Jansa waved her hands. "Sorry. Down here it is much the same. You might find the steward in your uncle's study. I can send one of the girls to fetch him for you."

"No, that won't be necessary," Marian said. "I shall find him myself. You may return to your duties." She turned to go, but Jansa reached out quickly and touched her arm, then recoiled.

"I meant no disrespect, milady," she said fearfully. "I apologize for my offense."

"You gave none," Marian said.

Jansa stepped so close that Marian could feel the breath on her cheek.

"Milady, please pardon me for saying so, but I would not trust the steward with anything you didn't want the prince to know." She glanced around, as if concerned that she might be overheard. "He might have served King Richard for years, but he has no loyalty to him."

Marian paused, thinking carefully about how to react. This could be some trick by Prince John, to lure her into saying something against him. It grieved her, however, that she had to even consider the loyalty of the woman who stood before her.

"Are you sure the steward has become… untrustworthy?" she asked at last.

The woman nodded gravely.

"Then I thank you for your warning and discretion."

"I've known you since you were a babe," Jansa said, "and I've watched as you grew. You are a good woman, and we place our trust in you."

We. Jansa was not alone in her suspicions, or her loyalty to Marian. A chill snaked its way down her spine as she prayed the same loyalty didn't get the woman killed.

"There is nothing more precious to me than your trust," Marian answered. "If there is anything that you think I should know, please send word to me."

Jansa dropped her voice even lower. "Milady should know that two of my girls saved one of the tapestries. It's hidden away where no one will ever find it."

Tears stung Marian's eyes. "They will forever have my gratitude."

"Would milady like a nice sweet?" Jansa asked suddenly. "One won't hurt nothing." There was a sound, and Marian turned her head. The steward entered the kitchen.

"I don't suppose it would," Marian said, watching him cross the room. His gait was easy, long arms swinging casually by his side.

"Milady, what are you doing here?" the man asked, eyes narrowing under beetled eyebrows.

"Can I not roam the castle at will?" she responded. "It is my home."

"Why yes, milady, of course. I just wondered why you would wander to this particular part of your home."

She sniffed, seeking to appear dismissive.

"I came to see about the preparations, since we have so many lords under the roof. Hospitality is one of the obligations of a king, so I anticipated that something had been planned in their regard. I was dismayed to discover there was not."

"The ones who can be on their way will be on their way, in short time," the steward said.

Marian sighed. "Well, then I hope they are not offended by this breach in protocol."

He straightened, pulling at his tunic. "I can assure milady that I acted on the king's order."

Prince, she thought.

Jansa handed Marian a small cake wrapped in cloth.

"Milady."

"Thank you," Marian said. She turned and didn't give the steward another word as she swept out of the kitchens with her head held high. A short distance down the corridor, out of sight of the kitchen, she stopped and leaned back against the wall. The stone was cold against her back, her body heat leeching away through the linen of her gown.

The castle felt suddenly stifling to her, the bare walls of it too close, the ceilings too low. She longed for the freedom of the outdoors. She needed to clear her head and think. She wanted nothing more than to grab a horse and ride with the wind in her face until she had put all this far behind her. There was work to be done, though. She had a feeling that whatever the reason for John's meeting with the nobles, it would be of great interest to her—and hopefully to King Richard, as well.

She turned, making her way to a hidden entrance that led to

the throne room. King Richard had often made use of it, and she hoped John had not yet discovered it. When she reached the door in question she stood for a moment, and then opened it just a crack so that she could see inside.

When she did, her blood ran cold.

Two men were on the floor—dead, from the looks of it. Noblemen. Her heart started hammering in her chest.

What is happening in there?

Will was mostly sober by the time he and Robin reached the castle. As they dismounted, a handful of noblemen he had known since childhood exited the main building, huddled together.

"Looks like we missed all the excitement," Will said. "I told you we'd be late."

"And I told you I didn't care," Robin replied. "I only came to keep your soggy self from falling off your horse."

As they walked up to the group, servants appeared, carrying the bodies of two men. Will blinked in astonishment as he recognized the face of old Minter. It was him, but it wasn't. The skin had lost its color and his eyes were fixed in death. Blood covered his clothes. His shock deepened when he recognized the other as Staunton. Companions in life, they were companions still, even in death.

"What happened here?" Robin asked sharply before Will could find his tongue.

Lord Brighton stepped closer and lowered his voice. "The king had them killed because they objected to the new way of doing things."

"And pray tell, what new way is that?" Will asked, recovering from his initial shock.

"Taxes, and lots of them. One half of our harvest and one third of our retinue."

"He can't do that," Robin said. "Winter is too close."

"I think Minter would beg to differ," Brighton said grimly.

"It's madness. We need our people—they are our responsibility, as well. Even if he takes some at sword point, how are we supposed to feed the rest with only half our harvest?" Robin demanded.

Will spoke up. "If the nobles stood together…"

"They won't," Brighton interrupted. "We won't. Locksley has already started licking the prince's boots. He volunteered to lead the tax collectors."

"Like hell he will," Robin growled, starting forward. Will grabbed his arm, knowing full well that he was endangering himself by doing so.

"Easy…" Brighton stepped in front of Robin. "Or you'll end up like Minter. Then who will look after your people?" He paused as that sunk in. "Locksley would be only too happy to bring them into his fold. And even if you manage to kill him and escape, the prince has decreed that any who fight the tax will forfeit their family's lands and the homes of those they protect."

"Robin, there must be a better way than that," Will pleaded. "Think of your mother. Think of your sisters." For a moment, however, it seemed as if nothing he or Brighton had to say would dissuade his cousin.

Then, slowly, Robin took a step back.

"If there's a better way, find it," he hissed, looking from one man to the next. He paused the longest on Will. Then he turned and, in a moment, had mounted his horse. "I'll give you a fortnight," he growled, jerking the reins and riding away.

"Fool is going to get himself killed," Brighton muttered. "I just hope he doesn't take a bunch of us with him when he does."

"From your lips to God's ears," Will muttered. He shook his head and took a deep breath. "Good day to you, Lord Brighton."

"No. It's not."

Will walked inside the castle. It was the last thing he wanted to do, but someone had to keep a cool head in order to help thwart the prince's plans, whatever they were.

It was hard to imagine what Prince John had in mind, that he would demand so much from his nobles. If he were building his own army, he would have specified that only able-bodied men be sent to him, but he hadn't. Perhaps he was just testing the loyalty of the nobles.

Or perhaps he was trying to break them.

Fixing a smile upon his face, he walked past more noblemen who were moving to exit the castle. Each of them wore a dour expression, all except for Locksley—whose smile was likely as fake as his own.

"I hear you are to be congratulated," Will said. Locksley inclined his head, but didn't answer, leaving with the others.

Will entered the hall that the men were vacating. At the far end Prince John sat on his throne, deep in conversation with the Sheriff. Will approached, stepping carefully around a large pool of blood gone tacky on the floor. He stopped at a respectful distance, waiting to be acknowledged.

At last the Sheriff left without a glance, and the prince turned toward Will, who bowed low.

"You have something to say?"

"Your Majesty, I just wanted to congratulate you on bringing the nobles so quickly to heel. It was a masterful stroke," Will said, letting the flattery roll off his tongue.

"You think so?" John asked, studying him.

"Absolutely. I always thought that many of them were far too impudent. Richard let them get away with it, much to his disadvantage. They will think twice now before questioning their king."

"As they should."

"My only regret is that my horse was too slow to allow me to hear you instruct them." Will said. John peered at him for a long, silent moment.

"Rest assured, you will be given all of the pertinent details," Prince John said finally. "You shall be a permanent member of my court, and henceforth shall reside here at the castle. You may send for your things. I can use a smart man like you, one who knows where the true power lies."

"You honor me, Your Majesty. I will do my best to be of service," Will said, bowing deeply again. He hadn't looked for such an invitation to come so soon, and he couldn't help but wonder if it was a sign of the prince's trust… or mistrust. Either way he would turn it to his advantage.

When it became apparent that the conversation was at an end, he turned, but before he could take a step he saw the cardinal being escorted in by a servant. Together they drew near until the holy man was standing next to Will.

"Your Majesty, may I present Cardinal Fran—" the servant began.

"What are you doing here?" the prince asked, his voice cold.

"My prince, I heard you were assembling the nobles," the cardinal said. "Since I had not yet departed, I thought I should attend as well. To offer my services as needed."

"You thought wrong," John said, waving a hand dismissively. "I have no need of you."

"But your brother often found my advice worthy of an ear."

"I am not my brother," the prince replied. "Since you are here, however, I will inform you personally of the new taxes that I am implementing."

"I heard some of the nobles discussing them outside."

"Yes, well, the church shall not be immune," John said, and Will saw the holy man stiffen. "It shall be expected to do its part."

"There is no precedent for that," the cardinal said, his voice admirably calm. "What is given to God's work must be used in the furtherance of God's work. If you were to make such a radical change in the relationship between the crown and the church, you would contend with Rome on that matter."

The prince leaned forward on his throne, his face twisting in a sneer.

"Let Rome come to me, if they wish to complain."

The Sheriff reappeared, stepping from behind the throne. Will shivered, and fought the urge to step back. He hadn't even realized the man was there.

The cardinal did step back.

"Your liege has tolerated your presence long enough," the Sheriff said, his voice little more than a growl. "Be gone, before I remove you myself."

Will sucked in his breath. It wasn't a lowly monk they were daring to order around in such a manner. This was a cardinal, an adviser to the pope himself. It was he who had been sent from Rome to discuss the Crusade with King Richard. The audacity they displayed in attempting to order him around was stunning. Yet the cardinal stood tall, his eyes shrewd and his hands clenched at his side.

"I would have a care," he said. "Men reign on this earth only at the pleasure of God. I would be happy to discuss with you the finer aspects of His will."

"Get out!" the prince roared, standing abruptly. There was going to be bloodshed. Will could feel it as a tightening in his stomach, a sickening sensation. He found himself stepping involuntarily toward the cardinal.

"It's time to go, old man," he said, looking meaningfully into his eyes. He'd have to beg forgiveness later for the disrespect, but for now it was important that Cardinal Francis leave before there was a fight, and that Will continue to earn the prince's trust.

"I will go, for now," the cardinal said, "but this shall not go unanswered." He turned and swept from the room, a thousand times more regal than the man who stood in front of the throne, the crown on his head slipping down over one eye. It was appropriate, Will realized, for surely power was blinding him.

CHAPTER NINETEEN

Marian swiftly made it back to her room, her head still reeling from everything she'd seen and heard. There was no use going to the cardinal with this—it would just be wasting precious time. Richard had entrusted her with the way to get hold of him, and she had something now that was sure to bring him home.

She sat at her writing desk, pulling out a piece of parchment and uncorking her inkwell. She dipped her quill in the ink, set it on the parchment, and began to write, recounting as bluntly as she could all that had happened. She was cautious about revealing her identity, and there were several coded ways she and Richard had used to communicate with each other over the years. So Marian wrote in a way that he would know it was she.

When at last she had finished she folded the letter and poured sealing wax upon it. She did not use her seal, though, knowing that, if her messenger was intercepted, it would be disastrous not only for her, but also for all those she cared about. She had no wish to see Chastity lying in a pool of her own blood.

To that end she thought long and hard about the messenger she would choose, as Friar Tuck had suggested. She couldn't risk losing Chastity. There was another whom she had decided she could trust, and already had been testing in a few small ways.

She tucked the letter into her bodice and made her way stealthily back to the kitchens, where she secured an apple. Then she headed for the stables. Murther saw her approaching and hurried to meet her.

"Begging your pardon, Highness, we're still clearing the stable of all the nobles' horses. Is there something I can help you with?"

"Walk with me," she said softly.

He looked confused for a moment, then nodded and fell into step beside her. Together they entered the stable and walked down to Merryweather's stall. The horse was happy to see her, but happier still to see the apple that Marian held out for her. Fortunately, there was no one else at this end of the stable.

"Do you know the way to the docks?" she asked.

"A'course Highness," Murther replied. "I was there when the king sailed for the Holy Land. Everyone was."

She looked into his earnest, young face. He was loyal to the throne.

And he was so young.

She took a deep breath, turned, and pulled the parchment from her bodice. She turned back to him.

"Take my horse and ride there now. Find a man named Donthos and tell him that I have sent you. He will direct you from there." She handed him the letter. "He is going to take you on a boat."

Murther's eyes grew wide, and he looked concerned.

"I've never been on a boat before." He pushed the letter into the pocket of his jerkin. "Don't they make you sick?"

She smiled at his naïveté, even as it panged through her chest.

"For some they do," she replied gently, "but if you can ride a horse, you can ride the sea. It's actually very exhilarating. I'm sure you will love it. But no one must know what you are doing."

"How long will I be gone for?"

"I don't know," she said. "Days at least. Perhaps weeks even." Then a thought struck her. "Do you need to tell your family?"

"No, Highness," he said. "I'm indentured to the stable. I live here. The stable master is the only one I report to." He dropped his head, sheepishly. "But he will be right angry if I leave. I will be jailed when I return."

She let out a sigh of relief. This, thank goodness, was something she could address, though she would need to be circumspect.

"Do not give it another thought—I will speak with the stable master," she said. "Then, when you return, I will see to it that you are freed from your servitude and given a plot with a home on it, as reward."

As wide as they already were, the boy's eyes went even wider. "That is *most* generous, Highness." He bowed. "I will do my best to earn it."

Marian thought for a long moment. "If you have any family who are indentured or otherwise indebted, I will make sure their obligation is released as well, and that they are freed or sent to your new holding, as you see fit."

Murther gulped. "Would that make me a lord?"

"No, but it is the first step. Property, then people, then profit to become a lord. Or you can simply remain a free man with a home, and the opportunity to make your own way."

He thought about it, mouth agape at the possibilities. Then he shut his jaw firmly with a sharp nod.

All he could say was, "Very, very generous."

The horse moved beneath Murther with long, sure strides and he thrilled at the feeling of the wind in his face. His insides were tight, adrenaline rushing through his bloodstream. He had been allowed to exercise the horses he tended before, but never out in the country, and rarely at more than a trot.

If he did as his lady had commanded, he would have a horse of his own, and more, as hard as it was to imagine.

Sherwood was haunted, so he skirted the edge of the forest, even though Lady Marian's warning about being unseen rang through his mind. The trees of the forest loomed on each side of him, gradually becoming thinner, and open sky hung over him the entire journey. The road he was on would lead straight to the water's edge. He'd follow it to the docks and the waiting ship.

He glanced up at the sky.

Bless Lady Marian for this chance to aid her.

Then he closed his eyes, enjoying the wind and the sun, exulting in the power of the horse beneath him.

Mayhap I will start my own stable.

He opened his eyes and smiled.

Something flashed across the road a short distance in front of him, darting from one clump of bushes to another.

Merryweather planted her front hooves, driving them into the hard-packed earth. Her body jerked short, rear legs lifting from the ground, still pushed by the momentum of her run. Murther pitched forward, his face slamming into the animal's solid neck. Instinctively his hands and legs clamped down, locking tight on the horseflesh under him.

His quick reflexes were the only thing that saved him from being thrown and landing on his skull. Breathing hard, heart pounding in his chest like a blacksmith's hammer, he held onto the horse's neck for a moment before straightening up slowly and pushing back over his ear the lock of hair that had fallen into his eyes.

What was that?

It had been too large to be a rabbit or even a fox. It was nearer the size of a wolf. Beneath him, Merryweather shook, muscles trembling under her sleek coat. The animal took a step backward, whinnying in fear.

"Easy, easy," he muttered, rubbing a soothing hand on the horse's withers. Merryweather jerked her head, baring wide teeth at him. Still she continued to retreat, hopping as if a snake were in the road.

He leaned back, jerking the reins to make her stop.

"What's wrong with you?" Murther kicked his heels and snapped the reins. "It's nothing. Let's go!"

Merryweather shook her head and snorted. He felt her lock up under him, and doubt crept in. Should he turn back? To find another path would cost him several hours on the journey.

"It was just an animal," he said, not sure if he was trying to convince himself or the horse. "It's already run off." Could it have been a deer? It might have been big enough, but it had seemed as if it was much darker even than a stag. He watched the bushes closely for any sign of movement. If it *had* been an animal, then likely it was gone, or at least far more frightened than he was.

It had to be an animal. No man moved in that way, or with that speed.

No *man*.

His fingers crossed his body. Sudden fear knotted his stomach and bile flooded his mouth. He choked it down and kicked Merryweather as hard as he could. She neighed in pain but refused to move. He kicked again, driving his boot heels deep into her side. She jerked and screamed the high-pitched scream of a horse in a barn fire. He kicked once more and drove his fists into her withers.

The horse leapt forward, shooting ahead at a dead run. Within a moment they were past the spot the creature had crossed. As it fell away in the distance, he breathed a sigh of relief.

The road flashed by under Merryweather's hooves. He could still feel her tension, her lingering fright, but the run was loosening her up. Nevertheless, a quarter mile of road passed before they both started to relax.

He sat up, pulling the reins to slow her down as they approached a large tree limb, hanging over the road. Just as they reached it, the limb shook. Something fell from the branch, knocking him from Merryweather's back. The horse squealed, dancing to the side.

Murther twisted, struggling to get up. Pain slashed across his back above his hips. Then he couldn't feel anything below the pain. Nearby Merryweather screamed in terror. He twisted his head to the side, trying to see.

Black fur, slashing fangs, and glowing red eyes filled his vision. Murther screamed for a long moment before the unholy vision opened its mouth wide, revealing what looked like rows upon rows of gleaming needles. The thing lunged, clamping down on his throat, cutting off his breath. His own blood spurted in an arc, landing hot in his eyes. It coated the wicked muzzle and gleamed as red as the unblinking eyes above it.

The Sheriff stroked the head of his pet as it presented itself to him, muzzle slick and damp. It dropped a blood-smeared piece of parchment into his free hand. After a moment he shook it open and read what he could of the contents through the viscera that stained it. There was no signature, but few people could have written the letter, which urged the king to come home.

He had been right to suspect that, after the prince's meeting with the nobles, someone would try to send word to Richard. That was why he had set his pet to watch the road to the docks. No doubt that was where the messenger boy had been heading. Perhaps he should have been taken alive and forced to reveal who had given him the parchment. Someone at the docks was loyal to Richard, as well. The prince should have been more cautious. Still, there was no need to tip their hand. Not just yet, at any rate.

His pet pushed up against his palm. He lifted it and placed it on his shoulder. In two turns of its body it had curled around his throat and closed its eyes, becoming a fur collar once again.

The ride home was one of the longest ones Robin had ever made. By the time he reached the manor he was spent. Still, he forced himself to climb the stairs. This was not news he could keep to himself.

Robin stopped just short of his mother's room. He had never once been inside. There were emblems that she had carved into the doorposts. She had told him when he was very young that they were magic, wards that would keep him—and him alone—from ever entering her bedchamber.

He had never believed that the markings were magic, but they might as well have been. He had never stepped foot across the threshold, not because the symbols kept him at bay, but because her hatred did.

As a child he had not understood when she would lavish affection on Robert, Becca, and Ruth, while at the same time shunning him. For the longest time he thought his dark coloring was the reason, that he was a shadow in a family of light and somehow unnatural. But years of his mother's apathy, and sometimes animosity, had cleared that from his mind. Still, he loved her because it was his duty.

"Mother, I need to speak with you," he called.

"Go away," she called back.

"It's important. Prince John has levied a tax. Each landholder is expected to give up one-half his harvest and one-third his retinue."

There was a moment of silence and then his mother appeared just inside the door. Her eyes were wide.

"That's preposterous," she said.

"Yes, but it is what he's demanding."

"We'll do no such thing!"

"While I share your sentiment, I'm afraid it's not that simple. Minter and Staunton tried to protest. He had them both killed where they stood."

Her face hardened. "So, they're good enough to die protecting their lands and families, but you are not."

He clenched his fists at his side as he forced himself to take a deep breath. "I'm not afraid of what he'll do to me. I am afraid for you, the girls, and our servants, though."

She waved away his fears with a dismissive hand. Then she pursed her lips in thought. "You know, there are some we could easily lose. Your father and brother have no need of any of their servants who have remained behind. And I've never liked that old man who wears the armor."

"I'm not sending Old Soldier to John," Robin said quietly.

The man had been one of Robin's few friends growing up. What his real name was, no one actually knew. He'd come into his father's service without giving one. One day he called himself an old soldier and the name had apparently stuck. When Robin was a child that was the name he learned.

"You're the man of the house now—you figure out who we should send away," his mother snapped.

Robin closed his eyes. He didn't want to send any, but he didn't see a way around it. "Lila, then—there's never been a thing she hasn't burned when it comes to meals," he said, naming the assistant cook.

"How dare you?" his mother hissed. "She has been with me since I was a girl. She came here with me when I married your father. You seek to hurt me, but must choose another way."

Robin hated thinking of people in terms of their usefulness. It seemed so callous. As much as he didn't appreciate being the object of his mother's ire, he was at least encouraged to learn that there were those she did care about, and was willing to defend.

"Fine," he said. "I will work something out." He turned and left before she could say anything else. It had been a gesture of respect on his part, going to her with news that would affect the manor so deeply. Clearly it had been a mistake. One he would not soon repeat.

The walls of the house were too small to contain him in that moment. He went downstairs and grabbed his bow and quiver before heading outside. He walked quickly, with purpose, and within the space of a few deep breaths he was in the embrace of the forest.

He closed his eyes for a moment and breathed it in. Sherwood, which had been more mother and father to him than his own parents. Robert had once joked that sap and not blood ran through Robin's veins. Times like this he almost felt it to be true.

He threw wide his arms, embracing all that was around him. An unseen wind rustled the tops of the trees far above and the sound seemed to echo, magnified by the thick trunks themselves until it sounded like a whisper, calling over and over.

Robin. Robin.

He knew why others thought the forest was haunted. For him the presence that dwelt there, that made the trees themselves seem to whisper to one another and to him, had always been a friendly one, a comforter and a guide.

"I need your strength and your guidance more than ever," he said out loud.

Robin. Robin.

Rhythmically, over and over, he could hear his name, and it comforted him as it always had in his darkest hours.

Marian could not sleep. She tossed and turned, her outrage and fear each vying for the upper hand. She tried to pray, but could not keep her mind on task. She just kept reminding herself over and over that soon Richard would be home and all would be set right.

Except for the families of the two nobles who lost their lives trying to stand up to John.

Anger ripped through her anew, tinged with a hatred she had never known before. It was so powerful that she began to shake. She rose with the dawn. She needed to do something before she went insane. So she dressed and hurried down to the stables.

The horse master met her there.

"Milady, I was not expecting you." His voice matched his hair, frazzled and distressed.

"It's alright. If I could just have a bridle, I can manage to get my own mount."

He shook his head sadly, clucking his tongue. "You cannot have your favorite."

Her heart skipped a beat. Someone at the docks should have returned Merryweather to the stables by now. "Explain yourself." Her throat was tight around the words.

The man dropped his eyes. "My stable boy was clumsy with her—she has a nasty cut on her leg, and another on her flank."

It was a lie—of that she could be certain. Murther wouldn't have returned her, *couldn't* have done so. He would be halfway across the sea now.

Still, she had to be sure.

"Show her to me," she said.

The man bowed. "As you wish," he responded. "Please follow me." He turned and led the way into the stables, and her fear heightened. Moments later she cast her eyes upon Merryweather. A freshly-stitched wound crossed her left flank, the edges pinched together by a strand of horsehair. The area had been shaved, all hair scraped away, and she could see that the wound, though treated, pulsed with an angry crimson fever. Another cut on Merryweather's leg lay open, covered in a thick ointment that caught dirt in its surface.

She reached out and put a hand on the horse's neck, and the animal jerked at the contact. Cooing to soothe her, Marian slid her hand up to her mane, which was crusted with a dark substance. She swallowed hard as she recognized it to be blood.

"You say a boy was careless with him?"

"Yes, milady, but not to worry," he replied. "The boy won't trouble no one no more. We've dismissed him from service."

With that the stall tilted, growing dark at the edges. Heat ran up her throat and her mouth went foul. She thought she was going to be sick.

Murther. Poor sweet soul. He was dead. Deep in her soul she knew it to be true. She had sent him on a mission, and now his blood was on her hands.

No. Not her hands. She held part of the blame for sending him, but someone else had done the deed. Yet who could have killed the boy? Who could have possibly guessed at his mission?

She had to assume that the letter had been intercepted, and that John knew there was someone who conspired against him. Most likely the Sheriff knew, as well. Neither had said anything to her, or hindered her in any way, so for now her involvement was still secret.

"Heal swiftly," she whispered to the horse. Then she forced herself to turn to the stable master. "I still require a mount." She concentrated, keeping locked behind her breastbone the tremor that threatened to climb into her voice.

"I will have one saddled for you at once," he said.

She nodded.

Half a turn of the glass later she pulled herself into the saddle of a beautiful white horse with long legs and a sleek musculature that vibrated with power. As she settled into her seat, the stable master handed her the reins.

"Her name is Snowcap. She's a bit headstrong. Good on the road or trail but if you point her at any obstacle, she'll jump it and you won't be able to stop her."

"I'll keep that in mind," Marian said, as she gathered up the reins.

"Steer clear of any river banks or fences and she'll do fine."

Marian pressed her heels to the animal's flanks, and moments later was free of the castle. She nudged the horse into a fast gallop, her dress flapping in the wind. Her riding clothes were still in the castle, waiting to be returned to their usual place in the stable. Her dress hiked up her legs, but there was none to see and her grief barred her from caring. The wind stung her eyes, pulling away her tears for the innocent stable boy who'd been killed in her service. She gave herself to the run, letting her mind go blank as she screamed into the air.

When her tears had finally stopped coming, she slowed Snowcap to a trot. She'd allowed the horse her own head, and the beast chose the road leading to the port. She steadied herself. Maybe she should head straight for the boat, trusting in God to get her there safely. She was the niece of the one true king— surely that would keep her safe from harm. Maybe she was the only one who could go. The only one with a position to take the *Kestrel* and fetch her uncle.

If she vanished, though, trouble would rain down on Chastity.

Her friend would have urged her to go, would've told her that she could take care of herself. Even if Marian could ignore the danger, though, Chastity wasn't the only one who might be forced to pay. There was the horse master who would doubtless be blamed if she failed to return. They might even go after Jansa, since the steward had seen the two of them talking. The very high profile that might keep Marian safe could also bring harm to innocents, and people for whom she cared.

She slowed her horse to a walk to let the animal cool down as the war raged on in her heart and mind. She looked up at the sky, gone iron gray with an oncoming storm, settling into the hypnotic rhythm of Snowcap's canter.

The horse jerked.

The animal's muscles coiled beneath her. Marian had learned to ride practically before she could walk, so well-honed skills kept her in the saddle even as her horse bucked and twisted in mid-air. A growl filled Marian's ears, dark and menacing. It sounded like no animal she'd heard before, rumbling like a wolf and slipping into a long sibilant hiss at the end. Her blood ran cold. She had no weapons with which to fend off any attack.

She peered closely into the brush by the side of the road and after a moment saw two blood red eyes staring back at her. A growl on her other side caused her to whip her head around, and she saw a flash of what looked like black fur. Her stomach twisted and a cold sweat broke on her skin. Evil seemed to permeate the very air she breathed, seeping into her lungs and poisoning her from the inside.

Whatever creatures they were, they were unnatural.

Jerking hard on the reins turned Snowcap's head, just as a beast of pure darkness lunged at her. Marian twisted, flailing as Snowcap reared. She lost a stirrup and her foot lashed out, thudding into the creature's skull. It fell onto the road with a hiss, monstrous, larger than a wolf. She heard the growl from its mate and knew that her lucky kick had slowed the one down only for a moment. She could not hope to fend off another attack.

She got Snowcap aimed back down the road toward the castle and kicked as hard as she could. The horse reared again, and Marian barely kept her seat. Dropping to all fours, Snowcap bolted down the road. She took a dozen strides and then kicked out with her hind legs, nearly sending Marian flying.

Marian heard a thud and knew that the horse must be fighting off one of the beasts. She kicked her in the ribs again and the frightened animal leaped forward as Marian held on for her life. She did not look back, did not turn at all.

Simply held on and prayed.

Snowcap's hooves slipped on the flagstone. The horse snorted and stumbled, trying to stop. Other horses in their stalls began to neigh and shake their heads at the commotion. The master of horse ran to meet her, grabbing the bridle and saddle, hanging his weight off her to steady the mare.

For a moment, Marian tensed, fearing that the horse would fall with her on its back, but the man's weight lent enough balance to stop that.

"Is everything alright, milady?" he asked.

"I thought she could use a bit of a run," Marian answered, slipping down the other side. Then she hurried out of the stables without another word of explanation.

She fled to her chambers. Her dress hung heavy with her own sweat and her fear left a bitter, stinging stench on the surface of her skin. Part of her felt silly, like a girl who startled easily, but in her heart she knew that wasn't the case. Something had been on that road—something that was not natural. Were they watching, waiting in ambush for anyone trying to go to the docks? Or were they simply predators looking for prey?

The cardinal's words about the symbols convinced her. This was a malicious incident. Whatever the source, she would have to guard every step she took, and warn Chastity to do the same.

She found the girl in her room.

"What's wrong?" Chastity asked, the instant Marian had shut and bolted the door.

"Do you have a dagger?"

"Of course."

Marian crossed to a small chest on one of the tables and lifted the lid. Inside was nestled a thin weapon. Rubies dotted the hilt and gold traced the blade, but it was made of good steel with a keen edge—a present from her father when she was but a little girl. She lifted it out and held it tight in hands that shook slightly.

"From now on, wherever you go, whatever you do, always be armed," she told Chastity. "Now I need your help choosing two loyal servants who we can trust completely. My messenger to the king... was killed... before he could make it to the boat. I will need to send others, two just in case."

"When do we need to send them?" Chastity asked.

"Tonight, so we have no time to waste."

CHAPTER TWENTY

Will was worried. Three days had passed since the prince's disastrous meeting with the nobles, and he had called another meeting, this one of nobles and freemen alike. He wouldn't tell Will what it was about, which just added to his unease.

He hadn't seen Marian in two days, but last he had she'd looked like a ghost. He was beginning to worry that something might have happened to her. If he didn't see her today, he'd have to make an effort to track down her servant girl, Chastity.

Come to think of it, I haven't seen her, either. He frowned at the thought.

"Important day, Will," John said, as he entered the great hall.

"Yes, Your Majesty. Although why it is, I'm still not certain," Will said, plastering an affable smile on his face.

John put a hand on his shoulder. "It's a surprise, my friend. You love surprises, don't you?"

Not your surprises, most certainly. He didn't dare say it aloud, though.

"Come, it is my understanding that our guests are already assembled," John said, gripping his shoulder hard.

Will looked around at the empty room with a raised eyebrow.

John laughed. Not a hale, hearty laugh, like King Richard used to give, but a thin, cruel laugh that made Will's flesh crawl.

"Not here," John explained. "This particular gathering is being held in the forecourt." Together they walked outside, where music met them. The courtyard was filled with people speaking to one another in hushed tones. There were enough of them that their voices still formed a cacophony. The band wasn't very good, more a clashing of instruments, but they tried, playing with gusto if not talent. In the courtyard a dais had been erected with three chairs placed upon it and guards all around.

Twenty feet from the dais stood a wooden platform. On it stood a group of posts with long ropes attached to them.

It was a gallows.

A sick feeling came over him as he realized that John hadn't yet had his fill of killing.

"So, it's to be a hanging?" he barely managed to ask through lips that were squeezed tightly together.

"Very astute of you," John said, in a teasing, playful manner that contrasted terribly with the fear of the crowd. For a terrible moment Will thought the prince might intend to hang *him*. John steered him toward the dais, though, and indicated that he should take the seat on the right, while John sat in the middle.

Moments later guards emerged from the castle, escorting Marian, who looked even less eager to be there than he was. She soon mounted the dais and took her seat on John's other side.

"You look lovely today, niece," John told her, a smile twisting his lips.

"Thank you," Marian said, although Will heard the strain it took to get the words out.

John clapped his hands together twice. The musicians ceased and a hush fell over the crowd. The courtyard was silent save for a distant sound of summer birds and the creaking of rope on raw wood. Will looked out, seeing so many faces he knew, both noble and freemen. He did not see Robin.

There were only a couple of women in the entire group. It didn't seem likely that John had done the decent thing by dictating that they remain at home so they didn't have to witness what was about to happen. No, he was sure their absence was deliberate, and likely malicious. He just didn't know why yet.

"By now you are all aware of the new way of things," John said to the hushed crowd. "The tax collectors will begin their work in the morning. Today, though, I wanted to give you a spectacle. One that will greatly entertain me... and hopefully educate you."

He signaled and a door was opened by a guard. Will found himself craning his neck along with everyone else to catch a glimpse of who might be coming out. He could see the flicker of movement, bodies huddled together. Then at last they stepped into the light.

A collective gasp went up from the audience. Three armed guards led out Lady Minter and her two nearly grown daughters. Following behind them, another phalanx of guards herded Lady Staunton, her two young sons—neither over the age of ten—and her daughter, who was the youngest.

Will blinked in disbelief. Surely this was some kind of cruel jest. He couldn't seriously mean to execute children. He turned to look at the prince. The man was still smiling, and there was a gleam in his eye.

Will dared not look at Marian, knowing that seeing her expression would only make it impossible for him to continue to play his part in this sick, twisted little game. As the guards led the seven up onto the gallows, Will leaned over.

"An excellent jest, Majesty," he said, his voice low. "Surely it's gone far enough, though."

"On the contrary, Will, I'm not taking it nearly far enough," he said, as nooses were fitted around the necks of the women and children.

A ripple of outrage ran through the crowd and Will felt a spark of hope. There were many of them—far more than John had soldiers. If the people rose up together they might forever rid themselves of this evil creature. He licked his lips, wishing he knew what to say to focus the crowd's energies in the right direction. Before he could say anything, however, John stood and held up a hand.

The crowd fell silent again.

"I am touched by the concern you show for the families of two traitors to the crown," he said. "I can assure you, however, that your sympathies are misplaced. These are dangerous times in which we find ourselves. In the absence of my brother, enemies to the throne have become brazen, attacking your very king. They hide behind children to perform their evil tasks. Well, I say, no more!

"While you traveled here today, my soldiers have visited your homes and have taken the youngest child in each. They have brought them here for safekeeping." He pointed up and to the left. "If you will notice the tower, you might recognize some of the faces there. Now, they shall remain safe within my care, and any man loyal to the crown has no reason to fear."

All heads turned. There, on a balcony halfway up the westernmost tower, stood a crowd of children, all young, none of them more than a head and a hand taller than the stone railing. Now that he saw them, Will realized that what he thought was the sound of birds actually had been the cries of the children, far above.

The prince sat down and Will regarded him with horror. The man was a monster. He was also brilliant. With one swift move he had quashed any thoughts of rebellion that might have been forming. He had lured the men here so he could kidnap their family members. Brilliant. Decisive. Evil.

His thoughts flew to his young nieces. Had Ruth been taken? Was that why Robin wasn't here—because he had intercepted the guards?

Or possibly even been killed by them.

Will struggled to catch his breath, though it felt as if his throat and chest were constricting. He had never thanked God so vehemently that he had yet to father children.

* * *

"Don't do it like that." Becca Longstride had her hands on her hips, looking down at her younger sister Ruth. They were only two years apart, but Becca had begun growing rapidly, stretching into the willowy height she would inherit from her parents, whereas Ruth still had the height of a normal child.

Ruth didn't look up at her sister, she simply continued twisting the hair on her doll. The hair was made of yarn.

"Don't be so bossy," she said.

Becca huffed. "But you are doing it *wrong*."

"It's my doll—there is no wrong."

"There is, too. You are supposed to be learning how to braid your own hair, not tangling it into a mess." Becca plopped down on the bench beside Ruth, bumping her with a hip. She reached out. "Here, let me show you."

Ruth jerked the doll to her chest and pushed off the seat. She walked toward the house several meters away from where they were playing, then turned toward her sister. Still walking backward, she thrust her chin out.

"I don't want you to show me the 'proper' way. I don't care. I'm a Longstride lady—" She shook her head to make her own thick locks of hair whip around her shoulders "—and I can wear my hair however I want."

Becca stood, meaning to chase her down and forcibly take the doll from her smartarse little hands.

Two soldiers came around the corner of the house.

Ruth didn't see them, still walking backward and waving the doll at Becca in defiance. Becca froze, and her heart skipped at their appearance. Both men walked with determination, their mail coats gleaming in the sun, and both had great swords hanging from their hips.

Then she saw the royal seal on their tabards, and relaxed. An eagerness sparked inside her. It wasn't uncommon for soldiers to come to Longstride manor, since her father was the king's friend. Maybe they came with news of her father's return. She missed him terribly.

She was about to call out a welcome to the soldiers when they both reached down. Each grabbed one of Ruth's arms in their wide hands. The little girl screamed as they jerked her from her feet. Becca watched her sister struggle, the doll falling into the dirt. Ruth kicked and flailed and screamed as she hung between the two men.

"Shut her up," the soldier on the left growled.

The one on the right pulled a burlap sack from his belt and jerked it over Ruth's head. She still screamed, but it was muffled by the heavy fabric.

"Better," the left soldier grunted, and he looked at Becca. "We're taking her to the castle fer safekeepin'. Tell yer ma. Order of the king." With that they turned to go.

Ruth's struggles slowed and she stopped screaming. Becca didn't know if it was exhaustion or a lack of breath that made her quit. The men lowered her to the ground and the left guard released, letting the other man drag her sister away.

Confusion that had boiled in her mind since the men appeared suddenly vanished and Becca was left with a cold, clear thought that came to her in her father's voice.

They are stealing my sister. Becca ran toward the men without thinking. Tucking her head into her shoulder she plowed into the left soldier, knocking him sideways. She bounced away, reeling but still standing, while he dropped to one knee, catching himself on his hands before he could eat dirt. Steadying herself she spun toward the soldier who still held her sister by the arm. She jumped, launching herself at him with her fingernails bared like claws.

His free hand snatched her up by the back of her hair before she could hurt him. Fiery pain washed over her scalp as he held her in one hand and Ruth in the other. Tears spilled from her eyes, blurring everything. She blinked them away and watched the left soldier stalk over, face knotted in a scowl.

"Little bitch," he said. His big hand swung back, and then came down on her head. Her vision went dark in a wash of agony that swept through her. The blow drove her to the ground, tearing some of her hair out in the other soldier's hand.

The left soldier stood over her, pointing down.

"Get up again and I'll *really* hurt you."

He turned away from her. Her head dropped, partially in pain, partially in shame that she was going to let her sister be taken. Then a weird animal noise made her look up.

Her brother Robin burst from the edge of Sherwood, running like a man possessed. He was filthy, covered in dirt from working the field. His always-dark face had gone even darker, veins bulging from his temples and cords standing out on his neck. He looked swollen to nearly twice his normal size, and colored night-dark by rage. His eyes bulged and his teeth shone wet in his mouth.

He had a shovel in his hand.

The left soldier raised his arm, yelling for Robin to stop. His other hand pulled on the handle of the sword that hung by his side. The blade was halfway free when Robin struck him across the face with the blade of the shovel. Becca watched as the dull edge sank into the soldier's face, caving it in on itself. There was no blood, no gore, the shovel blade simply fell into the space where the soldier's face had been and the man fell backward, Robin pulled along by his grip on the tool until he knelt on the dead soldier's chest.

A cry of triumph was wrested out of her and her chest felt hot and tight. Robin had killed the man who had struck her, and she was fiercely glad.

Ruth gave a muffled cry as the soldier who held her threw her to the ground and pulled his sword. Before Becca could shout a warning Robin's head jerked around, feral quick, as the soldier swung back his weapon to cleave him in two. Robin leapt to his feet, jerking on the shovel. The blade came out, painted red from mid-width to blade point, in a scattering of loose teeth and lumpy gore.

The soldier's sword flashed down, aimed to separate Robin's head from his shoulders, but her brother drove the tool forward, shoving it at the soldier's chest. The dull spade head didn't penetrate the mail shirt—it was too well made, the links of good English steel, but the impact jarred the soldier enough to halt his swing. The shovel slid up the slick mail, skimming metal on metal as Robin drove forward until it struck the soldier under his chin.

This time there was blood, so much of it that it sprayed Robin from brow to belt, painting him red like a demon. Becca turned her head from the sight just as giant hands circled round her.

The women and children on the platform stood with their heads bowed in their nooses. They didn't cry or wail, not the children, not the mothers of the children.

They've been drugged.

It was the only thing that made sense. Childless, Marian still had that maternal instinct nestled in her heart like a seed waiting for its season to bloom. It was there, the knowledge of the love one had for one's own child. She knew if it had been her on that gallows, and her children beside her, she would have screamed for mercy until her dying breath.

Her uncle sat beside her, leaning back in his chair and smiling—*grinning*. Will Scarlet sat on the other side of him and wore a sour face. She couldn't believe this was going to happen. She was going to watch people die. Innocent people.

She wanted to run to them.

She wanted to cut them free.

She stood, and the dagger in her skirts hung heavy against her thigh. It took all her willpower to keep from touching it through the slit cut in the seam that would allow her to draw it free.

"This can't happen."

Her uncle turned. "Oh, it will happen," he said. "These traitors will dance in the air for us."

"There are children."

"Do you know how old Cain was when he slew his brother Abel?"

The question drew her short. "What?"

Prince John waved his hand at her. "You are familiar with the story from your Bible, are you not?" She nodded. He leaned close, bringing his face near hers. "So then, how old was Cain when he first drew blood?"

Is this a trick?

Will leaned forward in his chair, looking intently at the gallows. Sweat ran down his face.

"Where did *he* come from?"

She threw a glance at where he looked. The Sheriff stood on the platform by the women and children there. They all looked at him, eyes wide and docile. His black armored hand rested on the lever that jutted from the stage, the lever that would release the trapdoor beneath the nooses.

The world slid sideways. It was all happening so fast.

"Niece of mine, answer the question."

The prince was so close to her, she could feel his breath on her cheek. Her face turned toward him but her eyes remained on the gallows, on the black-armored Sheriff with his hand on the lever.

"It doesn't say."

"Precisely!" Prince John cried.

The Sheriff jerked the lever.

The trap fell with a clap of wood and all seven of the people on the stage, two mothers and five children, dropped as if they'd stepped off a ledge. The ropes yanked, jerking them short. The wet crunch of separated vertebrae rolled across her, loud in her ears. The mothers and children bounced and dangled, swaying with their heads cocked to the side and their jaws crushed closed in the grimace of strangulation.

Will Scarlet turned away, fist to his mouth, struggling to hold back vomit.

Marian was numb, scrubbed raw by the short sudden violence of the hanging.

Prince John touched her face with his fingertips. She dragged her eyes from the swaying bodies to peer straight at him. His bottom lip hung out in a pout, and his eyebrows drew low over his eyes.

"The point of the question, young Marian, is that he could have been a child."

The dirt was packed tight, stomped down by all three of them. Robin knelt beside the unmarked grave. He'd sweated away the blood on his face and arms, but his shirt had turned black with it. Flies buzzed around him. He didn't brush them away.

"You gotta get up."

Robin didn't look at the man who loomed over him like a mighty oak. "Leave me be for a moment."

"I've done that, Lord Longstride," the fellow replied. "Time for you to be up and moving."

"That's my father."

The giant of a man pushed forward. "It's you, too. Now get up or I'll haul you to your feet."

"Dammit, Little John, leave me be."

John Little, known as Little John from the moment he became the biggest man in the realm, began to reach down for Robin. Then a spotted hand, still strong as steel, closed on his arm. Little John looked over. Old Soldier shook his head and removed his hand from the bigger man's arm.

He had a sword in his hand.

Little John stepped back, and Old Soldier knelt in front of Robin.

"First time?"

Robin's voice was dull, flat, when he spoke. "I don't know what came over me. I've been mad, but never before felt such... such *anger*."

"You've never before had two men try to kidnap your sister."

Robin looked up sharply. "Are you making fun of me?"

Old Soldier frowned. "No, son, I'm not. I'm explaining why you lost control, so you don't feel bad."

"I didn't lose control. I knew *exactly* what I was doing when I did it."

Little John drew in a sharp breath. "Jesus, Mary, an' all the saints."

Old Soldier cut him off with a sharp chop of his hand.

His eyes stayed on Robin. "Doesn't change the reason you did what you did."

"The world is falling apart. Why were the king's men trying to steal my sister?"

"I think this may have something to do with it." Old Soldier held the sword out, pommel first. He'd stripped the bodies of their mail and their weapons before burial. "This is new."

Robin looked. The pommel weight had been ground flat and inscribed with a symbol. Lines and whorls intersected, crossing each other in geometric eddies that his eye wanted to trace, but couldn't.

He shook his head. "The man personalized his sword. I've done the same to my bow."

"It's on both swords. Those men didn't look to be brothers, so not a family symbol."

"What is it?"

Old Soldier shrugged, his ever-present mail shirt shushed under the linen tunic he wore over it, steel links rubbing softly on the fibers. "It feels like there's something to it, some power. I'm old, but this is not a symbol used by any part of the Lionheart service." He ran a calloused finger over the symbol. Traces of color followed the lines where he touched it. "It's not natural. I'd guess magic."

"Magic isn't real."

Old Soldier raised his eyebrow. "Want to ask your mother about that?"

Robin said nothing for a long moment. "If those swords have magic symbols that make you steal children..." He shook his head. "I can't believe it."

"Believe that you saw two of the king's men trying to take your sister. You know King Richard—strength of character is one of his staunchest requirements of service. The soldiers he left behind wouldn't try to steal a child. Not without a revolt in the ranks."

Robin looked at the symbol again. "Magic." He shook his head. "Could be."

"We tell no one about this. If anyone comes by to ask, we never saw soldiers." Robin pulled himself to his feet. "And we do *NOT* show my mother that symbol."

Little John spoke up. "What if they try for your sister again?"

"We've got a lot of land, and a lot of places to dig holes." Robin looked in the direction of the house. "I'm going to check on Ruth. Work's done for the day."

"Good enough," Old Soldier said.

Robin turned away from the two men. They watched him go.

"If he hadn't cut through the woods, we could have stopped him from killing those soldiers."

"If I weren't old as this dirt and you big as this field, then we could have arrived to do more than watch."

Little John rubbed his face. "The viciousness of what he did…"

"I've seen worse."

"Have you done worse?"

Old Soldier considered his words before answering.

"Not with a shovel."

CHAPTER TWENTY-ONE

The woman kept crying. It shook her entire body as she huddled around herself, hands digging into her arms and shoulders. She rocked, the chair beneath her creaking with each movement. Her wailing filled the small home, swirling around the air like a wasp digging its way into the ear, burrowing its way deeper.

"Stell, pull yourself together!" her husband barked.

If Stell pulls herself together any more, Alan-a-Dale mused, *she will fold like a sheet*. He didn't smile at the thought, holding his face blank. Instead, he touched the man on his shoulder, long slender fingers barely brushing cloth.

"Let us step outside and give her a moment."

The man nodded and Alan motioned him toward the door. Together they picked their way over the objects littering the floor. Broken dishes, keepsakes, books, all pulled from the shelves by uncaring hands. The only chair on four legs was the one on which Stell still huddled. She stopped rocking and watched them leave the house, her eyes red and raw.

Alan ducked under the lintel and stepped out into the small garden. He had passed by this home just a week ago, and the front had been a riot of color so beautiful that he'd had to stop and compose a short verse. Now it was a churn of mud and crushed petals. He kept the verse in his heart. It would be cruel, not comforting, to share it with Stell and her husband now.

He looked at the stout man who turned in a small, slow circle. A tear tracked down his face as he studied the wreckage.

"Mayhap it will help to tell me what happened," Alan suggested.

"The bastards took my property! In the name of that false king that Richard left behind!" The man's voice was raspy, but loud. It carried out past the small wooden fence that surrounded his home.

Alan looked around sharply.

"Advice, friend," he said. "Keep your voice down with words like that."

The man glared at him. "Are you going to report what I said? If so, then good! Tell that imposter on the throne and his lapdog Locksley," he roared out at the sky and shook his fist. "Terrify my wife, take my things... I'll *kill* someone."

Alan stepped back from the man, who whirled at the movement.

"They've already come to my shop and demanded that I make armor and swords for fifty men, all as a tax! I'm expected to shoulder the cost of the ore, pay the assistant, and do the work. Richard already took almost everything I had on his fool chase across the ocean, but at least he paid for his. This black-hearted brother... that arsehole... just threatens." He spat on the ground.

"And I did it. I made his damned armor and swords and I made them good, put their custom marks on each, even though they demanded them in a time that meant I had to sleep by the forge. But *that* was my tax. *That* was my due. Then they come here, take my personal property, destroy more than they took. It's not right!"

"What did they take?" Alan asked.

"They took my dignity."

"What *property* did they confiscate?"

The smith looked up at nothing, thinking. He began listing things and counting on thick, calloused fingers.

"The gold left from Richard's payment, one third the food in my larder, a pair of new boots I was saving for the Christ mass, all the books my wife had, and an arm ring my dad took off a raiding Northman he killed." He closed his counting fingers and shook the fist they made. "And what they didn't take, they broke."

Alan-a-Dale nodded, letting the man vent his anger.

"I suffered through an apprenticeship under Smythe to learn this trade. Ten long, *hard* years of doing whatever that bastard wanted, all for scraps of bread, a bowl of water, and the ability to learn my craft. Ten years! I'm a craftsman. A *free* man. This is unholy, what's happened to me… and not just me, but all the shopkeeps in the marketplace. This so-called king is a greedy pigsuckler!"

Alan stood in the late afternoon sun beside the blacksmith in his destroyed yard and his upturned home. His heart lay heavy in his chest for the man and his wife, but it sank like a stone in the sea when the man looked up at him with tears cutting tracks through the grime on his cheeks.

"How will we survive this winter?"

The air in the hallway was stifling. The stones beside him radiated heat. It was midday and this was an outside wall. Sweat rolled under his brown woolen robe, skimming along his body until it soaked into the coarse fibers.

We should put in some windows for ventilation. He knew that it would never be done, however. The hall was too low for them to remove stones to allow the air to pass—that would compromise the integrity of the wall itself. Take out even one, and the outside wall became exponentially more likely to crumble under an attack.

An attack. The thought took him back. He still remembered being a child, early in his coming to the service of the Lord. He'd been at a monastery in the highlands held siege by the Sea Wolves, a motley, savage band of raiders and reavers come from the icy north to steal gold and rape women. The only things that saved his life—the lives of all the brothers there, and the lives of the villagers who hid with them—were the walls. Like these they were stout and thick, made of stones pressed tightly together.

The Sea Wolves had howled outside for ten days, drinking their wine and screaming for the monastery to send out the women and the gold. Do that, they said, and they would leave.

With sunrise on the eleventh day they had disappeared. Out of wine, out of food, and out of the berserker madness, they'd silently climbed back in their longboats and sailed away, possibly in shame but probably to hunt for easier prey down the coast.

A noise pulled him from the memory. Voices, and something else. He quickened his steps until he reached a hall that opened into an anteroom. A handful of brothers crowded around a door. The ones not under a vow of silence spoke in a murmur. Each man's face held a similar expression of horror.

They were gathered at the entrance to the monastery's library. The hubbub masked the sound of his approach. He stopped an arm's length away from them.

"What is going on?" he demanded. "Why are you all meandering about?"

As one they jerked around, puppets on the same string. Brother Dobbson moved close. He spoke low, his voice thready with anxiety, his words as halting as a newborn colt.

"Friar... I don't know... I..."

"Spit it out, man!"

Impacts sounded from inside the room.

Brother Dobbson's mouth opened, then closed, then dropped and hung open. Finally he could take it no longer.

"Move aside and let me see." Friar Tuck's wide hand fell on the man's arm, pushing to the left. Shoving forward he barreled through the group. As the last one stepped aside, he saw what had them in an uproar.

The library was in shambles. The handcrafted shelves were near empty, the floor littered with books and scrolls and parchments in oilskin sleeves. All of them were ancient. His eyes found pages torn from their bindings, leather older than the monastery itself cracked and broken from being dragged off the shelves and hastily tossed aside like garbage. These were the collective written knowledge of the order, each book meticulously scribed and bound. Many of them were singular, the only copy of that text anywhere in the world.

They were irreplaceable.

In the center of the room the bishop pulled another book from the shelf, flipped its pages through his fingers, and tossed it unceremoniously to the floor with the rest of them. At the sight of him treating the books so callously rage boiled inside Friar Tuck, and his guts went all greasy and hot. Before he could think he was across the room and his hands were curled around the lapels of the purple robes. Spittle flew from his mouth as he lifted the bishop off his feet and shook him. Fabric tore under his grip.

"What do you think you are *doing*?" he roared.

"Unhand me, barbarian!" The bishop kicked out, feet bouncing off the friar's thick midsection. Tuck shoved the man against an empty bookshelf. The wood cracked under the impact.

"Some of these books are priceless," he growled. "What gives you the right?"

The bishop's fists hammered down on Tuck's arms, striking a nerve on the left. Pain mixed with numbness and shot to the end of the monk's fingers. The bishop's feet touched the ground, and he swung his head forward.

Tuck jerked back, avoiding the impact of the bishop's head against his mouth, but catching some of it on his chin. Stars flared across his eyes, sending the room dark for a moment.

He dropped the man altogether.

Landing on his feet, the bishop lunged forward. Hands up and ready to fight, he tried to punch Friar Tuck in the face. The monk stepped back and the bishop stumbled over a small pile of books on the floor. Tuck winced as the sound of tearing cloth rose up from the man's feet. His hand snarled in the bishop's purple robe, pulling it tight.

The bishop cried out in pain as Friar Tuck swung back a meaty fist with every intention of trying to separate his opponent's head from his shoulders.

"Enough!"

The voice rang into the room. They turned to see the cardinal filling the doorway, lit from behind and radiating righteous anger. The other monks peered in from the doorframe, each struggling for a better view. He strode forward, cassock whipping around his legs as if it were driving him. Tuck's heart surged. Here he had an ally, someone of higher authority who wouldn't be afraid to challenge the bishop's position.

The cardinal glared at Friar Tuck.

"Have you lost your mind?"

The words were a dash of cold water against his face.

"Let him go," the cardinal growled. *"Now."*

Tuck opened his hand. The bishop fell, stumbling back. He caught himself on the wall. Pushing off, he pointed at Friar Tuck.

"The scourge!" he cried. "I want him scourged for daring to lay his hands on me."

The cardinal ignored his words, peering around at the destruction of the library. Then he fixed the bishop with his eyes.

"What are you looking for?"

"That's nothing with which you should concern yourself."

"My family donated the vast majority of these works," the cardinal replied. "I am *very* concerned."

"This is a library, and I am looking for a book," the bishop said, refusing to give ground. "That is enough for you to know."

Behind the cardinal's back Friar Tuck seethed. He glared at the bishop. What sort of a book could he be looking for that would warrant such destruction? Then a sudden sick feeling twisted his innards. He thought of the artifact brought by Alan-a-Dale. Surely he was wrong, though. How would the bishop even know of its existence?

As he stared at the man, his eyes caught a slowly spreading patch of darkness on the bishop's garish, purple robe. It was a mark, a series of lines that intersected in a weird way. His eyes began to water as he watched the purple linen turn dark, fiber by fiber. Then he glanced down at his left hand.

Wet red slicked his fingertips, already drying into a dark rust color.

He looked closer.

The symbol grew and his head began to pound, an incessant marching of soldiers inside his skull as the symbol grew solid. It lay on the bishop's forearm. Anger leeched away as he studied it, committing each line of it to memory even as his eyes began to feel as though they would leap from his skull.

"...I said, *to your chamber.*"

The cardinal's voice jolted him from his reverie. He looked up at his mentor. Francis's face had gone gray, the crow's feet by his eyes now carved deep as if by knife point.

With one last glance at the symbol, Tuck turned and left.

Alan-a-Dale followed the path, feet moving but his eyes not watching, traveling with a mind that churned like a river flowing over falls. His time with the blacksmith and his wife had marked his soul, mostly because it echoed what he had seen in other people who'd been visited by Locksley's tax brigade.

Brigands, more like.

He thought of the grimness that had settled on the land, starting first with the people who had been victimized, and spreading like a pox to their neighbors who simply waited with the dread of when they would receive the knock on their door. The hearts of the people had been bruised and left bleeding.

He pushed the thoughts from his mind, unable to dwell on them any longer, and focused on the one thing brought up over and over again by the homes he'd visited.

They were looking for a book.

No one knew what kind of book, but the thought of it made his shoulders tense. He'd not long ago brought a book into the care and keeping of Friar Tuck. Prince John arrived directly after, and now with force of arms he sought a mysterious tome. Alan was no believer in coincidence.

His dear friend Tuck had much to explain.

Friar Tuck couldn't sit still. He tried to lie down. He tried praying. He tried drinking from a bottle of brandy. Nothing took the edge off the anger that shimmy-jolted under his skin. So instead he paced the small chamber. Four strides from one side to the other, back and forth, again and again and again, each step a nail pounded into his rage.

The bolt on his door bounced against the wood door as someone tried to enter. He turned and reached out, yanking it open. It slammed against the wall.

"*What?*" he bellowed.

Cardinal Francis pushed in, barreling the stout man back.

"Shut your mouth," he said firmly.

Friar Tuck looked up at the taller priest, breath pounding out of flared nostrils and clenched jaw.

"Or what?" he said. "You would strike me, Francis? Be prepared for me to respond in kind."

"Then get it over with, if it will calm you," the cardinal said and he leaned back, arms stretched wide. "If not, then stick your head in a bucket."

For one blind moment Tuck almost did strike out. He could feel the impact of his fist on his friend's chest, feel the ribs compress inward, giving way under the force of his blow, collapsing from his strength. For one long moment temptation dragged at his very bones.

Then he looked at Francis's face.

The cardinal's eyes held no anger, no reproach. Instead they were filled with a simple sympathy, a love that made them soft around their edges as they peered into his soul and understood him.

The eyes of Christ.

He was forgiven before he could strike a blow.

Exhaustion fell on him like an avalanche, all the rage and anger crumbled into dust inside him. The cardinal put his hands on Tuck's shoulders.

"It's all right, my son."

"I'm sorry."

The cardinal chuckled. "No, you are angry and noble, and the two drive you to the same end. One is the horse, the other is the carriage."

"I try to pray it down," Tuck protested. "I truly do."

The cardinal leaned in, his voice a whisper so soft it was almost just a breath. "Don't," he said. "The prayers of a righteous man availeth much, but we may have need of the anger of a righteous man before we finish our time here." He stepped back. His finger moved up, pointing at his own eye, then reaching out to point at Tuck's. "You know you did wrong."

Friar Tuck touched his ears, and the cardinal nodded. Someone could be listening—the small monk's cell wasn't big enough to keep the sound of their voices from carrying.

"It's true," he admitted. "He was destroying things that were irreplaceable. I lost my head."

"He wasn't doing that." The cardinal's voice was stern. "He was searching for a book, for Prince John. You should not have interfered."

"I know. I am truly contrite of heart." Friar Tuck reached to a shelf, pulling down a parchment scrap and a thin piece of charcoal. Placing the parchment on his bench, he wrote, *Did you see the symbol?* Then he held it out. The cardinal shook his head, and Friar Tuck nodded.

"You will have to be punished," the cardinal said.

"I submit to your judgment in this." He quickly sketched the symbol on the parchment. As his fingers moved the charcoal they began to tingle. The lines wavered, squiggling on the thin sheet as he pulled them. His bowels churned, threatening to let go as he pulled the last line and thrust it toward his mentor, wanting it away from him, wanting the foul taste gone from his mouth.

"You will scourge yourself for five Our Fathers." The cardinal's eyes dropped to the scrap in his hand. His face paled, blood draining down his skin and leaving a chalk-white pallor, and he looked as if he was about to retch. He swallowed hard, folded the scrap, and buried it in his pocket.

He crossed himself with a shaking hand.

Are you alright? Friar Tuck mouthed.

Francis nodded and moved his lips. *We'll talk later.* He turned toward the door. Over his shoulder he spoke.

"Scourge yourself, my son. Scourge yourself and offer it up to the Lord as sacrifice for His wisdom and guidance in the coming days."

The door shut firmly behind him.

Tuck stood alone in the small room. After a long moment he untied the belt around his waist and let it drop from his hands. Pulling the hood of his robe he dragged it over his head and allowed it to fall to the floor as well. He stood in his braies, the cool air washing over him, raising gooseflesh across his body.

Head bowed, he reached out, grasping the knotted prayer cord from its peg on his wall. The rope was stiff and dyed dark with his blood, and there was a stain on the wall beneath the peg.

Wrapping the end of it around his fingers, he fell to his knees.

Glynna woke from a deep sleep full of tempestuous dreams. She panted, left that way by a dream lover who had fled back into the mist. The bed beneath her was damp, the sheets in disarray. Her body was tight, swollen and lush, but she felt hollow inside, carved out by unfulfilled desire. She lay for a moment, wondering why she had awakened before she could finish the dream.

Her mind drifted outward.

Someone was coming. Her ability to sense things had grown, becoming stronger each passing day and with each night she spent in front of her altar.

She'd heard no knock, not that she would have from her room. She rose and wrapped a dressing gown around her long, lean frame. Without bothering to light a candle, she made it downstairs and through the darkness to the front door. She leaned against it for a moment and imagined she could feel someone on the other side doing the same. She heard a whispering in her mind, soft, seductive.

Let me in.

She threw back the bolt and opened the door.

A man stood there. No, not a man, more than that—a demigod carved from the night itself. A crown of hair that shone white like the moonlight stood in stark contrast. She knew him from descriptions she had heard.

"Good eve to you, Sheriff of Nottingham," she said.

His mouth twitched at the corner. "And to you, my lady and witch," he said.

She took a deep breath. If it had been anyone else she would have denied it with her last breath, but something about him drew her. She wanted to tell him everything.

"Let me in," he said.

She moved back and he stepped over the threshold. She closed the door behind him. The man turned to her, then closed his eyes for a moment as if listening for something.

"Your son is away and your daughters are asleep." It was a statement, not a question.

"Both my sons are away, as is my husband. I gave the girls something to help them sleep. They haven't rested without aid since one of your men tried to steal my youngest."

He snorted. "Not one of mine. The king's men."

"Is that not the same thing?"

"Was your daughter taken? If you still have her, then it is not the same thing at all." He walked around the room, looking at the furniture and the decorations. His fingers trailed over the table where she kept a bowl of moonwater. The surface of the bowl shimmered as his fingers slid by. She watched him move, examining the items of her family's life. He was completely deliberate, every motion coiled with potential.

The sight of him caused something low in her stomach to clench, and suddenly she was warm and wet beneath her thin gown. The Sheriff turned to face her, closed his eyes and leaned his head back. He took a deep breath through his nose, held it, then exhaled and opened his eyes, pinning her with the intensity of his stare.

"Why have you called me here?"

She shook her head. "I haven't called you."

"Oh, I think you have," he said, taking a step closer.

Drawn like a moth to a dark flame, she moved closer to him, until she stood nearer to him than she had been to any man but her husband in many years.

"What are you?" she asked, reaching out to touch the armor on his chest. Her fingernails clicked on the carapace. She could feel the heat in her belly begin spreading throughout her body.

"I am your new master," he said, looking down at her. He took hold of the edges of her dressing gown and pulled it off her so that she stood before him in all her glory as a woman.

The fire spread faster and she closed the tiny distance left between them, pressing herself full against the cool surface of his armor. His hands slid down her back. The excitement that rose inside her was more intense than any she had ever felt, and she recognized it from her dreams.

"It was you, the day I created my altar. It was you who I worshipped." She knew it, deep down, like she knew the desire that painted the inside of her skin.

"Where is your bedchamber?" he asked.

"No, take me now, do it here," she begged.

"I want to see your altar."

"The room is warded. You won't be able to enter."

"I'm already there. You've already let me in," he said, his voice rough.

She took his hand and pulled him to the stairs. She made it to her bedchamber and was surprised when he crossed the threshold with her.

"Never doubt me," he said.

She led him to the altar and he looked down on it. "Very good," he said, picking up the black statue and holding it for a moment before placing it carefully on another table in the room. With one swift move he swept the rest of the items from the top of the altar.

He looked at her and she could feel his darkness wrapping around her, moving through her and it made her cry out in ecstasy before he lifted her in his arms. He lowered her naked form down upon the altar. She remembered that the day she had made it, it had been his hands she had imagined.

Now there was no need to imagine anything. She opened herself to him and he possessed her fully, taking her on the altar she had built to him. Her eyes rolled back and she screamed as pure darkness pulsed through her.

She didn't care who might hear.

The robe pulled away with a tearing sound as it separated from the wound on his arm. It had rooted, the blood drying into a scab that locked cloth and injury together, and the division of the two burned like fire. Pain circled his arm, spiraling up and into his armpit to stab across his chest and into the organs shielded behind his sternum.

His teeth bit into the leather strap to keep him from crying out. That damn friar had opened the wound. Carefully he pulled the sleeve up and studied what lay beneath.

Dark blood, near black but thin as water, pulsed from the lines carved into his skin. The edges of the cuts puckered, drawn tight by the red heat that surrounded the wound. In deep pockets he could see little balls of yellowish-white. Tiny violet-dyed threads clung to the tacky surface. It throbbed with each beat of his heart.

The source of the wound was Prince… no, *King* John. He had placed a shard of black glass against the arm. It had felt warm against his skin, made so by the hand that held it. John had murmured something that sounded like the buzzing of a swarm of flies. Then, clearing his throat, the king had spoken in a voice that was low.

"This is the symbol inside the book you shall find," he had said. "By this mark you shall know you have gained possession of that which we covet." Tilting his fingers down, the king sank the shard into the bishop's skin, causing it to disappear into his flesh.

He had tried to pull away, to tear free, but the king's grip had become iron, trapping him there to flail at the end of his own arm as his flesh parted like a furrowed field to a plow.

There had been so much blood.

CHAPTER TWENTY-TWO

"Thrice-damned son of a..."

Friar Tuck caught himself before he could finish the curse, but he was furious. Searching through the gold items that belonged to the monastery, he became more and more certain that several were missing.

It had to be the bishop. The toady had stolen away the irreplaceable objects, just to have them melted down to make that scepter for Prince John. It was unthinkable, and he barely managed to hold his tongue. Everything was backward and he reeled at the realization of how quickly things could begin to fall apart.

Change most often was a slow, torturous thing. The last fortnight, though, had thrown everything into chaos. The arrogance of both the bishop and the prince took his breath away. The tax collectors had been out in force for days, and he had heard the cries of the people who did not have the ability to give what the throne was demanding.

Francis had extended his stay, instead of returning to Rome as he had planned. Since his disastrous audience with John, who now called himself king, the cardinal had spent his days and the better portion of his nights on his knees in prayer in the chapel. His devotion was admirable, and though Tuck joined him frequently, his knees could not take the hard stone floor for as long as his friend's did.

The last time they had knelt together Francis had broken his silence for a moment. He had asked Tuck to send word to one or two whom he trusted with his life, and call them to a meeting so they might figure out God's plan for thwarting the evil that was creeping across the land.

Tuck had agreed. He was humbled by the faith the cardinal put in him. He thought long and hard, and in the end only called one other to the meeting. The bard could be trusted with secrets.

This was a truth he knew intimately.

It was with a great deal of fear and trepidation that he entered the cardinal's chambers. Most of the other monks were in the chapel, engaged in evening rituals, and the cardinal had sent the bishop to visit a monastery located a day's journey away.

When Friar Tuck entered the room, two other figures stood with Francis and Alan. They were silent, cloaked, and their anonymity made him fearful.

"Do not worry, good friar," the cardinal said, giving him a gentle smile. "Our guests have more to risk than we do." Tuck nodded and took a seat. After a moment the others did, as well. The cloaked figures both reached up and pulled down their hoods. He was startled to be staring at Maid Marian...

And Will Scarlet.

Tuck lunged across the table, his stool clattering to the floor, his belly driving the furniture forward to bang into his target. Grabbing the man's cloak, he wadded it in his fists. Scarlet cried out in pain and surprise as the big friar yanked him over the table and into his lap. Tuck's arms wrapped around his head as he crushed the smaller man against his chest.

Marian stood quickly, a dagger appearing in her hand. She swayed over the balls of her feet, unsure of what to do.

Alan-a-Dale had both hands on his friend's massive shoulder, trying to move him, but it was futile.

Scarlet kicked, hands pushing on the arms that held him trapped and were smothering him in wool-covered muscle.

The cardinal snatched up the bucket of water that sat by the fireplace and upended it on Friar Tuck's head. The water doused the monk, making him cry out, then spit and sputter. He let go as he wiped dirty water from his face. Scarlet sprawled on the ground, digging in his cloak for the hilt of his sword. His face burned red, a mix of anger and skin burn from the fabric of Tuck's rough wool robe.

Marian grabbed Scarlet by the shoulders, holding his arms while the cardinal stepped in front of the friar.

"Have you lost your mind?" he asked the drenched monk.

"He's Prince John's man!" Tuck replied. "He laid hands on you, and that I will not stand for."

Scarlet snarled. "You fat idiot! I'm not the prince's man, I'm a spy for the cardinal."

Friar Tuck froze, and looked up at the old priest who stood above him.

"Is that true?"

Francis nodded. "It is."

"Then damn me for a fool." Tuck shook his head, letting his hands drop to his side. He looked directly at Will Scarlet. "I'm sorry."

The cardinal patted him on the shoulder. "It's fine, Son of Thunder. It's only a misunderstanding."

"Misunderstanding!" Will shouted. "He tried to tear my head off! That's not a misunderstanding. A misunderstanding is when you don't know that your cloak must be the same color as your boots. This was attempted murder!"

Marian pulled him. "Ease yourself, Will," she said. "He knows now. He won't attack you again." She looked to the monk for confirmation.

Friar Tuck nodded. "I now understand your work, at least in part," he said. "It won't happen again, Will Scarlet."

"If it does," Will said with a growl, "I'll gut you like a... well, like a thing that should be gutted." He jerked away from Marian's hands. "No one lays his hands on me," he muttered, causing her eyes to widen with surprise.

Alan and Marian righted the table, pulling the stools back around. Tension sang in the room as Will sat and Friar Tuck stared. Once they each had taken a seat, the cardinal began to speak.

"We are here to stop a monstrous evil from dragging England into darkness," he said. "A time of strife long ago prophesied is upon us, when the king is absent and demons and creatures from our darkest nightmares will walk the earth. We five have seen the handwriting on the wall, and possess the wisdom to know what it means."

Will shifted uncomfortably and the cardinal turned his eyes on him.

"What is it you wish to say?"

"My grandmother used to speak of demons and monsters and witches," Will responded. "I don't believe in those things. I believe in evil, though—the killing of men and stealing of property. I have been in the king's court for a fortnight, and I see it every time I stare into his eyes."

"You mean the prince, not the king," Marian said, gently yet firmly.

Will waved his hand. "Forgive me, milady," he said. "Habit. Flattery is the one sure thing that gets me close to him."

"And we are grateful for your courage in doing so," Francis said.

"The point is," Will continued, "I don't know these prophecies you speak of. The prince is a man, a greedy, destructive man, but not a demon."

"I mentioned similar concerns," Marian said.

The cardinal put his hands on the table. He took a deep breath. "The signs are not to be found in the scripture. My entire life I have studied the lore of this land. Taliesin wrote a song, an epic, about a vision he had where Avalon fell to the darkness..."

"Who is Taliesin?" Will asked.

Alan-a-Dale leaned forward. "He foretold the coming of Arthur, the occupancy of Rome, the sinking of Atlantis. He was the greatest bard who ever lived, and he has never been proven wrong in his prophecies."

The cardinal tilted his head in acknowledgment of Alan's words. "He wrote about a series of signs and portents, a king going east and leaving his shadow behind, a black splinter that festers in the flesh of Avalon, the splitting of the mighty oak in a bed of ashes. This particular prophecy is also supported by many other sources that have varying degrees of veracity."

Alan tapped the table. "'The Unsingable Song.' I know it. It is only taught to bards once." His face lit up at the idea of new knowledge. "What sources corroborate?"

The cardinal turned to the slim man. "St. Joniesus echoes his prediction about the king leaving his shadow behind to hold his throne, and expands that it is conflict that draws him away and makes him 'fly across the water.' I take it to mean in a ship over the ocean."

"Go on," Alan smiled.

"Merlin warned about the splinter, lamenting that Arthur would not be here to pluck it free and drain the wound."

Alan tapped the table harder. "Yes! In the letter he wrote to Morgana Le Fey before she betrayed him for Mordred. Those lines have always bothered me. It makes sense now."

The cardinal nodded. "The pagan magi Melchior also spoke of the gathering dark and the splitting of the mighty oak. He mentions also the splinter and the shadow, but they are bare asides, unworthy of notice without the inclusion of the split oak."

Alan shook his head. "Melchior—"

The cardinal nodded. "I know. But he cannot be ignored."

Will Scarlet leaned forward, waving his hand between the two men. "If this is true, then what does he want?"

"If the shadow truly claims the throne, then the mighty oak of England is split asunder and laid to waste in a bed of ashes. The splinter festers, poisoning the land and destroying the people. Darkness then spreads to consume all of mankind."

"Then you should stop discussing prophecy and listen to what I have to say."

"What have you learned?" the cardinal asked.

"The Sheriff and the… prince… are thick as thieves, and neither of them has any love for the church. They're planning something big, but the prince has not yet invited me that far into his confidence. More tax money pours in every day, collected by Locksley thugs, but with the exception of the scepter, very little of it is being spent. That much plunder, I would expect him to buy horses, weapons, soldiers. He's vain enough he might even spend it to redecorate the castle more to his liking, pay some artist to paint him and that damned Sheriff as a mural in the throne room. He's done none of that, though, as far as I can tell.

"A wastrel might squander it on elaborate parties while his subjects starve, but he has no love of entertaining himself or others. I think they're stockpiling it for something."

"Do you think it is the prince's plan to usurp the crown?" the cardinal asked.

"Of that much, at least, I am certain."

"It is as we feared then," Friar Tuck said. In some ways it was a relief to have confirmation, even if it was of the worst possibility. He much preferred to know what he faced, than to constantly be fighting shadows. He did enough of that in his dreams.

"Do you know how they intend to accomplish it?" Alan asked.

"Not yet, but I'm working on it," Will said. "It is difficult. The prince trusts me more and more, but the Sheriff trusts no one. He's strange, like no man I've ever encountered."

"I'm not sure he is even a man," Marian said.

No one spoke for a long moment.

"Whatever he is, he must be stopped. They both must," the cardinal said.

"The people are crying out for mercy, but they are finding none," Alan said. "I have gone many places in the last few days. Women weep and men curse. They are overburdened with the taxes, and many have lost the ability to feed their families."

"The prince gloats over similar reports, and proclaims that this is just the beginning," Will offered. "Once he has finished this round, he will be looking for more."

"The tax collectors must be stopped," Marian said. "It is too much on the families."

"Yet the collectors are also men of this community," the cardinal said. "Killing them is not the way."

"Then the money must be returned to the people somehow."

"The nobles also suffer under this new tax, and cannot help the people," Will said. "They are lucky to feed those in their immediate households. More poor will go hungry, then die, if not helped this winter. And the prince still holds the youngest children of the Houses as hostages." He shook his head. "You'll not have support from them unless a total victory can be had."

"If the money the prince is collecting isn't being spent, perhaps there is a way to recover some of it." Friar Tuck thought of the bishop looting the monastery's treasures. "Someone has to steal it back."

Alan leaned forward before he spoke. "No one would dare be so bold," he said. "Any man caught doing so would be hunted down and executed."

"His family, as well, to set an example," Will added, his face paler than it had been a moment before. "It would be public, and gruesome. That is how this prince operates. No half measures. That's why he killed two of the nobles and hanged their families in public."

Around the room each person made the sign of the cross—all except Alan, who simply bowed his head for a moment.

"What we need is a man who is willing to stand up to the prince, perhaps one who has no family, so he has no one to lose," Francis said.

"Everyone has someone to lose," Marian argued. "If not direct family, then dear friends, associates. My own fear—of what he would do to some of the servants—has more than once stopped me from acting."

"And holy men, though long since separated from any family with whom they might have been born, still have brothers of the cloth," Will pointed out.

"Even if we could find a man with nothing to lose, he would have to be willing to risk his own life, to lay it down for the people. That is much to ask of anyone, especially one with no attachments," Marian said. "It is easier to risk your life for those you love than for strangers."

"Greater love hath no man than this, that he lay down his life for his friend," Tuck said.

"We must also remember," Francis said, "that this is more than a simple one-time theft of gold."

"It's true," Will agreed. "The prince will retaliate, take it out on the people, squeeze them harder."

"What we need is someone who can fight back against every injustice and rally the people to his side, someone who can become a symbol for which others are willing to fight," Francis suggested. "Perhaps someone we could even put on the throne, if we managed to remove John." He gazed pointedly at Marian, and she shook her head.

"I will do everything I can to help, but I can't be the public face, the one people rally around," she said. "Those dearest to me would pay the price. Besides, too many of the people are dismissive of me because I'm a woman. I wouldn't be able to rally as many as would be needed."

"Then I'm the logical choice," Alan said.

All eyes turned toward him.

"Based on what you are saying," he continued. "I have no family, no home even. Everything I own I carry on my person."

"You have friends," Marian protested.

"I do, and most of them are in this room. I don't think anyone else actually knows *who* I'd count as a friend. I'm the one who, on the surface of it all, has nothing to lose."

"It's true that you are well-liked, and you have the gift of persuasion in your voice. When you sing you can put people into a trance, change their emotions, rally them to a cause," Francis said thoughtfully.

"Forgive me," Will said, "but Alan is no warrior."

"Who said we needed a warrior?" Francis asked.

"As much as Alan is a logical choice, I'm not sure he is the *right* choice," Marian offered. "Yes, he is beloved, and yes, he can hold sway over people while he sings, but he cannot be singing for everyone all the time. And since he has no home, people will know there is always a possibility that he could leave, if things became too difficult."

"It's the truth," Tuck said. "He has no ties to this place, nothing that would convince others that he might be compelled to stay." He looked sideways at his friend. The bard frowned harshly, but the friar kept talking. "I believe he is of more use if no one knows that he opposes the prince. Indeed, the fact that he has no home is crucial. He could go places as needed, without raising suspicion. He is best used as he is—the bearer of news, the teller of tales."

"I agree, Alan," Marian said. "You have far more value there. Because of your station, no door is closed to you."

Alan nodded, and Tuck could see that he was relieved. It spoke to his character, though, that he had at least made the offer.

"As a spiritual leader I would also be a logical choice," the cardinal said. "Many would heed my words."

"And many monks would die in instant retaliation," Will countered. "The truth is, none of us here can be the symbol we need. We'd risk too much with capture. Each of us has a part of what is needed, yet none of us has the whole."

Suddenly Friar Tuck smiled. A snatch of a song came to him—a song he'd heard Alan sing once before.

"Then the answer is simple," he said. "We should strive to not be captured."

"Even if we are not captured, we will be recognized," Will protested. "Perhaps not you, but everyone knows the face of the bard, the cardinal, and the princess."

Friar Tuck shook his head, his grin broadening.

"When I came in here, I could not tell who either of you were, yet I've known you for many years." He shrugged and leaned back. "We need a champion, the people need a symbol. Who knows what kind of person lurks beneath a hood? It could be anyone. Maybe even someone of legend…"

There was a moment of silence as they all let it sink in.

Marian's eyes glittered in the low light.

A moment later Will began to nod.

"It might work," the cardinal said, "with God's help."

"If we do this correctly, we could all participate, yet make it seem as if every theft has been the work of one man," Marian offered. "A man who is not *any* of us. Who doesn't exist. Like the old children's stories." She turned to Alan-a-Dale. "Surely you know the ones to which I am referring?"

The bard nodded. "For many generations, there have been stories of a hooded bandit in the heart of Sherwood. It's part of the reason people believe the great wood to be full of haints and fey."

"Yes! Exactly," she said, her voice rising. "We could work together to bring back the Hood. Frequently the tax brigade uses the King's Road that runs through Sherwood. We can strike swiftly, and use the forest as a way to escape." Marian shifted on her stool, her eyes wide with excitement. "We will be holy terrors."

Suddenly the cardinal put his hand flat on the table with a smack, causing them all to jump. He glared at her fiercely.

"We are grateful for your counsel, Marian," he said, "but it is too dangerous for you to participate in this activity."

Marian stopped moving, jolted back to the here and now.

Will Scarlet slid his stool back.

"Dangerous?" Marian's voice was low, her words measured.

"No more dangerous for me than for the rest of you." Her hand rose as if she tried to pull in the intensity of her emotions. "I beg your forgiveness, Your Holiness, but when was the last time you held a sword? Alan is unaccustomed to them, as well, and Will is the same size I am. I was trained to fight by Richard the Lionheart himself. At this table, I have the best chance of survival in a conflict."

"The lady has a point," Friar Tuck said.

"And I have just as much to lose as anyone else," she continued. "Perhaps more."

"Will they miss you at the castle?" Francis asked. "How will you explain your absence?"

She shook her head. "John seeks neither my counsel nor my company, and I can be cautious." She leaned in, and peered from each man to the next. "You will not leave me out of this."

There was a long silence, which Friar Tuck broke.

"In truth, we could try to keep you safe behind the castle walls, but that seems like locking you in a box with two serpents just to keep you from skinning your knee," he said. "Soon every man, woman, and child in this country will be in peril, if we don't act against the prince and his mad dog of a servant."

"It is agreed then," the cardinal said. "The five of us shall don the hood, and take back what belongs to the people. I shall set some monks to sew five sets of matching clothes for us... discreetly, of course."

"I shall bring two sets to the castle when next I come," Alan said, nodding to Will and Marian.

"Before many days have passed, the hooded thief shall make himself known," the cardinal said. "Until then, keep watch, and send word if there's anything we need to know."

Will and Marian both nodded. Then the five of them bowed their heads while the cardinal said a prayer.

CHAPTER TWENTY-THREE

The thin fingers that clamped his forearm had a strength that had been earned by countless hours of moving over metal strings, committing to physical memory the notes of melodies that carried the history and law of an entire people.

Friar Tuck looked down at them, then back up to his friend.

"Hold a moment." The minstrel did not let go. "Please."

He nodded and moved to stand by the tall man as the others filed out of the room. At the doorway the cardinal turned, a queer look on his face. Without a word he smiled, made the sign of the cross toward them, and shut the door as he left.

The air in the room grew still.

"Do you think…?" Alan-a-Dale began.

Friar Tuck raised a wedge of a hand, silencing him. He held it there, listening for any indication that the cardinal had stayed by the door. Silence wrapped its arms around them. Satisfied after a long moment the priest lowered his hand.

"Now we may continue." He smiled up at Alan. "You kept me here for a reason."

"I did." Alan removed the hand, moving it up to run it through his own thick, sandy locks. "Two of them, actually. I've discovered in visiting several homes that the taxpayers aren't just collecting taxes. They're looking for something—a specific object. A book."

Friar Tuck crossed himself. "The bishop was looking for a book, as well, in the library here at the monastery."

"Are you pondering what I'm pondering?" Alan asked.

Tuck crossed himself again. "I do not know," he said, and there was doubt in his voice. "It seems more than just coincidence."

"To me as well. Whatever is in that book, I think the prince wants it."

"Which means he cannot have it." He thought for a long moment, and then added, "I should take a look, and see if I can figure out what it is he wants. That might help reveal some of his plans."

"Very true," Alan said. "Now, as to the second thing, we need to discuss what just occurred here."

"Oh." Wide shoulders slumped under brown wool. "That." He shrugged. "Well, it seems as if we've just started a revolution."

"Yet it seems like the rantings of fools and idiots," the bard said. "We are all doomed if we continue past the discussions of this evening."

"What the hell are you talking about?" Heat rushed through Tuck, the skin around his tonsure blasting bright red.

"Listen to me, my friend," Alan said, in a calming voice. "This is not a revolution. Tonight was just five angry fools, planning their own deaths. There is no chance that we can succeed."

Friar Tuck sputtered. "I thought I'd seen all the sides of you, Alan-A-Dale. I've never before seen a cowardly one."

"You still haven't, my fat friar." The bard drew himself up to his full height, stretching his frame the way he did when addressing a large crowd. The lamplight in the room threw his shadow against the wall, splattering it over the bricks. "Put away your anger and listen to me. Whatever you find in the book, we should not—*cannot*—use magic to fight this foe."

"On that we are agreed. Magic always comes with a cost. I have discussed that on more than one occasion with Cardinal Francis. I fear the price would be far too high. We are speaking of very powerful magic, after all."

"At least we are in agreement on that," Alan said. "Now hear the rest of what I have to say."

Friar Tuck crossed his arms and fell silent, yet he still glowered. Alan reached out, not touching him, just letting his long, delicate hands hover toward him.

"This plan will not work," he continued. "Not with the people who are involved. I am a student of history. As I said around that table, this has all happened before. And it has failed, time and time again." His hands dropped. "We need a man, a hero—a *real* hero—or we are all dead."

"A hero?"

"Yes. We need a Cu' Chuliann, a Finn MacCool, or a Lugh the Longhand. We need the extraordinary. What we have now are an old man, two children, a fat priest, and a man more suited to love than war."

The monk pointed a thick finger in Alan's face.

"You spend too much time in your stories, bard. There are no such extraordinary heroes, no legends, and there is no need for them. Ordinary people create change. I have an entire book that teaches us how a handful of ordinary fishermen turned the world on its ear."

"Ha! Ordinary," the bard replied. "How far do you think your church would have got if not for Peter, and after him Paul? Those were not ordinary men." Alan shook his head. "You forget how much of your book you've taught me. Peter was gifted with incredible amounts of sheer, stubborn will that enabled him to achieve his goals. You are mule-headed, but you are no Peter. I'm sorry. And the apostle Paul was a miracle, a convert who had the perfect tools of persuasion and the physical fortitude to survive beatings and prison and *still* convince people to follow him to a new religion."

Alan stepped close. "You had *hundreds* of Christians in the upper room, and yet you only ever hear about a handful. You only ever hear about the heroes."

He stepped back and dropped his arms.

"If we don't have a hero, this movement will die and we will all lose our heads."

Marian rode away from the monastery, relieved that something would be done to address the suffering of the people. Yet they needed to do more than that. They needed to fashion a plan—a plot to displace John, once and for all. The usurper was the problem, the manifestation of the sickness that was lodged in the heart of England. Stealing a few shipments of coins and material goods wouldn't be enough.

Lost in her thoughts as she skirted the edge of the woods, she didn't notice the man standing just inside their shadow. Not until he strode out in front of her. Startled, she jerked the reins and her horse reared. When the animal's hooves crashed back to earth she prepared to send him running.

Then she recognized Robin Longstride, staring up at her.

"I never meant to startle you," he said.

"It was my fault," she replied, recovering her composure, "for not being more mindful of my surroundings."

"It has happened to me once or twice."

"What are you doing out here?" she asked.

"Hunting."

Her eyes roved over him. The leather pants he wore fit well. *Very well.* His tunic was loose around his shoulders and gaping at the chest. A dirk the length of her forearm hung from his belt, and on his back he had both quiver and bow.

"So near dark? What game do you hunt?"

He stared at her. This close, his eyes looked near black, alive with a glittering intelligence that sparked at her subtle challenge. The long look pressed against her skin. With each moment that passed it grew, spreading under the clothes that hugged her so closely.

His gaze was intimate. So intimate that the need to move, to shift, to relieve the pressure of it swept over her. It was only her will—the fire in her belly from her mother's blood—that held her still in her saddle.

A tiny smile tugged the corner of his full bottom lip and the pressure broke, trickling down her body to dissipate, though not disappear. His voice was so quiet when it came that it barely carried over the short space between them.

"You would ask that." She didn't know how to respond, and he looked up before she could. "Would you care to walk with me for a while?"

She knew she should get back to the castle, but, as she had told the others, it was unlikely that she would be missed. She nodded and accepted his help in dismounting. The touch of his hand on her arm sent a thrill through her. When she was on the ground he removed it, and instantly she missed it. He looped her horse's reins over its head, and led him while they walked, side by side.

"How have you been?" she asked.

"Tired, but sleep is a terrible prey to hunt." He chuckled and it warmed her. "So I am out in the forest, struggling to come to terms with all of the changes in my life."

"The taxes?" she asked, as it was uppermost in her mind.

His features hardened. "They haven't yet come to Longstride manor."

She didn't like the look in his eyes. "Please, Robin, don't do anything rash."

He took a deep breath. He wanted to tell her about the man buried on his land. He couldn't. It would endanger her.

And she was a woman of kindness, not weakness, but a gentleness that soothed him. If she knew he had killed, much less how he'd done it...no.

He moved on. "That's what my father would say."

"I'm sorry."

"No, it's fine," he replied, and he relaxed a bit. "Truth is, I didn't really appreciate him or his perspective until I had to plow a mile in his shoes."

"Is it difficult to have him gone?"

"Even more than I would have imagined. I don't know how he has the patience for it all." He shook his head, a lock of dark hair falling across his eyes. "I'm not like him."

"That's not a crime, you know," she said softly.

"*He* thought it was." They walked along, not speaking for a moment. "I wish he was here now to tell me. I miss him, much as I wouldn't have believed it."

"He'll come back to you," she said, "and you are fortunate in that. I miss my parents every day, knowing that I'll never see them again."

"I'm careless to be complaining," he said. "I didn't mean to cause you distress."

"You didn't," she said quickly. "There's just... so much on my mind lately."

Silence fell between them again. For a moment she wanted to take him into her confidence, tell him what she and the others were planning. She was sure he would approve. She stopped herself, though. It wasn't her decision. She couldn't risk it, no matter how much she wanted to.

A rustling in the brush just ahead of them interrupted her train of thought. Robin was instantly alert. He tossed her the reins and slung his bow off his shoulder. The horse shied away from the sudden movement, and she had to hang onto the reins to keep it from bolting. Robin stepped forward, a long arrow at half draw.

From the side of the road burst a small dark shape. It flew across the gap as if it had been flung, running and tumbling to the other side. The horse started again, yanking Marian a step backward.

From the same part of the brush a wolf leapt onto the road. It landed on three paws, one of its front legs a ragged stump. Dark fur bristled along the hump of its shoulder as it turned toward them and bared yellowed fangs. It growled, tongue lolling out of a muzzle shot through with gray. The horse reared at the sight of it, pulling the leather straps through her hands, burning them in a sharp line. She held on, but barely, her eyes not on the horse but on Robin.

He ran forward, taking four long strides to put him squarely between her and the predator. It hopped on its three legs, growling loudly. Robin pulled and loosed the arrow laid across his bow. It flew swift and straight, thudding into the ground under the wolf's low-slung chest, striking so hard that the vibrating shaft smacked it across the muzzle.

The wolf snorted and jerked its head, hopping backward. It sneezed and looked up at Robin, who already had another arrow ready to fire.

"Go on and get," Robin said. "Don't make me kill you, old-timer."

The wolf looked across the road where its prey had disappeared, and then back again.

Robin took another step.

The wolf dropped its tail and barked once, sharply. It turned and bolted in the direction from which it had come.

Marian dragged the horse over to Robin as he walked to the arrow sticking from the road, plucked it free, and dropped it into his quiver.

"You didn't kill it."

"It was a lone wolf, old and crippled and expelled from his pack. He was just trying to eat. That's not worth dying over." Something passed over his face—a sadness. "Not worth killing over."

"What was it chasing?"

"I couldn't see. Perhaps a rabbit?"

Soft, mewling cries, and then a growling whimper, came from beneath a blackberry bush.

Robin hopped off the edge of the road and waded through the underbrush a few steps. Locating the sound, he parted the branches of a bush, stopped, and stared for a long moment. Before she could ask what he saw he stood up with a baby fox in his hands. The tiny creature wriggled and whimpered and her heart went out to it.

"His mother would never have birthed her kits this close to the road," Robin said. "He must have wandered off by himself, perhaps looking for her."

"You think something has happened to her?"

"There's no way to know, but he won't survive on his own. He's too young. Too small."

"I'll take him," Marian said impulsively.

Robin looked at her. "Are you sure?"

"Yes. We've had enough orphans in these parts. I won't see another."

"Have you ever raised a wild creature?"

"Once, as a child. This one will be wanting milk and warmth."

Robin handed her the tiny squirming ball of fur. She stroked him for a few seconds and held him close to her body for warmth. Within moments he had relaxed and fallen asleep.

"You're a natural mother," Robin said, his voice respectful.

"We shall see."

Robin straightened and cleared his throat. "You should be getting back. It will be full dark soon."

She nodded.

He held the fox and steadied her horse while she mounted. Once she was settled, he handed her the creature, which she carefully tucked into an inner pocket of her cloak. Then he gave her the reins.

"I might stop by the castle sometime," he said, then he added with a subtle smile, "to check on the little fox, of course."

"I'd welcome you any time," she answered, feeling herself blush. "For the fox's sake."

"Be safe on the road."

She nodded but made no motion to begin riding away. Again she felt the urge to tell him of her plans, but again she refrained. Robin had enough of his own worries trying to manage the manor in his father's absence. She didn't need to be adding to them.

"If there is anything I can do to help you," she said instead, "please just ask."

He smiled up at her, a full, dazzling smile that took her breath away. He didn't say a word, just let go of her horse and took a step back into the forest. He gave her a little salute, and she urged her horse forward.

Don't spoil the moment. Don't look back. Don't.

She turned and looked back. He was gone, disappeared into the forest from whence he'd come.

Chastity was waiting for her when she arrived at her room.

"You were gone a long time," the girl said. There was no disapproval in her voice—just curiosity.

Marian trusted Chastity with her life, but she didn't want to pull her in too deep. She couldn't risk putting her friend in danger. If she kept this plan from her, though, it would be the first time in years that she hadn't shared a confidence. So she reached inside her cloak and pulled out the baby fox, which looked up groggily.

"Look what I have found."

"Oh, he's adorable," Chastity cooed. "Will you keep him?"

"Yes. I need to get him some milk."

"I will go fetch you some supper and bring your milk," Chastity said. "Then we can talk all about it."

"All about what?" Marian's breath caught in her chest.

"About how you met Robin in the woods," Chastity said with a smirk.

Marian allowed herself a smile. "I do believe you are a mind reader."

"No, but I am a face reader, and yours is an open book."

Oh, Marian thought, *that may not be the best thing.*

By the time Chastity returned with the food and some milk for their new arrival, Marian had changed clothes. The baby fox sat on the bed watching everything with wide eyes. She thought she might have to soak a rag with milk, in order for him to suckle, but when Chastity set down a saucer he attacked, pouncing on the meal and able to drink it himself.

"So, shall we call your new pet Robin?" Chastity teased.

Marian rolled her eyes. "I can hardly do that. How would it look?"

"Well, then, what shall he be named? Lord Fox?"

"Too simple. Lord of the Greenwood?"

"Och, princess, that's quite a mouthful when he needs chastised."

"Perhaps." Marian tapped her chin with her finger. "I think for now I will call him Champion."

The fox looked up as if responding to his name, and she smiled. Heaven knew the kingdom needed a champion right now.

"Champion, Lord of the Greenwood," Chastity said, softly stroking the russet fur. "Long may he protect us all."

CHAPTER TWENTY-FOUR

The dirt under his feet was so hard-packed that no dust came off it as he walked, putting one foot in front of the other. A bead of sweat hung on the end of his nose, shaking with each breath. He watched it as a way to pass the miles from the mill to his appointed delivery spot, losing himself in the mesmerizing shimmer, counting to himself how many steps the drop would hold and when it fell, as they all invariably did, how many steps until another formed.

"Ho, boy! No need to go further. We can take that up for you."

Much turned at the booming voice, looking over the edge of the road and out into the field. Two men moved toward him, having left a team of horses behind. One man was older than his father, lean as a leather strap and looking twice as tough.

The other was a giant.

Much smiled as they drew near and lowered the crossbeam that held bags of meal and flour. Old Soldier put a hand on his arm, iron fingers squeezing the muscle. Pain shot through him, but he stood straight and didn't flinch.

"I swear, we could unhitch that team, put you in their place, and not miss a step," the grizzled old man teased.

Heat colored his cheeks. He pointed at the giant.

"He's the one you should strap into the harness. Little John can out-pull two horses easy. I saw him do it at the Beltane festival last year."

Little John threw his head back and laughed. "You were there?"

Old Soldier spat on the ground. "Everyone was there and you know it, you big lummox."

Little John raised his arms and flexed. Biceps the size of melons bulged against the short sleeves of his light tunic.

"Not everyone has heard of the Mighty John."

"Your head is bigger than your muscles."

Much basked in the warmth of their companionship, listening as the two men joked with each other in easy camaraderie. Deep in his heart he longed for a friendship like that, someone who wouldn't anger at a humorous insult, and would be there in times of need.

Little John reached down, grasping the crossbar in one hand and lifting it to his shoulder. Much had to pull his mouth closed at the sight of it. He knew exactly how much those bags weighed—nearly as much as he did. To see a man lift them as if they were empty shocked him. Silhouetted by the setting sun, Little John looked like a carving of Ogimos, god of strength and eloquence.

Suddenly there was silence, and a tension cut the air, drawing Much's eyes leftward to Old Soldier. The man's face had closed like a fist and his hand lay across the hilt of the dagger shoved into his belt, fingertips almost casually wrapped round it. His voice darted out, low and quick.

"See to, Little John. Stop acting a fool."

The giant looked down, and the grin plastered on his face cracked and broke and crumbled into his beard. He and Old Soldier both peered in the same direction. Much turned to look where they did.

Down the road came a company of mounted men, thirty strong. His eyes picked out the line of swords on all their hips, and many carried halberds or lances—even a poleax or two. As they drew near he recognized Lord Locksley at the head of the retinue, wearing his bright blue tabard over gold brazed mail. The men directly behind him were other nobles, and behind them rode a contingent of guards.

"What is this?" Little John said, watching them draw near. He looked at Old Soldier. "Do you think this is from the other day?"

Old Soldier leaned close to Much, so close he could feel the old man's breath on his face.

"Can you run?"

Much nodded.

"Then fly over that field and tell Lord Longstride that company is coming." He spat on the ground. "Bad company."

The door rattled in its frame, wood jarring against wood and sounding like thunder. The noise rolled through the house.

Glynna Longstride stepped into the great room, drying her hands from washing vegetables for the evening dinner. A thin, salmon-colored shift clung to her chest and stomach, sucking close to her skin with the water from the washing. She had been daydreaming, absentmindedly performing her task as she thought about the Sheriff. She accepted the sensation of wet linen against her skin, enjoying it and adding it into the texture of her reverie.

There was no servant to get the door—all of the house staff were out in the field. She pushed down the surge of annoyance that threatened to fill her chest.

The door rattled again as her hand fell on the latch. She jerked back, startled, the sound vibrating the air around her.

"Who knocks so fiercely on my door?" she cried.

A voice came through the door, muffled but familiar. "A duly appointed vassal to the king."

Through the wood she felt someone with whom she was familiar. She gripped and lifted the heavy bolt, sliding it from the iron ring in the doorframe and back into its oiled housing. Swinging the door open she spoke.

"Merl? What is the meaning of...?" Her voice died as she

saw the armed retinue of men lined up behind Locksley. His face softened as he saw her.

"We are here to collect the taxes for your household," he said, and he looked down at her collarbone, unable to hold her gaze. Then his eyes dropped even lower.

"We already gave to the war effort," she said. She pulled her shoulders back, standing proud without covering up. "My husband, a large portion of our belongings, and most of our people."

His voice dropped, low enough to not be heard by the other men at the front of the porch.

"This is different, *Gealbhan.*"

"*Do not* call me that." Her eyes narrowed. "I'm not your sparrow."

Red rushed to his face as he met those stormy eyes. He stared at her for a long moment, clearly admiring the line of her jaw, the curve of her neck. It was as if she could read his every thought— not that he was going to any great lengths to hide them from her.

Without turning, he spoke to the men behind him. "Search it all, take one third of anything with value, and remember to look for any books."

The men moved forward, pressing in. Glynna stumbled back. As they approached the door, some of the men stared at her, raw lust washing over their faces, turning their sneers into leers. And in that moment she understood all too well.

They will take everything.

Everything but what she held most dear. She trusted in the wards to hold on her room. She felt a slight moment of fear at the mention of the book. It couldn't be hers, could it? No one knew she had it, not even the Sheriff. Something inside her held it back from him, though she felt no guilt.

Lila. Lila might know about the book from the days when it had belonged to Glynna's mother. White-hot anger flared through her at the thought that a servant would have the audacity to betray her. Then she tucked the thought away.

She'd deal with Lila later.

There was a rush of sound behind her. Before a single invading foot could cross the threshold Robin was simply there. He appeared from nowhere, just suddenly moving past her. He twisted, kicking out with a muddy boot. The door slammed shut and someone outside howled, their fingers too slow to prevent being crushed by the impact. Leaning against the rough planks, he threw the bolt.

The door shook as fists pounded from the outside.

He turned, gripping her arms. His hands left smears on her smock. His eyes blazed in their sockets, teeth showing white in his dirt-covered face.

"That won't hold them long," he said urgently. "Gather the girls and anyone else who is here and go out the back before they get there. Don't return until after the sun rises again."

She nodded, taking in his words, understanding them. Yet she didn't move to comply, wrestling inside herself. Did she have enough power to stop these men?

Not without preparation. Not without ritual.

He shook her. "Go! It won't take them long to begin circling the house. Get your children to safety."

She nodded, blonde hair falling around her face.

Robin looked past her. "Go with her and help her."

She turned and saw the miller's son standing at the doorway to the hall. He didn't speak, just nodded vigorously. Moving forward he reached out and took her arm. His hands were far stronger than she would have expected.

"It'll be alright, milady," the boy said. "He'll take care of this." He didn't look at her when he spoke, though, tugging on her arm.

One thought ran through her head.

I always thought he was slow.

Looking at her son one last time, she allowed herself to be led around the corner.

* * *

Robin moved to the mantle of the fireplace. His fingers slipped across his bow on its pegs. Its yew seemed to grow warm as it called to him, an old faithful friend.

Reluctantly he pulled away from it and reached past, his hand closing on the leather-wrapped handle of an ancient hurley bat. It had been in his family for generations, passed down from father to son. The wood had cracked but never split, the ash grain worn smooth from hundreds of clashes on the field of a sport that was a cross between a child's game and murder.

He pulled it from its place.

"We cannot get through. The door is too stout!"

Locksley glared at the man, a landowner from the edge of the kingdom. He was like his holding, small and barren of any true value. His property had passed to him simply by dint of the fact that no one else wanted it. He was just a freeman with aspirations and a plot of rocky soil.

The other men stood back. One of the guards began to hack away with a poleax. Chips of wood fell into a pile at his feet, but because each swing caused the haft to strike the planks of the porch under his feet, he wasn't able to wield the long weapon effectively.

"Circle the house," Locksley said. "Find another way in."

The small noble nodded. He moved off to begin relaying Locksley's order. The remaining men turned and shuffled, moving off the porch and spreading to either side of the stone structure. Their feet stomped through flowers and herbs planted in shallow beds, trampling them and crushing the petals into the soil. Being shut out had turned their mood black.

Locksley watched them closely.

I should take command, rein in their anger before they destroy this house. His mind went back to a summer night, long ago in his childhood. A night he'd left his home and traveled across the county to see a flaxen-haired maiden. He'd been smitten, and neither the distance nor the late hour had dissuaded him. Her father was overbearing in his watchfulness, but a sound sleeper. Middle of the night rendezvous had been the way of their courtship.

He'd pulled his horse short of the field of clover where they would meet, wanting to slip quietly through the wood and surprise her in the moonlight. When he arrived, he found her in the arms of another. The two of them were like liquid moonlight made human, their fair hair and pale skin gleaming in the night.

He said nothing then, and he said nothing now. The men under his command stopped moving around the house with a clash of metal on metal, jerking him from his reverie. He stretched to see what was happening.

The men were being pushed back by a few farm hands and servants. A motley crew, they'd come around the side of the house, rushing toward his men with locked shields. The shields themselves were a mangled lot, dented and rusted, any paint long ago chopped away. The styles ranged a century at least, from one made of thick wood planks to a bronze scutum left behind by some Roman legionnaire to a few rough kite shields of hammered steel.

The men wielding them were just as mismatched. An old man, an impressive giant holding two of the shields, a handful of boys too young to have been taken to war, one woman stout enough to hold back two of his men, and a lone field hand hunched of spine but strapped with muscle from hard labor.

Only the old man held a weapon.

"What are you doing?" Locksley demanded loudly. His voice tore out of him, roaring out over the clash and the din. "Put them down, or I'll have you all lashed! We are agents of the king's authority."

His nobles and soldiers lunged forward, driven by his command. One of them thrust a halberd between the shields and pried an opening that the rest shoved through, splitting the line. His men stumbled past, turning left and right as they drew their swords.

The back of his neck itched as air passed over it.

The planks shook under his feet. He threw himself sideways, shoulder hitting the boards as a hurley crossed the space where his skull had just been. He rolled, stopping in a crouch, sword halfway drawn from its scabbard.

Robin stood in front of the door, hurley in hand and swinging back for another try. The planks still vibrated where the boy had dropped from the roof of Longstride Manor. He was bare-chested, filthy from the waist up, his dark hair matted with dirt. He looked like an ancient Pict—dark, savage, and full of murder.

The club swung again as he growled like an animal.

"Never threaten my family!"

Locksley twisted away, rolling on his knee and up to his feet in one smooth motion. His sword came out in his hand. As he lifted it, the hurley clanged off the flat of the blade, jolting a shock of pain all the way to his elbow. He held onto the weapon, but just barely. Swinging from his shoulder instead of his numb arm, he flailed out, opening some distance between him and Robin.

"Stand down, boy," he bellowed. "We're just here for the taxes."

Shoulders drawn tight, hands white-knuckled around the end of the club, so angry that his hair stood on end like a wild animal raising its hackles, Robin Longstride redoubled his efforts. He looked swollen, inhuman, his hatred driving his every movement.

Locksley took a step back.

He's going to make me kill him.

Robin lunged, hurley back and over his head, ready to fall like a boulder and smash and crush and grind into dust.

Locksley drew back his sword.

A cry broke the tension like a stone through glass.

They both turned.

The defenders of Longstride manor had been subdued, taken by sheer numbers and force of arms. The cry had come from one of the lads who lay face down in the dirt, his arm twisted viciously up and behind him in an angle the Creator had not designed it to go. Five men held Little John to the earth. Four held the woman.

The only one left on his feet was the old man wearing mail.

He hunched over, blood dripping from his mouth. His sword lay far from his reach behind a handful of soldiers who circled him. Still he moved, keeping them in sight, a wounded wolf more dangerous for his injury.

"If you keep fighting, we will kill them," Locksley said.

Robin glared at him.

"I would be justified in ordering their deaths," Locksley continued. "There would be no repercussion to me."

The boy looked from him to his men and back again. He swallowed, and it sounded as if he were choking. His voice rattled out of him as if each word had been strangled as it passed his lips.

"If we stand down, no harm will come to them?"

"Lord Longstride, we will still fight for you," the old man cried.

The giant struggled even more.

Locksley's gaze never moved from Robin. "On my honor. Cease and desist and they may leave here unharmed."

Robin's body vibrated. The hurley dropped to the end of his arm, thudding against the porch. He waved his other hand.

"Do not fight any longer," he said loudly. "Leave be."

Locksley's men looked to him for guidance. He nodded once, up and down. Slowly they stepped back, releasing Robin's men. The woman and giant leapt to their feet, their faces matched in twin snarls, their hands up in fists. The boys scurried toward one another, the two comforting the one whose arm now hung limp from his shoulder.

The old man picked up his sword, holding it naked in his hand. "What now, Lord Robin?"

Robin's eyes blazed.

"Let them take what they want."

"Your king appreciates your service," Locksley said with a sneer on his face and his words drawn out. "Now piss off before I have you arrested for resisting the tax brigade."

Robin stared at him for a moment, and Locksley tensed again, fearing a new assault. The boy just walked away.

CHAPTER TWENTY-FIVE

Alan's heart was heavy. He was traveling once again to see some who'd been paid a visit by Locksley's tax collectors. He still worried about the men searching for the book, and the revolution Tuck and the others wanted to start.

He needed to free his mind, to center himself.

His thoughts rolled over into song, composing all he had seen and heard into verse and melody. It began to flow inside him, his refuge the music itself. His feet stepped to the rhythm of the song in his head.

Then he stopped short.

The rhythm wasn't coming from inside him. No, it echoed through the green of Sherwood. Pinpointing its direction, he stepped off the path and began moving through the undergrowth, making his way deeper into the gloom.

The hurley cracked, splintering down its length in his hands. The rock against which he'd beat it remained unchanged. Robin Longstride grunted out his rage.

His fingers jammed into the crack in the ashen bat, pulling the two halves apart. Splinters drove into the calluses on his fingertips and palms, but he didn't notice, or care. Pulling across his chest, muscles taut with the resistance, he ripped the halves from the leather binding of the handle, tossing one, then the other. They flew through the forest in two directions. One struck a tree somewhere in the gloom, clattering tempered wood against living. The other simply disappeared, swallowed up by the darkness.

Leaping, he clambered up the rock like a feral creature. At the top he stood tall on its edge, looking over the glens and the hollows of Sherwood.

"Are you quite finished?"

He whirled, one hand clenched in a smashing fist, the other curled into a claw.

Alan stood on the other side of the outcropping, arms crossed, leaning against the stone behind him. The harp on his shoulder lay high, near his cheek, and he had tilted his head so that his face rubbed the smooth polished wood.

"How did you sneak up on me?"

The bard chuckled, keeping his face angled down.

"I am the last of my kind," he replied. "The Learned Brotherhood. We know the forest well, and it knows us."

"You are a bard, not a druid."

"All bards are druids... but not all druids can become bards."

Robin stared at him for a long moment. "Shove your riddles up your arse. What do you want, music man?"

"I am idly curious as to what that hurley bat did to deserve such brutal treatment."

The air between them crackled as Robin took a step forward.

"Are you mocking me?"

"Not in the mood for humor then," Alan said. The bard raised his hands but did not step back. "Well, then, let's see what reaction you have to this?" He paused for effect, then said, "Locksley."

Robin did not reply. Hands clenched in fists, he shook where he stood, caught between the struggle for control and rage. Alan stepped back, making distance. The darkness in Robin's eyes made him suddenly unsure if his status as a bard would protect him.

As the silence stretched on, he slowly reached up and undid the latches on his harp, sliding it over to his cheek. Fingers moving softly, he strummed the strings, calling forth a slow, sullen lullaby. The music tumbled out and rolled across the top of the leaf-strewn outcropping they occupied, a cool stream to quench a raging fire, lapping into its edges, pushing it down and down, smothering it oh so softly, oh so delicately.

Robin stopped shaking.

Alan hummed along with the melody, providing a grounding element to the song, a richness to the tune.

Robin's hands opened. He blinked, looking at the bard.

"Thank you," he said.

Alan strummed the harp one last time with a flourish, drawing the tune to a close.

"Would you like to learn how you can do something about Locksley and the tyranny of Prince John?" he asked, and Robin stared at him with new interest.

The scrap of parchment sat on the other side of the table. Even though it was surrounded by a circle of blessed salt and anointing oil, Francis could feel the symbol like grime on his skin. It was the one which Friar Tuck had given him, the symbol he had seen appear on the bishop's arm.

Francis had kept it, pondering the meaning, wondering why it had appeared on the other man.

He was using the scrap to test himself. It was a game, a contest to not snatch it up and burn it, to cleanse it in fire. He was being prideful, betting that his faith was stronger than the call of evil.

Dear God hold me fast.

Thoughts ran through him, chasing one another.

Why did the prince seek the relic?

Why did the bishop have this symbol carved into his skin?

What could that do to a man's soul?

Was the bishop willing… or coerced?

Was the prince given over to the forces of darkness, or was he their pawn?

The relic, a book bound in the skins of Christian martyrs, had been hidden. Safe. Or was it? The prince sought it, and had unleashed Locksley to root through the land. Now John had conscripted the bishop himself to search the monastery.

He crossed himself, murmuring the Lord's prayer.

Something fluttered, drawing his eye. The parchment had unfolded, the symbol now open to the air. It was darker than before. The charcoal looked wet, glittering in the candlelight.

Ave Maria…

His heart began to pound in his chest.

I am a prideful fool… Sweat rolled under his robe as he stared at the symbol. The light in the room dimmed.

Please save me from my arrogance.

Someone knocked on the door. It was just enough to break the hold. His chair fell to the floor with a crash as he leapt to his feet. His movement sent a small puff of air across the table. It struck the parchment, flipping it over and into the puddle of oil. The blessed liquid rushed through the thin skin, soaking into it. The charcoal broke free of its now slippery mooring and smeared, sliding through the oil in tiny streaks until the symbol was ruined, becoming an obscure smudge.

He crossed himself, fingers hitting hard on shoulders, skull, and breastbone, as he murmured a prayer of thanks and moved toward the door. Opening the wicket he found Alan-a-Dale staring back at him. He closed the wicket and opened the door, ushering him in. Then his eyes went wide.

Close behind came Robin Longstride.

He closed the door behind them and threw the bolt.

The bard swept the room with sharp eyes, taking in the oil-soaked parchment, the double rings of salt and oil, the overturned chair.

"Is everything alright, Father?" he asked anxiously.

The cardinal waved the question away, not wanting to answer it. He looked pointedly from Alan to Robin and back again.

"You have brought a friend."

"I have."

"It is always good to see any of the Longstride family. However, I wonder what reason you might have for bringing him here?" His brow wrinkled in a frown.

"I believe he is perfect for our plan."

The cardinal felt his face turn hard. "You keep a secret well, Alan-a-Dale."

"I've told him nothing."

"You've revealed that there is a plan."

Alan smiled.

"Well, there is that."

Locksley's men had left the place in shambles. As Glynna picked through the rubble in the kitchen her rage only grew. A step at the door caused her to turn. Lila was coming inside, walking carefully, her face filled with dismay as she looked around at the broken pottery.

"You! You told them about my book, didn't you?" Glynna demanded, striding forward and grabbing Lila by the hair.

Lila cowered before her. "I don't know what book you mean," she said, putting her hands up.

As if she could protect herself from me, Glynna thought contemptuously.

"The book of the craft that my mother left me," she hissed.

Lila's eyes grew wide and round. "I never... I never told *anyone* about that."

"Liar!" Glynna bent down and wrapped both hands around the woman's throat. She felt power coursing through her arms as she squeezed, beginning to choke the life out of the other woman. The more she squeezed, the more powerful she felt. Lila thrashed about, batting at her with useless hands as her face changed color.

"You knew about the book?" she demanded, easing the pressure a little.

Lila nodded, still struggling to breathe.

"My mother used it, didn't she?"

Again she nodded.

"And yet you never told me about it, or about her!" She hurled the accusation as she squeezed even tighter. A wicked laugh bubbled up within her and she did not deny it. This was power, real power. She held the choice of life and death in her hands. Her choice.

Her strength.

Her will.

Dark Lord take this sacrifice.

And then the light faded out of Lila, as though she were a candle that had simply been snuffed.

Glynna dropped her on the floor beside her. Black energy crackled between her fingers, tracing little shocks up her arm. The world was clearer, sharper, everything connected to her through her senses. Her tongue tingled as she tasted the air, suckling the scents from it. She looked down at the corpse of her servant and saw the bones of her.

"You were always a terrible cook," she said.

Robin knew what had to be done. Cardinal Francis and the rest, they were insane—but they weren't wrong. Morning dawned, and he had been up all night thinking about what they had told him.

He had finally come to a decision. His father had a distant cousin who lived in Scotland, the lord of a very small manor there. In the morning he would send Becca and Ruth. He would send their mother, as well, if he could persuade her to go. It would be safer for all of them, far from the prince or the Sheriff's reach. Freed from worrying about them, he could act as his conscience dictated.

He'd send Old Soldier and Little John to watch over and protect them. That way they'd be safe, too. Perhaps he would send away the entire retinue. Then, by God's beard, nothing could hold him back.

A quarter turn of the glass later he found his sisters in the stable, feeding treats to the horses as they so often did. He watched them for a moment from the shadows. It felt as if he'd been doing that all his life. Mother had discouraged a close relationship with them, and he regretted now that he hadn't fought her on it.

When they ran out of apple pieces Robin stepped forward. The girls turned and jumped. They had been that way since the incident with the soldiers, and it hurt his heart. Slowly they began to smile at him, but they were hesitant smiles, as though they didn't know what to make of his being there. Becca's eyes were especially guarded. She had seen what he'd done to protect them both.

"What is it, brother?" Becca asked.

He forced a smile onto his face. "I have a surprise for you girls."

"Tell us what it is!" Ruth said, eyes growing wide.

"You're going to go visit our cousin in Scotland for a little while. You'll get to meet more family, and ride horses all you want on green fields. You're going to love it."

"How long are we going for?" Becca asked.

"A few weeks, most likely. It should be quite an adventure."

"When do we leave?"

"In the morning, so you'll want to pack your things," he said.

"Is Mother coming with us?" Ruth asked.

"Yes," Robin said, hoping she would see the logic of getting her daughters to safety while things were so turbulent at home. "Now, you'd better hurry and start to get ready." Becca ran from the barn without a backward glance. Ruth walked over and looked up at him with solemn eyes.

"I'll miss you while we're gone," she said.

"I'll miss you, too," he said, tousling her hair.

She gave him a sweet smile, and then followed her sister toward the house. Robin stood for a few minutes, trying to gather himself together. It had gone better than he'd anticipated. Now it was time to find and tell his mother.

He was leaving the barn when he spied a figure exiting the house and striding toward him with purpose. He met her halfway between barn and house.

"What is the meaning of this?" she demanded, eyes ablaze.

"I was coming to tell you," he said. "It's for the best. With everything that's happening around here, the rumors I've heard of some of the atrocities committed by Locksley's tax collectors, I thought it would be a good idea to send the girls somewhere safe, until things quiet down. I think you should go with them for your safety and theirs."

"I am not going anywhere," she said firmly. "Neither are my daughters. You can't run us off that easily."

"I'm trying to protect this family," he said, through gritted teeth.

"I don't need your protection," she said, head held high. "I can take care of my daughters. They are perfectly safe with me around. So we shall be spoiling your plans."

He knew her well enough to know that there was no arguing with her when she was like this. He stared at her grimly for a moment.

"Why do you have to be such a bitch?" he asked, the words practically wrested from him. A lifetime of being at odds with her had come to a head. He regretted the words as soon as he had spoken them.

"Because you're a son of a bitch," she replied, turning and leaving him standing in the yard.

CHAPTER TWENTY-SIX

"This will never work."

"Shut up. They are almost here."

Will looked across King's Road. He couldn't see more than shadows on the other side, where gloom lay in puddles across the ground below the undergrowth of bushes. Marian was there somewhere, lying in those shadows as he did in his.

She probably had the good sense to not *lie in mud.*

He shifted, the ground squelching around him. He was already soaked through, a chill coating his skin, pushing into his bones. His face itched—by his eye, on the tip of his nose, across his entire chin. He fought the desire to reach up and scratch, to wipe away the soot-stained grease spread to hide his features. The others wore it, as well.

It was near the end of sunlight. Here, in the depths of the mighty forest, even just off the road, it left them enveloped in deep dusk, near night.

I'll never be able to shoot this thing straight. He picked up the crossbow and pulled it into his lap. Carefully, he laid a wooden bolt along its track, notching the string into the fletching. The tip was wrapped in boiled leather.

Not that it matters with no arrowhead.

A rattling sound jolted him, coming down the road, growing

louder and louder. He rolled up on one knee and sighted down the bolt, centering it on the spot between the two leaning hawthorns.

The rattling came closer, accompanied by the sound of horses at a gallop.

From the gloom of the forest stepped a figure, lean but broad of shoulder and carrying a rag-wrapped stick and a wooden pail. He set down the pail. Will recognized the person, despite the fact that a dark green tunic and hood obscured his face. If nothing else, he would know him by the bow slung around his shoulders.

I hope you know what you're doing, cousin.

Robin's plan called for both stealth and brash arrogance. Five against an entire brigade of armed men. Overpower them, take back the things they had collected from the people, and honor the cardinal's admonition that as little blood be spilled as possible. Hence the headless crossbow bolts. The elder priest wasn't there but his man Friar Tuck hid in the forest down the road, along with the lanky bard.

It all had seemed impossible, ready to collapse even before they had begun, and Alan had said so. Then Robin proposed a plan. An insane just-might-work-because-it-was-Robin type of plan.

Leaning against the base of the bush, he watched the road. The tax brigade broke around the curve, horses at full speed to beat the fall of dark. Even with the road, it was dangerous to be caught in Sherwood at night, and *very* dangerous to ride without light.

Twenty men rode forward, surrounding a cart pulled by a team. Sleek and low, the wagon rumbled with no sway, sitting heavy over the leaf springs on each axle, the iron box in the center full of something heavy.

Heavy like gold.

Leaning forward, Robin swirled the rag-wrapped end of the stick through the oil and pitch in the bucket. He straightened and shook off the excess. His left hand pulled out a coal box, flipped it open, and brought it to his face. Will saw the hot ember flare orange along the edges of the hood that was pulled down over his face.

The brigade drew closer.

Touching the ember to the rag caught it on fire, bursting in a flash to run up the oil-soaked cloth. It crackled and popped with greasy orange flame, black smoke from the pitch billowing into the gathering darkness as he raised the torch over his head. The harsh light cast his face completely in the shadow of his hood, hiding his identity.

At the sight of a man with a torch, standing firm in the center of the road, the tax brigade drew up short, pulling reins to halt their mounts. Mud churning under hooves, they halted ten paces from Robin. Locksley sat on the lead horse, and he looked down.

"Move off the road, you idiot," he bellowed, "and count your blessings that we stopped, instead of running you down as you deserve."

Will expected Robin to speak, to demand the gold, but his cousin made no noise, didn't even move—simply stood with his head down and the torch guttering over his head.

One by one the men behind Locksley began looking around, glancing at one another. Some laughed, short chokes of uncomfortable humor coming from a place of fear. The rest watched closely, waiting for Locksley to lead.

Horses began to shuffle, lifting their feet and moving their heads. They felt the nervousness of their riders, and reacted in kind. Ears pinned back, their eyes showed white and they snorted, teeth chiming as they chewed the bits in their mouths.

Still Robin did not move.

One by one the men began putting hands on hilts.

Will leaned forward into the screen of brush that hid him. He felt heavy in the center, as the number of their opponents weighed upon him.

This might've been a terrible idea.

* * *

Friar Tuck didn't have enough hands.

He needed one to hold onto the rope that tied him to the tree, another to hold the basket that vibrated in his grip, another to hold the tree because he didn't trust the rope to keep him in place, another to hold the burlap sack closed around the basket, and yet another to scratch the itch that had set up home under the edge of his belly.

It had been burrowing into his gullet for the last hour. Was it some insect, trapped between skin and cloth? Some creepy-crawly that would not stop until it reached his insides, where it would set up home and unleash a horde of baby insects who would scurry and skrim through his intestines until they burst from him in a flood of tiny legs and wriggly, segmented bodies?

No, it was probably just an itch.

An itch made worse because he could not spare a hand to scratch. So he shifted, rubbing his stomach against the rough bark. The leaves shook around him, brushing against one another and sounding like a hundred voices shushing him.

His nose burned from the sooty smoke that filled the branches around him. He looked down in the haze at the men gathered beneath the tree he clutched so dearly. Their horses began to shimmy and sway. None of them looked up to where he hung. All of their eyes focused forward on the man with the torch.

A knot of tension in his thigh began to squinge in on itself, building in intensity and spreading. Soon it would morph into a full-blown cramp.

I hope I can get down out of this blasted tree before that.

He tried to not think about the pain.

The hood blocked the top of his vision, cutting across it in a wavy line. He wanted to toss it back, but fought the urge. Anonymity was of the utmost importance—for Becca and Ruth. For the safety of the people left at Longstride Manor. Even for his mother.

He could see part of Locksley on his wide-chested white

stallion, and he fought the urge to plant an arrow in the man's throat. Longstride Manor had been ransacked by this tax brigade, these very men. Some of them were neighbors, some even friends of his father, and they'd followed Locksley's orders and destroyed Longstride property. Some of the things smashed had been new, some had been in his family for generations.

The memories crackled inside him like ice on a warm winter day—of his mother, stooping wearily to clean, and the sounds of his sisters sniffling to keep their sobs muffled. And worst of all was Lila, poor Lila, who couldn't cook anything without burning it. Some ruffian had choked the life out of her. Heaven only knew why. He had told his mother to get everyone out. Maybe Lila had just been too slow. His mother had discovered the body of her lifelong servant when they returned to the home. Anger burned in his breast for Lila, for all of them.

This is more than simple revenge. Now he had a plan. It was *his* plan.

He took a deep breath and began to speak.

At the sound of Robin's voice, Marian stopped moving, hand in mid-air, about to push away the branch in front of her. The words boomed out, rolling across the road like thunder. She was so used to him speaking in low tones that the sheer volume of it froze her in place.

"You men are thieves, stealing from the poor what little they have," he said, his voice disguised. "Sherwood has seen your actions, and the forest is angered by your very presence. You have been shaken, pressed down, measured in the balances, and found wanting."

As he spoke, Robin waved the torch slowly, back and forth, from one side of him to the other. Several of the men in the brigade crossed themselves and one cried out.

He spoke again.

"The weight of stolen gold is a millstone tied to your necks.

It drags your souls to Hell. Cut yourselves free from this burden, turn your faces and repent, and ye may yet be spared this night."

His voice dropped, and she had to strain to hear it.

"Refuse, and suffer the judgment of Sherwood."

Marian tensed, raising her crossbow and aiming.

The cramp in Tuck's leg cinched down on itself.

Will braced himself to keep the crossbow steady.

Smoke from the torch curled around Locksley's head.

It worked into his eyes, making them water. The horse under him vibrated, staying put but ready to break if he loosed the reins at all. It kept snorting, the sooty stench irritating its nostrils. Behind him came the sounds of jingling bridles and shuffling hooves. And murmurs.

Murmurs were disastrous to leadership.

He drew his sword, lifting the blade in the air.

"Step aside or I will ride you down," he demanded. "We are on king's business."

Then he was startled by a new sound. From under the hood came a sharp whistle. The man in shadows swung his arms with a flourish, flinging his free hand toward the mounted men and loosing an animal roar.

Noise leapfrogged from both sides of the road and two men behind him cried out as they were knocked from their horses by some invisible force. He jerked around as they tumbled to the ground. One man's animal reared, hooves kicking out and striking the face of the beast beside him. Chaos rolled through the group, men cursing and yanking at the reins of horses that danced and churned.

"Did you see that?"

"He knocked them off their horses!"

"Just a wave of his hand!"

This cannot continue, Locksley thought frantically. Then the man in the hood roared a command.

"Leave your ill-gotten gains and run, run for your miserable lives," he bellowed.

Locksley turned in the saddle, jerking his head back and forth, seeking a way to salvage the situation. In the dirt, broken by crushing hooves, he spied a slender object.

A crossbow bolt.

Waving his sword around in the air he began to shout at the men.

Tuck's leg jerked, pain ripping through his thigh and drawing it up into a fisted slab. His hand slipped on the smooth bark and he teetered left, his weight dragging him around. Letting go of the burlap-wrapped basket, he scrabbled to stop his rotation and wound up hanging by his waist, the safety rope cutting into the very spot where the itch had been.

He watched the turmoil below him and saw the basket fall, spinning free of the burlap as it turned. It smashed to pieces between the two horses that were teamed together on the wagon.

Marian stood, swinging her crossbow up in an arc. As she watched, a black cloud swarmed up between the harnessed team.

She could barely see it in the failing light, but she'd watched the basket fall and knew what it held, even though it was meant to wait for a signal from Robin. Black hornets in the gloom of the darkening forest, meant to be dropped behind the tax brigade to drive them forward and away while Robin remained safe in the smoke that would surge up from the bucket at his feet.

Something has gone wrong.

The horses began leaping and dancing in their stays, the

wagon of gold bouncing on its wheels as the animals tried to get away from the insects now free from their imprisonment, ready for war with any flesh they could find. The beasts fought each other, jerking in opposite directions.

The hornets spread like wildfire, driving their stingers into the men and mounts surrounding the gold wagon. Already shoved to the edge of panic, the horses bolted, some losing their riders, others carrying them away.

She swung her crossbow back and forth, looking for a target that would make a difference in the riot. In addition to Locksley's men, there were two of the king's guards present, one on either side of the treasure wagon. Both men's mounts plunged and twisted uncontrollably, screaming in fear as the hornets attacked them, as well. The man on the right unsheathed his sword and plunged it into his own mount's neck.

The animal screamed for a second, the sound strangling off as it tumbled to the ground and the man jumped off. He landed in a crouch and began to walk toward Robin. Horrified, Marian released her shaft, catching him right in the chest. It knocked him backward, but then he gathered himself and kept moving.

As though he didn't even notice it.

She drew her dagger, fear coursing through her. She had never heard of a soldier killing his own mount to keep it from carrying him away from a fight. Soldiers cared for their horses, knowing that they entrusted their lives to the beasts. She had never met the man who would willingly strike down his own animal.

Robin had foreseen this. When he had outlined this plan, he had warned them to be careful if any of the king's guard were present. The men who were kidnapping children were carrying swords with dark symbols forged into them. The blacksmith had told Alan that he'd been forced to forge weapons with strange symbols on them. Cardinal Francis had speculated that the weapons were infused with some sort of magic, forcing otherwise honorable men to commit atrocities—such as kidnapping children.

And killing their own warhorses.

Her stomach churned and bile rose up in her throat. Such a monster would not be stopped by anything but a deathblow, regardless of what the cardinal wanted.

On the other side of the wagon the other member of the king's guard struck down his horse, as well, and hit the ground with sword dripping blood. Both of them drew abreast of Locksley, unfazed by the chaos around them and the air of mystery around the man in the hood.

Marian glanced around frantically. Tuck was in the tree, and she couldn't see Alan or Will. Even if they had witnessed what was occurring, she didn't know if they would understand in time, or could respond fast enough.

As she lunged out of the darkness, she realized that it was up to her. Those who were running away might see her and realize that the Hood had help, but that was a chance she would have to take.

Robin stood his ground, watching and waiting to see what opportunity might present itself. He saw two of the king's guard, now on foot, advancing toward him, but he had a more immediate concern.

Locksley swung on him.

The man's face had swollen, skin bulging along the side of his skull. His eyes showed white all around the iris, gleaming in the falling dark. He yanked his horse around, foam flying from the animal's mouth, and, when it was aimed at Robin, he smacked the flat of his blade across the panicked beast's side.

The horse lunged, a thousand pounds of muscle and hooves churning the dirt as it flew forward. The noble held his sword over his head, a bolt of lightning ready to strike down the enemy.

Peace dropped into the well in the center of Robin's chest, washing over him as everything separated into moments, broken shards of time he could watch tumble apart. Tension sloughed off him and he leaned back, ready to react as the shards fell closer to him.

Locksley hurled a curse. It washed over him like a slow tide against a boulder.

The horse charged.

Torchlight gleamed off the razor-sharp blade.

Then they were so close he could see the lather bubbling on the war mount's flanks. Too close to dodge away.

Someone screamed.

Too close to not be run down.

Robin dropped the torch.

His foot lashed out, kicking the bucket.

It flew up, the liquid it held spilling in a wide fan of splatter. It struck the torch flame as it soared, and burst into a rain of fire. The veil of combustion swirled away and broke across the chest of the mighty animal. The horse dug in with its hooves, throwing its weight back, blindly trying to get away from the fire. Instinctual terror overwhelmed every ounce of training hammered into the mighty beast.

Locksley lost all control as the horse flung itself to the side, carrying him in his saddle. He held on as the creature bolted down the road.

Under his hood, Robin smiled.

His victory was short-lived, though, as he saw Marian racing toward the king's guardsman who was closest to her, dagger raised high in the air. His heart froze within him as he realized she was about to be killed.

Carefully laid plans scattered to the wind. He ran forward, knowing he couldn't reach her in time, shouting for help.

Will could tell from the sound of Robin's voice that something had gone terribly wrong. Through the smoke that burned his eyes he couldn't make out what was happening in the darkness.

He stood, trying to figure out what had gone awry. The smoke cleared for a moment, just long enough for him to see Marian plunge a dagger into the back of one of the two king's guards who had been present. Shocked, he staggered forward even as the man twisted around, raising his sword and slashing at her.

Marian jerked out of the way as the guard's sword whistled past her ear. Its passing seemed to superheat the air around it, though, and she found herself suddenly struggling to breathe. Her lungs were on fire, and her head was buzzing as if all the hornets they had released had taken up residence inside her skull. Pain traced its way through her, and she struggled not to crumple beneath it.

The sword. There is something wrong with the sword, she realized, even as the guard prepared to swing it again. Her dagger was embedded in his back, all the way to the hilt. She had thrust it where King Richard had once shown her. It should have passed through ribs and struck him in the heart.

Blood pumped from the wound, foul smelling and steaming slightly in the air. She grasped the hilt, shoving with all her might, but it would go no further into his body. Convinced of that, she tried instead to yank it free so she could stab him in the throat. It was lodged, however, and she cried out in frustration as he twisted, breaking her hold on the weapon.

She should have worn a sword. She knew how to use one, but Robin and Cardinal Francis had insisted. They had said that she wouldn't need it.

They had been wrong.

The brute twisted with a grunt and his sword came swinging at her. She stepped back and her foot slid on a pile of leaves slick with blood. She skidded, trying to regain her balance so she did not fall. Too late she realized that she *should* have fallen. The blade was set to catch her in the throat. She tried to move, but her feet just splayed more.

Suddenly the sword stopped in mid-air. Then it fell slowly to the ground, the flat of it striking her shin on the way down. Searing pain ripped through her, reminding her of the fire that had burned her as a child—the one that had claimed her parents.

She collapsed onto the ground, whimpering in pain, and the man crumpled beside her. There was an arrow in his throat, and his eyes were lifeless.

She looked up to see Robin towering above her, already notching another arrow in his bow. Behind him, the other guard lunged.

"Behind you!" she gasped.

Robin spun. There was no time to fire, so instead he impaled the man, gripping the arrow as tightly as he could. Blood flew from the wound, spraying across her face. It smelled horrible. He dropped his sword and the pile of leaves on which it fell began to sizzle.

Will Scarlet came running, crossbow up, but he was too late. It was over. Everyone else had long since fled. Throwing propriety to the wind, Marian yanked her trouser leg up and looked at her shin. The skin was red, and boils covered it as though she had been severely burned.

"What happened?" Will gasped, staring in horror.

Marian grimaced. More scars to add to her collection.

"Be careful," she warned. "There's something wrong with their swords—they're hot, they're burning everything they touch." She winced as she inspected the damage. She would need a healing poultice, and quickly. She couldn't help but wonder what kind of damage one of those swords would have inflicted if it had actually bit into skin.

Robin frowned as Alan came up to join them. "I've encountered swords like this before, with these markings. They did not burn, though."

"Perhaps they become hot when used in combat," Alan suggested. "They couldn't be that way all the time, or they'd burn through their scabbards and cripple the men and the horses."

Will crossed himself. "Magic," he whispered, as if until that moment he hadn't actually believed it could be true.

"Dark magic," Alan averred. "We're lucky to be alive. All of us."

Will looked around, and Robin followed his gaze. The road

was clear of men and horses, except for the treasure wagon team. The two animals had stopped fighting each other and simply stood, heads down and sides heaving from their efforts. The hornets had abandoned their attack.

"Where is Friar Tuck?" Marian asked, fear suddenly racing through her.

"Up here, waiting on one of you to help me down!"

The four of them looked up. The monk hung nearly upside down from the branch which had been his perch, held in place by the rope around his waist. His robe had fallen forward, so that it hung loosely over his head.

Alan was right. They were lucky they weren't all dead. As it was, she, at least, would forever bear the scars of this encounter. She dropped the trouser leg back down for modesty's sake, even though the rough fabric scraped against the tortured skin and made her bite the inside of her cheek until she tasted blood.

Marian needed treatment before the injury had a chance to turn foul and permanently cripple her. She didn't want to admit to any of the men, though, just how much pain she was in. She couldn't let them use it as an excuse to exclude her in the future.

MERLIN'S
TEARS

CHAPTER TWENTY-SEVEN

"Tell me what this means."

Richard's spy held the soldier against the alley wall, pressing his hand against the man's throat hard enough to hurt, but not enough to stop him from speaking. In his other hand he held up the man's sword. The symbol carved into the flattened pommel weight lay stark against the steel.

The soldier's eyes moved from the symbol to his assailant and back again. His mouth moved, sharp chin batting against the hand that held him as his tongue swirled around his loose teeth.

"Means I'm the king's man. What do you think it means?"

"I've carried a sword for the king. This isn't the lion."

"Wrong king. Old king gets on boat, new king sends the Sheriff 'round with new swords."

"This is John's mark?"

The soldier's eyes grew wide. The spy pressed harder.

"Answer the question. Is this John's mark?"

"It's my mark."

Something moved in the reflection on the soldier's eye. The spy threw himself sideways, swinging the man around with him. Two handspans of steel burst through the soldier's chest. Blood sprayed across his eyes, blinding him as he felt the quick burn of razor sharp steel scrape his chin.

Richard's man blinked, trying to see what was happening as the soldier jerked in his hands. Something tugged the soldier backwards and he shoved the corpse away from him. He wiped his eyes with his sleeve and swung the soldier's sword around.

His clearing vision saw sparks fly as the sword edge met steel. Red tears ran down his face as his eyesight cleared.

The Sheriff stood before him, weapon drawn and strange beasts at each side. The spy put his back to the wall, brandishing the sword in front of him.

The Sheriff watched him, his head tilted sideways like that of a carrion bird studying a corpse.

"Who are you?" he demanded.

The spy didn't answer.

"You feel familiar."

"You do not know me, scoundrel."

"Scoundrel? Me? That seems rather tame." The Sheriff swung his sword wide. "What's next? 'Ne'er-do-well'?"

"Villain."

"Villain I shall own." He smiled. "You still feel familiar." The Sheriff darted in, inhumanly fast, his sword licking across the arm of the spy. The spy swung the sword in his hand wildly. The Sheriff jumped back, and then reached up and with a long, pale finger scooped some of the man's blood from the tip of the sword. He stuck the red-tipped finger in his mouth, rolling his tongue around the tip of it.

"Ah. No wonder." Black eyes glittered. "I know your mother. She tastes the same. A bit spicier, but the same."

He lunged, thrusting with his sword. "Do not speak of her so!"

The Sheriff parried with a casual upswing of his sword. "Oh, I assure you, I have done much more with this mouth than speak of her."

"Liar! My mother is no whore." Rage burned hot inside Robert, powering his swinging sword.

The Sheriff danced through the flashing steel, stepping lightly, his armor clicking against itself with each move.

"Not a whore, but very wanton and near insatiable—worth the effort." He knocked Robert's blade upward.

Hot agony tore into the back of Robert's leg. He threw a glance down and saw that one of the Sheriff's familiars had slashed open his calf. He could see pink meat under the wash of blood that ran into his boot. He hacked down with the blade in his hand, planting the edge deep in the hackles of the creature. It fell in a convulsion and rolled away.

Robert barely had time to parry a swipe from the Sheriff when the second familiar struck. The creature dug claws into the back of his thigh, curling into the meat of the muscle.

The Sheriff lunged, thrusting his blade deep into Robert's stomach. He felt the sword pushing his organs aside, driving deep to punch out his back just to the inside of his kidney.

The pain made his body curl backward, drawing his spine into a clench. His fingers brushed long black fur. He closed them on the scruff of the familiar's neck and swung the animal at the Sheriff with all his strength. The sword pulled free of his guts as the animal struck the Sheriff in the chest. They fell in a tangle of slick-shined armor and light-eating fur.

Robert turned, his legs gone all watery as he stumbled from the alley and dragged himself onto the back of the first horse he saw.

Robin was in the forest near home. He needed time to think. The theft had gone as wrong as it could go. They were lucky none of them were dead or captured.

It had been his plan, too, which made him feel all the worse. He was beginning to wonder if a better course of action would be to head for the docks himself. They still hadn't been able to determine if either of the other two messengers had made it through. If so, King Richard could soon be returning. If not, they were all in serious trouble.

In the distance he heard the staccato thunder of a rider, coming fast and hard, headed for Longstride Manor. He was tempted to slip deeper into the forest and let the rider pass. He was the acting lord, though. Whoever was riding like that was either coming to see him, or was someone of whom he needed to be aware.

He unslung his bow and held it in his hand, not overtly threatening, but where he could bring it to bear quickly if he had to. He stepped out into the middle of the road and lifted an arm.

The horse came sliding to a halt in front of him, feet churning the earth. A cloaked rider sat the saddle, his face obscured beneath his hood. The man weaved. Robin looked closer and saw that the dark cloak was wet. At the same time he smelled the strong tang of iron.

He stepped forward, intent on helping the man. The rider slid sideways out of the saddle and Robin dropped his bow to catch him. He knelt, setting the man down on the ground as the horse danced sideways. He had been right—the man's cloak was soaked with blood.

"Robin." A hoarse voice said his name. "Robin, thank God I found you."

He reached up and shoved back the hood. A cry escaped his lips when he saw his brother Robert staring back at him.

"Robert! How? You're injured, let me see," he said, reaching to pull aside the cloak.

"Don't." Robert stopped him with a hand on his. "The wound is mortal."

"No!"

"It is," his brother said. "Listen to me. I have little time, and much to tell you." A froth of pink lay on his lips.

"Father?" Robin asked, heart in his throat.

"I do not know. The king gave me this mission. I boarded the ship and then snuck off before it set sail." His breathing hitched and he coughed, causing his eyes to close in pain. After a long moment he opened them again and continued talking, his voice half as strong as before. "I have been scouring the countryside as his eyes and ears while he is away."

"So much has happened," Robin said.

"More than you know. The Sheriff gathers witches and beasts that obey his command." Another cough brought dark blood to Robert's mouth. "Not like any creatures I've seen before." He coughed violently, and blood trickled out of his mouth. When he spoke again his voice was weaker still. "He's not human. I escaped. He couldn't chase me into the forest... don't know why."

"I'll kill him," Robin vowed, his throat constricting tight. His brother was the best warrior alive, but Robin was a hunter, and he would stalk the Sheriff as he would a beast of prey. Then he would put an arrow through his throat.

Robert grabbed Robin's shirt. "Stay away, he's dangerous. John, too, though he doesn't look it." He coughed again, bringing up more blood. The end was near. Robin had seen too much death in his life to pretend that the gray creeping into Robert's pallid face was anything else.

"I thought him a... spoilt little prince but he's... dangerous and..."

Robert drifted to a stop, his eyes closing. Robin shook him lightly.

"No, no, no, no... stay with me."

Robert opened his eyes again. "Love you, little brother."

"I love you, too." Tears ran hot down Robin's face.

"Mother was wrong... to treat you as she did. Sorry... didn't stand up... to her."

"That was never your place."

Robert's head lolled, and then he seemed to gather his strength. His grip on Robin's hand tightened slightly. His words slurred, barely a whisper.

"There's more. Henry... in Scotland, drawing nobles to himself... amassing... a conscripted army, preparing... to make an assault on the throne."

"Better he sit on it than John," Robin said fervently. An invasion by Henry would almost be welcome, if for no other reason than it would occupy John's time and take his focus away from whatever schemes of his own he was hatching.

"It will destroy England," Robert wheezed. He coughed, and still more blood came up, covering his chin as it dribbled from his lips. Tears began to roll down his cheeks.

"Brother, England is all but destroyed," Robin said. "I think only a war could save her."

"You, Robin," Robert's voice was only a breath now. Robin bent close, his ear practically to Robert's lips. "You will save," Robert whispered.

"Save what, brother? Save what?"

Robert's hand went slack, and Robin turned to look him in the face. His brother was gone. His eyes were fixed on something he alone could see. As Robin reached up to close them, bitter sobs wracked his body.

There would be no saving. He had failed.

Robin was like a man possessed. No matter how many armed guards entered Sherwood with a cash box, they always ended up fleeing in terror. When Locksley finally ordered his men to ride far out of their way to avoid the forest, the Hood still managed to ambush them on the road.

The legend of the guardian had so taken hold in the minds of those guarding the gold that more often than not they turned and fled without a fight. The only ones who stood their ground were soldiers of the king's guard, and he had learned to kill them quickly. Fortunately they did not accompany every shipment.

He had taken to leaving his comrades behind, stalking the tax brigades, hoping to find the Sheriff escorting one of them. Thus far he had been unlucky.

One by one the soldiers had fallen, dropped in quick succession by noose, stone, and arrow that had come from the dark of Sherwood. He was the only one left, and the wagon under him rocked violently as he whipped the horses until their skin flayed open in red lines that opened and closed in rhythm with their mad gallop.

He drove them like the devil, praying neither of the animals would turn a hoof and fall. Suddenly something heavy landed beside him on the bench. He turned his head. A man in a hood stared at him, face lost in the shadow. All he could see were the whites of the eyes and a mad snarl of a smile—the grinning visage of the Angel Of Death.

A booted foot lashed out, kicking him in the face and driving him backward. He tumbled off the wagon that roared down the king's road. He screamed both times the wagon's wheels ran over his arm, crushing it into uselessness. The hooded man dropped down behind the wagon, his bow in hand.

The soldier didn't see the arrow that killed him.

"'Tis not a man."

Locksley turned to his right. "Shut up, fool."

"It's not our fault," the man responded. He shook his head, beady eyes as wide as they could get in their deep sockets. "One way or another, he knows."

"I said, be *quiet*." Locksley struck fast, the back of his fist lashing out across the nose. The man dropped to one knee, and Locksley drew back his hand to deliver another blow.

"Hold."

The command came from behind. Locksley forced himself to remain stock still as his man slumped to the ground.

"Lift him up, and let him speak," Prince John said from his chair. "I love a good ghost story."

Locksley stepped away, returning to his original position, looking straight ahead. Prince John lounged on a curved settee, sinking into the cushions there. Beside him on a matching divan sat Will Scarlet. Both men wore velveteen robes patterned through with gold thread. Locksley couldn't tell, but they appeared to be a matched set.

Perhaps it was merely a coincidence.

The prince shifted, looking up at a man who stood to the left in a shadow of his own making, all light subdued by the black armor that encased him.

"I'm not the only one who wants a ghost story," John said with amusement. "Am I right?"

The Sheriff of Nottingham inclined his head in agreement, and there was no humor in his gaze. So the prince indicated that Locksley's man should stand.

"Rise and finish your tale of horror and ghouls."

From the corner of his eye, Locksley saw the man climb to his feet. He held fingers over the place where the blow had split the skin. It leaked thin blood along each side of his nose, and it ran down like thin streams of red tears. His voice was thick when he spoke.

"You cannot blame us for the loss of the taxes," he said. "The spirit of Sherwood keeps taking it. We've all seen him—just ask anyone. You cannot fight a ghost."

The prince glanced at Locksley.

"You disagree with his assessment?"

"It is a man—it has to be," Locksley replied. "A tricky bastard for sure, but he isn't the stuff of legend. Such a creature doesn't exist. No, he's flesh and blood, like you or me."

"Then why haven't you stopped him?" John demanded. "He's been disrupting your efforts for a month, and yet you're no closer to apprehending him."

Locksley had nothing to say.

"What makes you so certain this highwayman is a ghost?" the prince said to the bleeding man.

"Like I said, I seen it with my own eyes."

"Well, that settles it." The prince lifted a goblet from the table beside him and took a long swallow. "Clearly you are an expert in the matters of spirits, able to discern the truth about them."

The man looked belligerent, and stuck his chin out.

"I know what I know," he said stubbornly. "Me mum were a bit of a witch."

At that the prince leapt to his feet, flinging the lead goblet at the man. It flashed across the room, striking him in the face almost exactly where Locksley had split his nose. The man cried out in pain and dropped to his knee again. This time he did not rise.

"*There are no ghosts in Sherwood!*" the prince screamed.

The Sheriff was there, standing next to the man. Locksley had not seen him move. The armored man's hand flashed once, driving against the sobbing man's chest. When he pulled away he held no knife, yet blood gushed from a wound. Feebly the man raised his hands, reaching for something he could not see. His eyes had gone blind.

The Sheriff stepped back, and the man fell over, and a puddle of his own blood began to appear around the still form.

The prince sat back on his chair, and the Sheriff strolled back across the room to again lean against the wall. Locksley looked over at Will Scarlet. The man looked down at the threads of his robe, as if nothing out of the ordinary had occurred. No emotion could be seen in his expression.

"What is the current bounty placed on the outlaw?" Prince John asked.

"One hundred gold pieces," Scarlet answered, picking at a loose thread near the cuff.

"Double it," the prince instructed. "Two hundred gold pieces to the man who brings me the head of this... ghost."

Locksley did not move.

"Did you not hear me?" the prince said.

"I beg your pardon, Your Majesty," Locksley responded, "but gold doesn't buy what it used to."

The prince raised an eyebrow. Locksley knew instantly that he was perhaps half a moment from tasting the Sheriff's wrath, as well.

The prince sighed heavily. "Very well, make a note. The man who brings me the ghost's head will receive two hundred gold pieces, and he will be granted immunity from further taxation."

"As you wish," Locksley said, bowing deeply. The truth was,

for two hundred gold pieces he'd do almost anything to bring the hooded outlaw in himself. As the chief tax collector, he'd done much to hide the majority of his own wealth, knowing he would need it to feed the people in his care when the winter struck hard.

Besides, there had to be *some* reward for doing the crown's dirty work.

"And what of the book?" the Sheriff asked, his eyes piercing.

Locksley shook his head. "It has not been found."

"Are you certain it has not been taken by this hooded outlaw?"

"Absolutely," Locksley replied. "There has been no sign of it." The symbol on his arm burned under his sleeve.

"Then you will continue looking—search every nook and cranny for it," Prince John said, his displeasure obvious. "You *will* find it, or there will be consequences."

"Yes, Your Majesty," Locksley said, bowing his head and reminding himself to be grateful that he was being allowed to continue looking, instead of lying beside his fallen man. That could just as easily be his blood spilling onto the floor.

"Go," the prince said, with a dismissive wave of his hand.

At last, an order he was happy to obey.

Will watched Locksley go. It had not been easy, worming his way further into Prince John's confidence. The Sheriff didn't entirely trust him, but even he was beginning to overlook Will's presence, more and more.

"Locksley hasn't found the book, and neither has the bishop," the usurper said, rubbing his forehead and glowering in frustration. This was the third time he had mentioned the missing tome, but Will knew no more about it than he had before.

He debated about whether or not to speak up boldly and ask about its nature, or to just sit quietly and hope to be ignored. Before he could make a decision, the Sheriff looked in his direction.

"These words aren't for other ears," he said to his master.

"You're right," John sighed. "You may go, Will." The prince waved him away.

Will stood and bowed. Skirting wide of the body that was cooling on the floor, he moved to leave. Halfway to the door he turned.

"If there is something you're looking for, perhaps I could be of help?" It was a calculated risk, but as the prince's "right-hand man," then it might seem stranger for him *not* to offer his assistance in the search.

The prince looked at him for a long moment.

"That will be all."

Will bowed again and left the room, letting the door shut of its own accord. There was an imperfection on the frame that he knew would prevent it from closing completely. On the other side he held his breath, listening, hoping he could overhear whatever they said next.

"Human agents are worthless."

Prince John shrugged. "I wouldn't agree with that."

"That is because you are one."

"An agent?"

"A... human." The Sheriff moved to the table that held the wine. He lifted a crystal glass and filled it halfway with a dark whiskey poured from a decanter. "We need the grimoire that is bound in that book." He strolled over to the dead man who lay on the floor, and stared down at him with abstract interest.

"Your wizards and witches have turned up nothing?"

"They are human, as well."

"No one knows where the cursed thing is," the prince said.

"Someone does." The Sheriff squatted beside the corpse. Long, pale fingers grabbed the tunic and lifted, raising the dead man up to his knees. "The monastery is the storehouse for such things, is it not?" The hand switched from the back of the corpse to the front, holding it steady.

"The bishop has searched its library, and failed to find anything."

"He needs more motivation." The hand squeezed the blood-soaked tunic over the half-full glass. Crimson trickled out, plopping into the whiskey in fat droplets. They, in turn, swirled in delicate patterns, the mixture filling the glass to the lip. The Sheriff stood.

The corpse fell forward with a wet smack against the marble.

"He's devoted to our cause," John said, "or at least what he thinks is our cause."

The Sheriff took a sip. "I've heard rumors that this ghost who steals the tax money is finding a way to give it back to the people. Village children see him as a good fairy who brings food and treats and protects them."

"This ghost is tightening the noose around his own neck, and those of any who may be protecting him," John said, anger growing in his voice. "The people are stubborn enough as it is, without having someone to give them hope. They need to be taught a lesson."

"You have something in mind?" The Sheriff took another sip, the mixture leaving his lips with a trace of color they normally didn't have.

"Give me a moment."

The silence was broken only by the sound of the man in black taking the occasional sip from his glass. Finally he spoke.

"The tax scheme was your idea. It was supposed to be a cover for finding the Grimoire of Relics, to strip away the hope of the people, and to pull them from the protection of the church."

"It would work, save for the Hood," John muttered.

"Regardless, it has failed," the Sheriff responded. "Whether it is because of this outlaw, or because it was a flawed idea to begin with, we cannot know for certain."

Prince John rose to his feet, feeling his face burning.

"Do not blame this on me," he said. "If you have a better plan, then do not withhold it."

The Sheriff smiled, his teeth stained red. "Need I remind you of my role in this?"

John fell back on his seat. "No," he said. "No. I remember."

"Then think of a new scheme, one that the Hood cannot spoil, and let us be done with it. I have waited long enough."

Prince John put his chin in his hand.

Something the outlaw cannot affect.

He sat up straight.

"I have it."

The Sheriff rolled his hand, indicating that John should continue.

"They say if a man doesn't have his health, he doesn't have anything. Disease is what we need, to thin the herd and break those who remain." To John's surprise, the Sheriff's black eyes widened.

"Why, little prince, it may be that humans aren't worthless after all. That is truly an inspired suggestion."

"Thank you," John replied, careful to hold in his delight.

"You should have started with it," the Sheriff added wryly, "and saved us all these weeks of labor."

Prince John waved away the insult. "Can you do such a working, on such short notice?"

"Harnessing the sorcerers in my care, we can conjure up something suitably effective."

"Good," John said. "Make certain we have just enough potion to keep a handful of us safe," he said. "It will thoroughly demoralize our enemies more than anything we've done to date."

"I will begin preparations tonight," the Sheriff said. "Are you sure, though, that you have the stomach for this? That you feel not a whit for these people?"

John snorted. "Father banished me from England years ago. I have no love for anything here, and I'm happy to see its people dragged to Hell."

The Sheriff smiled. "Soon enough, little prince."

* * *

Will heard footsteps drawing close, and he moved away swiftly, losing himself in another part of the castle. His heart pounded in his chest.

What they were talking about... it was impossible, wasn't it? He had never believed in magic or curses or the fairy folk who supposedly still lived in Sherwood. He had thought all the stories his grandmother told were nothing more than that. Fairy tales. Yet he himself had seen the burns inflicted on Marian by a cursed sword, that night of the first raid. Since then he had begun to doubt, to think that maybe magic *could* exist.

But a plague? That was something entirely different—so much bigger than a burning sword. Could Prince John and the Sheriff really conjure such a thing? They seemed to think so. So, either they were both insane, or it was possible.

Yet how?

A hand landed on his shoulder and he spun, startled.

Marian jerked back, hands up at his reaction.

"Damnation, Marian," he swore. "You startled me."

"I'm sorry."

"No, it was not your fault," he said, waving aside her apology. The truth was it was good that she was able to sneak up on him again. That meant her leg was healed, or nearly so. Until now she had been walking with a limp, favoring the burned limb. He took a deep breath, grateful that she seemed better. Then he looked her in the eye.

"I need to talk to you, and the others. Something is happening."

Marian had known that both the prince and the Sheriff were evil men, but she had not dreamed they would contemplate something so profane. She prayed that such magic was beyond their reach.

After Will told her, he left the castle to warn the cardinal. She didn't go with him. It wouldn't be good for them to be seen together.

That night she stayed up praying until the dawn that God would deliver them from the hand of darkness that was closing around them. Champion had curled up in her lap, keeping her company, but was falling asleep on the watch. Still, stroking his fur brought her some comfort as she agonized through the long night.

With shaking fingers, Agrona lifted the lid to the black oak box beside her pallet. The dry must of bone wafted out, filling her nostrils, calming her immediately. It was joined by the sickly-sweet carrion scent of rotting meat. She'd only been able to save the shin of her sister and it lay inside, nestled with her mother's bones as the meat attached to it broke down and began to fall away.

She shut the lid as the Mad Monk folded himself to a sitting position beside her. He bowed his shaved head toward her. Slick patches of scar tissue glimmered in the torchlight. His voice was a low tenor.

"Necromancer."

"Sorcerer."

He smiled. "I would love to have a morsel from your collection."

They had done this dance for weeks.

Every day.

"No."

"You have not heard my offer."

"Nothing you have is worth what I possess."

His hand slid into the sleeve of his robe. When it slid out it held a white feather with a red tip. In the center of the feather blinked an eyeball. It looked mostly human. The folds of the lid were wrong, and it was inserted into a feather, but it was an eyeball nonetheless.

She could feel the power of it pulling at her. Her nipples hardened.

"Is that...?"

"It is."

She gaped at him in awe. "So the stories are true. You succeeded."

He shook his head. The skin in the center of his tonsure was waxy. "Had I succeeded I would not be here right now. I did not catch the angel, but I did manage to pluck two of these."

The eyeball blinked, and it jerked something inside her.

"Why would you trade that for bones, when you aren't a necromancer?"

He smiled crookedly. "I… *knew* your mother when she was alive. I would like a keepsake of her."

Agrona didn't know what to say. The implication of his tone struck her. She would be sure to ask her mother about it later. She would never parcel her out in such a way, no matter what was being offered.

But now she had to find a way to acquire that feather. Before she could speak, however, the magic in the room shifted. It rolled across her.

The Mad Monk was on his feet, feather tucked away and out of sight.

She stood in one fluid motion and found the Sheriff in the center of the room. All the practitioners who were present had turned, and now watched him. He smiled at them and stroked the fur collar around his neck.

"My children, I have a task for you."

CHAPTER TWENTY-EIGHT

After three weeks, the monastery had run out of sheets. Bodies were being wrapped in blankets, and soon those would be in scarce supply. Before long the dead would lay in the clothes in which they fell. They would no longer be faceless.

Friar Tuck laid a hand on the young man's shoulders. The man's neck twisted as he turned his face up, while his form stayed draped over the small body that lay perfectly still on the woolen blanket in which she would be wrapped.

The young man's face had been sucked tight to his skull, made hollow by a lack of food, a lack of sleep, and a lack of hope. His eyes had sunk into his cheeks, the lids red and chafed from tears being rubbed out of them. He was a candle whose wick had been snuffed out.

The friar knelt beside him. His hand crossed his body and the young man mimicked him out of a lifetime of habit.

"What was her name, son?" he asked, keeping his voice low.

"Tessa."

Friar Tuck looked down. Tessa's face was serene, beautiful in her final rest. The pox had only marked her throat and just under her hairline. This close to her, he could see that the sores had closed, fading to the waxy pallor once the body ceased generating the fever that turned them angry and red. Dried sweat left a glistening of miniscule salt crystals that made her skin shine.

He prayed she'd been too young to be a mother.

"I need to perform the benediction, son."

The young man didn't move.

"Could you come back, Father?" he asked, his voice cracking a bit. "I know it needs doing, but if you don't then it means she's not really gone, and I need her to not be gone just yet."

It was a simple request, spoken clearly.

He was commissioned by the church to care for the dead in the moment of their passing. It was his duty, sacred and undeniable.

Without a word he stood and left the young man with his Tessa.

"If I had known it would feel like this, then I would have suggested sacrificing *everyone*."

"Don't act giddy."

"Is it unbecoming?"

"No, little prince, it is annoying."

"I feel drunk."

The Sheriff lifted a jeweled knife from the table, one used to break wax seals on missives and epistles. He turned it in long slender fingers, spinning it in a sunbeam from the window. The faceted crystals refracted the light, shooting it around the study in a dozen colors.

Prince John leaned forward. "Pretty."

The Sheriff flipped the knife into his fist and drove it into John's arm.

The finger-length blade punched through skin and muscle to strike bone. John stared at the knife protruding from his arm.

He sniggered.

Then giggled.

Then both of them laughed.

* * *

Cardinal Francis swayed on his feet. The world around him moved in jumps and starts seen through a haze of exhaustion.

He'd spent the last several days first at the infirmary and then moving through the courtyard and various hallways that had been used when the sick began coming in droves. He did what he could to help with the physical burden of caring for the sick and dying, and spent much of his time making hard decisions about distributing provisions.

Francis did not want to attend this secret meeting. It was the least of his concerns in the face of such suffering. Yet Will and Marian had been insistent, and so he now made his way to the cell they'd been using for months.

Looking left and right, up and down the hall, he entered the room. Everyone was there before him, already seated.

No one stood as they normally did, and exhaustion was stamped on every face. Friar Tuck pulled the chair out beside him, gesturing for the cardinal to sit. The rotund monk had been in the thick of caring for the sick, and it showed in looser-fitting robes and the dark circles under his eyes.

Marian had spent her days here, as well, doing much the same as the rest, providing comfort as best she could and assistance to the brotherhood. The exertion had made her paler, her skin nearly ivory white and stark against the dark of her tresses. Darkness smudged under her eyes and gave her beauty a haunted quality.

Alan's body curled, weary of being straight as he'd spent every moment combing through the nearby parts of Sherwood, using his vast druidic knowledge to locate any medicinal plants to be had, attempting to replicate a healing elixir mentioned in the legends of the land.

Robin had grown darker still, pulled into himself. Any time not spent holding Longstride Manor together was devoted to hunting like a fiend, trying to help provide nourishment to be given to the sick. He'd driven himself to the brink of his prowess, but had no ability to stop. He scowled, arms crossed, looking eager to be gone again.

Only Will Scarlet showed no sign of stress or strain—if anything, the troubled time had burnished him like a coin in a pocket. He leaned forward.

"This is the prince's fault."

No one spoke.

"Did you hear me?"

"We heard you," Friar Tuck said.

"And?"

"And there's nothing we can do about him right now." The monk pushed away from the table. "We all have tasks to perform."

"Wait!" Scarlet said. "Hear me out. He is behind this plague, he and the Sheriff. Perhaps if the prince was... gone... the plague would be lifted."

Friar Tuck rounded, slamming his hands on the table and leaning over it.

"This is a plague, Will Scarlet. No matter how it started, I don't think it can be stopped by... what? By killing a man? Even if he is the one responsible."

The cardinal laid his hand on Tuck's arm.

"Listen to him," Marian pointed at them. "He's not being foolish. We know from the prophecies that Cardinal Francis has shared with us that an evil splinter will poison the land. Perhaps it is time that splinter was plucked out. Perhaps, as with any splinter, once it is removed then the flesh can heal."

Friar Tuck sat back down, and Scarlet continued.

"I have overheard even more conversations between the prince and the Sheriff," he said, his words carefully measured. "This pox isn't their ultimate purpose. It is evil magic they have made to destroy the spirit of the people. They have something even more terrible planned. I am sure of it."

Francis blinked the exhaustion from his mind. "Did you hear anything about how to stop this sickness?" he asked. "Anything about its nature that may help us?"

"No."

"Then we are doing all that we can." He stood. "We must continue our efforts."

"But if they are responsible, then surely this can be stopped?"

"That may be true," the cardinal replied, "so it becomes your task to find out how. You remain in their confidence. Until then, we can only carry on ministering to those who have been stricken. We dare not make a move against the prince. Not now. We have too much else to worry about. And I can't condone murder, no matter what type of monster he is."

"But..."

"Will Scarlet!" Francis roared. The younger man's eyes widened. "People just outside that door are suffering. Either they are dying, or losing someone they love dearly. Do not call us back here until you have found a way to stop this."

"I did not mean..."

Robin stood, cutting his cousin off.

"You've spoken your peace, now go back to the castle," he said. "We have work to do."

He walked from the room without a second glance.

"It does not work. We might as well be pouring water down their throats." Friar Tuck pulled his fingers from the neck of a man growing cold in death.

"No help with the fever?" Alan asked.

"Just enough to ease the delirium, so they are fully aware when death comes." He stood and thrust the jar at the bard. "Your potion is a failure."

Alan took the jar, its contents sloshing. "I sought help from the local medicine women and hedgewitches..."

"Find better help," the monk growled, shoving his finger towards the container. "That is no good."

"There was no help. They are gone," Alan said. "All of them. This was my own meager attempt at medicine."

Friar Tuck looked at his friend, feeling a hard twinge for insulting his effort. It was swallowed up the moment he looked around the room at the dead and dying. He sighed.

"Has there been progress locating the elixir?" he asked. As he did, Alan's jaw tightened.

"If there was, would I have brought you this pitiful attempt?" he replied sullenly.

"No, I don't suppose so." Tuck knew what this might mean, and the thought chilled him to his soul.

The shadows twisted around him. With every step they seemed to slither out from under his foot just before it touched the ground. He was used to the shadows back in Sherwood, which almost seemed alive thanks to the movement of the sun and the wind that rustled through the trees. This was different. These shadows had substance, a kind of weight to them.

No one else moved in the castle. It was quiet and empty, unlike anything he'd ever seen in it before. The whole place felt bewitched, a weird energy in the night air. He would hear whispers and every time he turned, sure that someone was behind him, he found an empty hallway. Yet the whispers continued sliding over each other, even as the shadows did, just soft enough that most moments he doubted he was hearing them at all.

Perhaps it was simply his own blood, rushing through his hearing in the dead quiet.

He remembered a childhood game he had played with Marian in these very halls. Hide-and-seek, it had been. In his memory, the palace seemed alive then, full of light and merriment. Even his father was less stern when he was there, and his mother had glowed like a radiant angel as she laughed and talked with others. Those days seemed like the echo of a distant memory, though, and it was hard to reconcile them with the present.

Ah, Marian.

His chest tightened at the thought of her. Had she known what he was doing, she would have tried to stop him. She would remind him that he would be killed. If not in the immediate fray, then he would surely hang later.

If he looked into her eyes, he would turn from this path.

That was why he couldn't tell her. That was why he couldn't tell anyone. What he was doing was right. It might save them all. All except him, of course. His father wouldn't be surprised. He'd comment that Robin's temper had been destined to bring him to a bad end.

Let the old man be right about this. He could go to the grave with that and so much more on his conscience, as long as he was able to free England from the tyranny of the usurper. Saving the people—particularly his well-meaning friends—was all that mattered.

The truth was, Will had been right. The prince had brought this upon the people and the prince needed to be stopped. One way or another. He just prayed that Marian had been right, that removing John would be like removing a poisoned splinter, and that the land, the people, could begin to heal. At the very least he hoped no more devilment could be rained down upon them as his friends searched for a cure.

A door opened and Robin flattened himself against the wall, scarcely daring to breathe. A servant exited the room, scurrying down the hall in the other direction carrying an empty food tray. Robin paused, waiting until the girl was out of sight. He was pretty sure he recognized her. Chastity. She'd been with them, hiding and seeking so long ago.

She must've come from Marian's room.

It wasn't good, the fact that Marian was taking her meals so late and in isolation. He'd have to speak to her about that. It made it possible for someone to harm her, and for her absence to go unnoticed until it was too late.

He shook his head. After tonight he wouldn't be around to warn her. Then again, after tonight she would have no reason to fear. So he continued on, sliding silently past her chambers.

He almost entered, the doorway pulling at him, drawing him like a moth to a candle flame.

All he wanted before he died was to see her face once more.

He gritted his teeth and forced himself to keep going. The sooner this was over, the better off she and the others would be. He came to a set of stairs leading down into the king's bedchamber.

Just thinking about the prince, tainting all that belonged to King Richard, made his blood boil. The cowardly wretch hid behind Locksley and his tax collectors and the Sheriff and his soldiers. The people suffered because of them all. Strike off the head and the body would cease to function. There might be short-term chaos, but he trusted the remaining lords to handle it until Richard's return.

Just outside the heavy door he paused. He drew his dagger from his belt. The prince did not deserve a swift death, but he would receive one nonetheless. He paused and pulled the hood up, concealing his face, though he knew it was a useless gesture. He reached out a hand and tried the door.

It swung inward easily and silently on greased hinges. Robin stepped inside, closing it quietly behind him.

The room was much darker even than the hallway had been, and it took a long moment for his eyes to adjust. The whispering took on an urgency. Maybe whatever was making the sound was unhappy that he was there.

He took three steps forward and the whispering changed into a low moaning that caused the hair to rise on the back of his neck. There was something unnatural at work here. He didn't have time to think about it, however, so he pushed it from his mind. His eyes were drinking in the dark and translating it for him to see.

His prey lay in the bed on the far side of the room.

Asleep.

Robin strode quickly forward, his footfalls light on the stone floors and undetectable to human ears. Years of hunting in Sherwood had taught him to be as silent as one of its wild predators. He was halfway to the bed when something grabbed at the back of his shirt. He spun, knife raised, prepared to slash at whoever was there.

There was nothing.

He turned back, setting his jaw. He closed the rest of the gap between him and the king's bed. Prince John lay on his back, eyes closed and lightly snoring. Robin raised the knife high and brought it down with all his might, aiming for the black heart beneath him.

An inch from the body the knife slammed into something. The jolt vibrated up Robin's arm, enraging muscle and nerve from wrist to shoulder. Pain slammed into him and he lost his hold on the knife. It toppled over and hovered just above the prince as if on a cushion of air, then slid away like rain off a leaf.

It clattered on the floor.

Invisible hands grabbed Robin and threw him backward, pinning him to the wall next to the door. The voices that at first had whispered and moaned now screeched, screaming into his ear. The sound slipped under his eardrum and into his head, vibrating in his skull. He writhed in anguish as white-hot knife cuts slashed behind his eyeballs.

A sinister laugh cut through the noise.

The prince rose off the bed and gained his feet without ever having sat up. He glided toward Robin, feet not touching the ground. The laughter grew louder, more maniacal as he drew near.

"Think to murder me, would you, outlaw?" the prince said. "You're not in the forest now, protected by your spirits. You are in my world, and I can assure you that the spirits here are under my command."

Something struck Robin in the stomach, then the chest, feeling like tiny fists. They drove into him, punching deep, driving to bone where they stayed. The pressure was intense. He thought his bones would snap at any moment.

Then it changed.

The pressure opened up.

Then the biting began. He couldn't see anything but he felt

teeth, tiny, razored teeth, chewing into his skin. Panic crawled into him—something he'd never felt before. It was alien, foreign, and inescapable, digging hooked claws into his psyche. Prince John spat out a word, guttural and inhuman, and something sharp as a knife slashed him across his left thigh.

He struggled not to cry out.

"What have you sold yourself to?" he asked, grinding his teeth together to keep a scream from following the words out of his mouth.

More laughter came pouring out of John, along with more shadows that filled the room all around him.

"I am the master here," the prince said.

Robin pushed the panic away, driving it from his mind. It still sat in his skull, waiting to pounce and destroy him, but he had to *think*. His bow and quiver were still strapped to his back. He had them in case he'd needed to fight his way in, or had been lucky enough to try and fight his way out. He twisted an arm behind him, struggling to reach an arrow. He couldn't even lift the arm over his head.

His fingers scratched at the leather, pulling at the knot in the quiver's stitching.

Slowly the prince slid closer and Robin twisted, pulling, clawing, his fingers beginning to bleed. The knot began to give, little by little. At last he could wriggle a finger in there, his fingers pricking against the sharp edge of an arrowhead. He dug deeper, trying to widen the hole he had made.

"You have been quite a bother, outlaw, but now you have come to me. Your arrogance, your presumption, shall be your own undoing."

Keep talking...

Robin closed his eyes, breathing a silent prayer as he pulled on the arrow with all his might. He was still being hit and scratched. Something bit him just over the fourth rib on his right side and he couldn't contain the cry of agony as he felt the flesh being torn from him.

"You are nothing," John hissed, standing in front of him now. "And now you will return to the nothing from which you came."

The arrow slid free, dropping through his fingers. He caught it just below the fletching and opened his eyes.

"After you." He thrust with the arrow. It struck, catching the prince in the throat. The man hissed in pain and fell back. The forces pinning Robin to the wall disappeared, and he dropped to the ground. Pushing through the pain, he scrambled to his feet. The prince pulled the arrow out of his throat and dropped it to the ground.

There was no blood.

Robin grabbed hold of the door, opened it, and flung himself into the hall. The weapons he had were no match for the prince. He had to warn the cardinal and the others. They needed to know what he had seen. He would have given his life to end the man's tyranny, but now he had to live to help them find a way to stop the monster he had just faced.

Moving rapidly, he was up the stairs and into the main hall when he heard the door open behind him.

"Guards!" The voice was piercingly sharp.

Robin wondered why. It would be easier for the monster to chase him down and finish him. Perhaps the prince didn't want to risk having anyone else see him as he truly was.

He ran down the corridor, his mind racing, trying to plan an escape route. Every step brought pain that threatened to drop him at any moment.

He needed help.

He didn't know where in the blasted castle his cousin might be. He couldn't call out. So he searched for a doorway as he stumbled, looking for anyplace he could hide. Noise began to fill the halls behind him, the guard roused by the prince's calls.

He wasn't going to make it. He would never find his way out. And he was getting weaker with every step.

He would be captured and killed, and no one would know.

Marian. He could at least warn Marian. That way someone

would know, and be able to warn the cardinal. Without conscious thought he turned toward her room, stumbling his way down the hallway.

His hand was on the door when she opened it. He fell inside, crashing to his knees and clenching his teeth in pain. He pulled himself into the room and she slammed and bolted the door.

"Robin!" she gasped, dropping down next to him. Her eyes swept over him, taking in his injuries. He was bleeding on her floor, and he wanted to say something, tell her he was sorry. The world swam before his eyes, until all he could see was her face. "Who did this to you?"

"The prince," he managed to say, although it hurt his chest to speak. "He... he can control... something. Demons... shadows. I couldn't kill him."

"My God, Robin," she said, taking his face in her hands, scanning the room for something she might use to help. Tears streamed down her cheeks.

"I failed you," he whispered, struggling to move. He couldn't, though. He could see his own blood pooling on the floor. There was so much of it. "He's not human." She had to know, to understand.

"Don't talk, I'll get help," she said, standing to go.

He grabbed her wrist. "You have to tell the cardinal."

"I will, Robin, I swear," she said firmly. "We'll tell him together."

The darkness came for him suddenly and without remorse.

CHAPTER TWENTY-NINE

Will woke to a pounding on his door. He rose, throwing on his dressing robe, and answered. Chastity stared at him, her eyes huge and white-ringed.

He conjured up a smile for her.

"What can I help you with, lovely lass?" There were all sorts of things with which he'd love to help her. All of a sudden, being so rudely awoken didn't seem so bad.

"My lady needs to see you," she said. "Now."

"You are summoning me for Marian?"

She shook her head, refusing to speak. There was a streak of blood on her sleeve.

"Let me dress," he said.

"There's no time."

"At least let me bring my clothes." He scooped up the items he'd worn earlier that day, which he'd left crumpled on a chair. Closing his door, he followed Chastity into the hall. When he expected her to turn right, though, she turned left.

"Where are we going?"

"Be quiet!" she hissed.

Whatever could have made her speak to him in that tone must be serious indeed, he mused. He followed her through the castle, winding, turning, until even he had no idea where he was.

He heard angry shouting at one point from at least a couple of different voices, and realized something was happening outside. He didn't bother trying to seek out a window, however. The sound, coupled with her fear, made him step even faster.

At last they came to a corridor he did recognize, and he realized she had taken him by a very circuitous route to Marian's room. There had to be a reason for the caution. She knocked— four times in rapid succession—and a moment later he heard a bolt being pulled back.

He hurried into the room behind Chastity, and Marian herself threw the bolt again. She turned around to look at him. She wore nothing but her nightclothes, and he made a point of not seeming to notice.

He did notice, though. Marian was lovely when dressed, elegant and regal, with the bearing of royalty stamped on every inch of her. Seeing her in the thin cotton gown she wore to bed, her hair loose and free, his body responded. She had an air of wildness to her. He'd seen her fierce in fighting, but the energy in her now was of a much more wanton potential.

"Pull it together," she said, and he realized he had been standing there without saying a word. "I...*we* need your help." She grabbed his arm. Before he could ask her what was wrong, she turned and pointed toward the bed.

He followed her gaze.

Robin lay crumpled on the floor near it, his face white as death and blood everywhere. Will leapt forward, his clothes falling to the floor in a heap. He dropped to his knees beside the body, everything forgotten in the panic.

His cousin bled from a dozen wounds, and he lay in a twisted heap, contorted and broken. Blood-soaked bandages were pressed over his ribcage and a tourniquet was tied around his one thigh.

"What happened?"

"He tried to kill John."

"And the Sheriff caught him?"

"He said the prince did."

Will looked up at her, an oath on his lips.

"John? But how? He's dangerous, but no match for Robin in a fight."

"Damn it, Will! He didn't give me details! Robin said he commanded shadows. That he wasn't human."

Through the window Will heard more angry shouting. Additional voices had joined the hue and cry.

"They're searching for him outside," he said. "He needs a doctor."

"I can't get out of the castle to fetch one," Chastity said.

"Then we need more clean cloth, water—whatever you can find. Needle and thread, as well," Will said. Chastity bobbed her head and headed out the door.

Seconds later she was back. "They are searching throughout the castle for him," she said. "Every room."

Marian nodded. "Get what we need, but make sure you don't get caught." She glanced around, then snatched up a dirty shift from her hamper. "As you go, trace the corridors nearby and look for any blood he may have left. Wipe it away if you can. If you get caught…"

"I'll tell them it's my time. They won't question further." The curly-headed girl stepped back into the hall.

"And don't return until after they have searched this room," Will called.

Chastity nodded her understanding and then left.

"What are we going to do?" Marian asked as she bolted the door again.

"I would love to believe that the prince and his men wouldn't have the gall to search your room, but I know better." He looked around, weighing his options. He nodded to himself. "We must prepare. Help me get him onto the bed."

It was a testament to the faith that she had in him that she didn't ask why, just ran to his side to help.

"We need to carry him to the far side. If you can get his legs, I think we can do this."

Already the covers on Marian's bed were tossed back. Clearly she had retired for the evening when Robin made his unexpected appearance at her door. He caught movement out of the corner of his eye, and saw a tail disappearing under the bed. Marian must have acquired a pet.

Robin, why didn't you tell me what you were going to do? Will thought, not realizing he could be this angry and this frightened, both at the same time. They picked him up and, after much staggering, got him around to the other side of the bed and then up onto it. Once he was in place, Will pulled the covers over him.

Then he peeled off his robe and used it to mop up the couple of obvious blood puddles. Finished, he shoved the garment under the covers next to Robin.

"That will never work," Marian said, an edge of panic to her voice. "They will see him there, won't they? They'll be able to tell someone's in the bed."

Will paused. He knew what he had to do, but he needed her cooperation.

"Marian, what would you do to save Robin?" he asked.

"Anything." Her voice was intense, her eyes unwavering.

"So would I," he said. "Also... I'm sorry." He stepped over to the door and unbolted it.

"What are you doing?" she asked, eyes widening. "They'll be here any minute!"

"I know, and when they come, we'll have to let them in anyway. This will just look more... natural."

"Natural?" she asked as he walked back toward her. He could hear the guards in the hallway. They'd be there in seconds. Marian narrowed her eyes. "What are you sorry for?"

"This," he said, as he came to stand right next to her. His clothes already lay in a heap between the door and the bed. His bloodied robe was safely hidden away. He stepped close enough to touch. Marian stared at him, eyes widening in shock as she realized how little he was wearing. She'd never seen a man in this state of undress before. He was bare-chested, and below he wore just his braies, the thin linen covering only to mid-thigh and cinched loosely around his waist.

Before she could react he pushed her onto the bed and dove on top of her, laying his body across hers. She drove her palm into his chin and his teeth crashed together, biting the edge of his tongue. His mouth filled with pain and blood. Her eyes flashed with fire and she swung at him again. He grabbed her arms, trying to pin her to the bed. She fought and bucked, nearly tossing him off.

"Stop it, Marian!" he hissed. "On Robin's life, this is necessary!"

She froze, her body locked in place, muscles singing with tension.

"This is the only thing we have time for," he said. "Trust me."

Marian looked into his eyes and he looked back, willing her to see his good intentions.

She lay back onto the bed beneath him, her body still tense.

"I'm sorry," he whispered again, softly. She was a good woman, and she didn't deserve the shame that was about to rain down on her. She would do anything to save Robin, though.

So would he.

Seconds later her door flew open and they both reacted, her with a little scream. Will seethed inwardly. The dogs hadn't even bothered to knock before charging in. He marked the faces of the four men who entered. If he lived through this, there would be retribution.

The Sheriff came last.

Even though Marian struggled beneath him, Will took his time sitting up, and when he did his skin felt hot, flushed. Marian cringed behind him, and her body blocked them from seeing the lump that Robin made.

"Men should knock on a lady's door." Will put a touch of anger and a touch of arrogance in his voice. "What is the meaning of this rude intrusion?"

"How did you get in here?" one of the guards demanded.

Will turned to him. "I knocked. You see, that gets you a much... warmer reception." His voice lightly mocked. His reputation as a rogue would be the thing that saved them all.

One of the guards leered at Marian. Will leapt from the bed and crossed the room in three strides, trusting his spectacle to keep them from looking beyond her to the far side of the bed.

He shoved his chest against the offending guard.

"You will not look at the lady that way," Will warned.

"Not so much a lady, is she?" the guard said.

In one swift move Will snatched the man's own dagger off his belt and stabbed upward. The blade sank deep into the man's forearm, scraping between the bones. Will jerked the blade out in a splash of blood, slinging it around the floor as he did so. He hoped it would cover any of Robin's blood he might have missed. The guard crumpled to the ground, holding his arm and howling. Will dropped the knife on top of him.

He glared at the other three guards.

"You'll get the same, if one word leaves this room."

"Worried about her reputation?" the Sheriff asked.

"No, mine." Will turned to the man in the black armor, pouring smarm into his words. "The ladies love me because I'm discreet. I make them believe when I tell them that there's never been anyone else in my heart. When they find it not to be true, they know they can count on me not to reveal their indiscretions—for which they are immensely grateful.

"A rumor such as this, substantiated by the king's guard, would ruin me at court." He stepped close to the Sheriff. Being that close made Will's skin crawl, but he forced himself to stand there and lock eyes with the man. He dropped his voice low. "It took me years to talk my way into her bed. I've never worked so hard at anything in my life."

"Why the effort?"

"I would tell you to just look at her, but that didn't work out so well for the last man who did."

"I believe the outcome would be different, if you tried with me."

"She would still be worth the try," Will replied. "She is above me in station."

"Except for a moment ago, when she was beneath you," the Sheriff sneered.

Will forced a smile. "Granted, but if her protectors found me out, one of two things would happen. I would be executed, or I would be forced to marry, in which case I might as well be dead."

"Marriage is akin to death?"

Will sighed. "I'm a very simple creature. I only want one meal in my life, but I want it from as many kitchens as will serve me."

The Sheriff's eyes flicked past him to Marian, then back to him.

"Let's go," he said to his men. Then he turned and strode outside. The three guards picked up their fallen comrade and carried him from the room. Once they had gone Will shut the door, bolted it, and then sank onto his knees, shaking like a leaf in the wind. He buried his head in his hands and thanked God his ruse had worked.

He could hear Marian behind him, moving around. She didn't say anything, for which he was grateful. He didn't want to face her. Not yet.

A soft knock on the door, four times in rapid succession, and he started to his feet. He opened the door a crack and found Chastity carrying a bowl of water. He let her in and then bolted the door again.

When he turned he saw that Marian was wearing robes over her nightdress. Her cheeks burned red. She walked around to the far side of the bed and uncovered Robin. Chastity quickly set the bowl on a table next to the bed.

"I came as soon as they were gone," she said, her voice almost a whisper. "How did you keep them from searching the room?"

Marian looked at Will and then turned her eyes down.

"We gave them something else to look at."

* * *

"You saved us all with your quick thinking," Marian said quietly. She didn't look up at him, starting to work on Robin. "Thank you. Truly."

"I only did…"

"Will—" Marian cut him off.

"Yes?"

"Get the hell out of my room."

Will nodded. He started to go, picking up the clothes which were still in a heap on the floor. At some point in all the stress, they seemed to have forgotten the fact that he was half-naked.

"I'll just dress before leaving," he said.

Marian nodded and turned, giving him whatever dignity she could at that point. Chastity, on the other hand, stared unabashedly, pink rising in her cheeks.

I had no idea she fancied Will, Marian thought tiredly. She didn't see how that could end well for either of them. Then again, she was one to talk. Will and Chastity stood a better chance at this moment in time than did she and Robin.

CHAPTER THIRTY

Marian had been humiliated. Worse than that, it was the most intimate contact she'd ever had with a man. She wasn't squeamish, but given the circumstances it left her unsettled, feeling like she needed to wash it all away.

Yet she was grateful for what Will Scarlet had done. If it weren't for his ruse, the Sheriff and his men most certainly would have found and killed Robin. She could only imagine what the prince would have done to her and Will. And just like that, their revolution would have been over scarcely before it had even begun. It gave her a sick feeling in the pit of her stomach, just thinking about it.

She and Chastity cleaned and bound Robin's wounds to the best of their abilities. Something beyond her imagining had caused deep claw marks and a hideous wound on his ribs, leaving jagged teeth marks along the edges.

"He's going to be lucky to live out the night," Chastity said, when they had done all they could.

"Then we will just need to have faith," Marian said, as she pushed a lock of hair out of Robin's face. His skin felt hot to the touch. It worried her more than she cared to admit.

"We won't be able to smuggle a healer in here tonight. Nor a priest, if things…"

"He won't have need of a priest," Marian said firmly. "As for the healer, we'll get one when we can."

Chastity tucked a corner of the blanket under Robin's leg. "I don't think we should move him."

"I agree," Marian said. "They've already been here. They're not likely to come looking again. He should be safe enough." She glanced up at Chastity, who swayed on her feet. "You should go get some sleep."

"Not before you."

Chastity came to stand by her.

"Get some rest, princess," she said. "I insist."

"Alright," Marian agreed. There was nothing more she could do but pray, and she'd been doing that for hours. Chastity could keep watch until the morning. Then they'd see what was to be done.

She glanced around foggily.

"Go ahead and sleep in your bed," Chastity said, a teasing tone in her voice. "I won't tell anyone that there was a man in it."

If only you'd seen me earlier.

She couldn't come up with a witty response, so instead she just nodded in resignation. She lay down, but didn't pull the covers up. That way she would be ready to rise at a moment's notice.

She felt hands shaking her, hard.

"Marian, *wake up*."

She recognized the voice as belonging to Chastity, and forced her eyes open to see the girl's worried face.

"He's cold, he's shaking, and I don't know what to do," Chastity said.

Marian turned and saw that Robin's form was indeed trembling. She reached out a hand and discovered that where his skin had been hot to the touch, it was now ice cold. Chastity had already pulled the blankets up over him, and added what others Marian owned.

She glanced around the room, her mind grasping for what to do.

"Start a fire," she said. "We'll drag him over next to it." Chastity nodded and flew to the far side of the room, where she busied herself thrusting wood into the fireplace. Marian moved close to Robin and put her arms around him, holding him, trying to warm him. The thin shift she wore offered almost no barrier. His skin felt cool as wet clay against hers.

"Don't you dare leave me," she whispered to him. She began to rub his chest as fast as she could, trying to get his blood moving. He groaned, muttering under his breath, but she couldn't make out any words.

Within moments the fire roared to life. Somehow she and Chastity found the strength to carry him to it. Marian held him there as Chastity wrapped more blankets around them. Soon Marian was sweating freely, the fire and the blankets stifling her, but she willed that warmth, that life, into him.

Finally, after what felt like a lifetime, his skin began to warm and he stopped muttering. His limbs ceased twitching and he fell into a deep sleep. She looked up and saw that the sky outside her window was beginning to lighten with the coming of the dawn. They had made it through the long, dark night.

She hoped that was a sign.

Much was worried. Everywhere his father sent him to make deliveries, the pox had been before him.

The family of masons was his latest delivery and as he walked slowly up to the stone house a sinking sensation curled in the pit of his stomach. It was quiet, far too quiet for mid-afternoon.

He stopped a little way from the house, hesitant to go any further.

"Hello?" he called out, hoping to hear a friendly voice.

Only silence greeted him.

Carefully he set down his grain. He walked forward. The door hung partway open. He leaned forward, careful not to touch anything, but still trying to get a glance inside. What he saw turned his stomach. He ran a few feet away before retching.

When he'd finished he stood, wiping his mouth on his sleeve. They were dead. All six of them were dead, their bodies in a pile in the middle of the floor. Who could have, no, who *would* have piled them that way, he had no idea. They were covered in open sores and flies.

It was best to get away from the place, and quickly. He picked up his grain, wondering who was left to take it. He turned and began to walk, not going anywhere in particular, just getting away as fast as his feet could carry him. He had gone nearly a mile down the road when he heard someone calling for help.

It sounded like a girl. He hurried on and found her just around a bend. It was a servant and she lay on her side just off the road, up against the embankment. He stopped well away from her when he saw that she had the sores on her, as well.

"Please," she begged him. "I was sent to get help. They're sick. They're all very sick, and I can't find my master to tell him."

"Who is sick?" he asked.

"My lady and her daughters."

"I know it hurts," he said. "I will go get help. Tell me the names."

"Lady Glynna of Longstride."

CHAPTER THIRTY-ONE

Friar Tuck barely held in a curse when he saw the Miller's boy walking toward the monastery, a girl draped in his arms. He held open a door so the boy could pass inside the building, and then led them to the dining hall. All around the room the sick lay on what thin pieces of cloth were left. The boy found an empty spot on the floor and set her down.

Then he stood and gazed solemnly at the friar.

"She came from Longstride Manor. She said that the ladies of the manor are all sick, and that no one knows where Robin is."

A chill touched Friar Tuck's heart. Was the cursed pox going to claim all of England before it was through? He and the others who called the monastery home had been taking turns tending to the sick and praying for God to lift the blight from the land. All except the bishop.

"Thank you for bringing her," he told the boy.

Much nodded gravely. "There's something else. When I went to the Mason's villa, they were all dead."

"God rest their souls," Friar Tuck murmured. More good people struck down. He was beyond anger, too exhausted for it. Instead he was just deeply grieved.

"Someone had stacked their bodies in a pile, like firewood, in the middle of their home."

Friar Tuck frowned. "Are you sure?"

"I saw them with my own eyes," Much insisted. "Who would do that?"

"I don't know, but it doesn't sound good," Tuck admitted. Actually, it sounded like the devil's own handiwork, but he didn't say so out loud. There was no need to scare the lad. He cleared his throat.

"Well, you'd best be off."

The boy hesitated, staring intently at him.

Friar Tuck pulled at the collar of his robe. It was getting hot inside. Stuffy, as well. Sweat had been pouring off him in tiny rivulets all day. The one that had found its way down his spine was especially irritating.

"Where am I to go?" Much said.

"Go home, lad, that is the best thing you can do at this point," Tuck advised him.

"Friar?"

"Yes?"

"You don't look well."

"It's this heat," he said, wishing he had something with which to mop his brow. "I never do well with the heat, and it's sweltering in here. It's a wonder I don't melt like snow in the summer."

"Friar, it's not hot in here at all."

Tuck stared at the boy as he wondered which one of them had lost his mind. It had to be the boy, he concluded, because anyone with any wits at all could tell that it was hellfire hot.

"Honestly, boy, are you alright?" he asked, as he swatted at a fly that buzzed around his face. Sweat had rolled down his forehead, and now a bead of it hung off the tip of his nose. He was getting dizzy. He was too tired. He'd been working too hard with no sleep. He needed to rest himself a little while. Maybe just an hour or two would help.

The cardinal appeared in the doorway. "Friar Tuck, I need to see you in my study."

Tuck nodded, took three steps, and fell down face-first.

* * *

Much jumped backward with a cry as Friar Tuck landed on the floor near him. The large man had fallen so swiftly that the boy hadn't a prayer of catching him. One moment he was standing, and the next he was not. For a terrible second he wondered if the man had been struck down by God.

The cardinal rushed over and Much backed up, bowing his head to show respect. His father had told him that a cardinal was second only to the pope.

"What's your name, son?" the holy man asked, his voice sounding rough.

"I'm Much, the Miller's son."

"Help me roll him over, good Much."

Much dropped down and grasped the friar's thick shoulders. He pulled and the cardinal pushed, and together they rolled the friar onto his back. Once they had done so, Much stood up quickly and backed away.

"His face!"

The cardinal had also seen the red blotches springing up on Friar Tuck's skin. He looked grimly at Much.

"He's been stricken," he confirmed.

"Is he going to die?" Much asked as he stepped back a couple more feet. He didn't want Friar Tuck to die, but in his mind he kept imagining his body piled on top of the bodies of his family. He didn't want to think it, but he couldn't help it.

"No," the cardinal said. "He will not."

That made Much feel a little better. The cardinal was a wise man and a good one. Maybe God would listen to him.

"Help me move him some more," the cardinal instructed.

After a moment's hesitation, Much complied. He thought they were going to place the friar next to the others, but instead they moved him into the cardinal's study, which was covered in books and scraps of parchment. The smell of old leather and new ink made him wrinkle his nose.

Once they had the friar on the floor in a position that was as comfortable as it could be, the cardinal looked at him.

"Thank you, young Much. I think it's best if you went home to your family now."

He nodded and scurried out of the room. Outside the monastery he noticed the sun sinking low toward the horizon. He hurried, moving faster. He wanted to make it home before it was dark. The tiny village below the monastery looked peaceful in the fading light. He hoped it didn't mean everyone was dead.

Lenore ran up the road to her house, slingshot in hand. She had been targeting some rats down by the woodpile when she'd seen the soldiers coming up the road, headed for her home. Her father was there—he'd know what to do.

She was out of breath when she made it in the door and both her parents turned to look at her. They had been sitting at the table and she could tell from the looks on their faces that they'd been having one of their serious talks, the kind they didn't like her to hear.

"What is it, Lenore?" her mother asked, voice tense.

"Soldiers, coming this way."

"It's time," her father said, voice and face hardening as he stood to his feet. He looked at her. "Lenore, hide yourself."

When he used that tone of voice she knew better than to ask why. She ran toward the back of the house. There were barrels stacked by the back door. They contained food supplies, but also some of the goods that her father would sell on his journeys. She crouched behind them, straining to listen.

She heard raised voices. Then, clearly, "I'm surprised to see you both alive."

"The pox has not hit us, thank God," she heard her father say.

"Just as well, merchant, someone has to be left to pay the king's tax."

"He's no king of ours," her mother said, voice ringing, defiant.

Lenore felt her heart begin to pound.

"He is," the strange man said, "and he will have his due. Half of everything you have."

"The devil take him," her father said. "We have nothing that can be spared."

She heard something, the sound of a fist striking flesh. Then scuffling as of a struggle. Her heart pounded harder in her chest. Then she heard her mother cry out, a loud, wailing sound that turned wicked at the end. More scuffling, a thud.

Lenore risked peering over the edge of a barrel.

Her parents lay on the ground, unmoving. A man stood above them, sword drawn and dripping with blood. She bit back a cry as she realized he had killed both her parents.

Her head spun as rage vied with her grief. She clutched the slingshot tighter, wishing that she was David from the Bible stories and that she had a stone big enough to kill a man with.

She didn't, though, and she knew instinctively that if she made her presence known she'd be swiftly joining her parents in death. Or worse. Her father had warned her about being taken unawares by strange men.

Lenore knew what she had to do. She had to run. Get as far away as fast as she could. She could go to the monastery. Her father had always told her that it was a safe place.

She kept low as she moved to the back door. The men were all starting to go through the kitchen, greedy hands grabbing at her parents' things. None were looking her way as she seized the knob and twisted. She eased the door open, made it outside and shut it.

Then she ran for all she was worth.

Alan-a-Dale was on his way to the home of the blacksmith and his wife. It would be his last stop for the day. At the moment he was the only one free to deliver food, medicine, and a little money to the people. Friar Tuck and the cardinal were busy tending the sick. Will and Marian were at the castle attending a gathering—one at which he had not been invited to play.

He was relieved, rather than offended. He was not in the mood to make merry in front of the prince. Not while so many suffered. The songs in his heart that day were only dirges. Of Robin's whereabouts he had no idea. That was often the case, though, with Lord Longstride.

It had been a dark day. By his calculations at least one in three people had been infected by the plague. There wasn't even a logic to the sickness. Sometimes only one person in a home was infected, and other times the entire family. A home might have been spared entirely, yet be surrounded by death on all sides. He struggled to make sense of it.

If the prince had truly cursed them, then it seemed as if there would be a method to the situation, but so far he'd discovered only madness. Young and old, male and female, rich and poor... all were at risk. The lack of a pattern frightened him the most.

The food in the sack on his back weighed him down. He was used to traveling much lighter than this. His feet were weary, and that was the state of his soul, as well. The mind and body were connected in all creatures, but he had long ago realized that he felt the connection more strongly than others. It was part of his calling, his gift.

Days like this, it felt more like a curse.

He rounded a bend and the blacksmith's house came into view. He stopped abruptly. There were a dozen horses outside, including two that were laden with various packs and objects. Three guards stood outside. Two more came out, carrying items from the house that they fastened on the beasts.

Alan found himself in the rare position of being speechless. The guards were robbing the family of everything that could possibly be melted down or sold. Not a sign could be seen of the victims of this heinous act.

Another guard came out of the house, followed by Locksley, and Alan felt the anger rising within him. He stepped back out of sight, though, before any of the brigands could spy him, but not before noticing that the brand new flowers the woman had planted were being trampled underfoot.

Locksley began barking orders at his men. A minute later Alan heard the horses heading down the road. Leaving his hiding place, he walked slowly toward the house, wondering what words of comfort he could possibly bring to the family in such an hour of anguish. Suddenly the scant few items in the sack on his back felt as if they weighed next to nothing, far too humble a gift for those who had just lost everything.

He tried not to look down at the ruined flowers as he stepped up to the door.

"Hello?" he called softly.

There was no response.

He walked inside, expecting to find the family devastated.

Instead he found them dead.

He gasped and froze in place. Their pox-marked bodies were stacked one on top of the other in the middle of the room, their unseeing eyes no longer able to witness the atrocities committed against them and their home.

Alan backed slowly out of the house. The prince's tax collectors had committed their greatest atrocity to date. They had stolen from the dead.

CHAPTER THIRTY-TWO

Marian didn't know which angered her more—the fact that in the midst of the people's suffering, the prince chose to host a ball, or the fact that nobles from all over England, those who hadn't been taken by the pox, had actually come to attend it. The very act seemed like the ultimate in cruel jests.

She knew why they did it, though. After the hangings most had fallen in line, terrified of crossing John in the slightest. They did as they were told. So they came to the ball, and she could see more than one concerned parent cast their eyes toward the upstairs where they believed their children were still being held captive.

The truth was Marian had no idea where the children were kept. Chastity had learned that they had been moved in the night, though no one seemed to know where.

Marian herself was given no choice but to attend. The prince had commanded it, and these days she needed to be very careful about choosing her battles. Yet she was participating in one small act of rebellion. Instead of being downstairs in time to play hostess and greet all the guests, as she always had for King Richard, she tarried in her room until she was sure most people had already arrived.

The usurper's insult provided an unexpected opportunity, as well. With so many people milling about, Will would be able to smuggle Robin to safety. The Lord of Longstride had spent the last day in his cousin's room. While he was stable enough to travel, he was still a long way from healed. Will had made arrangements for him to be taken from the castle, but he had not shared the details.

When she finally descended to the great hall, she did so with a smile frozen on her face. She wore a burgundy gown shot through with gold threads, and small gold rosettes tied up extra bits of fabric all around. She wore her hair meticulously coiled atop her head, going out of her way to look her best, hoping that it would portray strength and confidence. With a small twinge of regret she wished Robin had been well enough to attend. She was sure he would have said something very flattering.

There were more in attendance than she would have guessed, although a few faces seemed to be notably absent as she strolled through the room. She passed a small cluster of women and nodded to them. None of them returned her greeting, instead dropping their eyes or looking suddenly away as though they hadn't seen her. It was odd, but Marian kept walking. She saw a few more women glance her way then hurriedly turn to start whispering among themselves. She glanced down at her dress, just to make certain nothing was amiss, but everything seemed to be in place.

Finally she approached another cluster of women and stopped next to them.

"Good evening, ladies." She tried to sound pleasant.

A couple ducked their heads. The woman in the group who usually held the most sway addressed her in return.

"Good evening to you, *Maid* Marian," the woman said. And there it was. They were mocking her. Word had spread that Will Scarlet had been found in her bedroom. Once loosed, nothing could be done to recapture it.

She should brush it off, think of something witty to say, or ignore it completely. One girl leaned in and whispered something to another, and they both began to giggle. Marian felt anger tracing its way through her body, and she spun on her heel, eyes searching for Will.

Spotting him, she crossed the room to where he chatted with a lord. Marian walked up and before she could stop herself she slapped him across the face.

The lord hastily excused himself.

Marian pulled back her hand to slap him again, but Will caught her arm with a lazy smile.

"My dear friend, one strike is proof that you have been offended," he said glibly. "Two strikes is evidence of shame." His grip was surprisingly strong, and she swallowed a whimper of pain. Seeing it in her eyes, he eased the pressure, then released her.

She lowered her hand, but anger still smoldered within her. It wasn't Will's fault, she knew that, but he was the only one to whom she could express it. More than that, it would be expected. Given the circumstances under which they had been forced to create the charade, they had to carry it to its logical conclusion.

"I never wished to be romantically linked with you either," Will added with a sigh, his eyes flashing.

"I should imagine it would increase your prospects."

"Quite the opposite. No one wants to see herself in competition with you."

"They mock me."

"Only because they fear you," he said. "Mockery is the only weapon they have."

Marian forced in a deep breath as she reminded herself that, in the end, it didn't matter what the others thought.

"On a happier note, our friend is safely on his way," Will said, his voice low enough that it couldn't be heard by anyone else. To someone standing nearby, it would appear as a lovers' spat.

"That makes this easier." Marian relaxed a little. "Tell me something."

"Anything you want."

"The things you said about me to the Sheriff. Were any of them true?"

Will sighed. "Most of them. It's why my words were believed."

She nodded, considering the answer.

"I'll tell you something you didn't ask," he said, "if you want to hear it."

"How would I know?"

"As lovely as you are, and you have been beautiful since childhood, you have always belonged to another."

"I've belonged to no one."

"Are you lying to me, or to yourself?"

"You are a scoundrel, Will Scarlet."

"It has been said before."

Will put his hand to his forehead, rubbing it and scowling.

"Is something wrong?" she asked.

"It's just… hot in here. I think I'm getting a headache."

Despite the number of people who were present, the room most certainly was not hot. If anything, she had noticed it seemed a bit chilly. Then again, without the tapestries on the walls, it always felt that way to her.

"If you'll excuse me," he said, "I think I need some fresh air."

"Do you need me to get you something?" she asked. He didn't look right. Perspiration glistened on his forehead.

"No, I'm sure I'll be fine," he said. He started to walk away, but after six steps his knees buckled. Marian started forward, but Will caught himself before he fell. She moved in front of him and put a hand on his arm, concern outweighing any thought of how it would look that she was touching him.

He was sweating more profusely now, and his eyes had gone glassy.

"Marian, I don't think I'm doing too well." The words slurred together. Then she noticed a red spot on his neck that hadn't been there a moment ago. Even as she watched, it seemed to grow. Moments later a second one appeared.

She involuntarily crossed herself in fear.

"I think you've been cursed with the pox," she whispered.

* * *

Robin found himself struggling to stay awake and stay on his horse. He remembered very little since fleeing from Prince John's chamber. Most of it was random images that seemed to come to him unbidden. He could see Marian's face one moment, then Will's. Over and over in his head, though, he heard Marian begging him not to die.

For her sake he would not.

Will was responsible for getting him out of the castle and onto the back of a horse. At least, he was pretty sure it had been Will's doing. They were headed now for the monastery, and from the brief snatches of conversation he heard between the two monks who were escorting him, he guessed that the conditions there had to be awful. More people were being struck with the pox.

They were moving at a snail's pace, and at any other time it would have made him unlivable, but this evening he was grateful to have the gentler stride. His wounds were barely holding themselves together, and he didn't want to do anything to risk opening them up.

If only he'd been able to kill the prince.

They had not understood the true nature of their enemy, yet Robin would not make the mistake of underestimating him a second time. He just hoped the cardinal would know of something, *anything* that could kill a dark sorcerer.

He kept fading in and out of consciousness, which made it hard to judge the passing of time. At last, though, they arrived at their destination. Robin considered it a minor miracle that he was actually able to walk inside under his own power. He had to find the cardinal, and tell him what he'd learned.

The man was in his study, his face pinched with worry. Robin moved inside, struggling not to fall down, and the cardinal looked up at him.

"What in hell did you think you were doing?" he asked bluntly.

"I tried to kill the prince, and put an end to this nightmare," he replied.

"I'm not sure which is worse, the fact that you did something so foolhardy without consulting me, or the fact that you failed and have therefore put him on even higher alert." A vein in the man's temple was pulsing, and his face was twisted in rage.

A dull ache throbbed through his body, making him edgy.

"What I did was right. I'm only sorry I failed," Robin said. "But in failing, I've learned far more about our enemy than we had guessed. He has dark forces at his command, shadows—demons. They attacked me, and I barely escaped. Even though I wounded John, it was nothing to him."

The cardinal cursed under his breath and Robin pretended not to hear him.

"Things have taken a turn for the terrible," the holy man muttered. "The first part of what you have said does not entirely surprise me. The fact that you wounded him and nothing happened, that is cause for a great deal of worry."

"How can we stop a man we can't kill?" Robin asked.

Robin turned his head slightly, having noticed something out of the corner of his eye. There, lying on a pad on the floor, unconscious and covered in red marks, was Friar Tuck.

"Cardinal, I need to speak with you!" a familiar voice said, pulling his attention away from the monk. Moments later Marian appeared in the doorway, and she started at seeing Robin. Her cheeks were red, as if made that way by the wind.

"I'm so glad you're alive," she said, stepping toward him.

"As am I." To his surprise, however, she turned her attention back to the cardinal.

"I have just come from the castle," she said. "Something's happened, and it couldn't wait, so I rode here as fast as I could." She paused, then added, "Will has been stricken with the pox."

The news was like a slap in the face, and the world swam before him. Robin grasped the edge of a table.

"So has Friar Tuck," the cardinal said, indicating the large man's form. Marian cursed.

The cardinal shook his head. "This is very bad."

"How long will he live?" Marian asked, her voice hardly a whisper.

"A day, maybe a little more than that, and then they will be lost to those of us left here on earth."

CHAPTER THIRTY-THREE

"There has to be a cure," Robin said.

"There's not," a new voice said. Alan-a-Dale came in, closing the door behind him. "Some things are best discussed in private, even now," he said. "Especially with the bishop prowling around."

"Quite right," the cardinal agreed.

"What's happening?" Friar Tuck asked, struggling to sit up. "Why am I lying on the floor—it's filthy down here."

"You've been stricken with the pox, old friend," the cardinal said sadly. "Please, conserve your strength."

"Bring the bishop here," Tuck replied. "I'll try to give it to him."

"Alas, I'm not certain that would work," Alan said. "I cannot detect how it is spreading, or how it is choosing its victims. The only thing we *can* confirm is that for every three people, one is sick or has died. What's more, Locksley and his men are pillaging the homes of the dead."

Robin cursed. "I should have killed him years ago."

"It's too late to worry about the past—all we can do is try and salvage the present. So there will be a future," the cardinal said. His eyes narrowed as he stared at Robin. "Tell the others what's happened to you."

Robin quickly related the details of his attack on John, and how he had nearly been killed by the prince and his dark creatures. Alan turned pale when he described the invisible demons.

"Your wounds were terrible," Marian said. "Chastity and I did what we could to clean and bandage them. As it was, we were afraid you wouldn't live out the night."

"It would seem Robin has a wealth of natural resilience," the cardinal mused.

"I still hurt," Robin said.

"His guardian angel was watching over him," Alan said, casting a significant look at Marian.

"So now we are faced with the fact that the prince cannot be killed. At least, not by conventional means," the cardinal said. "Our task has become that much more impossible."

Robin couldn't stand any longer. His weak legs were about to betray him. Rather than collapse on the floor next to the friar, he found a chair.

He had always been one to heal fast. Given the nature of his wounds, however, and from whence they had come, he wondered if they would heal at all. The cardinal would know, but he didn't want to ask about it in Marian's presence. She had enough worry on her mind and a heavy enough burden on her shoulders without adding his troubles, as well.

As the others discussed the latest developments, Robin found that he was becoming light-headed. He struggled to bring his focus back to bear on the conversation, even though all he really wanted to do was find a quiet place to lick his wounds and go to sleep.

Then suddenly something he had heard pierced through the fog that seemed to be enveloping his brain.

"What did you say?" he asked, turning to look at the large monk.

"Much, the miller's son, brought in a servant girl he'd found on the road. She had been sent looking for help." Tuck paused, as if struggling to find the words. "The pox has reached Longstride

Manor. She said that your mother and sisters were infected. I'm sorry, Robin."

Everything seemed to stop.

His mother. His sisters. Will. Friar Tuck. All of them had just days, maybe only hours to live, unless this thing could be stopped. Alan had said there was no cure, but he had to be wrong. If the curse was brought on by dark magic, then surely there was a way to break it.

"There has to be something we can do," Robin said. "I will not stand by and watch all of Nottingham wither and die because of this monster."

"I know you're a fighter, Robin," Marian said, "but what we need right now is a healer, or someone who can manipulate magic in order to fight back." Her voice was soft and her eyes shimmering with unspent tears.

"Then let's find someone who can do that," he said. "It's either that, or learn to wield magic ourselves." He waited for a word of admonishment from either the cardinal or the friar. Instead the two men exchanged curious glances.

"Indeed, gentlemen, I believe you are right," Alan said.

What? Robin thought, and he turned to look at the bard. "What are you talking about? They didn't say anything."

"No, but they were thinking it." Alan leaned forward. "We have long been discussing whether or not to use magic to fight back. The problem is with magic there is often a terrible price to pay, and we have not been certain until this moment that it was worth it." He paused as if reluctant, and then continued. "Legends speak of all sorts of powerful magics, most lost to us today."

"Most," the cardinal said, "but not all."

"What do you know?" Robin demanded, leaning forward in the chair. Shifting his weight made the wound in his side howl in agony. The pain was good, however, since it helped him focus. "What have you been keeping from us?"

"There are many relics of the old world that have been guarded by Sherwood and, indeed, by this very monastery," the cardinal said. "These are things of power, infused with different types of mysticism."

"Since the pox struck, we've been focused on seeking the answer to a single question," Friar Tuck said. "Is there something that can combat this terrible assault on the realm?"

"We think there is," the cardinal interjected.

Alan nodded. "There are stories about an elixir that can turn ordinary water into a powerful healing potion. But it can also be used as the deadliest of poisons."

"It was once used by the druid Merlin to fell Mordred, the wizard king who had begun enslaving the land," the cardinal added.

"Like Prince John," Robin said.

"We can only assume that there are similarities, but we don't know the extent of Mordred's evil and his crimes," the cardinal replied. "What we have of the story focuses more on Merlin and the elixir."

"Where would I find this elixir?" Robin asked.

"We have been trying to discern that very thing," Friar Tuck said, and he struggled to speak, sweat pouring off of him. "It was hidden. Lost. Deep in the heart of Sherwood."

"If it fell into the wrong hands," the cardinal explained, "it would be a potent weapon. Thus it is protected by the fey spirits and guardians of the forest. They will not surrender it easily."

"Have you not heard?" Robin said, knowing full well the irony in his words. "I am one of the guardians of the forest."

"Yes, you have taken on the role," Alan said, "but I'm not sure your brother spirits will recognize you as such."

"Then I will force them to do so."

"Robin, your wounds are severe," Marian protested. "You are too weak to go."

"Who else can do this?" he asked. "No one knows the forest as I do. I grew up in the shadows of its roots and boughs, and I have traveled within its bounds every day of my life."

"That is truth," Alan said, "but you will need more than your skills as a woodsman and a hunter. You will need to persuade the fey to help you, and not kill you. These are creatures well outside of your life's experience."

"Tell me."

"I don't know what you may wind up facing, if you can find them at all, but the fey are not like us. They do not understand how fragile we are compared to them. They are rule-bound, but by their rules, not ours. They view us as children... no, as toys to be played with and discarded when broken."

"Perhaps Alan, as a keeper of the old ways, would be better suited," Marian suggested, but Robin shook his head.

"Alan isn't a fighter," he said, "and if the fey cannot be persuaded, then we will need to fight to retrieve the elixir. And— no offense—the bard has nothing personal at stake. I stand to lose my entire family."

"Lord Longstride is right," the cardinal said. "We need a champion, a warrior. Besides, Alan has already tried and failed at persuading the fey to help him retrieve the elixir."

"Just tell me whatever else you know," Robin said. "And Lord Longstride is my father."

CHAPTER THIRTY-FOUR

"There is a chapel in the woods, a safe place where items can be dropped off and picked up," Friar Tuck told Robin, his voice quavering.

"I will take you to it," Alan added, "but farther than that I cannot go. Even though I am a bard of the old ways it would seem there are places in this forest where even I am not welcome."

Robin nodded, and pushed himself to his feet with a grunt. It took determination not to collapse, but he managed it.

"I'd like to have a word with Robin," the cardinal said. "Alone."

Marian hesitated, but then she nodded, and Alan followed suit. Together they left the room.

"I'm going to need a little help," Friar Tuck said.

"You can stay where you are," the cardinal said. He moved forward and placed his hands on Robin's shoulders. "You are taking upon yourself the mantel of savior," he said solemnly. "It is a burden I would wish for no man to carry, but prophecy has indicated that one man must."

"I'll do what I can," Robin said, not knowing what else to say. He had never seen himself as anyone's savior.

"No, you must do better than you can," the cardinal answered. "I know you, Robin Longstride, and despite your faults—many though they may be—you are a *good* man. I need you, *we* need you, to become a great man. That means maturing and taking responsibility, not just for your own actions, but those of the others you command."

"Yet I command no one," Robin said.

"That is where you are wrong. Though you may not see it, others follow you without question, look to you for leadership and confidence. You must accept that, embrace your destiny, or we shall all fall into darkness."

Robin swallowed hard. Even standing was difficult. He didn't know about prophecies, and he certainly didn't see himself as a leader of men. Something had to be done, though, and time was running out.

"I will do what I can to live up to your expectations," he said. He wanted to call the older man insane, yet he had too much respect for him to do that. What was more, every moment wasted meant more needless deaths, and brought his family closer to doom.

"I will bless you before you go," the cardinal said. Robin bowed and accepted the ritual. The cardinal uncapped a vial of oil. Placing some on his finger he touched it to Robin's forehead, murmuring a prayer. When the holy man had finished Robin dipped his head in thanks. As he turned and walked to the door, it felt as if his steps were steadier than they had been when he'd arrived.

Marian and Alan waited just outside the room. He gave Marian a slight smile, afraid to say or do anything more.

"I will keep watch for you at the edge of the forest, by the crossing of the King's Road and Church Road," she said.

He nodded, his throat tight with emotion. Then he turned to Alan.

"Let us make haste."

Scant minutes later the two men were on horses and headed away from the monastery. It was dark, but the moon was out and full, transforming the path into a silvery ribbon that they could follow. Robin realized that it was the first time he'd ever seen the bard astride one of the animals, instead of on foot.

"You can ride a horse," Robin said. Normally he would have preferred to travel in silence, but the pain and the exhaustion were threatening him again, and he needed something on which to focus, so his mind didn't drift away.

"I can, but I don't often choose to."

"Why? It's faster."

"Faster is not always better. My feet know the roads I travel, but my eyes do not."

"Then can we trust your eyes tonight, to get us to the chapel?" Robin asked.

"Once we reach the forest, I will proceed on foot," Alan said.

"Then what are we waiting for?" Robin asked, kicking his mount into a gallop. Beside him Alan did the same. The wind whipping his face felt good, invigorating, but after a time even that sensation dulled. So Robin dug his fingernails into his palm, the pricking pain breaking through the numbness that surrounded him.

She was cold.

She had been so hot when she lay down. Like a fire had been stoked inside her skin. She'd been a furnace, burning away the dross. She had lain down and offered all that fire to him, pouring it into the darkness that came for her.

Then she sat up. The little statue was still in her hand. Lines from its edges had been pressed into her palm.

The cold still touched her thighs. She looked left and right to the small forms next to her. They'd been so hot when they crawled in the bed beside her. They looked peaceful, sleeping, their skin closed from the pox marks. She looked at them and felt nothing. No sorrow, no pain, no joy.

She only felt one thing.

Her hand drifted, pressing against the slight swell of her stomach.

* * *

They finally arrived at the edge of the forest. There Alan dismounted and tied his horse to one of the trees at the very edge.

"Sorry, my friend," the bard said to the beast. "I need you to be here when I get back." He stroked the animal's face.

The forest itself was massive. Robin had explored so much of it in his life, yet he knew that he had seen but a small portion of it. And he had never come across a chapel. Neither had he encountered any fey or guardians, with the exception of the magnificent stag.

There had only been so far that he could go without risking his father's wrath. The older man had not approved of the amount of time Robin spent in the woods, and had forbidden him to stay away from home for more than two consecutive nights.

"Is the path wide enough for this beast?" he asked, as he patted his animal's neck.

"It is, and it's best you take him and conserve your strength," Alan offered.

That was precisely what Robin intended.

Alan took a torch from his saddle and lit it using a fire pot. Both men were apprehensive about taking fire into the forest, but there was no help for it. Robin was in no condition to make his way in the dark. The moonlight would not pierce through the many branches of the trees, and they could not wait for the coming of the dawn.

The bard led the way and Robin urged his horse to follow behind. Once the creature had placed all four feet squarely beneath the canopy, Robin felt something, as though the air itself were crackling around him. His horse clearly felt it, too, for the animal stopped, startled.

Alan turned and looked at him questioningly, then slowly nodded.

"Demons are not permitted here," he said. "The forest is tending to your wounds."

"Then why do we not bring the people with the pox here?" Robin asked. "Would Sherwood not heal them, as well?" Indeed, already his pain was easing, particularly over his ribs.

Alan shook his head. "The pox is a curse that has spread, but it is still a disease and it acts like one. Your wounds were inflicted by supernatural creatures, and while the wounds themselves are not evil, their makers have left their trace on you. That is what the forest is burning away—the taint of the demonic magic that harmed you. You will not be healed, but any residual presence will be removed, making the wounds less bothersome."

Even more important, Robin felt his mind becoming clearer, his thoughts sharper. This was a vast relief, because if the things he had been told were true, he'd need all his wits about him. When the crackling at last faded he was able to nudge his horse forward, and the animal went willingly.

The torch in Alan's hand cast intense light in front of them, but also caused shadows to leap and weave about in some sort of macabre dance. When Alan would look back, the light playing off his face made it look like a skull.

Robin paid careful attention to where they were going, so that he could return the same way. The monastery was just to the south of the great forest. The paths they followed had been familiar to him. However, where he would have turned to the right to travel toward his home, they instead turned left and very swiftly entered a section of the woods he did not know. He was grateful that the bard was leading the way.

They wound several more miles into the forest, going deeper and deeper. Twice Alan had to replace his torch with a fresh branch he'd found on the ground. When the last one finally began to die out, light was beginning to appear. He carefully stamped out the last of the embers.

"We are almost there," he said. Robin nodded, relieved to hear it.

A handful of minutes later, the chapel came into view. To Robin's surprise, while it was overgrown, it looked like a plain chapel of the sort that could have been plucked from anywhere else in the region. Vines were twisting over it and tree roots snarled the stone path that led to the door.

"What is it doing here?" Robin asked, hard pressed to imagine who would have come all this way to pray.

"It is acting as a safe harbor," Alan replied.

Robin dismounted and tied his horse to a tree near the entrance. His hand was on the door when he turned to look at Alan.

"Are you coming?"

The bard slowly shook his head and took his instrument from his shoulder.

"I have been inside many times, but not today I think." He began to strum the instrument, creating a strange, haunting tune that made the small hairs on the back of Robin's neck stand on end. Turning again, he pushed open the door of the chapel and stepped through.

The inside was as unremarkable as the outside. Most churches were filled with decoration, frescoes and paintings, statues of saints, crucifixes. There was nothing here save plain wood benches and an unadorned altar covered in a plain white cloth. He walked to the front of the chapel, briefly glancing at the simple altar, his fingers moving from habit in the sign of the cross. He didn't know where any magic items might have been left, and his cursory inspection turned up nothing unusual.

Outside, Alan stopped playing and Robin made his way back toward the door.

As he exited he asked, "What am I supposed to do now?" Then he blinked in surprise as he realized that the bard was gone with his horse. He took several swift steps forward, eyes probing in the dim light, but he saw no sign.

From what he had been told, there were fey and other guardians in the forest. Time was running out for his friends and his family, so this would be a good time for one to show itself.

"I need help!" Robin shouted at the top of his lungs.

Leaves shook on a nearby tree, and he swiveled his head in that direction.

A small bird gazed back at him.

Robin felt his desperation mounting. It was as if he could sense his loved ones slipping away from him. Anguish tore at his heart and he fought back a cry of pain that came, not from his body, but from his soul. Struggling to get himself back under control, he finally turned back toward the chapel and stopped.

A small creature, covered in splashes of blue pigment, stood in front of the door staring at him.

CHAPTER THIRTY-FIVE

Robin stared back in astonishment. Then he stepped forward. On longer inspection, what stood before him looked like a man. Tiny and distorted, but close enough to be human.

"What are you doing here?" Robin asked.

The tiny man shrugged. A gnarled black stick in his hand helped prop him up.

"You called."

He must be referring to the song that Alan was playing, Robin thought, but he didn't say anything, since he wasn't sure what would happen if the creature figured out that he hadn't been the one who had done the summoning.

"You're here to help me?" he asked instead.

"That depends. What is it you want?"

"I am searching for a healing elixir once used by Merlin," Robin replied. "It's a matter of life and death."

The creature turned its head, regarding him sideways.

"'Tis not so easy to get the things Sherwood hides," he replied. The creature's voice was a soft melody that carried to Robin like the song of a river over stones. It tended to swallow its 'O' vowels, but he quickly grew used to the inflection. "The forest is ancient. It has many secrets it enjoys keeping, and is loathe to give up." Suddenly the tiny man had a pipe in his hand. It appeared in a sleight-of-hand trick, and Robin missed where it came from. He stuck it in his mouth and began to puff. "You look hale enough for an infant, though," he said between puffs. "Why do you need an elixir?"

Robin's hopes were buoyed. The creature hadn't denied the elixir's existence.

"A curse has been placed on the land," he explained, "a pox that spreads. I need it to heal my family, my friends, and the others who have been afflicted."

"Then the answer will be no," the creature replied. "It's not Sherwood's problem."

"It's *my* problem," Robin insisted. "My mother, sisters, and cousin are all sick. Others—too many others—as well. All of them are innocent of any wrongdoing, save the fact that they have fallen under the rule of an evil man."

The strange creature scowled. At least, that was what it looked like. He turned and walked half a dozen steps, crunching through dried leaves to a patch of bright flowers growing near the chapel.

"Did you hear that?" the creature asked, addressing his question to the flowers.

Suddenly, one of the blossoms exploded upward. Robin blinked as he realized that it hadn't been a flower at all, but rather a faerie dressed in a gown the color of the bloom on which she had been sitting. Even tinier than the man who had addressed her, she rose in the air and flew close to his ear, whispering to him.

The larger creature nodded rapidly, listening in rapt attention. When she had finished, the faerie floated back down and landed on the ground next to him. The piles of leaves that lay there were nearly taller than she was.

The blue creature turned toward him. "Your quest is futile, pale knight," he said flatly. "You should go home."

"Futile?" Robin replied, letting the word sink in.

The man nodded firmly, waving the pipe at Robin. "Yes, futile. Fruitless, vain, useless, to no effect one way or the other," he said. "Need I continue?" Without waiting for an answer, he turned away and made as if to depart into the forest.

"But *why*?" Robin demanded, his voice becoming louder. "Why is it futile?"

"Because your mother and sisters are already dead," the creature told him.

Robin took a step back, feeling as if he had been struck. Pain screamed through his mind, and he could only compare it to the moment his brother had died. Then he forced it to the side, focusing on a single idea.

It can't be true.

The creature didn't even know who he was, let alone who his family might be. This was just a ruse—it *had* to be, to trick him into giving up his quest.

It's not going to happen.

"You're full of shite," he said, throwing it out there like a challenge.

The creature stiffened, and he straightened ever so slowly. "Not after me morning constitutional, Robin Long-of-stride."

"How do you know my name?" Robin asked, panic nibbling at the back of his mind.

"I don't know your name. *She* knows your name," the creature said, indicating the flowers the fairy had been resting on. "She heard it on the wind, and she knows more, as well. It is too late for them, the wind said. Your family are dead, and your enemies close on your home to steal it. With you away, they may succeed.

"Go home," he continued, not a hint of scorn in his voice. "Save it if you can, and leave this elixir business well enough alone."

Robin's knees gave way beneath him and he crashed to the earth. He grabbed great fistfuls of dirt and leaves and tried to focus on the sensations. He was in Sherwood, the place where he always felt most at home, the place where he'd longed to run as a child, never to return.

The fairy could be lying.

Or the blue creature might be.

Has to be.

His father's voice crawled through his mind. Words from childhood stories.

The fey never lie. They're tricky bastards, but they are honest about it.

He felt the truth of it in his heart. They were gone, and he wept with grief and anguish. Pain rocked through him and he screamed to the trees and the dirt and the animals. Anything that would listen.

Then in his mind he saw Friar Tuck, lying on the ground in the cardinal's study, his face covered in red sores, sweating, and striving so hard to be brave. His mother and sisters might be dead, but Tuck wasn't. Neither, hopefully, was Will, or the rest at the monastery.

The cardinal's words came to him now. He was wounded, injured in body, mind, heart, and soul. He was a broken man who never could be made whole again, but there was something he could do still to help others. Something he *must* do, with every last ounce of strength.

Anguish passed, and his old friend anger filled the hollow place. It lay in his stomach, quiet but there. Growing louder, stronger.

He pulled himself to his feet.

"Give me the elixir," he told the creature.

"If your friends are dead, too, would you still seek it?"

"If you keep asking questions like that, I will seek it just to take it from you."

"Well, if you feel that way about it," the creature said, "then follow me." He turned, and began to wind his way through the trees.

Robin forced one foot numbly in front of the other, the tiny creature always five paces in front, even though his legs were half the length, and he leaned on his stick with each step. Through thickets they walked, up hills, and across the occasional clearing. Robin had no idea how far or how long the journey lasted. The forest remained dark and the air strange.

Then at last they came to a stream, and the creature stopped, allowing Robin to catch up.

"Cross it," the creature said.

"What?" Robin asked.

"It's a stream," the little man said. "Surely you know how to cross a stream." He looked up. "Or did your people send a dimwit to fetch the elixir of the great and mighty Merlin?"

The flames of anger fanned inside him, but Robin pushed them down. The stream looked shallow, peaceful water flowing lazily by. He should be across in four steps, perhaps five. He stepped into the current, and everything changed.

Suddenly it was moving incredibly fast, and the ground gave way beneath his feet, plunging him into icy water that was well above his head. He floundered, seeking a foothold on the bottom of the river, but there was none—it had dropped away. The other side, which had seemed mere steps away, now looked far beyond his reach.

He could barely even make out the far shore.

Robin twisted and his eyes landed on the creature who stood passively on the shore, leaning on his short cane and smoking his tiny pipe. The man shook his head.

"You're beyond my help, boy. You've angered the river by dismissing her so easily. She's gonna show you something, indeed. You're on your own."

Then Robin was carried away. He could feel the wound in his side threatening to open up, the seal on it softening. His fatigue returned, far too much to be crossing a swollen, turbulent river. His hands grabbed at the rocks on the edge, trying to find something to grasp.

The rocks were slippery, the water a torrent.

He forced himself to take several deep breaths, and he focused on the images of Will and Tuck. He twisted back and faced the opposite shore—his goal. It seemed far away. It couldn't be, though. Not in reality, even if it was in his mind.

"I think you may kill me," he muttered.

DEBBIE VIGUIÉ ⬥ JAMES R. TUCK

Drawing a deep breath, he slipped under the surface and began to swim. Seconds later he reached the other side and pulled himself up on the shore. He collapsed on his back for a moment, gasping and coughing up some water he had swallowed.

Slowly he sat up and looked to the other shore. The stream had returned to its natural width, babbling gently over the rocks. The strange creature was no longer there. Robin twisted his head, searching everywhere for him, but the blue man had gone.

Robin dragged himself slowly to his feet, pulling air into his lungs, and with it new purpose. He had to keep going. He had made it across the river, and he had to move, to obtain the elixir. So he put the cursed stream behind him, and started walking.

CHAPTER THIRTY-SIX

After walking for what seemed an eternity, at long last he came to a large clearing. It was covered in a carpet of short sweetgrass and tiny red blossoms, bordered on one side by a stream. Whether it was the same one in which he had nearly drowned, he couldn't tell.

In the center of the clearing stood a lone figure, and he walked toward it. It was another creature painted with blue smudges, similar to the first but this one was larger, fully formed with long limbs and sleek muscle.

"Welcome," the creature said, inclining his head.

"Is this the heart of Sherwood?" Robin asked.

The creature chuckled. "This is not the heart of the forest. More like an arm, perhaps even a leg. There are many things in Sherwood. Some to heal. Some to kill. Some to see the future. Some to see the past. Some to illuminate the present. Each kept safe by a guardian."

"I want only one thing," Robin said. "Merlin's healing elixir."

"That is here."

"May I have it?"

The creature shook its head side to side in rhythmic motion, the top leading and then switching direction, undulating back and forth like a flower caught in a breeze.

"Nothing is mine to give or take," it said. "You address the guardian, and see if you may win it from him."

"Win it?" Robin asked. "So it is a contest?"

"Isn't the whole of life a contest, Long-of-stride? You are much like your grandfather, and your father." The creature tilted its head, contemplating Robin. "And your aunt Rhiannon."

"I don't have an aunt Rhiannon."

"Your father's sister."

"But he…" Robin shook his head. There was no time. "Where is this guardian I must fight?"

The creature pointed toward the stream. Robin moved toward it, steeling himself for whatever might come next. Next to the stream stood a large boulder. On it sat a young man who had not been there just a moment before. With a narrow face, pointed ears, and eyes far too large by half he, too, was dressed in green, mostly leaves that looked as if they had been sewn together. He was bare-chested and barefooted, as well. One foot with abnormally long toes dragged back and forth through the water, as its owner gazed down as though deep in thought.

Robin approached and stood for a few moments, waiting to be acknowledged. The young man's hand darted into the water, snatching out a fish that had nibbled at his toes. It thrashed in his hand, flashing silver off its scales. The young man flipped it into the air and watched it fall back into the stream with a splash. After a moment he went back to dragging his foot through the current.

Robin cleared his throat.

"Are you the guardian of Merlin's elixir?" he asked.

"Called that by some," the young man said. "Fish are dumb." He looked up at Robin with wide, green eyes the color of newly budded leaves.

"I need the elixir," Robin pressed. "There are many in England who have fallen sick. A dark wizard has put a curse upon the land, and his pox is killing innocents." Thoughts of his mother and sisters stabbed into him.

He pushed them away.

"What you say might well be, but what has that to do with me?"

"The land is being poisoned by this monster," Robin persisted. "It's only a matter of time before Sherwood feels his evil, as well."

"Your kind heart is much admired," the young man said, "but go away, for I am tired."

Robin felt anger flaring white-hot. This small, delicate-looking creature stood between him and life for his friends and family. If forced, he would wring its neck and take what he needed. He glanced uncertainly at the stream, wondering if it was the source of the potion, or if it was somewhere else, hidden safely away.

"I need that elixir," he said. "I'm prepared to do battle with you to get it."

"You don't know the battle's begun. How could you hope to see it won?"

Robin's hand lay on the hilt of his knife while he tried to decipher what the creature had told him. The large blue man had said that Robin would have to *win* the elixir. His mind began to spin. So he took a deep breath, and answered.

"The hour is late, my patience is low…" He paused to think, "…but without the elixir, I will not go."

Yes.

The boy sat up.

"Even if you play my game, my answer will still be the same."

The bard would be much better at this than I.

"You may not care or have a heart, but I am sworn to do my part."

"Then speak it now to the air, and tell me why anyone should care."

"Death comes to all in time, even to boys who love to rhyme. That does not mean we should embrace the night. All are tasked to stand and fight. I've come far, and through much strife…" His mind tripped, stumbling as he reached for the words. His chest drew tight. "And I will take the elixir, that gives back life."

"Then convince me now, for you must, that any beyond the forest are just."

"I know a man whose Lord has bled. Without this potion he's as good as dead," Robin said, thinking of the good friar, and all he had done to try and help the people.

"For one holy man you may speak more, but for the elixir give me four."

Robin blinked, not sure if he understood what the insane child wanted. Four what? He prayed it was only to know that there were four other good people beside the friar.

Taking another deep breath, he continued.

"One a lady, fair of face, fights as a man in man's own place. Another with tongue of solid gold speaks for the people with a heart so bold." He swallowed hard as his thoughts flew to his little sisters. He had been told they were dead. He prayed it was not true, but he might not want to tell the boy of them, in case they were. "A holy man of station high, yet he gathers all the lowly nigh. A man who'd risk his own dear life, to cut off the hand that holds the knife."

He wasn't sure if that was what the boy wanted, or whether his answer even made sense. He waited, holding his breath.

The creature regarded him. Finally he spoke.

"For six good souls tried and true, the elixir now I give to you."

Robin tilted his head to the side, not knowing who the sixth good soul might be. As if sensing his confusion the boy continued.

"Of your five friends, you spoke so true, but number six, my friend, was you."

Robin blinked hard. He found it strange to think of himself in those terms. Flawed? Yes. Belligerent? Definitely. Perhaps others saw something in him that he didn't see in himself.

The boy leaned down and dipped his hand in the river. The waters which had been trickling peacefully suddenly churned violently, swirling around his hand. A few seconds later he lifted it out, and instantly the waters calmed. In the boy's hand was clutched a tiny silver bottle with a cork in it. He held it out, and Robin took it and tucked it inside his tunic.

It was such a tiny bottle.

How could it save so many lives?

"One drop per bucket is all you need—the water, the earth, the elixir, the seed. If you drink Merlin's tears you will find your fever clears."

Robin nodded. "My thanks you have, it now is true, and so I say good day to you."

"That the sun does drop, the hour is late, but first a word concerning fate. With another you must strive, if you hope to stay alive." The boy held up his hand and pointed. Robin turned to follow the line of his indication, and his eyes landed on a tree a fair distance away. Something protruded from it.

A single black arrow.

For a moment he felt his heart stop.

Robin.

He shook his head, certain that something had called his name. Yet there had been no sound. He turned and glanced at the boy, who shook his head solemnly before returning his attention to the river.

Robin.

He began walking toward the arrow, his eyes fixed on it. There was something about it that pulled him, as if he wasn't even telling his feet to move. They were doing so on their own.

Robin.

Then the voice in his head was singing, softly as a lullaby. He fought the urge to close his eyes and listen. His body began to sway slightly as he walked, almost dancing to the tune that played in his mind. Suddenly he was close, only a moment away from reaching out to touch it.

Yet the boy had said that he needed to strive with another. What would the guardian of the black arrow want? Would it be a game of words? Of wits?

He heard the ringing of a sword being pulled from its sheath, and spun as his hand went to his own dirk. An enormous man towered over him, his face twisted in a snarl, naked steel in his hands.

This would be a game of weapons.

CHAPTER THIRTY-SEVEN

R obin barely had time to pull his knife from the scabbard before the arrow's guardian brought his sword down.

He deflected the blow using the thick spine of his blade, gritting his teeth as he felt the flesh tearing over his ribcage where he was wounded. Blood flowed down his side, but he forced himself to keep his eyes on his opponent.

"I am going to take the arrow," Robin informed him.

"That arrow is death," the giant said, circling. "It kills whatever it pierces."

"All the more reason I need it," Robin said. With the arrow he could finally put an end to the prince and his black magic schemes. "I have a great enemy I need to take down."

"You worry about him, when I stand before you?" the man asked. "He is either a great foe, or you a great fool." He thrust and Robin spun, feeling the blade graze his already injured side. He sucked in his breath with a sharp hiss, but forced himself to refocus. He lunged and the man blocked.

Blows rained down on both sides. They each twisted, turned, blocked. Robin finally scratched the other man's cheek, but was unable to do more damage. He was losing ground and losing strength. The earth beneath them became trampled, Robin's blood mingling with the dirt and turning it into mud.

His hands were sweat slick, sliding on the dirk.

He was losing. He had to do something soon or it was all over, and he couldn't let that happen. So he gave way under the next blow, then again—maneuvering his body toward the tree with the arrow, allowing the bigger man's blows to drive him where he wanted to be. When he was close enough, he reached out with his left hand and yanked the arrow free.

In that moment his opponent jumped forward and twisted Robin's arm. The arrow spun out of control and then sliced through Robin's tunic, stabbing him in the shoulder.

The huge man let go and stepped back, a look of anticipation on his face. Robin reached up and yanked the arrow free of his flesh, spun it in the air, and then plunged it into his quiver.

While the giant gawked at him, Robin lunged forward, knocking him to the ground. He brought his blade to the man's throat even as he stood on the sword to keep him from raising it.

"Do you yield?" Robin panted, blood and sweat flowing freely off of him. The other man nodded, so he eased back, but kept his knife at the ready. The giant stood slowly, leaving his sword on the ground.

"We must look," he said, pointing at Robin's shoulder where the arrow had struck him. Robin frowned and, with his free hand, peeled back the torn edges of the tunic. As he did so, the giant peered eagerly.

"The arrow has branded you," he said. "Truly, it is yours now."

"What does that mean?" Robin asked.

"You claimed it by pulling it from the tree, and the arrow chose not to kill you." The man pulled up his own tunic. Along his left side was a scar very similar to the wound Robin had received. "It chose you to be its next guardian. It is now your responsibility to protect it."

"I'm not sticking it back in that tree," Robin said. "I have things to do."

"You will be back," the giant said. "This forest is home to the arrow. It will always seek to return here."

"That may be so, but it will have to wait," Robin said. "I'm leaving now."

"Yes, you have much work to do, and it is late. Perhaps too late." He tipped his head forward in salute. "Thank you for freeing me from my prison." With that he turned, stepped away, and faded from sight.

Robin stood for a moment, panting. The arrow *had* been calling to him. He knew it for certain, and if it would mean an end to the nightmare that gripped the land, he would gladly return it to its home.

Now, though, he had work to do.

Glynna was worried. She recognized the signs, the subtle changes, even though it was early days. She was with child. The thought of carrying *his* child, the thought of placing the infant in *his* arms, filled her with an unholy joy, but it was tempered with her concern for those in her household who might find the timing of this pregnancy suspicious. She calculated the number of weeks since her husband had been gone. She might be able to pull off the charade that it was his, at least until it was no longer required.

She had considered for many months bringing her daughters under her tutelage, introducing them to the magic that her own mother had kept hidden from her. She saw now, though, that they were just a distraction. Perhaps it was the best of all situations that they had come down with the pox.

She would miss them, but her grief would be nothing compared to the joy of raising this new child with her master. She stared at the little black vial of liquid that sat on her altar. He had brought it to her in the night, a cure for the pox. He had left it while she slept, but whispered to her in her dreams what it was.

There was enough to share with her daughters.

She had meant to, but then she thought about the baby. If it was an only child she could devote everything to it. She wouldn't be distracted by others demanding her attention.

Truly, this was the child she had always been meant to have. She could feel it inside her already. She could almost swear it felt her, too, that it knew she was its mother.

She uncorked the vial and drank it down, shuddering as it burned all the way. After the fire passed a tingling set in. At last she looked down at her arms and saw the red marks vanish as though they had never even been there. Her master loved her, protected her. How much more would he love her when he found out that she was carrying his child? Then again, maybe he already knew.

Her smile grew broader.

After what seemed like an eternity, trudging through the gloom, Robin staggered out of the forest. Sherwood had never felt so large to him as it had stumbling away from the chapel. Somehow, though, he knew the way.

Marian, Alan, and the cardinal were all waiting. Marian was the first to see him. With a cry she jumped up and ran forward. Her cheeks were flushed when she reached him.

"You're alive," she said, sounding relieved beyond measure.

"Barely," he said, summoning a smile.

"Did you find it?" she asked, still a bit breathless.

"I did." Then her eyes took in the wound in his shoulder.

"Robin, what happened to you?"

"It's a long story," he replied. "I'll tell you later, when we have time."

Together they joined the others.

"Did you succeed in your mission?" the cardinal asked, not bothering with a formal greeting. In response Robin pulled the silver flask out of his tunic.

"One drop in a bucket of water," he said.

"Let us find some buckets then."

* * *

At the monastery they gathered around a bucket filled with river water. Robin handed the flask to Cardinal Francis, who uncorked it and very carefully tilted it over the bucket, allowing a single silver drop to splash into it. When he was done, he carefully sealed the flask again.

They all stared at the bucket. Robin, for his part, was waiting for something to happen. He expected the water to change color or consistency, for there to be boiling or vapor.

Nothing happened.

"Is that it?" he asked, looking up at the others.

"What were you told?" the cardinal asked. "Were there any rituals, words, something we might be forgetting or overlooking?"

Robin thought back. "'One drop per bucket is all you need— the water, the earth, the elixir, the seed.' Those were his exact words," he said.

"What if it was all a ruse?" Alan said. "We know the liquid can also be used as a poison—what if that is its *only* purpose? We might be dooming someone to a horrible death, worse than the pox itself."

"Well then, we'll just have to test it on ourselves," the cardinal said grimly.

"But none of us has the pox," Marian pointed out.

"I know, but there is no one else we can ask to try it," he replied.

Robin picked up the dipper that was on the table next to the bucket. He filled it with a little of the water and then brought it to his lips. The water was cool, but he only drank a little.

Then he handed it to Alan. The others took turns drinking, as well.

He began to feel warm all over, like he was heating up from the inside. He shifted on his feet uncomfortably, trying to avoid panic. He'd managed to get the bleeding stopped from his various wounds before coming out of the forest, but they were burning now, feeling hot and itchy.

He began to twitch, and he noticed Marian reaching toward her legs, a strange look on her face. A moment later the cardinal gasped, and Alan rolled up a sleeve to inspect his arm.

It was a ruse! Robin thought desperately. The heat grew until he felt as if he was on fire. Then there was a final blinding burst...

...and it was gone. With a start he realized that he felt good. Better than he could remember having felt in a long time.

"My legs." Marian lifted her skirts up ever so slightly. "I had scars, but now they're gone."

"The same with my arm," Alan muttered.

The cardinal nodded, his eyes wide. That was when Robin realized his ribs weren't hurting. He moved his hand there, expecting to feel the raw wound. Only smooth skin met his touch.

They all had been healed, Marian realized, of everything except for a chevron-shaped scar on Robin's shoulder. That was the only one remaining between the four of them.

It is a miracle, she thought, afraid even to say it.

"I think the elixir works, praise the Lord," the cardinal said.

"Now to get it to the people," she said.

"I'll tell the monks to gather as many buckets of water as quickly as they can. Marian, you work here. Alan and I will split up the town, and go to the ones who could not make the journey," Cardinal Francis said.

Robin was already in motion, grabbing the bucket and moving toward the stable.

"I need to take some to Longstride Manor," he said.

"Will is here. Chastity brought him and a couple of others. I'll see that he gets the elixir first," she promised.

"And then Friar Tuck."

CHAPTER THIRTY-EIGHT

Will couldn't remember ever being so grateful to see anyone in his life as he was to see Marian.

"Did it work?" he whispered.

"Drink this," she ordered, shoving a small cup at him.

With a shaking hand he grasped it and did as she said. Moments later he could feel heat flaring through his body. His first reaction was fear, but then his mind began to clear, and he could breathe easier.

After a few more seconds he struggled to a sitting position. All around him he saw monks administering water to other victims of the pox. And all around him people began to sit up, their skin clearing of the red marks.

"It's a miracle," he breathed. "Praise Jesu and all the saints." Everywhere around him people lifted their voices, proclaiming the same.

He was dying. Friar Tuck knew it as sure as he knew anything in the world. He had been drifting in and out of consciousness for a while. When he woke again, he was still in the cardinal's office, but his mentor wasn't there.

Bishop Montoya, on the other hand, was. Tuck felt his lip

curling as he wished he could do something about the man before he died.

As if sensing that he was awake, the man moved closer, confronting him, eyes gleaming with an unholy light.

"Your sins have found you out," he declared, his voice shaking with excitement. "It was only a matter of time."

Friar Tuck blinked at him. "What are you talking about?"

"I knew there was something about you, even before you dared to lay a hand on me," he said, his voice almost a hiss. "You have no respect for authority. It's been you who has been working to undermine our new king, you who has been plotting to steal the tax money and keep it for yourself."

Friar Tuck gawked in amazement.

"That money belongs to the people," he blurted out. He was instantly angry with himself, for he knew it might be taken as an admission of guilt.

"No! It belongs to the rightful ruler of this land," the bishop said, practically pouncing on his words.

"While the king is away, the people and all things that belong to him must be safeguarded." Tuck shook his head, and the pain made him regret it instantly. He needed to make better arguments, but he could barely string words together to form a sentence. He could hardly think at all through the raging fever.

"It doesn't matter," he said finally. "I'm dying." At least he could rob the bishop of his final victory.

"Oh, but it does matter," the cursed man answered. "You see, I know everything. You talked a lot while you were delirious. I know all about your allies."

"I have no allies," Friar Tuck bluffed, fear rolling through him.

"Ah, but you do. The cardinal, Longstride, that minstrel, Will Scarlet, and even the harlot."

Tuck stared at him in horror. He had to stop the bishop from speaking about what he knew.

"You can't—" he began.

Before he could finish, Montoya moved abruptly over to the

door of the study. He threw it open and Friar Tuck could hear people outside. They were singing... something had happened. The bishop turned then, a twisted snarl on his face.

"Perhaps they will save you, just in time for you to be hanged."

"What do you mean?" he asked.

The bishop just smiled and slipped quickly out of the room. All Tuck could do was pound the floor weakly and choke in impotence.

CHAPTER THIRTY-NINE

"Do you feel that?" Prince John asked. It was as if an invisible ripple ran through the air as magic shimmered, then broke apart.

The curse was broken. He blinked in astonishment. He had no idea how it could have happened, or who could have done it. The power that had flowed to him from so many deaths, so many *sacrifices*, suddenly stopped. Where before he had felt so invigorated, now he felt terrible, weak.

He let out a long groan.

"This cannot be," he said. "My plan, the execution... it was *perfection*."

"Shut up, you fool," the Sheriff growled. "I feel it far more acutely than you ever could." His face was twisted in an inhuman snarl.

"Yet how can it be?" John responded, hating the whine in his own voice. "There is no one with the skill to oppose us. And worse, we still haven't found—"

"What part of 'shut up' did you fail to understand?" the man in black snapped, and he reached for the prince, who shrank back into the throne. But the Sheriff stopped himself, and stood as if it took all of his strength to control himself.

"You will live," he snarled. "If you say another word about

your 'perfect plan,' you will die by my hand, the final victim of the pox." With that he began to pace.

Rapid footsteps sounded on stone.

"Your Majesty," the newcomer said loudly, causing the Sheriff to utter a low growl and turn. "I bring news…"

The house seemed empty when he arrived. Robin had ridden the horse as fast as he could while still managing to balance the precious bucket of water and not lose any.

He raced upstairs to his mother's bedroom, thinking to find her there. The room was darkened. He stepped forward, and an invisible hand threw him back. Some of the precious water splashed up on his chest and he cursed as he steadied the bucket while trying to regain his balance.

He blinked in shock. His mother had not lied. All those years ago she really had warded the door against him. How could she have managed magic such as that?

He'd never know, unless he found her quickly. He ran to each of his sisters' rooms, but they, too, were empty. When he saw the emptiness, felt it in his soul, he made it outside and started toward the road.

He knew where they would be.

The tears felt strange on Old Soldier's face. The last time he'd cried he'd been a younger man. Anasai had left him while in childbirth, taking the little bairn with her. Then the tears had run off the sides of his cheeks and dripped from his jaw.

Now they lost their way, running along the creases and the seams of his face, tickling through wrinkles and lodging in the coarse gray hair that covered his chin. Beside him Little John bawled like a fool, his grief—like everything about him—swelling into the space and looming over everything.

The hole was dug, deep enough to keep them down, wide

enough to lay them side by side. Nearby some of the women were wrapping the girls in sheets before he and Little John would lower them in.

He looked over the heads of the others gathered there, each of them sad in their own way. Some for what they'd lost, some for what they thought they'd lost.

A dark figure stepped from the house and onto the road, moving toward them with quick steps.

Robin could taste his own fear as he moved toward the others. He saw the two shroud-wrapped bodies, both too small to be adults.

Becca and Ruth. His chest squeezed at his heart as he fought his own panic and grief. Maybe it wasn't too late. He pushed the grieving women aside, and fell to his knees, dragging one of his sisters onto his lap. It was Ruth. Tears ran as his fingers dug the cloth from her face and pried apart her ashen lips. They felt like wax. He scooped out a handful of water, dripping it into her mouth. It sat there, spilling from the sides as her head lolled against his chest. Nothing changed, no magic healing.

He held her tight and cried until they pulled him away.

There was a footstep. He looked up and saw his mother. She was dressed in white, but hers was not a shroud like his sisters now wore. Her skin was clear, healthy. He stood slowly.

"They told me you had the pox."

"I did," she said, with a serene smile.

How could she be smiling when her daughters were dead? It was beyond his comprehension.

"What happened?"

"It was a miracle," she said, her bright eyes shining with the fervor of belief. "An absolute miracle."

Robin very much doubted it.

* * *

The doors of the castle had been thrown wide and left open without attendants.

The bishop's purple robe dragged the floor as he walked toward the throne room. He would start there and continue to search until he found a servant. He imagined how pleased the king would be to learn the names of the traitors who were stealing the tax shipments. It could only cement their bond, and elevate him further in the monarch's esteem.

Crossing the threshold he found King John sitting on the edge of the throne. His man, the Sheriff, paced from one side of the dais to the other. They did not look up until he was halfway across the room, moving toward them as fast as he could.

His mind filled with all the rewards the king would bestow upon him.

"Your Majesty!" he cried as the two turned toward him. "I bring news…"

"Hold, man," the monarch warned. "Bite your tongue."

Suddenly, violently, the Sheriff stepped in front of the royal, blocking him from view. King John fell silent.

Montoya's pace stuttered, halting.

"But you should know…"

The Sheriff appeared larger than he had a moment before. He snarled, lips curling over his teeth.

"The pox… the people…" Still the bishop struggled for words. "The Hood…"

"What did you say?" the Sheriff demanded.

Montoya stammered, looking for a clue as to how the Sheriff might want him to answer.

"The pox is broken," he said. "A cure has been found."

King John stood, shaking his head and violently waving his hands.

Darkness flashed, and what felt like dust flew across Montoya's face, coating the wet surface of his eyes. He blinked rapidly, tears bursting from ducts, trying to wash his vision clear. He wiped at them, and it hurt.

The Sheriff was there before him, basalt chestplate nearly touching his nose. Hot breath washed over him, smelling sickly-sweet like carrion.

"*Aegrotatio Egrotatio.*"

Sweat poured out of his skin, soaking the robe he wore as his body began to burn from the inside. Fever struck like lightning, setting his blood to boil. His muscles gave out, dropping him to his knees as his bowels let go.

He knelt in his own filth.

His tongue ballooned, filling his mouth.

The king stepped up beside the Sheriff. He looked down at Montoya as the bishop clawed at his collar, trying to tear it open, to somehow, in some way, make a tiny space for even a sliver of air to find his lungs.

"Well," the king said, his voice becoming fainter over the pounding of his blood in his veins, "you are nothing if not a creature of your word."

The Sheriff nodded, little more than a dark shape now as the world blurred out of sight.

"Enough of human agents," he growled. "It is time for a new plan."

Montoya fell face first onto the marble floor, and a sore burst on his cheek. Without knowing why, he slowly slipped away into darkness.

Robin heard the horses first. He didn't see the men until they rode from the side of the house. Five of them—Locksley and four others. The noble held a rolled parchment.

Robin stepped through the door, and stopped at the edge of the porch. They rode slowly toward him, then sat on their horses looking down at him.

He didn't speak, forcing them to break the silence.

Locksley held up the scroll. A fat clump of wax, royal blue in color, held it together. Though it wasn't visible from where he stood, he knew it had been pressed with a royal seal.

A humming came to his ear. From the quiver on his shoulder. He ignored it.

"Do you know what this is?" Locksley said.

"Don't care."

"You should," the noble responded. "The king has awarded Longstride land to my keeping. This makes it official." He tossed the scroll to Robin. It tumbled through the air, hitting him in the chest and falling to his feet in the dirt.

Pull me out and put me in his throat.

You can do it before any of them can move.

He ignored that, as well.

Locksley spat on the ground. "Read it or not. It's still binding. This property is mine."

Robin took a deep breath. Even on this side of the house he could smell the forest. He looked up the road. The people were all just shapes and silhouettes, still huddled around one spot in the consecrated earth.

He looked up at Locksley.

"I'd like to gather my possessions from inside."

Locksley sneered down at him. "I'll allow you ten minutes, and only what you can carry."

Robin turned and walked back inside the house, shutting the door behind him.

He gathered the lamps first, picking them up and carrying them through the house, going room to room in a systematic search. In his sisters' room he found an old one, handed down from woman to woman in his family for generations untold, its body cracked but somehow still holding oil.

That one he didn't empty.

In the kitchen he opened the small iron door on the fire pit. Warmth radiated from inside the oven. Using tongs he dug out a coal that began to glow orange as he brought it into the air. Raising the wick on the ancient lamp, he touched the coal to it. One small puff of breath and the wick caught, the oil blazing to life.

He dropped the coal, set the lamp on the table, and watched the wick flare and flicker. He thought of his mother. Of his sisters. Of his father across the sea. Dead or not, all of them gone.

With a sweep of his hand he knocked the lamp from the table. It crashed to the floor, glass exploding across the surface as oil ran fast and free. The burning wick lay down in the oil, igniting it in a tide of cleansing fire. The flame had just reached the end of the spreading puddle, catching its edge as it collided with the trails of oil he'd tracked through the house, from all the other lamps he'd found.

Fire ran like children, chasing through hallways and into rooms, leaping quickly onto anything that would hold it dear and let it burn.

Without looking back, he walked out the door and into the forest.

EPILOGUE

As winter came to Sherwood, the first dog soldier crawled from its glass womb.

In the bowels of the castle it lay on the cold stone, soaked in potions and saturated with dark magic, while the Sheriff gently picked shards of glass from its skin and sang to it a lullaby of death and destruction.

ACKNOWLEDGEMENTS

First I have to thank my amazing co-author, James, who has been a joy to work with and who has made this book so fun. I'm so glad we've had the chance to work together. A huge thank-you to our fantastic editor Steve Saffel, who believes in this series as much as we do and whose enthusiasm and passion have been greatly appreciated. Thank you to an amazing agent, Howard Morhaim, who worked hard to make this happen. There are so many at Titan who have helped tremendously with the creation of this book. Thank you to: Alice Nightingale, Nick Landau, Vivian Cheung, Laura Price, Natalie Laverick, Miranda Jewess, Julia Lloyd, Tim Whale, and Paul Gill.

Thank you to our fans who have been eagerly anticipating this book. Your excitement has added fuel to our own and we're so thrilled to be able to finally share it with you. Thank you as well to Rick and Barbara Reynolds, Juliette Cutts, Ann Liotta, Chrissy Current, Calliope Collacott, Rita De La Torre and Jason De La Torre for their encouragement and support.

–DV

Thank you to Debbie. An idle conversation on a panel at Timegate has resulted in this book and this series and it rocks! Thanks to D.E.O Steve Saffel who did drive this book further down the road than we were originally going to go. Thank you to Howard Morhaim and his staff. The behind the scenes Titan posse which include: Alice Nightingale, Nick Landau, Vivian Cheung, Laura Price, Natalie Laverick, Miranda Jewess, Julia Lloyd, Tim Whale, and Paul Gill. Thank you to every merry man out there no matter your gender, you are welcome one and all to our Sherwood. Special thanks goes to Krista Merle for being a sounding board.

I couldn't do any of this without my darling dear, Danielle Tuck.

–JRT

ABOUT THE AUTHORS

Debbie Viguié is the *New York Times* bestselling author of more than three dozen novels including the *Wicked* series co-authored with Nancy Holder. In addition to her epic dark fantasy work Debbie also writes thrillers including *The Psalm 23 Mysteries*, the *Kiss* trilogy, and the *Witch Hunt* trilogy. Debbie plays a recurring character on the audio drama, Doctor Geek's Laboratory. When she isn't busy writing or acting Debbie enjoys spending time with her husband, Scott, visiting theme parks. They live in Florida with their cat, Schrödinger.

James R. Tuck is the author of the Deacon Chalk series. He is also a professional tattoo artist, an accomplished photographer, and podcaster. He lives in the Atlanta area with his lovely wife Danielle.